SHIELD OF RUIN

The Ruined Destiny Series: Book One

S. H. Blodgett

Dedication

First and foremost, none of this would have been possible without my husband, Ian Blodgett. I'm entirely blessed to have such a supportive life partner. I love you to the moon and back!

To Gramme, who encouraged my passion for reading, thank you for all of those visits to the local Books and Bagels shop! I forever have a place for each book you gifted me on my shelves and an even bigger place in my heart for all of those memories.

To my family who shaped me into the person I am today, I will always be grateful. The support you all have given me has made this journey possible.

Thank you all from the bottom of my heart!

CHAPTER ONE

SAYRA

As Sayra rolled her armor-clad shoulders, she steeled herself for the coming minutes that would decide her fate. Only one victory separated her from the dream she fought tooth and nail for. A dream her brother had sacrificed his life for.

Freedom.

A short nun garbed in ivory robes stood in the marble corridor. Her hand gestured for Sayra and her opponent, Netta, to pass through the open doorway into the arena beyond. "Remember, display your prowess in battle to impress the observing Arcanists. One of them will purchase your guardianship should you graduate."

Which means I'll never see my homeland again, Sayra thought, her hand tightening around the worn pommel of her sheathed sword. *I'll no longer be forced into a life unenviable by my worst enemy.*

Sayra inclined her chin in acknowledgement, her heartbeat thudding loudly in her ears as she stepped forward. Just as her feet were about to cross the threshold into the arena, Netta's words sent an icy chill down her spine.

"Maybe if your brother asks nicely, the Goddess could trade your life for his so it won't be wasted when I cut you to shreds," she said, her dark eyes pulling at the ends. Netta tsked, her head angling down at Sayra.

Sayra knew a smirk was beneath Netta's helmet. Her nose flared, her desperation the only thing that kept the last string of her self-control intact. Grinding her teeth, she forced her dented boots to clack across the modest stone floor. Arcanists, the revered majik-wielders who protected the dwindling population of mankind, watched with burning gazes from above. They were tucked away on the second-floor viewing level, a rune-engraved column of marble at each end of the rectangular arena.

Lanterns flickered generous light across the marble walls, and a large window on the ceiling collected thick flakes of snow falling from the sky. The overseeing combat monk, Batar, gestured for Netta and Sayra to bow their heads in prayer for a safe battle. Or as safe as it could be given the last round ended with an acolyte nearly losing her entire left leg. For the prayer, Sayra mumbled some vague words, acting the part of someone who believed in the church's faith.

She breathed in, falling into an offensive stance as Batar signaled for them to be ready. A dozen feet away, Netta haughtily pulled her sword. A single brow quirked up. Exhaling, Sayra tuned out the dozens of men looking down at her and pushed back the fear of failure. Most importantly, she twisted her body so no one saw when she flipped a crude gesture at Netta.

Netta's eyes twitched, a wild grin crossing Sayra's exposed face.

Hag.

"May the final round commence!" Batar stepped back out of harm's way.

The grin slipped from her face as Netta charged. A hush sounded from the men watching as Sayra dipped low. A sword swung wide in a powerful arc, narrowly missing Sayra by a foot as she danced around Netta's slower body. Sayra attempted to sidestep, drawing her own blade across Netta's chest. Metal weakly glanced by, not even scratching the armor plate as Netta recovered with a vicious strike.

Sparks flew from Sayra's back as she half rolled, half stumbled out of Netta's reach. Relying on her strength, Netta swung her sword in wide, powerful arcs, each blow intended to cleave through Sayra.

Only a minute in Sayra's form was becoming sloppy. A grunt escaped her lips as she blocked a rough blow. She knew the only way to win was to use her nimbleness to her advantage, so she became more daring with her dodges. Her mind tracked each movement Netta made, waiting for the opportune moment.

It became a lengthy dance of Sayra navigating deadly blows. Occasionally, the edge of her blade would glance off Netta's in a minor deflection.

But then, she made a fatal mistake.

Netta feinted left, and Sayra fell for it.

Steel raced for her neck, and Sayra barely raised her sword in time to lessen the impact. A double-edged blade bit into her combat-worn breastplate, just beneath her collarbone. Netta's robust arms strained as she attempted to deliver an incapacitating blow to end the match.

Muscles quivered throughout Sayra's upper body as she held Netta's blade at bay with a lesser-skilled hand, a low grunt escaping her teeth as her hulking opponent shifted her weight forward. Sayra's right boot drug back into the snow-dusted stone, her spine bending backward.

Steel screeched further toward her shoulder, Sayra's own sword clashing on her plates from the force. Then her mind surged elsewhere. Her brother's mauled face flashed in front of her, his last words haunting her ears.

It's okay, Sayra.

It's not okay, she wanted to shout, feeling the world crumble around her as gleaming, daemonic eyes shifted to her next.

Sayra's labored breath hitched in panic, her mind struggling to repress the memory and instead focus on the match at hand. Netta pounced at the opening of weakness and drove her shoulder into Sayra's chest.

A strange sense of vertigo overcame her as she went airborne, Sayra's sense of self snapping back to reality when the ground rose to meet her. Her bare head bounced off the ground, and she tasted blood in her mouth. For the millionth time, Sayra wished her culture allowed head coverings of any sort.

Only years of extensive training had kept Sayra's grip firmly on her sword, despite the way the world teetered around her. The onlookers—sadistically intrigued—leaned over the ivory-wrapped marble railing to glean a closer look at the trial's last match between the weakest acolyte in her class and a brutal opponent.

It was Sayra's last chance as an acolyte to graduate into a Valkyrie, an esteemed guardian who protected the few remaining men in their world.

And she blew it.

"Truly a shame that our noble Arcanists have to witness such a disgraceful performance from a girl who hoped to protect them from daemons. From a girl who can't even win a fight," Netta tutted, stepping over Sayra. Narrow ebony eyes shined with victory behind her helmet. "Perhaps this performance will ensure that the likes of a Faendan remain within their failed empire. Arcanists don't need weak Valkyries guarding them."

A murmur rippled through the crowd at that, one Arcanist raising his hand to quiet the unrest. Netta sprung then, lifting her dull blade high above her. Alarm raced through Sayra at the devastating blow racing toward her stomach.

Moving her steel-clad arm to intercept the two-handed attack, Sayra knew it was a wasted effort. *Too slow.* The arc of her blade would never clash in time with the other, her loss imminent.

For years, she had fought harder than any other to overcome her weaknesses, and while there were few that mattered, Sayra believed she had finally amounted to more than her family thought possible.

And... for what? To fail in her last trial? Her jaw clenched, teeth protesting from the force of it.

I can't lose.

What happened next was incomparable to anything Sayra had ever felt. A rush of cool, tingling energy coursed through her body. It pressed against her skin, begging to be released.

Majik.

While Sayra could certainly feel it as it dispelled from her body and wrapped itself around Netta, it moved unseen. A force that was designed to be discovered by a new sense, unnoticed by the ones she previously relied on.

Time slowed, Netta's blow slightly slower than it should have been. Unwilling to sacrifice her impossible advantage, Sayra hastened her arm, narrowly deflecting the blade into the dirt a hair's breadth away from where her stomach had been.

Too close for comfort.

Swiveling with a dancer's grace, the flow of time resumed with fury, rippling across Netta's gaze as she beheld Sayra wringing a leg around her own. Sayra expertly maneuvered her weight, stealing her opponent's limbs from under her while gaining the high ground. Metal clanged into stone, and Netta's sword dragged on the ground beside her.

The tip of Sayra's blade drew a thin line of blood from the sliver of skin showing on Netta's neck. Their battle-flushed faces were feet apart and bearing expressions of mirrored disbelief.

Batar removed himself from a corner under the second-floor walkway, his ivory robes swishing against the dark gray of the floor. "Sayra von Lykken has—"

The young woman trembled with rage under Sayra, her voice screeching out with indignation before the overseer could declare her loss. "She used majik to win!" Netta cried.

Silence was all that remained in the declaration's wake, Sayra's still form unsure of whether to release Netta. Guilt gnawed at her gut as the truth of the statement rang in her head, though she knew it to be partially false. Majik was a force solely wielded and manipulated by men. Women never had the capability. An Arcanist had interfered on Sayra's behalf, one to whom she owed a lifetime's debt for the victory.

It was a truth she'd *never* confess to Netta.

Her eyes flicked to meet Batar's incredulous ones, his mouth firmly pressed into a severe line. Purple flushed through his tanned skin, age lines becoming more prominent at his anger at the interruption.

A deep voice lazily drifted from above, its tone reflecting someone in a position of authority—one whose word demanded unquestioned obedience. "That's ridiculous. The acolyte relied solely on her abilities to score the outcome. I, among the other Arcanists, would have seen majik should it have been summoned by a *female* no less," the figure said, his charcoal cloak rippling as he waved a hand at the display before him.

Chuckles sounded from a handful of Arcanists, the notion of Netta's claim completely inconceivable. Batar dipped his bald head in acquiescence, his features regaining their stern composure before shifting toward the sprawled acolytes before him. Folding his arms parallel, he raised his chin and glared at Netta's disbelieving face.

"As Prince Emrys confirmed, no majik resulted in your ignominious loss. This false accusation will reflect harshly on your accumulative scoring for graduation, Netta," Batar said. He practically growled the words.

Netta forcefully pushed Sayra aside, her eyes writhing with the promise of vengeance. Sheathing her sword, she took to the hallway, exiting into the depths of Saint Highburn Monastery without a final glance at the crowd eagerly lapping the unfolding drama. Sayra gathered herself and pulled back her shoulder blades. A grim line shaped her mouth at the inevitable encounter they'd later have. Replacing her own sword on her left hip, she threw her waist-length braid behind her.

Commotion caught her attention in the balcony. Several nobles quietly conversed with the Arcanist who cleared her name. The dark prince Emrys Navarre. He was notoriously known for his affinity with majik's ominous fire element, his persona embodying the aftermath of the fiery destruction he was capable of. A wink from his gray eyes widened Sayra's, the realization striking her swifter than a snake's bite. A miniscule smirk pulled on a corner of his mouth before his attention returned to the other chattering Arcanists.

For a moment, Sayra was caught off guard by the force of his attention. Her brows knitted together in response, and her mind circled the confusing realization she had gleaned from that tiny, seemingly insignificant interaction.

The dark prince ignited majik in her somehow, something Sayra had only felt when her brother had showed off his majik to her long ago. Prince Emrys had been sly about it, so the match appeared natural to spectators. Such raw talent... and he was only a fledgling Arcanist.

A chill raised bumps on her skin.

Sayra owed *him* the debt.

Batar stepped toward her, his hands rolling up parchment he annotated with the outcome of every match. Clearing his throat abruptly, the monk regained her focus before speaking. "Sayra von Lykken has emerged as victor from the final trial of strength."

Polite clapping sounded from above, lifting her chin and setting her spirits soaring. Sayra had accomplished what everyone else thought she'd grandly fail at. The fruition of her four years at Saint Highburn Monastery at long last revealed itself: her path as an Arcanist's Valkyrie. Without any doubt, she would follow in her late mother's footsteps. A woman whose name was revered within the surrounding lands and the Holy Family that ran the monastery before she died.

To Sayra, it mattered not *how* she emerged victorious, but rather solely that she *did*. Besides, it wasn't as if *she* had cheated.

Bowing her battered form, she took the cue for dismissal and retreated into the hallway Netta had moments before. It stung that the Arcanists barely applauded before turning to chat amongst themselves.

Two nuns closed the oak doors behind her, silencing the chatter on the other side. Within the safety of the empty hallway, Sayra rolled out her stiffened neck, removing a scratched gauntlet to free a hand. She brushed back loose strands of wheat-tinted hair across her sweat-slicked forehead, her metal-clad feet clanking against the marbled floor as she neared an interlocking section of corridors.

A heavy weight settled on her. The knowledge of her debt to the dark prince dampened the victory Sayra should have been reveling in. She only saw the prince in passing before today, only the whispered rumors shedding light on his elusive persona. She wasn't one to gather debts, so she felt strongly obligated to the Arcanist who brought her triumph. In her homeland, to owe another was an immense burden. It was better to stand by oneself than to grow weak and rely on others.

Should he not have acted, though...

Sayra would have been forced to concede her aspirations of becoming one of the best Valkyries within the surrounding countries. Forced to admit she could never one day redeem herself by saving the lives of others.

Now, though, she could make amends.

Nothing sounded more glorious than an hour-long soak in a scented tub to her aching muscles, the thought nearly making her groan at the lengthy wait ahead of her. The acolytes' trials officially concluded with her match, and the scores for each were to be tallied by the officiating monks to determine who would graduate.

Distracted, Sayra didn't notice the gauntlet until it slammed into her chest. She fell roughly to the ground, her armor clanging as Netta's creaked around the corner. A grunt escaped her mouth as Netta hoisted her breastplate, lifting Sayra's torso toward her scathing face.

"You will confess to the instructors," Netta seethed. Her disgusting breath twisted Sayra's nose. "I don't know how you used majik, and I don't give a shit where you learned it, but I felt you using it to slow me down."

Repressing the urge to headbutt the hag off of her, Sayra instead chose to do something infinitely more satisfying. After all, she knew what ticked her rival off. A laugh bubbled from Sayra's throat, a fake restraint shattering at Netta's ludicrous claim. "Everyone knows we can't use majik. It's not my fault your logs for arms weren't fast enough. Just accept your loss, and move on before you become the laughingstock outside of the monastery too."

With a noise of disgust, Netta threw Sayra's shoulders to the ground. She worked to keep the wince from her face, every aching bruise flaring at the abrupt movement. Still, the slight victory warmed her stomach more than the fear of being discovered.

Should they unearth the dark prince's machinations, Sayra could only imagine the consequences of cheating for herself. The least of which was bringing grave dishonor to her family, degrading their traitorously earned noble status and ruining any opportunity for her younger sibling to enter the esteemed Saint Highburn's Academy for Valkyries and Arcanists at the monastery. Not that she'd give a flying *dritt*—a swear word from her home tongue—about their general welfare. Only her younger sister held a place in her heart.

Ahead of her, Netta stormed into the classroom and slammed one of the thick wooden doors with every ounce of her fury. Sayra knew if Netta had stayed any longer, her thinly spread self-control would shatter and get her expelled. After all, Valkyries were supposed to be above reproach in their holy duty.

Well. That was fun.

Finding her feet, Sayra felt a pop in her spine as she followed in Netta's footsteps. Double doors opened to reveal that year's class of acolytes spread across an enormous chamber filled with chalkboards recently erased. The other young women gathered around sturdy oak tables barren of their normal study materials, many standing in collected groups with some resting in the maroon velvet chairs.

Sayra immediately spotted Netta at her usual table, tucked away in the back with her group. Several furious pairs of eyes locked on her the moment the heavy doors shut, and it took every ounce of her resolve not to stick out her tongue at the imposing image they believed they presented.

Some of them should have chosen a trade as a court jester instead.

Sayra would be an esteemed Valkyrie soon enough, and it was high time she rose above the pettiness she allowed herself to indulge in one too many times. Deciding instead to politely smile, she couldn't help but relish the snarling wrinkle of Netta's toad-like nostrils. Turning on her heel, Sayra made for her friends' table in the front, permitting one flick of her thick braid before her back flipped to the ever-troublesome group of brawny rivals. Despite her admirable effort of restraint, she knew at some point there'd be *helvete* to pay when they managed to find her alone.

"Netta and the hags are positively livid. You beat her, right?" asked Kimimari, drawing Sayra's attention toward the acolyte who appeared to personify the word intimidation.

Between her ebony swirl of intricate flames lacing up her arms, strong voice, obsidian hair and eyes, and severe facial lines, she was easily one of the most terrifying girls in their small cadre. A muscled arm draped over her helm, the rest of her body a picture of knightly posturing with her alert stance and ever-observing narrow eyes.

An auburn head swiveled Kimimari's way from across the table, her prim face affronted. "Of course, Sayra won Netta," Lynn rebutted, her heavily accented words lifted from her native tongue of Faenda.

Whereas Sayra had learned foreign languages from a young age, her childhood friend, Lynn, hailed from a lesser house within their home province and suffered extensive difficulties studying the common language at the academy. With the Droden Empire absorbing their homeland, its prosperity had significantly declined along with chances for females to learn the common tongue. Only due to Sayra's lineage was she afforded more luxuries, languages being one of import if she were to be married off for a suitable price. Though she had avoided an arranged marriage with a swift enrollment at Saint Highburn's Valkyrie Academy. A choice her father had no ability to control, even though he currently held an esteemed position within her conquered country. Betraying his own council to remain in power within a new empire did that to a man. He only would have gained more clout if he had succeeded with Sayra's marriage.

Throughout the last four years, Lynn had achieved a suitable degree of proficiency that allowed her to communicate what she intended to convey. However, she was still subjected to ridicule.

"Sayra *beat* Netta," Nes corrected Lynn, thrumming her manicured fingertips on the maple wood of their table.

Out of all the acolytes within their year, Nessika—Nes to Sayra—was easily the most attractive with her smooth darker skin, fully curved lips, high cheekbones, and stunning, heavily lashed, icy eyes. She'd been outcasted due to it. Beauty wasn't a trait coveted among Valkyries. Many presumed she'd flunk out the first year, though they were woefully wrong when she pummeled each of them with graceful ease in the sparring ring. Her hand-to-hand combat was unparalleled, her rank within the top of the class all but guaranteed upon graduation.

Lynn sniffed, but Sayra spoke first to cut off what was no doubt a terse reply with one of her own. "It was close," she grudgingly admitted, bracing her leaden arms against the polished wood. "But I was fortunate to exploit an opportunity to counter."

"Will you have graduation?" Lynn asked, the slight from Nessika all but forgotten in her concern. Her warm, earthy eyes flicked between Sayra's, tiny light freckles bunching around her nose.

Sayra chewed on her lip, considering all of her exam results thus far. In the written and field practical examinations, she succeeded in achieving top marks in her class; however, she only managed to secure one victory out of the five combat matches, all of which weighed heavily on one's score.

But she felt good. Confident. Excellent scores for two out of three were more than others received. Many didn't do well on the practical, and Sayra was more than proficient when it came to protecting her assessors from hypothetical daemon attacks.

Finally, Sayra dipped her chin. "I will. Netta's overall score in this examination was likely much higher than my own and as a result of her loss, should have increased my score quite a bit."

"I have much excitement." Lynn smiled, glancing at each of their cadre in turn. "We shall graduate all as Valkyries."

Sayra politely nodded and smiled when appropriate as the conversation continued. Her mind milled around the experience of majik and the cumbersome nuances of the matter. For one reason or another, whether mischievous or self-serving, the dark prince saw fit to interfere with her match. And she didn't like that one bit. It didn't sit right. What intention would have compelled him to do so, and why would he allow her to know of his interference?

Perhaps he thought her to become subservient, revering his holy *ræva*—yet another of her favorite swear words. Sometimes, Sayra preferred the finesse of her home tongue. While the whole incident could be rounded up to innocent boredom, she had a hunch it was anything but.

She spotted more than a handful of Arcanists spying on them during practice sessions. Many of them were likely up to no good. But until they were full-fledged Valkyries, acolytes weren't permitted to interact with anyone outside of their circle at Saint Highburn Monastery.

Several ancient doors opened opposite of the corridor in which she previously entered, the vast array of acolytes standing at attention as their superiors flooded into the chamber. Robes of ivory filled the perimeter, one prominent exception striding her way to the front center of the boards. Whereas the hundred acolytes' armor was dulled from mock battles and bore an array of damages, hers was a radiant ivory of perfection—edged with the finest runic gold lettering and adorned with the cape of the Holy Valkyrie. A stunning depiction of the warrior goddess mid-combat, flaring across the velvet, the likeness of the monastery's renowned cross carved below her left clavicle.

Out of the corner of her gaze, Sayra noted Lynn's reverence as the legendary Sanctus Catara Zefare of the Holy Family herself folded her arms behind her torso, taking in the acolytes eagerly awaiting her verdict. Despite herself, Sayra couldn't repress her own excitement at her cumulation of extensive training, and the moment she could finally feel something other than guilt with every morning she awoke to.

Not a scuffle sounded as the professors' steps halted. Nor a breath released until the words were spoken.

"Acolytes," Catara began. Her hazel sight seemingly marked each individual with a sharp astuteness akin to that of a lion with its prey. "For four years, you have striven to perfect your blade, bled to enhance your senses, and sacrificed to devote yourself to the protection of humanity's future." Closing her eyes, her platinum bun crested her head as her chin lowered. "For four years, you've endured extremes in the name of the Goddess and her blessed Arcanists, those we are sworn to protect from the ever-growing influx of daemons that threaten us with imminent extinction. Without Arcanists, every civilization's majik wards would fail, and our people would perish. With our very lives, we must ensure this never comes to fruition."

Swifter than lightning, Catara drew her blade and pointed it directly toward the center of the chamber. Above the pommel, the crest of house Zefare shone in burnished gold. Ferocious was too tame a description for her wild and determined countenance—an image painters could only hope to achieve in their most glorious of works.

"Do you still strive to uphold these values?" she roared, her passion resonating with the gathered crowd.

Sayra set her chin a hairsbreadth higher when she shouted in unison with her sisters. "We do!"

"Then, no matter what results you are given today, know that each of you has accomplished all that a solemn population could ever hope for. In your pursuit to follow our Goddess's will to become protectors of Arcanists, you have sacrificed much. You will sacrifice much more to keep Arcanists from dying. To give them that extra second to cast a spell to save their lives and that of others. In this endeavor, we have never been more successful. Let us spare a second of silence for those who have given their lives thus far in pursuit of this honor." Catara sheathed her blade and bowed her head in remembrance.

Closing her eyes, Sayra nearly shivered at the chill that raced down her back. Everyone present felt the gravity of the moment. They were all faced with the knowledge they could have rejected the Change—a majik bestowing acolytes with enhanced abilities, senses, and regeneration—upon entry into the academy. The day was scarred into their memories when the Grand Priest of the Holy Family visited to bequeath the Goddess's mark upon the nape of their necks. Only two-thirds of the acolytes survived in their class alone, the mark too great a power for some, leading to death. It was a blessing only females were chosen for the duty, else the ever-dwindling population of men would have since perished.

"May the Goddess watch over you all," Catara murmured, resuming her initial stance with her hands clasped behind her back.

"And over you," they responded, the formality ingrained from years within the monastery's Valkyrie Academy, a sister school to the Arcanist's Academy across the grounds.

Waving a hand toward Batar, an instructor of hand-to-hand combat and an Arcanist, Catara stepped aside as the monk unraveled a fresh scroll inked with brackets of names. The girls all sharpened their focus, Sayra becoming impatient from the lack of an immediate answer. The announcement was finally to be known to all, and she desperately hoped for an elite position. Her chances of making something of her life would be remarkably better if she held a greater responsibility.

There was always the chance of receiving a minor house, in which case she'd be sequestered to a single village for a lifetime. Awful. What a waste of her second chance at life. Though it wouldn't be nearly as horrible as it would be not to graduate at all.

Their combat instructor cleared his throat, every pair of eyes on his calloused hand as he wove a spell of majik. "We shall announce first those who graduate with honors, those who will receive the duty of guarding prominent Arcanists hailing from esteemed households across the kingdoms, empires, and nations alike..."

After all, Saint Highburn Monastery hosted students from every country on the continent.

Batar's voice droned on, the list of names passing by in an achingly slow manner. Sayra shifted her weight in annoyance, but when Nessika Onai's name was called, pride blazed inside of her at the accomplishment. Nes truly was one of the best candidates, and when her name was majiked onto the board, Sayra's countenance ever so slightly broke as a smile fought its way to the surface.

When the list reached thirty-eight, Batar returned his sights to the acolytes, each of them drinking in his every word. "Next are the graduates who will receive positions specially elected by the Grand Priest himself. Those who have the honor will have the holy duty of protecting the monastery, duty stations throughout the continent, and the Goddess's will," he explained as if they hadn't had the brackets drilled into them from the day they arrived.

Sayra wished he'd skip the formalities and simply copy the entirety of the list on the board. It positively killed her not knowing whether she'd graduate or if she would be assigned to an Arcanist. She only had one dream, one future she chased more than anything. While being assigned to the monastery could still lead to it, she desired nothing more than protecting her own Arcanist. After her brother died, Sayra would wreak havoc before allowing anyone else under her watch fall to a daemon's menace.

Ticking her jaw from side to side, she refrained from tapping her foot as names appeared before them. Twenty-nine were called for that bracket, none of which were her cadre.

"Two brackets remain," Batar announced in a gravelly voice. Sayra's heart pounded in response. "Those who will be assigned to lesser nobles and the unfortunates who will not be graduating with the title of Valkyrie."

Sayra gritted her teeth, ardently praying to their supposed Goddess or whatever greater power would grant her wish. Yes, it was completely awkward for her, a Faendan, to be praying at all. The very essence felt contradictory to the majority of her people. But if it worked for most of the land, perhaps there was something to it. Even if the believers looked silly doing so during their weekend congregations.

Of course, Sayra supposed she should be less critical. The slow incorporation of religion into her homeland decades ago allowed her to attend Saint Highburn's Valkyrie Academy in the first place. An individual without religion wasn't welcomed to walk within the monastery, let alone reap the wealth of knowledge and majikal benefits of the Goddess's grace.

"This year, due to the limited number of Arcanists present in your year and available positions elsewhere, seventeen acolytes will be unnecessary. Those with the lowest rankings will not be named and will be required to remain within the classroom after the next bracket is revealed," Catara said, her expression reflecting the serious nature of the next group.

Batar resumed his majik list. "And so, those in the third bracket are Zena Lekahr, Netta FeShire, Kimimari Hayashi..."

Sayra held her breath, elated to hear Kimimari's name called, though disappointed Netta's was among the chosen. Five names had been called, none of which were hers or Lynn's. Swallowing hard, Sayra's dark brows knitted together in concern.

Seven names.

Her fingers twitched, itching to know the outcome.

Eleven names.

Sweat beaded on her forehead, her vision tunneling on the ever-growing list of names.

The thirteenth name was called: Lynn von Naykarn. Her friend visibly swayed beside her as relief flung through her body, her future secured in the Valkyrie's ranks.

Fourteen names.

A slight tremor raced through her hands, her nervous energy seemingly a tangible force about her. With each passing person called, she felt her eyes grow a margin wider.

Fifteen names.

Please, please, please, she silently begged, a thing she hadn't done since she lost *him*.

"And our final graduate ranking at number eighty-four in the class, Allera Benevski."

Sayra had failed.

"No," she whispered, her voice so soft that no one beyond Lynn could hear it. Her friend's head tilted forward, a small gesture in tribute to the gravity of Sayra's loss.

Not that any of it mattered anymore. Sayra had failed, and her words carried no weight beyond her own bubble. Whether she remained collected and composed no longer affected her future. Posture was irrelevant when you held no value in their eyes. She'd be forced to return to her family in disgrace, having no purpose other than to be married off to some wealthy gentleman with a strong, noble lineage so she could contribute to humanity's growing population. The notion sickened her to no end.

Perhaps Sayra could escape and become a mercenary for hire, protecting anyone who could pay from the Horde of Daemonkind roaming the untamed land between civilizations. Any fate would be better than that of a *wife*, doomed only to produce heirs at all costs. She wouldn't share a husband with another for the sake of having as many sons as possible. Marriage used to be a sacred thing once, from what her mother had shared before she passed. Before the ghastly daemonic specters began hunting down men, drastically reducing the ratio of genders to a scant one male to every ten females continent-wide.

Recently, it was rumored the ratio had gotten even worse.

Only females were spared from the violent ending of a daemon's wrath. It was an anomaly when they died without provocation, only occurring when a female chose to fight back or run. Thus, they made up most of the remaining population of humankind, making them the ideal candidates for chancing their lives to protect the remaining men. Most of the monastery staff members were female as well as all the acolytes. Few monks aided in their education, those who did being masters in their trade. Sayra didn't mind. Not when the situation permitted her to become a warrior rather than a homemaker. Women weren't given many choices otherwise, only a gifted handful provided opportunities to excel in different trades.

Well, except in the southern democracy of Highlands. There everyone was equal in standing and considered apostates for forsaking the Goddess and rebelling against the faith with widespread violence.

It wasn't an appealing life to Sayra. She liked her violence in small doses. Preferably against the hags.

She had strived to be able to make a difference in the world, going as far as receiving the Goddess's mark and clumsily learning swordsmanship. As her friends glumly exited the whispering room to clean up after the day's conclusion, she couldn't bear the pitying glances or the reassuring hand Lynn placed on her shoulder before she followed the others. It was only when Netta stormed past, roughly clanging into her back, that Sayra snapped out of her downward spiral with a pissed expression.

There were options she could turn to before resorting to a return to her homeland. After all, undergoing four years at the academy earned her some prestige, even if she didn't graduate. She was only nineteen years old. She had options.

Right?

Chapter Two

SYLVEN

It sickened Sylven to watch the acolytes' training and to know they'd all die for absolutely nothing. Just as his sister had when the Arcanist she protected watched her die by the claws of a daemon. The man hadn't lifted a single finger to help.

A sneer crept across Sylven's face, his inclination to be independent ironclad. As an Arcanist, he would never equate a Valkyrie's life to that of a temporary barrier. He endeavored to show Arcanists they could be just as effective as Valkyries, if not more so.

"As you're quite aware, your future Valkyrie might fight in this final match," Rys drawled, his carefully maintained expression looking over at his closest friend, Sylven. Rys was known as Prince Emrys to almost everyone else. His fabric, a mild black, contrasted against the mass of navy uniforms clogged around the marble handrail that barricaded the fifteen-foot drop into the acolyte's training arena.

Sighing deliberately, Sylven rested his head against the wall, his withering glance not appearing to have any impact. "You take me for a fool if you think I'm going to abandon my own values in favor of hiring one of *them*." Which Rys knew. "Why are you pushing the matter yet again?"

Rys draped an arm on the handrail. "Perhaps I was trying to convince you to join me in observing."

Sylven repeatedly bumped the back of his head into the marble wall. The moderator, Batar, if he recalled correctly, announced Netta and Sayra would be fighting next. The names didn't mean much, though he did see other Arcanists whispering as they pointed at the young women emerging below.

A stocky Arcanist nudged his friend a couple feet from Sylven. "The bigger one is brutal. Netta's a beast when it comes to these matches."

His shorter friend nodded eagerly. "Netta's going to win for sure." Brown eyes fell on Sylven as he listened in. "What do you think?"

A scathing frown crossed Sylven's face. "I'm terribly sorry. Have I not made it clear enough in the last two years at the Arcanist Academy that I have absolutely no vested interest in this?"

The stocky Arcanist rolled his eyes, taking the conversation down a notch so Sylven couldn't overhear any longer.

Rys's eyes had a calculated glint to them, causing Sylven to pinch his brows. "One of these two has caught my interest and may end up contracted with me." A sly edge clung to his words.

What was he up to?

Sylven's fingers drummed a restless pattern against the rich material of his navy cloak. Eventually, his curiosity won out. Stepping forward, he tilted his head to look down at the two acolytes. A blonde, scrawny girl swiveled her foot nervously as she squared off against her opponent. The plates of metal hanging from the acolyte's frame were ill-fitted. Not only did she appear to disregard the protocol for helmet usage—the entirety of her sun-tanned face exposed—but she had a golden fabric tied around her lengthy braid that would only prove to be cumbersome in a genuine battle. It would be far too easy for someone to pull her hair, and for what? To look pretty?

It was painfully obvious that acolyte didn't belong within the ranks of her peerage. She was much less physically capable, a longshot to score the feat. The other girl was a mass of muscle, her back to Sylven and Rys.

It didn't boost his confidence when he noticed the scrawny one discreetly flipping off her opponent in a manner that only a handful of observant Arcanists could spot from their second-story perimeter. Sylven's expression tightened as he met Rys's eyes.

"Tell me you're not favoring the small one in this farce," he said.

The prince only quirked a corner of his mouth in response.

Groaning, Sylven shook his head. "I can't watch this."

Rys's stormy-gray eyes scrutinized Sylven as he returned to his reclusive corner for a second before flicking back toward the afternoon's last match. His light skin contrasted against straight onyx locks. A regal, unforgiving edge made his appearance just intimidating enough that everyone kept an extra foot of distance as they observed the combat below. Sylven knew of no other who had such extensive control over their emotions. Rys was a marvelous actor when necessary, making it difficult to decipher when he was truly portraying his innermost self. It had been a problem since the day they met.

Yet, people still gravitated toward him. The prince of Acacea was a second son with no hope of inheriting his father's throne. Somehow, though, he commanded more attention and respect from his peers and superiors than Rys's elder brother, Vander. Perhaps it was because of Vander's roguish personality. Perhaps it stemmed from his lack of reservation that Rys excelled at maintaining. Whereas Rys kept a cool demeanor, Vander's was gallingly welcoming and open.

It never ceased to baffle Sylven.

Silence overcame the small arena, bringing with it a sense of relief that Sylven could soon leave. When he heard Batar call out the victor's name, he could have *smiled* at the prospect of returning to his training. It peeved him to no end when the instructors mandated they observe the acolytes' final trial before graduation when he wasn't even contracting one.

Wasteful.

Pushing himself off the wall, Sylven had only stolen a single step before an enraged shout arose from inside the ring.

"She used majik to win!"

The accusation cut through the air, leaving a single moment of stunned silence before the Arcanists began crowding forward. It took him the blink of an eye to process the outrageous claim. Sylven's feet moved of their own accord toward the handrail. His shoulders brushed against another's as he shoved his way beside Rys, a grunt of annoyance sounding from the Arcanist he bumped into.

Sylven ignored it. He was far too invested in the false claim and the unfolding drama.

The first thing Sylven noted was the scrawny acolyte with dented armor standing with her sword awkwardly positioned over her opponent's neck. The beefy acolyte appeared outraged, obviously furious *that* girl bested her.

Still.

There wasn't the slightest chance she manifested majik, and it had to be a desperate ploy on the loser's agenda. No female could wield the gift. It was a male's bane to wield against daemons, a blessing from the Goddess that allowed them to protect the others.

Rys's voice snapped him out of his wandering thoughts. "That's ridiculous. The acolyte relied solely on her abilities to score the outcome.

I, among the other Arcanists, would have seen majik should it have been summoned by a *female* no less." Arcanists around him laughed openly at the thought of women wielding majik.

"If that were the case, then daemons would attack females too," one Arcanist snickered nearby.

Sylven's brow crinkled, taking in the prince and his declaration. It was rare for him to flout his authority, and even more so to show interest in something as paltry as a loser's wild claim. The overseeing monk accepted the validation without hesitation, but Sylven didn't. As Batar chastised the lying acolyte, Sylven whispered to Rys, "Out with it, Rys. What are you up to?"

Sylven's eyes flicked between his prince and the acolyte that squirreled herself into Rys's small scope of interests. The former's statuesque expression returned to the girl below as her body was roughly shoved aside by the retreating loser. Her lengthy, wheat-hued braid trailed down the middle of her head, swaying lightly when her sharp green eyes twisted back toward Prince Emrys.

Despite the tiny tells, it wasn't until Rys returned her perplexed expression with a subtle wink and smirk that Sylven knew he had an underlying agenda with his interference. After all, every movement made, word uttered, and portrayal expressed had a purpose for a personal motive of his. Prince Emrys had initiated another constructed ploy, and Sylven knew it would be yet another plan that proved irksome and exceedingly tedious to fulfill. Rys had a tendency to involve him regardless of his individual choice in the matter.

A muscle twitched beside Sylven's eye, his mind puzzling over what the connection was between Rys's agenda and the acolyte he defended. "Rys, why are you vouching for her?" His words came faster and faster as he spoke them. "She's dismal at best, she has an attitude problem, and she clearly has no sensibility to protect her head with a helmet in a *sword fight*. Speaking of swords, she can barely wield one. No one will bid for her."

Sylven was quite certain the girl would die if she fought a daemon, and her Arcanist with her.

"I don't think I've ever heard you so interested in an acolyte before," Rys replied, an amused shine lighting his dark eyes.

Sylven threw up his hands in exasperation.

Abruptly clearing his throat, Batar regained control of the proceedings with a stern expression. "Sayra von Lykken has emerged victorious from the final trial of strength."

The girl—Sayra—lifted her chin defiantly at the sound of polite clapping on the arena floor, lowering her battered upper body in a shallow bow as if somewhat offended she didn't receive a hero's applause.

Rolling his eyes in blatant annoyance, Sylven scowled at the snow-crusted rooftop window as the final trial cleared out. Rys politely returned conversations with a handful of the pestering Arcanists who stole the opportunity to further their graces with him. Running a hand behind his neck, Sylven grew restless at the passing minutes—until movement shifted his focus toward the oncoming duo of Arcanists.

What a drag, Sylven thought.

Reluctantly, he placed himself by the prince's side, subtly gesturing to the company walking toward them. A silent exchange of acknowledgment flashed between them, Rys politely excusing himself from the discussion of tomorrow's ceremony of the Old Covenant.

Leaning against the cold railing, Sylven inclined his chin, giving a carefree appearance. Beside him, Rys pulled his shoulders close, his expression unwavering in the face of the incoming heir of the Droden Empire. After all, the small sovereign entity of Saint Highburn Monastery hosted the elites from every kingdom, empire, and coalition on the continent, providing an unparalleled education to the scant population of men in order to establish ties within each country.

Average in everything, with the minor exceptions of his bulking frame and sharp tongue, Kenji Haru posed more of a threat to Rys's Kingdom of Acacea than any lingering daemon beyond the towering monastery walls. Kenji's burgundy cloak flared about him. The differing colors both he and Rys boasted signaled their elevated status within the monastery.

"Austere as ever, Sylven Astor," Kenji drawled in his deep tenor, halting a matter of feet before him and sporting the grin of a wolf.

Sylven's mouth twitched down in displeasure, reluctantly repressing the desire to rise to the bait.

Gold-brown eyes drifted toward the prince, thick brows lifting just so. "Emrys, Emrys, Emrys," Kenji sighed, giving an awed shake of his head. "What a wonderful batch of fine acolytes this year, don't you say?" His arms stretched out, palms up, to emphasize his point.

Sharing a courtly nod, Rys said, "Indeed. I believe us to have sound guardians and a promising year ahead of us." He clasped his hands. "If rumor is to be true, I hear you won't be partnering with a Valkyrie of this class?"

Kenji's square face became sly, a hand flaring out with relish. "I'll indulge you just this once and lay rest to the rumor. Yes, rather than contracting with a lovely Valkyrie from this year, I intend to hire elsewhere."

One of his usual lackeys, Cage, jerked his head toward the sparring ring, locks of his chestnut hair swaying just above his copper-flecked eyes from the movement. "I'll put in for a Valkyrie, though. Despite others having—"

Kenji's narrowed eyes flicked to the shorter Arcanist, his pointed glare a warning should Cage continue.

Clearing his throat, Cage appeared slightly sheepish as he said, "Anyway, I'll be joining you two at the class ceremony in the morn." He shuffled his feet, turning his face toward the ground.

Shaking his head, Sylven tapped his hand once against the marble. A short walnut lock of his hair swayed just above his brow. "As I've been saying for years, I have no intention to bid." His brows lowered to emphasize his seriousness in the matter.

"I'll have to express my deepest condolences then," Kenji replied, his expression displaying his surprise and underlying amusement. "My convictions of you have been misplaced."

Sylven shifted his weight forward, folding his arms across his chest in irritation. "How so?"

"I thought you were simply vying for attention all along. Trying to further emphasize your aversion for your fellow Arcanists and the invasive covenant foundation." A slow, devious smile grew on the heir's face as he spoke, each word directed to incite a reaction. "You seemed the sort."

I am not some petulant child running around spouting lies to get noticed. I've always meant what I've said, Sylven thought. His nostrils flared, his impulse driving him forward a step toward the Droden heir before a voice cut in.

"Will we not be enjoying your company tomorrow during the Old Covenant ceremony then?" Rys asked, giving Sylven time to cool off.

A short laugh escaped Kenji's mouth. "I'll be there to reap the benefits. I've been waiting far too long to contract with a Valkyrie. Without a doubt, I won't miss the ceremony. I'll formally sign with my chosen one as well. She'll be attending despite not being in this class."

"Excellent. Not to say that our conversation has gone too long, but unfortunately, I have business of the highest import to attend to before the eve grows much later," Rys said, his tone clearly conveying his lack of regret for the interruption.

A flash of disappointment crossed Kenji's face, that viper's smile ebbing away. "I suppose I'll look forward to your company during the bid. Until then." The words echoed around them without the dozens of bodies that were once present. He dipped his flattened chin, beckoning to Cage as they swiveled toward the winding staircase that descended into a corridor encircling the arena.

Releasing a pent-up breath, Sylven flexed his hands from the balled-up state they had fallen into. "I will never understand how you can routinely manage conversations with the likes of *them* and not become embittered over time."

Rys rested a hand on his shoulder momentarily as he stepped past, permitting a shrewd grin to crack through his demeanor. "All part of the endgame, my friend." He paused at the stairwell's entrance, his face tipping toward the arena with a near-imperceptible glance at the same passage the unseemly acolyte, Sayra, took minutes before. "They are but pawns in the path of a rook." Descending the steep steps, he murmured to himself, "And the long-anticipated time has come for the second rook to chance its first action."

CHAPTER THREE

SAYRA

Glaring at the back of Netta's helm, Sayra remained standing beside her seat in the ever-quieting classroom. The monks, nuns, Catara, and Batar all remained behind, silently observing the unfolding scene before them. Their eyes were assessing, constantly picking apart every movement, noise, and expression of the remaining handful of failed acolytes. It was nearly eerie being assessed in such a manner as the last graduating Valkyrie exited the room.

It felt surreal.

Four years of training. Four years of promises they'd all graduate—until this semester, when they shared there were too many acolytes and not enough Valkyrie spots. It never made sense to Sayra and her cadre. Could they have such a thing as too many? Regardless, the Holy Family running both academies on the monastery grounds had left room for no questions.

People died in abundance still. Despite the precautions men took when traveling between cities, such as traveling during daylight, having guards or Valkyries escort them, and staying along the main routes, there were still occurrences where someone stayed outside too close to nightfall. Some were ill-prepared, not bringing an extra wheel, and their carriage broke down in between two safe havens. Others were downright stupid and didn't factor in certain distances.

Extra Valkyries could mean more guards for the cities and for travelers. Was there any way Sayra could convince them of that?

She chewed on her tongue, her mind desperately whirling with possible ways to ask. Her eyes crossed with Catara's, and something caught her attention. For a second, Catara's lips pressed together, her eyes darkening with... regret? Anger? Sayra couldn't discern what. Catara twisted away, signaling to the two nuns.

Both nuns moved to close the grand doors without a glance at any of the acolytes. Did whatever came next require secrecy? What *would* come next? Especially considering they all bore the Goddess's mark, which majikally enhanced physical abilities but didn't grant the ability to wield majik. Would they be forced to work at the monastery in a different capacity? Perhaps they'd work as regular guards? If it weren't taking every ounce of self-restraint to maintain her wavering composure, Sayra would question the odd behavior.

Footsteps echoed down the hall the acolytes had walked out of. The nuns halted their movements on either side of the doors, choosing instead to reopen them to allow passage for the incoming person. A majority of the failed acolytes either didn't notice or didn't care after the news they'd received, selecting instead to stare blankly at the floor or ceiling while awaiting their next order.

Strands escaped from the young girl's tight, mousy bun, clinging to her sweat-slicked brow as she entered the somber room. Her voice was breathy as she announced her arrival with a bow. "Monk Batar, I have a missive for you from the Grand Priest to be read immediately."

"Bring it here, child."

She carefully handed the scroll over to Batar, who opened it without further delay. The runner turned tail, rushing back to deliver the next letter her job demanded. Sayra's eyes were pinned to the scroll in Batar's hands, occasionally attempting to decipher the message from the hints of surprise his lifted brow and deepening facial lines betrayed. Seconds passed before he wrapped the paper back into its original shape and tucked it into one of his many pockets within his robe. He pulled out his original list of acolyte names and brackets. With a quick nod of confirmation, he turned toward the chalkboard and muttered a single spell under his breath.

Transfixed, Sayra's eyes widened as additional letters majiked onto the board, Batar's voice ringing out through the quiet chamber.

"We have one additional request from an Arcanist at the last second. We shall select the next highest-scoring acolyte to accompany him as a Valkyrie," he informed the crowd, his hand dropping from the board at last.

There, scribbled in chalk, were three new words under the lowest bracket.

SAYRA VON LYKKEN.

Sayra didn't believe in the Goddess the church preached about. Not when her homeland revered the very ground they walked on and nature itself. But at that moment, she thanked whatever greater power was watching over her.

Elation sang through her very soul, an energy like no other, revitalizing her spirits. Sayra nearly forgot to bow before exiting to follow the other graduates. Catara's gaze trailed her the entire way as she left the forbearing classroom and the sixteen acolytes who couldn't leave with her.

While Sayra felt empathetic to those left behind, she couldn't believe she was returning to the dormitory. Despite herself, a relieved grin spread across her face when she entered the acolytes' central courtyard. Rays of sunlight shone through breaks in the massive clouds above, creating the illusion the white marble every building was predominantly made of was radiating as a source of light itself.

Sayra was practically skipping with relief and joy across the snow-crusted cobblestone pathway, weaving through towering pines. One of the well-sheared bushes twitched alive as a snow rabbit darted across her path and disappeared into the plentiful shrubbery. Her feet guided her to the entryway of the dormitory, three stories of windows flurrying with the activity of those preparing themselves for an evening's celebration. The sharpened-steel ends of her footwear nearly scraped into the stone stairs leading to the stunning vine-wrapped structure. Her hands caressed the silver handle that would allow her to join her sisters, her intentional pause permitting her to savor the memorable moment.

She'd prove herself an asset regardless of her lowest graduating score and what others believed she was capable of. Oh, she was going to wreck *helvete*—hell—making a name for herself.

A devilish grin split her face as she twisted the lever, only freezing when a familiar voice called out to her.

"I believe it's time we speak," the dark prince said, pulling her gaze to his snow-spotted form. Prince Emrys stood so ridiculously still across the courtyard he could have been mistaken for a statue had it not been for the ever-shifting intelligence behind those unmistakable eyes.

Well, *dritt.*

A surge of annoyance rose in her like a snake. Two factors played into the frown that spread across her face and the fists that clenched as her armor clanked through the courtyard to stand in front of Prince Emrys.

Firstly, she knew she owed a debt for her place within the Valkyrie's ranks. The thought irked her more than Netta's flat and blotchy face, and *that* said something. Secondly, he absolutely spoiled her grand entrance back into the Valkyrie fold. Time was ticking. She didn't want someone to discover she was joining them before she could make a dramatic appearance.

Prince Emrys held up a gloved finger, murmuring soft words to form a spell. A shimmer encapsulated them as his hand fell. "We may speak freely. I've ensured with majik that no one may overhear us."

Sayra could feel it too. A cold breeze seemed to kiss her skin as it passed.

Perhaps she should have shown more self-restraint when speaking to the prince for the first time, but he was far too calm about the situation for her liking and could have had her expelled if he was caught. Besides, she once maintained a similar station to the prince's status. A thought that curdled in her stomach.

"Why did you use majik during my trial?" Sayra hissed, her nostrils flaring as she restrained herself from decking his insufferable expression of indifference.

Amusement twitched his brows, the inflection in his voice not conveying the sentiment. "I had no hand in that."

Bewilderment made Sayra fold her arms haughtily. She detested being left in the dark. Her sense of reason began to kick back in and berated her for speaking out of place. The Arcanist was a prince after all.

"Well, then who else?" she ground out. Politer.

"You."

"Females can't use majik," she stated as if it were the most ludicrous thought imaginable. Which, next to her becoming anything but a Valkyrie, it was.

Prince Emrys's face grew grave. His eyes assessed her to the point where she felt her defensiveness escalating. "I wouldn't lie on this matter, Sayra, nor would I waste my time pranking an acolyte when I've gone to great lengths to ensure you'll be graduating tomorrow. At this very moment, we may no longer say females are incapable of using majik—for you are the first."

Sayra opened her mouth to say something, but nothing came out. Her mind whirled as she processed the last few hours. It was painfully obvious to her she had felt the majik as it rushed through her. Even when her elder brother had practiced the Arcane Arts, Sayra only felt a brief breeze of energy around her. Similar to the prince's spell to protect their privacy mere seconds ago. What Sayra felt earlier that day had been vastly different. Never had she felt majik with such potency.

While she'd never crossed direct paths with the Saint Highburn Monastery Arcanists, as every acolyte was strictly forbidden to leave their small slice of the training grounds, Sayra was loath to admit the enigma that an Arcanist's majik had gripped her interest. She'd seen it before with her brother, of course, but it was held closely to every Arcanist's chest, similar to a deep secret, the power used only to solidify their political standings, protect themselves or others, and—in obvious circumstances—train.

If there was one Arcanist who could determine where majik was being used, it was Prince Emrys. He was famous for his exceptional majik prowess and the unique ability to discern when another used it in his vicinity. If he determined it came from *her*, not many would question it ardently.

What did it say about her that *she* could feel majik?

The possibility scared her. She only wanted to be a Valkyrie. There wasn't even the smallest part of her that wanted to be an Arcanist in earnest. And if that brief usage of majik in her final trial hadn't been enough for her to become a Valkyrie...

"What do you mean you ensured my graduation?" she questioned, vividly recalling the runner who had entered with the scroll, requesting an additional acolyte. Her shoulder blades pulled close, her irritation forgotten in her need for answers.

The prince shook his head once. "Not a concern. I have to be somewhere else in a matter of minutes. My presence here is only a formality," he deflected, a flake churning between them in an endless spiral.

Sayra's brows pinched, her previous irritation flaring up. An unnatural silence descended as snow fell in earnest, neither of the two moving despite the icy kiss of flakes against their faces.

"This must remain confidential. You cannot share this with anyone or attempt to use majik again. Your life will be forfeited if you do," he cautioned, two gloved hands reaching back and placing his hood over his head. "Don't take this warning lightly. Covering for you once is manageable. A second instance, however..." He trailed off, his chin tilting down toward her. "That would garner the wrong faction's attention and, with it, swift, decisive action. The kind that will end with your body in a grave and your death a mystery to all who knew you. There's a reason women aren't Arcanists, and it isn't because of the Goddess's will."

"If you knew, then why wouldn't others?" A part of Sayra, a part she didn't want to admit, was terrified. Why would she be killed for having majikal ability? How could she hide it when she didn't know how she used it in the first place?

And what did he mean it wasn't the Goddess's will? Wasn't that what everyone believed?

Prince Emrys shook his head, his deep voice lowering a notch. "No one else will know so long as you refrain from using it further."

Without a second glance, he headed toward the Arcanist dormitory, leaving a multitude of questions in his wake. Sayra stood there for a moment before she decided to act.

"I don't want to owe you for keeping this secret!" she called out, stepping after him. "Besides, I didn't intentionally use it. How am I supposed to avoid it if I have no control? None of this makes any sense! I—"

The prince turned so quickly she nearly bumped into him. Creases deepened the skin surrounding his forehead, firmness lining his chiseled features. "You must not speak of this again so loudly," he advised, his voice edged. "You are fortunate I placed a sound-distorting spell on our perimeter in case of eavesdroppers. I shall also warn you that the walls have ears in the monastery."

Sayra felt her gut churning at that, and questions, so many *questions*, rose to the top. How was it that she alone could wield majik out of every female? Who would hunt her for it? And how did she perform the majik in the first place? Waving her arms to either side, she said, "You cannot just drop all this on me and expect me not to ask questions. You owe *me* that much."

To her credit, she managed not to shout any of that, although she couldn't help the glare in her eyes.

The Arcanist barked a dry laugh, his face growing exasperated. "I can count the number of people who would talk to me with such candor on one hand."

Sayra took that as a compliment.

Prince Emrys sighed out his nose and continued. "Unfortunately, I do not have the time for a lengthy discussion. For now, heed my warning, and when an opportunity arises, I promise that I will discuss your situation then. You owe me nothing when I am part of the reason you're in this situation."

Sayra's eyes widened, her mind more confused than ever. How was he responsible for her having majik?

Before another question could form, the prince beat her to it. "At this time, I'm sworn to secrecy by a higher power than myself. We have a matter of weeks before the next semester commences. Allow me this period to seek what I must to help you upon my return to Saint Highburn Monastery. Until then, this secret must remain between us."

The world spun slightly as Sayra inhaled, collecting her patience. Her mind compartmentalized the information. In her nineteen years, she never once used majik before today. A couple of weeks wouldn't hurt her to wait for more answers.

Prince Emrys turned, raising one brow mockingly as if asking for permission to depart. Something in Sayra wanted to test him, to see if she could trust the inscrutable prince. In Faenda, there was one gesture that meant more than any other when it came to oaths. Pressing her lips together, she held her forearm out vertically, raising her chin. Without hesitation, he responded in like to the Faendan motion and met the scratched metal of her arm with the expensive leather of his, the X symbolic of a vow made in her culture.

Sayra's eyes were unflinching, her tenacity shining through with clarity as she held him to the oath. Grudgingly, she couldn't help but admire his response as she inclined her head to meet his gaze. His resolve was blatant and his knowledge of how to act when presented with a Faendan vow impressive. Whether it was the attractive pull of sincerity or the gut feeling that told Sayra the enthralling man was one to be trusted, she accepted the miniscule act as good faith. When he left the courtyard, she stood vigil and digested everything that threatened to rock her off her feet.

CHAPTER FOUR

SYLVEN

Sighing in defeat, Sylven folded his hands behind his downcast neck. A well-inked paper balled up in front of him held his gaze, unfortunately not burning to ashes from the force of his glare. While it might have ruined his cherrywood desk, he'd be more than willing for the sacrifice if it meant he could procrastinate on his responsibilities. Closing his eyes, he ran through dozens of acceptable replies he could write back to his father and mother that wouldn't be saturated with his revulsion for their choice of topics.

During his time at Saint Highburn Monastery, his parents had an incessant need to ensure their preferences for him to acquire a contract. The term *Valkyrie*, however, was too offensive for him to even *think*. Their blatantly conveyed pleas fell on deaf ears, including their secondary desire for him to begin considering females to court within the esteemed echelons of Acacea's elite.

Ridiculous.

Sylven swiped the paper across his desk, knocking it directly into the waste bin already packed with discarded papers. He had delayed opening the letter for two days. Between Rys's scheming and his studies, he had no desire and little patience to motivate himself to do so.

Tomorrow, he thought. *I'll respond after the Old Covenant ceremony and fill it with blatherings about the festivities so it distracts them from my vague responses to their pestering questions.*

That way, he could support his friends as they formed a contract with their Valkyries while procrastinating just a tad longer. Win-win.

Knocking sounded at his door, a voice barely loud enough to pierce the solid oak reaching him beyond it. "Sylven, you promised me that you wouldn't feed me to the sharks."

"Stop complaining. I'm getting up now," Sylven grumbled, knowing Waylen couldn't hear him. Sliding his chair back, the flame to his scented candle flickered, and with it, a strong waft of pine rose from the melting wax.

Smoothing out the wrinkle in his navy frock coat, he opened the door to find a sour-faced blond boy impatiently tapping his beige leather shoes. "It starts in three minutes. You said you'd meet me in my room," Waylen said accusingly, the expression of frustration unnatural on his otherwise good-natured face. "That's all I asked for on my twentieth birthday last week, and you said it wouldn't be a problem."

"You are practically dragging me into this horrible affair. The least you can do is allow me a few extra minutes to lament the loss of my evening."

Rolling his bronze eyes, Waylen pushed off the door's frame and began making his way toward the reception hall. "It's good for you to be in public at least once a month, you know. Otherwise, you'll end up a hermit." From the tone of his voice, he was only half joking and obviously peeved. Even his steps were louder than necessary as Sylven trailed behind him.

A small knot of guilt wound in Sylven's chest. He didn't have many friends, Waylen and Rys his only two in the Kingdom of Acacea. Sylven's father was King Navarre's right-hand man throughout the king's twenty-eight-year reign, making Rys his brother in all but blood the moment each was born. Waylen entered their circle when his parents, the Rothlanders, were attending court. Not many children of his standing were within the port territory his father's duchy oversaw. For years, Waylen remained at court with them under the care of his mother. All of their parents were closely knitted together, always frequenting each other's estates. Waylen remained closer to Sylven, however. His respect for Rys placed a sort of distance between him and the prince.

"All right, all right." Sylven ran a hand through his short and somewhat disheveled locks. Catching up with his friend's longer stride, he relented. "I apologize for the wait. It was unintentional." At the questioning peek of Waylen's gaze, he added, "I received yet another letter from my parents. They are as demanding as ever, and in my efforts to not throw a book against the wall, I completely forgot what time we were to meet."

"Even I'm amazed at their persistence." Shaking his head, Waylen sighed. "Don't worry about it. I'm excessively concerned over this whole ordeal. I know whoever I end up with will be just fine. I can't help but doubt regardless."

The duo turned into the bustling reception hall, the sight never ceasing to amaze most occupants even if they hailed from a noble house. It was a grand project of architectural mastery, a stunning work of white-veined granite, carpeted with plush burgundy running wide down the center. Two staircases adjacent to opposite walls curved upward to connect to the second floor, and an enormous dais rose to create a third floor in the center. Hosting an exceptionally skilled orchestra, the third floor was surrounded by intricate wooden carvings in the likeness of vines cascading down the walls and intertwining around railings along the stairs. Chandeliers of the clearest crystal floated from the arched ceiling, filling the space with soothing light. A plethora of voices were chattering around, barely discernible from the lively music rebounding off the walls.

Waylen cursed beside him as they crested the second floor, dashing toward a massive central table laden with stacks of paper and nuns monitoring the commotion about them. Already, a majority of his class waited in lines; the luckiest of the bunch had already fulfilled their bid and enjoyed a flute of champagne on the sidelines.

Coattails and waistcoats of every shade imaginable decorated the Arcanists. Sylven's nose wrinkled in distaste at the incessant need of the generational majority to display their gauntlets at a formal event. The claw-like contraptions encircled the backs of their hands, clasping along the palm in polished, dull points. Each pair was handcrafted for their owner, the metal and embedded jewels hues of their choosing. It recently became a fad to display them outside of training and combat, another feather in their plumes.

Sylven understood and respected the use of gauntlets as necessary. There weren't any other means of boosting one's connection to the power of majik deep within the earth. Especially since majik stemmed from individual ley lines that could run too far away from an Arcanist's reach if not assisted by a majik-enhancing device such as the gauntlet. He'd never sport them to appear mightier than another as the rest of his class did. It was an excess of privilege, and—

He stopped.

Taking a deep breath, Sylven forced himself to dispel the lingering annoyance. He promised Waylen his support after all, and it would weigh heavily should he let one of his childhood friends down.

Sylven quietly walked to Waylen's side, taking in the intricate leather-bound binders of the graduates' profiles and the bids for each in the noble category below.

His light-colored brows were bunched in concentration, the cap of Waylen's pen tapping incessantly as his eyes scanned for a particular name. Across the table, a distressed commoner muttered to himself upon seeing the current competition for his preferred tier-three graduate.

Bidding wasn't a financial affair. No, that lump sum was cleared the moment their dues for the Saint Highburn's Arcanist Academy were fulfilled. Rather, it was based on Arcanist rankings at the beginning of their fourth year's winter break. Whoever ranked first would get the ultimate pick, whether he wanted the best or worst of the tier he was permitted to bid on. Each Arcanist was given one slot, and if a higher-ranked student bid over theirs, then they'd be given the opportunity to rebid during the second or third round of the evening.

A draft wafted through the hall from the arching doorway nearby. Three distinctly dressed individuals silently glided toward the central table and ignored any attempt from the serving staff to take their fur-lined cashmere cloaks. The Zendiya oligarchs had arrived to stake their claims, a trio as elusive and reclusive as a black widow tucked into the crevices of an abandoned cabin in an uninhabited forest.

While Droden and Acacea had their everlasting cold-shoulder rivalry, Zendiya was a den of vipers fighting amongst themselves for power in the permafrost-covered northern country. The current Arcanists attending the Saint Highburn were simply a futile olive branch held toward the collective powerhouse of countries in the vicinity to maintain peacetime. A symbolic gesture to share their intention of avoiding war due to a collective need to survive the daemon invasion while simultaneously pandering to the monastery. In return, the Holy Family running

Saint Highburn provided cathedrals and spread their religion through each country, trained their Arcanists with the continent's most brilliant minds, and provided the highest caliber of Valkyries to protect the elite in every country.

The Holy Family granted legitimacy to the current trio of oligarch's claim of power in Zendiya's aristocracy. Only the three oligarchs from their country reaped all the knowledge and protection offered within the monastery. Any other Zendiya Arcanists had to learn from trial and error or any home-grown academies offered within their home country. It placed an enormous advantage on Arcanists who attended Saint Highburn's Arcanist Academy.

Besides, every country knew the more pious they proved to be, the more the Goddess blessed their lands with further Arcanists. It was purely beneficial to ally with the Holy Family and receive the Goddess's favor.

Sylven couldn't be more relieved to live in Acacea. After all, the Goddess gifted him with majik, and he couldn't be more grateful.

Nikolay, Arseny, and Yakov each hailed from a separate family, though they were the only three students at the academy hailing from Zendiya, and due to it, the trio solely stuck with their own company, refusing any social gatherings or partnering with others. Their white cloaks and uniforms were a firm separation from the rest of the Arcanists. In a way, Sylven respected their avoidance of unnecessary indulgences.

"All right," Waylen breathed, his shoulders slouching in relief. He carefully replaced the pen next to the binder, stepping out of the line beside Sylven. "It seems that fortune may be on my side. None in the top fifteen have bid on the acolyte I prefer, so the goddess may smile on me yet."

"It appears all but a few have bid. Many are already indulging in the pastries and drink," Sylven noted, a corner of his mouth turning down at his next thought. "Rys hasn't made an appearance yet. I wonder what's holding him up."

A sly grin passed Waylen's boyish face. "Emrys has already placed his bid," he said, gesturing toward the array of goods across the hall. "Let's grab a bite before they get stale."

Surprise flickered across Sylven's face, his pause placing him a step behind Waylen. The varying shades of three blond and light-eyed oligarchs passed by them as they crossed the hall, not one bothering to glance in his direction despite them being feet apart.

Sylven wished he could be among them, ignored by all and respected for it.

"I can't believe Rys managed to sneak in and escape before we arrived," grumbled Sylven, reluctantly accepting a raspberry macaron from Waylen's plated mound of rainbow treats. The baked goods smelled fresh, a variety of fruity scents rising from the serving table.

"I only wonder what mischief he's managing at this hour," Waylen replied between bites, his eyes nervously pinning each student approaching the table.

Folding his arms, Sylven shook his head, and his voice stayed low. "Rys is up to something. When he meddled in the acolyte proceedings, he all but gave that away," he said, observing the nuns as they began tallying the results of the first round.

A frown crossed Waylen's face, his eyes drooping ever so slightly, though there was no hint of jealousy in his words. "It must be nice to have no care about the results of the round."

Nice indeed.

Rys easily ranked first in their class, making whichever pick he bid on a guaranteed outcome. Sylven bore no small amount of pride for his friend at his accomplishment. His overall scores made him one of the Holy Academy's finest Arcanists to grace the halls in the centuries since it was established. Not even Vander Navarre, the crowned prince of Acacea, could compare with his current marks, and he was in his final year at the academy.

Across the room, Sylven spotted Kenji and Cage laughing amongst a group of Arcanists from the Droden Empire. His face turned sour as Kenji caught his eye with an unabashed grin. The Droden princeling raised his flute in a mock salute.

Sylven wanted to raise something else in a rude gesture.

"Waylen!" Trenden, a lanky Arcanist who would inherit the title of Baron in the Astor duchy, called out. His pale hands adjusted a button on his navy overcoat as he greeted them. "Benjamen and I have placed our bids, though both of our first picks are likely to be taken. How do you fare?"

Shrugging, Waylen tapped the edge of a cherry macaron on his porcelain plate. "I was fortunate enough to bid on my first preference, but we'll see." His brow pinched. "I hope you were both able to pick someone you feel is a suitable guardian."

Benjamen, the son of an earl in the Rothlander duchy, scratched behind his freckled ear in nervousness. "I'm entirely unsure, though I do hope so. After all, we all attend the Arcanist Academy, largely in part due to the promise of acquiring a Valkyrie. Any trained guards pale in comparison to them, and having that reassurance of protection when traveling between city—or country—warded zones is the only thing stopping my anxiety attacks." A shudder raced through his broad frame.

"I refuse to ever travel in the open again without one. I just hope my Valkyrie will live up to the legendary status their kind have."

Sylven breathed out loudly through his nose, Trenden's hazel eyes wincing slightly.

"Except for you, of course, Lord Astor." Trenden dipped his head respectfully.

A frown creased Sylven's face. "For the last time, at the monastery, we forgo titles in deference to the Holy Family and the Goddess."

A small apology slipped from Trenden.

"We are all students on these grounds." Sylven's frown deepened as he met Benjamen's green eyes. "What Arcanists should realize is this academy stands as a school to equip us with knowledge of majik and how to use it to protect ourselves and others." His eyes narrowed. "It is *not* an excuse to hide behind a Valkyrie's sword for the rest of your life and to neglect the potential the Goddess gifted us. None of us should use this academy as a status boost or unearned prestige when there is real worth to be had in the knowledge gained here." His hand pointed toward the monastery walls.

Trenden politely grabbed a champagne flute from a nearby table, drinking it with a tenseness in his body Sylven knew to be from the conversation.

Holding his hands up, Benjamen rightfully looked a shade sheepish. "Well, familial obligation forces some of us here."

Trenden nodded at that, placing his empty flute on a passing serving nun's discard tray.

"Others are aiming for the hefty salary of an esteemed position afterward. The fame is great and all, but for many, the pay is much higher than their station would otherwise grant. For myself, I simply want to graduate and return to working on my family's estate. The freedom to travel with a Valkyrie's protection, both from daemons and any political enemies, is the only bonus that benefits me," Benjamen explained.

Two Arcanists from Droden breezed by, their voices greeting the four from Acacea as they passed. Sylven didn't bother to acknowledge them.

Waylen sidestepped next to Sylven, likely noticing the angry set of his jaw.

Benjamen plopped a whole lemon macaron in his mouth, his eyes darting between Sylven and Waylen.

"Without Valkyries and the premise of this part of the academy, many students likely wouldn't have attended," Waylen reasoned. "If not for that, then the Goddess wouldn't have been able to reach and uplift the other countries as she has."

Conversation throughout the hall seemed to dwindle, a handful of monks moving to the bidding tables.

At Sylven's scowl, Waylen continued, "Think about it. All royalty and many of nobility from each of these countries have had their sons sent here. Here, we weave ties deep within each surrounding country when we graduate and disperse. In this way, it has unified our continent and allowed the spread of the Goddess's faith." He gripped Sylven's higher shoulder with a smile.

The unspoken words lingered in the air. *It's what brought an era of peace to the continent.*

Ultimately, it *was* what led to a theocracy across most of the continent, with the Holy Family running Saint Highburn Monastery at the forefront of power. Sylven felt his resolve soften at that. The last thing he wanted was to return to an era of war, and the Holy Family excelled at unification.

"Plus, some of us don't have the majikal ability to fight daemons." Trenden sighed, his wavy black hair falling to either side when he looked at the ceiling as if searching for answers. "Some of us have majik that is only good for healing. I need a Valkyrie if I'm to live after an encounter with a daemon because I can't heal daemons to death."

Nodding in agreement, Waylen rested his hands in his black trouser pockets.

Trenden seemed to remember he was speaking with his future duke, pulling his shoulders back and straightening his spine. His eyes met Sylven's once more. "I still take my classes very, very seriously. I agree that it's crucial to learn about our majik, the ley lines it comes from, and how to spell cast safely."

Taking a second, Sylven forced himself to swallow his anger's lingering dregs. They were decent points, and it wouldn't be seemly to make a fuss in public over his stance. Even if most Arcanists couldn't admit to themselves they didn't take the curriculum seriously, Sylven knew most could easily fight daemons if they lived up to their full potential. Many famous Arcanists regularly took down daemons with little to no help from their Valkyries. Rys himself could.

It made students purely lazy and neglectful to write off their own efforts with the excuse of contracting a Valkyrie. Except Sylven, of course. He thrived with the world-renowned education the monastery provided. Rys and Waylen were much the same.

The head monk of the bidding event—an Arcanist instructor of fire named Dryd, if Sylven recalled correctly—held up a hand and patiently waited for the vicinity to quiet. His deep voice echoed across the hall, lacking the soothing music emanating from the still orchestra.

"The results of the first round are posted. Those spoken for have been removed from the selection and moved to the northern end of the table for viewing. Those left may now return for the second round of bids," he said, gesturing for the musicians to resume their art.

Waylen hastily discarded his plate, moving with the mass of students rushing to glean the results. A handful of downcast young men didn't bother searching for their outcome; rather, they elected to reinstate their bids with trudging feet. When one's class rank was low enough, it was near impossible to win any bid in the first or second round. Should Sylven have thrown in a bid, he would have been behind Rys by a slim margin with his ranking.

Not that he'd dare. He was above having a Valkyrie, much to his parent's distaste.

Thankfully, it seemed Waylen ranked high enough to secure his preferred acolyte, judging by the elation in his eyes as he passed the binder to the next student in line. There was even a certain lightness to his steps as he rejoined Sylven.

"Seems fortune has smiled upon me—and you, Sylven. My business here has concluded." He grinned, clapping his friend between the shoulder blades.

Thank the Goddess.

Relief made him loosen a breath, the small excursion into the unnecessary scene already testing his patience. "Excellent. I'm grateful all went well for you." Gesturing in the general direction of the Arcanist dormitory, Sylven said, "I must return to my winter readings. I enrolled in Advanced Principles of Wind Manipulation next semester, and already a select group of concepts has proven challenging."

Thick brows shot up in shock. "Even for you?" Waylen asked, somewhat baffled there was any topic that could stump Sylven's natural inclination for his majik elemental affinity.

Every Arcanist had one affinity toward a single element. Wind, a challenging one to work with, was Sylven's.

He answered with a disgruntled noise, walking in silence beside Waylen as they exited the hall and followed the candlelit corridor to their rooms. The doorway opened to their dormitory when they were steps away, a noir-clad figure emerging with an expectant expression.

"Remarkable timing," commented Rys, his chin dipping in greeting. He widened the door and held a hand toward the building. "There are matters I'd like to discuss in my chamber if your schedule permits."

Curiosity nipped at Sylven, his mind concluding the prince was about to divulge an aspect of his latest scheme with them. "I have a spare minute," he replied, nodding his thanks as he passed Rys. Their shoulders were of equal height, though Waylen's rose short by an inch.

"Is this another lecture on the importance of taking classes pertaining to political affairs?" Waylen sighed, trailing behind Sylven and tucking his hands into his trouser pockets. "Because I believe it to be far too late to switch classes at this point in time."

"Actually, it is very much possible to do so if you wish," Rys offered, the note of amusement catching Sylven's attention and dread.

Narrowing his eyes, Sylven twisted his head to pin the prince with his gaze. "You didn't," he grumbled, stilling beside Rys's door.

An enigmatic quirk of the prince's lips was his only response. Sylven and Waylen waited in anticipation, each taking up one of the few spare ebony plush chairs Rys stored beside his modest table. Sylven's foot bounced off the burgundy high-pile rug, his sight searching for clues between the elegantly carved—yet bare—desk and dark fabric-clad sleigh bed. The room was immaculately clean and organized, with textbooks and notes all filed into shelves and cabinets.

Rys took a seat beside his desk, leaning forward as if the weight of his next words propelled him to do so. "I have acquired an acolyte for you, Sylven. Tomorrow, you are to contract with her at the Old Covenant ceremony," he calmly informed his friend, his relaxed countenance contrasting with the severity of his words. "Our fathers were more than eager to make the bid on your behalf when I mentioned your willingness, pulling strings even if it meant hiring an additional Valkyrie from a pool that hadn't graduated."

A second passed. Then another.

Waylen blanched, leaning as far back into the chair as it would permit. Sylven's jaw ticked to the side, his chest rising with a deep breath in a vain attempt to leash his fury.

It failed.

"How *dare* you," Sylven seethed, his hands gripping his knees and causing pain. At that moment, it was the only thing keeping him from leaping out of his seat and storming out of the room. He still had half a mind to.

"I've already invited your family to the ceremony on your behalf and secured one I believe will be beneficial to you and your future responsibilities," Rys said without apology, his imposing gaze unwavering.

Gritting his teeth, Sylven couldn't withhold his impulse any longer. Bursting from his chair, he pointed an accusing finger at the prince's infuriating neutral expression. "You had no right to condemn me to such an invasive and burdening contract with one of *them*," he shouted, chest heaving and fists purpling as they balled at his sides. "You are fully aware of my standing on this matter. So, why? Why would you subject me to this against my will? How can you call yourself my brother in all but blood when you take such actions?"

Waylen shook his head in disapproval. "Emrys," he bemoaned, moving his hand to pinch his nose below furrowed brows.

Rys waited for an opening before responding. "This is for the best, Sylven. You know as well as I that your own goals are unachievable without the aid of a Valkyrie. You can't maintain the charade forever. You're far too intelligent to lull yourself into believing that you'll survive many encounters with the daemonic Horde." A steel glint reflected in his eyes, his already strong facial angles becoming more severe.

"Besides. Our duties fall first to our kingdom, and I selfishly must insist upon better protection for you if we are to proceed as a united front. For years, I have hoped you'd grow out of the negative perception you've bolstered of the Valkyries. For years, I have respected your outlook and opinions to the point of offending those held in high esteem in numerous courts. While some have been understanding due to Jess's—"

Sylven slashed an arm through the air, his eyes positively murderous. "We will not speak of it," he snarled, nose wrinkling in disgust at the disgraceful audacity of the prince.

The incident was far too personal, still fresh and haunting his waking life. He chose not to contract with a Valkyrie to honor his sister, Jess, and for Rys to knowingly ignore that... "You have crossed the line. You've pushed so far beyond it I can't recognize what your limitations are anymore. I'm sorry, but we can no longer be friends since you've taken it upon yourself to manipulate my life, *Prince* Emrys." Bitter satisfaction grew in Sylven's stomach at the ever-so-slight flinch of Rys's face at the formality. "No friend of mine could betray me so."

Before another word could be uttered, Sylven slammed the door behind him, his last glimpse finding Waylen pale and horrified and Rys with eyes whirling from a myriad of undefinable emotions. As he stormed down the lengthy dormitory, his steel will hardened to his one and only goal.

He'd become the first successful Arcanist to hunt down daemons without the presence of Valkyries. Even if it meant Sylven had to break the forced contract by a prince who thought he knew better. All the

Arcanists before him who died weren't half as dedicated as Sylven, and he'd show the world Valkyries weren't the only solution.

CHAPTER FIVE

SAYRA

It was unfathomable that Sayra could use majik, a force so elusive it only selected men. Even then, it gifted only a portion of the ever-dwindling population with the ability to use it. Humanity's survival was becoming more and more of a concern over the last decade and a half, especially when more babies were born female than male. Majik was a great, perhaps the best, method to eliminate the daemons that sought their prey in the night.

If she should be so fortunate to wield a capability with vast potential, shouldn't she learn how to sharpen that tool as well? Would it not benefit whomever she contracted with, along with giving hope the paradigm of majik was shifting?

If females could be born with the potential to be an Arcanist, the church would begin their search for others like her. *Finally*, they could regain authority over the earth and the creatures erupting from its seemingly endless fissures.

The thought of one of those earth-dividing rifts sent a shiver down Sayra's spine. It was common knowledge daemons kept crawling out of those impossibly deep rifts, but no one ever survived a journey close enough to look inside. In recent years, the Horde, a collective name for daemons, had been growing in numbers and ferocity. It was terrifying to the majority and infuriating for her. Sayra was itching to take to the outside, prepared to eliminate any daemon they crossed paths with.

Without consciously moving them, Sayra was surprised to find herself staring at her hands splayed in front of her. Her fists clenched.

Oh, she'd get her answers from the dark prince. There was no way Sayra could tolerate being ignorant for long, and if he decided to take his own sweet time to fulfill his end of the bargain, she'd do some reconnaissance of her own.

Her boots found their place outside of her dormitory entrance once more, and she held her chin high as she entered the bustling corridor.

A *drit*-eating grin split Sayra's face from ear to ear as she sauntered down the hallway, a trail of whispers spreading in her wake. A commotion of activity livened the first-floor common room ahead, girls excitedly chatting about next morn's ceremony from what snippets she could hear. Acolytes gathered around the beige couches dotting the perimeter, the roaring fireplace decorated with varying swords collected through centuries, and the entryway to the higher levels.

"What the *hell* are you doing here?"

Chatter ceased immediately. Bewildered eyes searched for the voice's owner and the one the statement was directed at. A path cleared as the wave of girls separated in front of the stairwell, four incredibly pissed females emerging, each directing their unnecessarily hateful eyes at Sayra.

Hags.

She shared a feline grin, propping a hand on her armor-clad hip with enthusiasm. "Why? Don't I live here?" she asked in an innocent voice, basking in the attention of the crowd and the drama she was stirring up.

"You failed. You don't belong here," a snarky voice chimed in behind Netta's tense frame. Jayde, a towering brunette, glared at her with almond-shaped amber eyes. The acolyte had done more than her fair share of bullying when it came to tormenting Sayra and her friends.

Sayra's grin widened further, her head tilting just so, as if to give the impression of looking down on the taller graduate despite their height difference. "Actually, I've been requested to graduate and will be assigned an Arcanist." Switching her sights to a furious Netta, she added, "It's too bad about your ranking. After all your constant assurances of your above-par performances, I would have thought you to at least pass in the second bracket of graduates."

Netta's eyes flashed with an unparalleled ire, her feet taking an involuntary step before she remembered their company. "You will pay for this, Sayra," she promised in an unnervingly deep voice, the tone chilling to Sayra's ears. "I was to graduate in the first bracket if it wasn't for your cheap ploy in the ring. I know you cheated, and one day, I *will* end you."

The tension in the air was palpable. Every person present hung on every word. Only the crack of the fire startled some out of their trance as Netta and her pals remained insufferably in Sayra's way.

Her lips flattened, jaw ticking to the side at the threat. Head high, she refused to rise to the bait and strode forward, her path directly between Netta and Jayde. Never would she allow some paltry threat to shake her. She was Sayra von Lykken after all, and nothing would ever prove an obstacle to her life's purpose.

"*Du kan prøve,*" she said in Faendan.

You can try.

Bumping her shoulders into theirs, Sayra didn't so much as glance back as she took to the stairs, knowing full well she was stoking the flames. But what was life without causing some trouble? Besides, she absolutely savored the anger left in her wake. Turning into the second-floor corridor, where activity flurried as normal, Sayra noted the serving staff carrying boxes of personal items from a few rooms. Their steps were hurried and the rooms nearly bare as she passed and peeked into each. Ralla, Beaul, and Xena's belongings were being removed, all three not graduating in the morn.

Strangely quick. Sayra frowned, making it another three steps before a shriek sounded from ahead.

"Did you have pass after all? Always I knew success for you!" Lynn's short braid bounced around her ecstatic heart-shaped face, her arms squeezing the breath from Sayra's chest. A burgundy ribbon ran around her hair, catching the nearby candlelight with a shine.

"I did," Sayra wheezed, cheekily grinning at Nes as she, too, emerged from her own room at the commotion.

Lynn hopped back, appearing in the process of cleaning her armor from the looks of the discarded pieces scattered across her wooden floor and the jar of polish open beside a pile of rags.

"About time," Nes commented, relief flickering behind her cool façade. Crossing her arms, she tweaked a manicured brow at Lynn and fixed her errors. "Did you pass after all? I always knew you would succeed."

Rolling her eyes, Lynn waved an annoyed hand at the corrections. "Bjørn will be coming?" Caution rolled in her tone, each word lifting with her thick accent into a hesitant question.

Sayra shrugged, maintaining an air of indifference, even though her mind was raging at the name tossed her way. "My father never thought I'd succeed, so he sent his condolences a week ago." Her lips drew into a fake smile in response to her friend's pitying expressions. "It only makes tomorrow that much better for me since he won't be there and the look on his face that much more enjoyable when he learns of my success."

Both nodded in agreement as a nun rushed by, and they moved out of her way. She carried a giant box in her hands.

Nes tilted her head. "So, what exactly happened after we left?"

Lynn's wide eyes anchored on hers with eagerness.

Hesitating, Sayra had to decide then and there just how much to divulge. Would she trust the prince to honor his vow? For some illogical reason, she didn't entirely believe him. Trust never came easily to Sayra, but she couldn't deny the gravity of his earnest desire to help her. His motivations were unclear, the actions he took unknown, but there was an allure about his countenance she couldn't shake.

Sayra crinkled her brow at that. *I bet he flaunts his mysterious persona to all the ladies.* Besides, while she loathed to admit it, she was a bit paranoid about his warnings. Telling a lady someone may murder her if she spoke the truth would do that.

"Sayra?" Lynn whispered, her eyes concerned.

"Sorry," Sayra apologized as her mind snapped to a decision. "An Arcanist decided at the last minute to contract with a Valkyrie, and I was next in line."

"The rumors are true then," Kimimari said, her lengthy frame intimidating enough for the nuns to go around her as they emptied rooms. The rest of the women moved aside each time. "We all made it to graduation!" A full grin split her face, and a disbelieving laugh escaped Sayra's mouth in response.

"I can barely believe it myself," Sayra admitted, her face an echo of their combined happiness and relief. Lynn even appeared tearful.

The evening quickly passed with reminiscent chatter and inquiries about the future. They shared a hasty meal in the acolyte dining hall, then started preparations for the ceremony. It was oddly peaceful throughout the night, knowing they had completed their basic training at long last and were finally guaranteed spots within the elite society. It was a privilege, albeit a perilous one, where they would need not for basic necessities and could secure a comfortable retirement.

Could.

Life wasn't guaranteed in their profession—one that often proved fatal if the assigned Arcanist traveled frequently. They were all familiar with the consequences of their duty and ready to lay down their lives for the greater purpose. Many did to give their Arcanists time to protect themselves or fight back against daemons. Sayra's mother included. And possibly Sayra too, if she ever made one simple mistake in the heat of combat.

The potential for death haunted many of their darkest nightmares in the late hours of night.

The group finally retired for the evening, armor polished and belongings packed, and Sayra felt an odd twinge in her chest, a pestering feeling as if everything were about to change. A new life was about to start. One where nothing would be familiar. Rather than feeling dread, however, she longed for the challenge. For the opportunity of a new tomorrow. One where she could leap out into the world and claim what was rightfully hers. While she wouldn't ever inherit her birthright, she aimed to collect what her mother left in her stead all those years ago when she perished.

A mantle of honor.

Sayra would become a legend, rumors of her sweeping as far north as the lands of Zendiya and trickling down to the southern country of Kevsha. She'd slaughter every daemon she encountered, defending her Arcanist against any foreseeable threat. Even if she got the worst one of the lot, anyone who attended the academy held prestige and required her skillset. It was, after all, why they hired a Valkyrie in the first place. It would be a tedious journey for redemption, but she fell asleep that night with every confidence it was within her grasp.

Sayra would make her belated brother, Brevn, proud.

⬥

Images tortured her. With a beheaded body prone against the floor, a daemon of hellish origin and uncanny strength caressed entrails while lifting its gaze to meet hers. Its gory mouth wickedly grinned at her. Sayra knew it wasn't a lack of ability or speed that kept it from brutally murdering her next but a sick sense of cruelty that left its prey frozen and numb. It was indescribable. That majikal fear daemons captured their prey with dulled the senses, blocking the urge that normally told a human to *run*. The roaring in her ears drowned out any sound other than her own painful heartbeat and the slow screech of vicious joy emitting from the creature. It was an agonizing crescendo of everlasting torment that would carry well beyond the threshold of the afterlife, the knowledge of it a fate worse than death.

Sayra hid like the coward she was behind the wards of her home, a bleeding wound stretched just below her eyes. It was minor. So incredibly small in comparison to the two dead men scattered before her.

Because of her.

It's okay, Sayra.

Brevn's words haunted her far beyond the confines of the unshakable memory.

She'd been so selfish, so incredibly stupid to defy her father and run outside their web of safety. Sayra felt that incapacitating dread as something evil sprinted toward her. She froze as an enormous monstrosity knocked her to the ground with a single sweep, her body rolling through sticks, dirt, and fallen leaves. Cuts littered her skin, but the only thing

Sayra noticed was the claw pinning her torso down in the following second, another hovering over her face.

She didn't realize the screams were coming from her, not when her brother leaped from the wards with Lynn's brother in tow, and not when the daemon lifted its glistening claw from her face to pounce on them instead.

So fast... It was all over in less than the time it took to stumble the dozen feet back through the wards.

Sayra's eyes snapped open, glazed with pain and clammy as she blocked the memory from her mind once more and set to the task of readying herself.

Even as her nimble fingers wove her strands into an elegant braid, they trembled. Though it'd been years, the memory of losing Brevn and his friend was far too fresh. The thin line where that claw had raked under her eyes and across the bridge of her nose ached, and her mind immediately worked to repress it.

Without the proper time to repair her armor at the blacksmith, Sayra would have to attend the ceremony with what the church provided as a ceremonial outfit. A dark, burnished-gold tunic of the finest fabric buttoned vertically down her torso, a black collar tight against her neck. The fabric dipped into two sharp points, one over each thigh, and was snug along her arms until they reached black cuffs with the sigil of the church sewn in gold. Black vines of fine lace trailed down from the rigid shoulders, the overall look paired with polished leather boots and trousers of a similar shade of black.

While she didn't have many left, Sayra managed to locate a charcoal *slør* that matched well enough for the occasion. She wrapped the thin fabric around the length of her braid, the handkerchief-like material tied by the nape of her neck. As she stared at herself in her bathroom mirror,

Sayra wondered if she'd ever be content with leaving her hair down. A corner of her mouth dropped as she considered it. Women in her culture were supposed to be married to keep their hair loose.

Not a chance.

It was a shame, though, since Sayra was stunning when her long hair was curled.

Although others would typically accentuate their eyelids with a swish of color, their skin brushed with powder and lips shaded red or pink, she refused. She was presentable enough.

It was a solemn yet eager affair as the graduates winded down the seemingly endless corridors to the Great Hall, one of the few rooms that connected to the main body of the church and the Arcanist academy. A majority elected to wear a similar uniform to Sayra, but a select few, notably in Netta's circle, wore brand-new armor sets decorated with capes just like Catara Zefare's. The second set must have cost a small fortune, an option only available to those hailing from wealthier families across the lands.

The moment Sayra ran from her family, she was financially cut off. The stipend given to acolytes had helped her scrape by.

The line of graduates collected outside the southern set of doors, which were made of beautifully carved chocolate-stained oak. Batar and a handful of monks maintained their silence as the procession began, a string of grand music barely perceptible through the thick wood and dark marble. No one was able to stand still for long. A scuffle of feet or clang of armor would occasionally echo through the small antechamber. A monk's sharp eye would then quickly spot the culprit, and silence would return.

Sayra could only imagine the magnificent hall and what the ceremony would entail. From what the instructors had explained, it would be a small affair of church officials—perhaps the esteemed bloodline of the Holy Family themselves would be present—and the families of those partaking in the ceremony. At the northern end, the Arcanists would be gathered, awaiting their cue to make their own grand entrance. No graduate on her end knew who they'd be paired with. Of course, rumors had already circulated that certain acolytes had a *feeling* they'd be paired with one of the few royal candidates due to their outstanding performances.

Sayra couldn't care less who she was contracted with, so long as she could fulfill the role of a Valkyrie. However, the thought didn't ease her nerves in the least. She felt like she was on the edge of a precipice, the yawning depths opening before her. Everything she had fought for, tooth and nail, was about to pay in dividends. The debt she owed to a life that saved hers, to her beloved dead brother, was about to begin repayment.

It made her mouth warble for a heartbreaking moment. A moment that only happened because of *him* and because of his love for his little sister.

Sayra would bring the world to its knees in his name.

Music pitched into a grand cascade, doors widening to the spectacle beyond. As the neatly ordered acolytes filed in, Sayra couldn't help but gawk at the grandeur displayed before her.

So much cobalt, the tint chosen as the Holy Family's standard.

Gold-marbled molding crowned the rectangular ceiling, and a dozen crystalline chandeliers with golden accents were paired across the length. The candlelight bathed the walls and the dozens of gigantic columns in a stunning shade of gold, the color similarly reflected on either side of the marbled floor's cobalt aisle runner. Plush chairs of cobalt velvet lined either side of the carpet, and two hundred occupants clad in fabrics and silks of the finest make expectantly observed from their cushions.

Banners of the church fell from the image of heaven painted far above, the countries they represented marginally smaller beside those. The hall was nearly unreal, almost as if they were inside a treasure chest filled with valuable gilded artifacts adorning the walls.

It was the first true hall of the monastery Sayra had seen. They'd never been allowed to wander through a majority of the grounds.

Across the hall, the line of Arcanists streamed in unison to their own steps, their goal to reach the elegantly robed archbishop grandly presented in the epicenter of the building. Sayra fell last in line, according to her graduation rank, and while a more self-conscious individual might have found less pride in that, she strode with confidence and a dancer's grace. She wasn't naïve enough to believe her presence didn't capture the audience's attention. After all, she hailed from the conquered Empire of Faenda, and her family name bore weight and distinction.

Feet stilling, Sayra stood at attention when both leaders of the lines kneeled before the holy sigil of the church, the archbishop's voice echoing through the hushed hall. A voice nagged at her that she should pay attention to the words of the man. That she should *not* be attempting to peek ahead to witness the first contract in the making.

But when did she ever listen to the voice of propriety?

Straining to maintain a composed stance while navigating over shoulders proved tricky, but at last, Sayra managed to catch a glimpse of the ceremony. What she saw widened her eyes.

The dark prince kneeled across from Nes. Both heads bowed reverently as the archbishop gave his pleasantries and introduction to the gathered crowd. A minute ticked by, the formal portion of the speech giving way at long last to the ceremony. The archbishop raised his hands in prayer, only lowering them upon its conclusion. His voice was methodic. The words flowed with a smoothness that captivated all but

Sayra. Her eyes were only for one man, and it wasn't the holy one clad in snow-white and etched with gold. Rather, it was the figure who struck a remarkable presence in his granite-gray frock coat, each layer darkening below to the shade of anthracite.

Her eyes were glued to Prince Emrys's downturned face, a jolt running through her when his head rose at last, and those impossibly gray eyes somehow marked hers from the notable distance. Sayra refused to flinch or to acknowledge any wrongdoing on her behalf.

Sayra was extraordinary at reading others, a knack she developed at a young age. Perhaps that's exactly what got her into mischief. The talent of knowing which buttons to push and when to push them was how she wormed her way into many fights. She couldn't help it; it brought too much gratification when her sharp tongue did the work of blades. She knew she had more weapons at her disposal than a simple hunk of metal—a dagger that only needed an ear within sight to strike true.

Some marks proved tricky in that regard, but Prince Emrys was a whole other challenge. There was disingenuity to the expression he portrayed, but his eyes were a complex whirlwind of too many emotions to identify—an intricate knot of thread she couldn't untangle. There were moments where one would emerge more prominent than the others, and she could only presume it to be an accident on his behalf for that brief window of openness. An ordinary eye would never catch his lapse.

At that moment, Sayra hadn't a clue of what he was thinking.

The prince's eyes returned to the archbishop's, the majikal aspect of the ceremony about to commence. Both individuals rose, clasping their right hands over the space between them. The archbishop gently rested his palm over them, an awe-filled silence reigning as he uttered words of majik aloud.

Lackluster was the only way to describe what transpired, which according to Sayra's perspective was absolutely *nothing*. The duo stood to polite applause and exited the small passageway behind the archbishop and a portion of the audience. From there, Sayra lost interest and tuned out the array of proceedings until her turn neared. Both Kimimari and Lynn contracted with respectable-looking Arcanists, though not ones she recognized. Sayra only knew of a handful of titled individuals prior to her entry at the academy four years ago, none of whom were the lesser nobility her graduation tier would contract with.

Sayra counted ahead as the pairs dwindled, noting the Arcanist she'd be contracting with well in advance—one who apparently would rather glance in any direction but hers. Whereas the prince was near impossible to decipher, her Arcanist was the complete opposite. He was an open book, his bearing irritated with his pinched brows and unhappy frown.

His jawline was strong, and he had short, wavy hair cut above his ears and eyes. Eyes an average girl would swoon over. Hazel, mixed with a prominent ring of bronze around his pupils, with long lashes and thick, dark brows. To Sayra, he looked to be the same height as Emrys but a tad broader in the shoulders. He did appear rather dashing in his emerald frock coat, though any charm he might have wooed another with fell short due to his sour appearance.

Sayra fell onto a poised knee, bowing her head in mock respect to the foreign religion the Holy Family preached. While she had no belief in their faith and stayed true to her roots, she'd happily comply if it meant she could achieve her vision.

"Arcanist Sylven Astor and Valkyrie Sayra von Lykken. Should you both be willing to partake in the Old Covenant and faithfully serve the church in your endeavors, take now each other's hand," the archbishop said, his words finally reaching Sayra's ears.

Her hand stretched out a beat ahead of the Arcanist's, his unwillingness slowing his efforts. Their hands wrapped around each other's—one noticeably larger—and his eyes at last lifted to meet hers as the archbishop placed his palm in position.

"*Unio*," the archbishop murmured, the jolt of magic flaring alive from his palm and racing through her. What felt like hours passed in a second, her mind floating adrift out of her body.

Sayra's limbs froze as her mind linked with the Arcanist—*Sylven Astor*. For the first time in her life, Sayra saw herself in another's eyes. It was bizarre, almost as if she drifted into a deep sleep and slipped into a dream instead. She expected to wake in her bed with the first trace of dawn entering through her window. Though she supposed that was to be expected when the bond took hold of their very souls, merging a fine bridge between them.

The scar she bore wasn't as prominent as she previously assumed. It was a thin line, pale against the tan of her skin and fading as it crossed her face. Sayra wasn't completely vain, but between her striking light eyes and delicate features, she was quite proud in that moment to bare a scar that contrasted with her non-warrior composition. After all, compared to the other Valkyries, she was gangly. It was no wonder they constantly pegged her as weak.

Sayra would work harder for it, if that was at all possible. Four hours of sleep per night should be doable, the extra hours allotted to weightlifting more than beneficial.

A flurry of emotions crossed her mind. Surprise, unease, and frustration were the most prominent. It took her but a moment to question them, wondering why she felt that way.

Her eyes widened.

It struck her then the emotions weren't hers at all; they belonged to *him*. She could only wonder what he thought of her, likely believing her to be a self-absorbed sort of creature.

Blinking, Sayra returned to her own body, though his emotions were still present in her mind. *That will prove tricky to differentiate*, she thought, resolving herself to grow accustomed to the new development.

"May the Goddess watch over you both," the archbishop said, bowing his head in a shallow gesture.

"And over you," they responded in kind, rising and exiting between the rows of onlookers.

Dread kicked her deep in the gut, her eyes flicking toward Sylven as he gazed awkwardly at a family seated beside him. A man acknowledged the Arcanist with a self-satisfied nod, and a tiny girl and boy radiantly beamed beside their pleased mother. His family. They had to be. Sayra concluded they must not have been on the best of terms if the Arcanist had such a reaction toward seeing them.

Nuns opened the doors for them. The corridor stretched toward the reception hall where she knew she had to introduce herself to her Arcanist and his family before winter break officially began. Sunlight streamed through the mosaic glass, cascading a rainbow of brilliant tones onto the walkway before them. The doors clicked shut, and without a second to spare, Sayra felt Sylven's anger spike before he turned on her.

"I'd like to make this very clear from the start." His brows sank dangerously low above his furious eyes. "We will not be collaborating in any sort of manner. Your presence here is but a formality I must acquiesce to for the time being. I never willingly signed up for this, and I will rid our contract the moment I am capable."

Sayra tilted her head just so. "Oh, come now. I'm not *that* bad." She hated the tiny flicker of hurt she felt at his growing fury.

Sylven stepped forward. "You," he emphasized, eyes narrowing. "You are nothing to me but a major hindrance and inconvenience. I would like to make it painfully obvious that I despise everything about you."

Clenching her jaw, Sayra had to force the words rising out of her down. Otherwise, she just might have made an irrevocable mistake. It was almost as if someone had turned the tables on her. Saying all the right words that dug into her insecurities, words that pressed the knife a fraction deeper. The crack widened, but she could, and *would*, withstand it. Sayra had endured much worse than petty insults from a pompous noble, and besides, once he got over his obvious issues, things would work out. Sayra permitted him to take the lead, biting her tongue as they entered the hall.

Anima, the duo of Arcanist and Valkyrie alike, were scattered across the room, conversing with one another. A sizable group was plating spinach quiches and other hors d'oeuvres beside the tables laden with mid-morning snacks while others collected in small groups on the nearby raised dais. Sayra was admiring the artwork of lacing vines when a man immediately spotted her Arcanist and ventured over, his Valkyrie, Jayde of all people, in tow.

"Sylven!" called out a youthful-faced Arcanist, his brown eyes anxious as he approached. "I haven't talked with you since..." The boy shared a pointed look before frowning at her.

Sayra frowned back, wondering why everyone was incredibly unpleasant that morning. Jayde took a serious stance beside him, her amber eyes sizing Sayra up. Immediately, Sayra threw on a dazzling grin, her voice as friendly as if she'd been speaking with Lynn. "Jayde, how great it is to see you. I truly hope you are well, and I am so grateful that Netta is so *pleased* with her position. I sincerely know of no other who deserves it more than her."

Jayde's eyes flashed, lips pressing into a flat line as she crossed her arms. Before the tall barbarian had the opportunity to retort, Sylven cut in.

"I have no interest in speaking to either of you after that, Waylen. And if you're here on behalf of *him*, you are more than welcome to take your leave as I have nothing to say." He glowered, appearing on the verge of storming out.

"I'm not here for Emrys," Waylen started, lines creasing across his forehead.

Sayra's eyes darted at the name. She analyzed the new Arcanist, attempting to determine the connection between him, Sylven, and the prince. Obviously, things were tenuous at best between the three of them, leading her to believe they might have been friends. The prince had mentioned the lengths he went to in order to secure her a position, and between that and Sylven's exceedingly rude behavior, Sayra assumed he was forced into things.

"I sided with you on that matter, pointing out his error. You both need to talk this out. I'm sure there is a resolution that can be reached." Waylen frowned, concern evident in his tone.

Sylven scoffed, his head shaking at the ground. "I have not the patience to deal with this right now," he said bluntly, turning toward a lone corner of the room and abandoning the conversation.

Sayra stole a glance at Waylen, who appeared equal parts frustrated and stressed, and volunteered, "Sayra, by the way." A quick wink at Jayde, and she was off to her moody counterpart.

Doors opened to a flood of voices as the previous audience entered the reception hall, Sayra dodging the influx of people as she slowly made her way to Sylven. By the time she reached him, his presumed family had accumulated around him with an additional two faces. One appeared to be a younger brother of around eleven, the other unmistakably a seasoned Valkyrie. Both females in the family wore frilly dresses bedecked with jewels of varying shades. The men wore typical frock coats, though theirs appeared to have actual gold embedded into the cuffs and collar. Even the Valkyrie had the finest armor Sayra had ever seen, comparable to Catara's.

Sylven's parents were aristocrats, and judging by the make of their clothes and the way they carried themselves with obvious superiority, they held high standing within their court. That only bemused Sayra further. Why had she been assigned to Sylven if he was such an important figure? The prince had pulled some strings, seemingly going as far as forcing one of his subjects to take her on as his Valkyrie. That was what her logical mind concluded, anyway. There were still pieces she couldn't quite comprehend, the gap too wide for her to deduce any specifics regarding her alleged majik and why the prince cared about her predicament so much.

Even if he claimed he had a hand in it, how would that be possible? They hailed from two different kingdoms.

Then there was the matter of her life being at stake should she share the information.

Hazel's eyes caught hers as she approached, and Sylven's mood immediately darkened further. Really, Sayra was impressed anyone could be so glower. Bowing her head respectfully, she stood beside her grump of an Arcanist and listened attentively to his father's continued conversation.

"It's given me cause to doubt certain perceptions I once held in regard to your stay at the academy. I must say, we were quite ecstatic to learn about your change of heart. We simply must celebrate at the manor," he said, his profile eerily similar to his son's in terms of facial structure, wide shoulders, and near-identical height of six feet.

Dread swam in her stomach once more, stemming from Sylven's probable distaste at the idea of prolonging his stay with his family. Or maybe that Sayra would be present. Before he could reply, his mother curtly cut in.

"This is your Valkyrie, hmm? Introduce us, Sylven," she chided. Her eyes were an almond-shaped version of Sylven's and picked apart Sayra's appearance. Disapproval shone in them the longer she dissected her.

A pin of alarm raced through the bond between them, and Sayra realized Sylven hadn't the faintest clue of her name despite it being announced during the ceremony. It only made her slightly smug since he was being an absolute *dritt*. Sylven shuffled in place, running a brief hand behind his neck before facing her.

"This is my father, Duke Everis Astor, and my mother, Duchess Tianne Astor. My sister Lina and brother Regen," he introduced, holding out a hand toward each. Both siblings had similar brunette hair, theirs as wavy as their mother's. Lastly, he turned to the Valkyrie. "Korine is my father's Valkyrie and has been a part of our family for twenty-three years."

An auburn bun dipped in acknowledgement at Sylven's words.

Before he blundered the remainder of the introduction, Sayra stepped forward to continue on Sylven's behalf. "My name is Sayra von Lykken. It is my pleasure to formally meet your acquaintance," she presented, lowering her head and crossing an arm over her heart before rising. It was a custom in Faenda for greeting esteemed individuals.

Surprise shot through her mind, followed by increasing suspicion. Sayra wondered what exactly was running through Sylven's mind.

"Lykken," echoed Everis, his emerald eyes interested. He turned his head, dipping his chin to make it even with hers. "Duke Bjørn, the previous emperor of Faenda, is your father then?"

"Yes, Duke Astor. Making my mother Arene von Lykken." Out of the corner of her sight, Sayra noted Korine's eyes widened. Even Tianne seemed taken aback before resuming her critical gaze.

Sniffing, Tianne flattened an invisible fold in her dress. "It is only proper after all. My Sylven deserves only the best." A whiff of sarcasm wafted from the words.

"Our condolences on her passing," Everis said, his tone genuine. "It was truly a loss felt across the world."

A pang of longing filled Sayra's heart before she could repress it. She despised sympathy, especially when it came to her home life. "I appreciate your words and am proud to carry on her mantle. I hope to represent the name well." It was all smoke up their *røva* but necessary for Sayra to establish a decent understanding with them.

"If your pedigree is so remarkable, then how is it you graduated at the bottom of your class with no exceptional capabilities?" Tianne's thin brows lowered over judgmental eyes.

Refusing to shrink at the criticism, Sayra held herself higher with a straight back. "I'm not afraid to confess that my skill with the sword may not exceed that of my classmates, and due to it, my placement was lower. My academic performance, in addition to my practical application skills, were exceptional. Those scores don't reflect as highly, however. Thus, my lower ranking. What I lack in one minuscule portion of my training I compensate for tenfold in my other capabilities."

Painted lips turning downward, the mother only replied with a stiff, "We shall see."

"Sylven, we expect both you and Sayra to be prepared for the journey once lunch has concluded. We'd like to celebrate properly upon our return to Acacea in our traditional manner," Everis said, leaving no room for negotiation as he turned to speak with other dignitaries from his country.

Lina squeezed by her mom as they turned to go, sprinting a few steps to leap into a tight embrace with Sylven. "I'm soooo happy to see you, Sylv." She grinned, a tooth missing from her top row.

"And I you, Lina." He smiled, though still tense from recent events.

It was sweet to see Sylven change from being unapproachable to nearly doting on the young sibling. Sayra tucked that information away for later in case she ever needed ammunition to agonize him with.

"You're so pretty!" Lina whispered to her, enticing a small grin to form on her lips. "Why are you with him?"

Sylven immediately reddened, both from embarrassment and annoyance. "Lina, I believe it's time to return to Mother. I promise we'll talk all about the cool things I've learned later, okay?"

Lina pouted, reluctantly returning to where their parents were nearby. The moment she was by their side, Sylven began moving toward an exit, briskly crossing the space and all the chattering people in between. Sayra stared wistfully at the excitement, wishing she'd had an easier time of it. She was in a bizarre limbo where she didn't know where she stood. On the way out, feeling more like a stalker than a Valkyrie, she spotted Lynn for a moment before being swallowed by the crowd. She wished she could go share in the celebration with her friends, but she knew her duty lay with Sylven.

The door was inches away from shutting before Sayra caught it, swinging it wide and following the Arcanist through the windblown courtyard. Snow crunched under her boots as she caught up to him, her exasperation getting the better of her.

"Sylven, could we have a civilized conversation?"

"No," he replied.

He kept walking, making his way along the exterior of the dining hall and curving down in the direction of the Arcanist dormitory. Sayra struggled to keep up with his fast pace, eventually electing to jog ahead and block his path. Sylven huffed, throwing out his hands in contempt. Sayra could feel the storm raging in his mind. Resentment. Cynicism. Bitterness. All those words only described a portion of what she could interpret, and it tempered her own irate mind before she lashed out.

"Please," she said finally, her hands held out in caution as if a dangerous animal paced in front of her.

The bond between them blew up in outrage.

"You have no right coming into my life like this! None of this is what I wanted. Can't you understand that? I need some semblance of privacy right now, an ideal I cannot even be granted due to this damned contract that I was forced to enter!" Sylven shouted. A muscle feathered on his clenched jaw when he pushed past her.

Grinding her teeth, she brushed back past him and halted his steps once more. "Do you think I had a choice in who I worked with? Can you at least be somewhat respectful of the fact that I am not your enemy? I'm here to *help* you!" Sayra took a step toward him. "You are your own person, and if you truly didn't want to contract, you could have simply elected not to. You had a choice in all of this."

Sylven's eyes looked murderous. He leaned his head forward, his voice low, and said, "Go pack your things, and meet me outside of the reception hall an hour after noon. Until then, stay the hell away from me."

Sayra spun away, unable to stay in his presence any longer lest she punch the *ræva*. How did her mother ever handle having a contract? What had she gotten herself into?

Chapter Six

SYLVEN

Never had he felt so isolated before. Not when he left his family, and not even when his closest sibling passed away defending an ungrateful Arcanist. Sylven, more than anything, didn't want history to repeat itself. He didn't want to begin to view his Valkyrie's life as dispensable. He could watch over himself and would do everything in his power to force her to formally request breaking their contract. If both parties agreed, the Holy Family could acquiesce, though the Valkyrie seemed dedicated enough, and it was near impossible to break the Old Covenant without an immensely justifiable cause.

A part of him felt awful for the words he used with the Valkyrie, but he couldn't allow himself to establish any ties with her, lest she grow on him or the other way around. He needed an easy break.

Besides, none of that anger was for her.

Sylven could feel the world crashing in on him, the weight too much for his shoulders to carry as he stumbled down the hall, finally slamming the door behind him in his chamber. A button caught on his frock coat as he removed it, the fury coming to a crescendo with a shout so full of pain and betrayal he tore off the fabric, throwing it into the trash. It gathered on top of his pile of trashed letters, his back sliding down the wall as his face fell into his palms.

Why? Why did Rys do this to him?

The prince was fully aware of Sylven's past and just what it would mean for him. Sylven felt trapped between his parents' expectations and those of his friend. No, brother. Rys was like a brother to him, one of two people who knew him more than anyone else in the world. He couldn't fathom the reasoning, couldn't comprehend why Rys wouldn't have been straightforward and discussed the matter more before altering his life. Rys and his damned plans would be the death of him. Sylven should have known what it would lead to when the prince stepped in the day before the trial.

Too late.

Sylven never cared to admit his true feelings, no matter the person. Now some unknown nineteen-year-old girl knew his every emotion, and she'd soon know his thoughts once they mastered the nuances of the covenant bond. His were far worse than her own intrusive flares of emotion, the hurt and anger of the Valkyrie only further inciting his own. If they were to continue with classes in the next semester, she'd grow capable of becoming even more invasive, even more burdensome. Sylven despised the very thought of it. He couldn't express in words how it made his skin crawl. Given his family had actually met her, his chances were growing slimmer he'd be able to get rid of her. They wouldn't permit it if he went to the Holy Family to request the contract be broken, especially knowing her background.

Damn it.

Rys had somehow wormed Arene von Lykken's daughter into the contract. Sylven's father was surely enamored with the pedigree since the legend had been a personal Valkyrie of the Holy Family. Yet another victim of the inflated egos and incessant laziness of Arcanists. Sylven didn't want to be the reason Arene's daughter followed in her mother's footsteps into an early grave. And for what?

Nothing. Nothing at all.

Sylven sat there, unable to comprehend Rys's betrayal and the inescapable burden chaining him down. He had half a mind to pray for answers, but a spiteful part of him didn't trust there were any prayers good enough to satiate his fury.

—◦✦◦—

Sylven's nose was buried in a book as the overly embellished carriage rolled through the country hills of Acacea. The wealth in the simple contraption was ridiculous, and his family happened to have two. His parents and siblings traveled in the first for the day's entirety. The second had been thoughtfully reserved for him and Sayra to converse. Naturally, he refused, rejecting any attempt the Valkyrie made to talk. Infuriatingly enough, she wouldn't shut up and kept chatting every fifteen minutes or so. They were eight hours into the journey, an insufferable two hours remaining, and he struggled to ignore the impatience the Valkyrie felt, working to focus on every emotion that was his.

Sylven had previously thought he knew the definition of unbearable. He thought he knew many things. Yet, he couldn't have been more wrong.

Unbearable was the creature who kept pestering him with unnecessary questions. It was the girl who couldn't stop moving some portion of herself at all times, whether it was an armored foot tap or a head bob to some internal melody. It was the ex-Faenda princess sitting on the plush sapphire cushions across from him, currently draped over the seat and humming to one of the latest operas released by some famous singer or another.

It drove him absolutely and irrationally insane.

If it weren't for his reading, he would have had to feign sleep during the duration of the trip and count the seconds until they reached the manor. He even offered her a book just so she'd finally, *finally*, quiet down for a scant period of time.

Of course, she didn't care for reading.

Closing his eyes, Sylven stole a moment to breathe deeply through his nose. Only when night began to near, and the sun danced lower on the edge of horizon, did the Valkyrie begin to still. Sylven could sense her alertness, her attention focused outward as every majikally heightened sense of hers searched for daemonic threats. Even Sylven's nerves began to act up, every minute ticking by with his ears straining for the things that go bump in the night.

Sayra suddenly shot up, alarm racing through their bond despite Sylven's continued attempt to ignore it. He glared with blatant hostility at the excessive movement.

She likely forgot to pack her favorite cloak, he thought.

Then, the horses stalled, neighing in fear. It was something they did when a threat approached, one that incapacitated them.

"Stay inside," Sayra ordered, reaching for some foreign weapon on her hip. In a singular deft movement, she opened the door to the chilling evening breeze and leaped out.

It caught him completely unaware, but even more so when an alarm shouted from the lead guards. That was when he felt it. The presence of the Horde. The fear snuck up on a person. It was a nagging feeling in the back of his mind, slowly inching through his body until he wondered if he was having a panic attack. The closer a daemon was the more irrational and all-consuming the fear became. And right then, Sylven could hardly breathe. His chest felt constricted.

That only meant one thing. It was approaching fast.

The daemons shouldn't be out yet, Sylven cursed. *And now our horses won't move until the daemons are dealt with.*

Cracking open the door, Sylven took in the area. Their forested surroundings were dim beneath the clouds. The remaining daylight gave some sight around the trunks of trees, but evening was too close to see much more.

The sight outside was ominous, and both Sayra and Korine were communicating, the latter taking a defensive position beside his family's carriage and Sayra outside of his. His limbs felt weighted down, sweat beading on his brow. Truthfully, he couldn't fathom how the Valkyries were capable of their movements, the effortless way they held their weapons at the ready. Sylven couldn't hold himself straight under the pressure that bared down on his shoulders, forcing him to kneel inside the carriage. His heart pounded, lungs pleading for air as his eyes frantically searched for the enemy.

He wished the academy had included training on how to combat fear earlier in their education. For all her distasteful traits and her infuriating presence, Sylven couldn't help but feel a sliver of grudging admiration for the fearlessness in which Sayra acted. Even with it not being his first daemon encounter, the effects of their evil presence still held a vice grip on his chest.

While Arcanists could acclimate to the fear and endeavor to train their minds to withstand it, similar to a Valkyrie, Sylven had another year in his educational career to approach that line of study. After all, one had to have a mastery of majik before even considering taking on the Horde.

Arcanists were *supposed* to rely on Valkyrie protection, but Sylven refused to be sidelined even when disadvantaged. He rested a clammy hand over the cross on his chest, forcing his breathing to slow into deep pulls. He could have sworn the cross grew warm over his heart, the Goddess sharing her strength. Gritting his teeth, he managed to righten himself. His breaths came fast, a part of him desperate to prove everyone wrong about his aspirations and leap into the fray himself.

The small forest-encompassed glen was empty save for their presence on the trail. Sayra's voice spoke softly to him. "Can you cast any sort of barrier around the carriages, horses, and guards?"

Sylven knew his family's protocol. "My father already has." It was embarrassing just how breathy he sounded. It was a knock to his ego.

"Excellent. Korine is covering the front. I don't know you well enough to assist me, but if you see an opening, signal, and I'll move out of the way," Sayra murmured, both hands grasping some sort of chain. "Would have been nice if you had shared some pertinent information on what you're capable of." Her tone held more than a hint of resentment.

"Really?" he said, his voice incredulous at her timing.

"Really?" Sayra mimicked, her head shaking in disapproval.

Unbelievable.

Sylven realized the tight knot in his chest had loosened enough for him to breathe easier. It irked him she knew just what to say to ease out some of that paralyzing fear. The effect was immediate, his mind clearer and the shakiness subsiding enough for him to think somewhat logically. He knew he'd have to if he didn't want his emotions to affect his Valkyrie. Steadying his breathing, Sylven descended from the carriage to grudgingly stand beside her, taking in the scene further.

Guards were posted around the disturbed horses, four in total wielding swords and round shields. Such a stark contrast to the Valkyries they posed. Even with the best guards money could afford, the bulky muscle mass and exceptional sword work of a honed man could never compare to the superhuman speed and strength of a majikally-enhanced Valkyrie. Valkyries didn't wield shields, not when every dreg of their speed and strength was required to match daemons. Sylven witnessed Korine humble the guards time and time again, well beyond the point where any average man's ego would have lashed out.

Adrenaline raced through his veins. The fear was still present but suppressed enough for Sylven's mind to remain clear. That he could work with. For four years, he dove into texts and studied long hours while others spent their time chatting or playing various board games in the common rooms. He waited for the next daemon encounter to prove himself capable.

He took a step closer to Sayra. Then another, his eyes wildly searching the dense trees around them.

Leaves shook ahead of the first carriage, snow falling in large clumps as a monstrosity emerged. Nine feet of pale, leathery daemon raced toward him, obsidian eyes piercing him and renewing the fear in his soul.

Muscles bulged across its enormous form, and back-bent legs ate the distance with a speed he'd never witnessed before. It was grotesque, from the knarred horns around its triangular head to the half-decaying flesh flapping on its body. The smell alone nearly made him retch, and he was fifty feet away.

Far too close.

Korine pitched forward, lashing out with a slash that was immediately intercepted by a tri-clawed arm. A screech sounded as the steel-like talons scraped down the blade. Sayra brought up the rear with a chain-based weapon too far away for him to decipher.

A sharp object flew forward faster than he could blink, impaling the beast's shoulder with a sickening noise. It roared in agony, kicking back a taloned foot and nearly catching Sayra, if it weren't for her ducking into a tight roll under the daemon. She jumped to her feet, pulling hard on the chain and causing the daemon to slip in the snow, the metal tightening until it lost its footing.

Trees swayed to Sylven's left, pulling his attention to a second form rushing toward them. One daemon appearing was rare, but *two*? He swallowed hard, his eyes widening in dawning horror. A tremor ran through his hands, the ability to move forgotten as logic struggled to linger in his mind.

His heart skipped a beat, mind racing through a list of spells he could utilize and settling on one that would slow the beast in its tracks. His distress pulled Sayra's attention to him, causing her to receive a powerful kick to the chest.

No.

Sylven's eyes went wide as the talons dented her chest plate, her body whirling in the air until the ground rose to meet her. Korine rushed it, resuming battle with the daemon while Sayra rose from the ground, her eyes locked on Sylven's.

"*Fy faen*! Fight!" she yelled at him. Her green eyes were fierce as she pulled her chain-like weapon free and sprinted to him.

Sylven breathed again. *She's okay.*

Sayra took in the space between her Arcanist and the daemon, and her terror raced through the bond when she found herself too slow, each step not long enough to clash with the daemon before it would tear him apart. It was on him to do something.

"Get in range of the wards!" Sayra shouted, desperation flooding her eyes.

Sylven could feel the panic overcoming her and saw her eyes glaze over as if she were running in another place—toward another face. Her emotions churned as if he were already dead.

He raised his unsteady hand, the daemon two dozen feet away with its claws outstretched for his head. Victory gleamed in the monstrosity's eyes, knowing its prey was helpless before its might.

It was now or never. Sylven had always sworn he could take on the Horde. What good would he be if he couldn't uphold his vow?

Behind it, fallen branches littered the forest line, scattered across the snow. His eyes honed on them.

"*Commutatio!*" he yelled, his voice awakening the power within the earth.

Claws were inches from his nose when the powerful words took hold. Sylven's body disappeared only to reappear thirty feet behind the daemon where one of the branches once was. His majik had traded their places. The daemon let out a skin-crawling roar when it discovered its prey was switched with a wooden limb.

The strength of the magic required nearly brought Sylven to his knees. Without his gauntlets, his connection to the ley lines was strained, the energy he needed to use costing more to withdraw. He cursed the dependency he had, but more so, he cursed his own false sense of safety. Sylven had fallen into the complacency commonly shared among the Arcanist community and their reliance on Valkyries. Since the initiation of the guardians, deaths had become far scarcer. A fact he knew only proved their worth. His jaw clenched at his own infuriating conformity.

Frozen just ten feet from him was Sayra, and when he jerked his head to check on her, it shocked him to find tears pooling in her eyes. From their bond, he knew it was not stemming from her own injury but something deep-rooted that rose to the surface.

Despite whatever her deal was, Sylven knew he had to pull through and finish the daemon on his own. Even if it peeved him that she chose then, of all times, to have a breakdown.

Arene's daughter his butt.

The daemon was rising, shaking its heavy head venomously before kicking the ground at its feet. Cawing sounded far above. A murder of crows circled in his field of view, an eager edge to their dance in the sky as they awaited their feast. The daemon charged then, picking up speed as its steps became steadier. Summoning his will, Sylven gathered power before releasing his next spell.

"*Commutatio!*" he cried out, the edges of his vision flickering briefly as the energy left him and the beast disappeared, a crow flapping in confusion where it had once been.

In the cloudy early evening sky, a daemon screeched as it fell a hundred feet to the ground, incapable of anything but bracing for impact.

Sayra stared as it slammed into the slushy snow, disoriented and seriously injured. Breathing heavily, Sylven struggled to step toward the daemon, failing in the end and collapsing onto his knees.

Sayra finally appeared to snap out of it, pulling her weapon out and swinging what appeared to be a spear tip attached to a bulky chain. At the last second, she spun, twisting the chain around her torso, causing the sharp end to arch across the daemon's throat and cut deep, black blood spilling liberally into the snow.

Korine finished off the other daemon in an efficient manner, turning to report it to his parents once she cleared the vicinity. The release of plaguing fear was instantaneous. Even the horses began nickering, stomping in impatience.

Sylven felt a flicker of disgust that his father hadn't deigned to help, even if he himself was seeking his father's approval for the very thing

Arcanists weren't known for: fighting daemons. Stepping close, Sayra's face was grimmer than ever before, her weapon somewhat clean from dragging it through snow and recoiled at her hip.

"What was that?" Sylven glared at her, his mind focused on her hesitancy to help him. "You could have gotten me killed." Struggling, he managed to regain his footing.

Snarling, Sayra threw out her hands in disgust. "You didn't want a Valkyrie to begin with! I tried to help you despite that!" A hint of her accent tinged her words, leaking through in her frustration.

"Why didn't you help our son?" snapped Tianne, climbing out of the carriage and storming toward them. Ghostly pale, his mother was a vision of pure wrath, and Sylven saw his opportunity to be rid of the Valkyrie at last.

As if reading his mind, Sayra stepped toward him. Her brows were upturned in the middle, and her eyes more solemn than he'd ever seen them before. "I can explain, but I swear on my life I'd never put you in harm's way," she whispered, her eyes flicking between his. Large dents pushed into her gut from the impact of the creature's claws, very likely causing incredible discomfort, though she didn't show it.

Closing his eyes for a moment, Sylven knew he was at a crossroads. He could play along and pretend Sayra had intentionally abandoned him, even though his gut said otherwise. It was a crime punishable by extreme measures and would absolutely ruin her career. But could he be that cruel? Two other pairs of eyes were on him—Korine's confused and his father's furious.

Sylven decided then and there.

No matter what others might condemn him for, he couldn't possibly be that vindictive to another. He swore to himself that he'd discover an alternative way to dispense with Sayra.

"I commanded her to stay back, Mother. I've always insisted that I could handle myself, and I believe I proved that today," Sylven said warily, appearing as if a breeze could knock him over.

Splotches grew on his mother's face as she approached him, a hand whipping out so quickly Sayra hadn't even comprehended what happened until she felt Sylven in pain. She became still, her relief and guilt flooding through his mind.

He was already exhausted, his body feeling the need to crumble in on itself, but he wouldn't permit that weakness. Not when there was something left to prove. So, his reddened face rose to confront his parents as they retreated to their carriage, his father turning to speak before following his wife.

"You'll not do something so foolish again," Everis ordered, his eyes flashing beneath furrowed brows.

Sylven worked his jaw as he and Sayra sat back in the carriage, his exhaustion numbing him to the sting on his cheek and any interest in learning his Valkyrie's excuse. For once, Sayra didn't make a comment as he rested his head. She loosened the dented plating around her torso, her eyes distant all the while. Sylven closed his for the rest of their travel.

They unceremoniously crossed into the Astor duchy wards, posted wooden signs pointing to nearby cities and the paths to them. The distance was written beneath each, a crucial detail if one was planning to travel outside of the wards between duchies or countries.

No one spoke when they arrived at the manor soon thereafter, nor when the serving staff aided in unloading their luggage and directed them inside the three-story stone home. The last bit of daylight turned to nightfall, and with it, Sylven's will to tolerate anyone else evaporated.

He ignored everyone blatantly and headed up the foyer's winding, carpeted staircase to the residential third floor. Not once did his eyes wander toward the painful portraits of his broken family. Perhaps for the first time, he couldn't even mentally chastise the excess his family flaunted in the manor—not the bejeweled sconces, excessively plush and spotless cream carpeting, or rich décor flown in from exotic countries across the Randen Sea.

Sylven made for the luxurious shower in his chamber, briefly cleaning himself before dressing for a long night's rest in his maple four-poster bed with the finest navy down comforter money could buy. While the monastery boasted suitable dormitory rooms for their stations, nothing quite beat the quality of his home. His feet sunk into the carpet as he dragged himself into the silk sheets, hair dripping but indifferent to the fact. That night, he fell into a fitful sleep, nightmares plaguing the duration of his slumber.

The Horde was attacking them all over again. Sylven's fear collapsed him to the snowy ground, his cloak piling around him as he clutched his chest.

The Valkyries fought both daemons, Sayra slowly retreating to keep her footing after back-to-back lunges from her opponent. Fangs snapped on her chain, catching it between teeth and yanking her weapon from her grasp.

Terror froze Sylven's arms as snow cascaded in a calmness that contrasted with the terrible scene before him. *Act!* he wanted to shout at himself. *Help her!* But his mouth couldn't form the words as the daemon's claws found purchase around her legs, swooping the Valkyrie's feet from under her just as she attempted to dodge its attack.

Still, Sylven couldn't move.

Another rotten limb pinned Sayra's struggling body into the snow. The daemon's maw glistened as it screeched in victory, raising its claw to deliver a death blow. Sayra's chin rose in his direction, her eyes pleading with him to help before it was too late. Her face was etched with desperation, but all Sylven could do was watch. Watch as the daemon impaled her chest with several impossibly sharp talons.

Sayra let out a bloodcurdling scream, crimson spraying across the daemon's flaking flesh. Her body flailed, growing weaker by the second.

"You're letting her die just as I had," Jess whispered in Sylven's ear, his sister's eyes full of accusation.

His fingers dug into the earth beneath the snow, every fiber of his being disgusted in himself as Sayra's screams faded. He couldn't look away from the scene, bearing witness as the daemon's teeth tore Sayra's head from her body. Bone and tissue separated, blood gushing from severed arteries and veins. Nausea rolled through Sylven's stomach as the daemon tossed her head toward him, the object rolling to a stop at his feet.

"Run. Run like my Arcanist did when the last drop of my blood left my body," Jess said soothingly, her hand gripping his shoulder. "After all, you got her killed by being *weak*. You saw the fear in her eyes, yet you allowed her to work for you. To throw away her life for you. Run now, before yours is lost too. *Run.*"

Despite everything he believed in, despite his resolve, Sylven ran.

Gasping awake, he breathed heavily as he sat up in his bed. His heart thudded in a rapid rhythm, the panic slowly receding as he convinced himself it was all a dream. He pulled himself from the comfort of the sheets, morning sunlight dappling his walls.

Knocking sounded at his door—not long after he had dressed in charcoal trousers and a simple, long-sleeved white shirt. His fingers deftly buttoned it up to his collar before opening the door to find a maid, passing on his parents' wishes for him to join their morning meal in the dining room.

When he found his way to the second floor, he picked up chatter and the distinct voice of Sayra answering an endless barrage of questions. Her voice brought back the nightmare. Sylven blinked several times, reassuring himself everything was fine. Still, he hesitated outside in the hall, the doors open for him to eavesdrop on the clinking of cups and shuffling of fabrics, the conversation nearly drowning the mild flurry of activity.

"The *slør* represents availability to court, though women who deem themselves ready for such a process accent the fabric with a small lace bow at the top, just at the nape of the neck," Sayra explained, eliciting an *ooooh* from Lina. "Every female of marriageable age wears one in my homeland."

Sylven's mind visualized that strange wrap that surrounded her braid. He supposed it made sense it was a cultural tradition rather than Sayra's inclination for accessories.

Chair legs scraped the tiled floor, Lina's voice rising in question. "So, where is your bow?"

His mother tsked, her cup replaced with a clink on porcelain. "I do apologize for her forthrightness. It is improper to ask such questions, Lina." Her voice was stern, if not slightly exasperated.

A warm feeling, mixed with bittersweet melancholy, twisted his heart. Sayra's heart. The feeling of sharing her emotions was foreign to Sylven, yet he continued to listen. It was normal to hear a tale when spoken but unusual to feel it along with its speaker. It intrigued him. Slightly.

"It is of no offense to me, duchess. I have a younger sister of my own who asks similar questions," Sayra explained. She then addressed Sylven's seven-year-old sister. "I'm not to marry, little Lina. I'm a Valkyrie, and as such, my life is dedicated to another cause."

The kitchen doors swung open down the hall, Sylven lurching forward before he could be discovered. The velvet curtains were drawn wide, revealing a frivolously decorated maple table laden with half-eaten pastries, fruits, bread rolls, and tarts. Sunlight barreled in beyond the outside patio, making him squint as he rounded the table to sit at the open chair beside Sayra. Regen was missing, leaving only his sister and parents in the room. Dabbing her mouth delicately, Tianne folded her napkin before meeting eyes with Sylven.

"I do apologize for my outburst last night, Sylven. I was... It's been a long time since we've dealt with the Horde, and I acted partially out of heightened emotion," Tianne assented, meeting his level gaze with a solemn one. "However, you cannot act single-handedly in the future. You'll put your life at unnecessary risk. Can you promise me that you won't?"

Folding his hands across his lap, Everis observed his son with a judging eye.

Resentment swept through Sylven's chest. The willpower it took to outright glare at his mother required almost more than he contained. It was the same song regaled at every opera across the world. Different circumstances, same results.

Whereas his father was stone, his mother was the storm that weathered him. One day, she'd be as light as a feather, prancing from one room to another, taking up random tasks and hobbies in each. The next, she'd be screeching at them all with a watery apology given at the end. Sometimes, Sylven couldn't tell which side of her he'd get. It was a struggle, a task he, for once, didn't feel like contesting.

"I accept your apology, Mother," Sylven said, his voice tinged with fatigue. It wasn't physical, just mental. All caused from the last forty-eight hours and begun by those he was close with. "Regarding your request, I suppose I have no choice on the matter now, do I?"

He toasted his tea in Sayra's direction, drinking deeply before picking at his breakfast. The Valkyrie was torn between annoyance and regret, the latter giving Sylven hope she might feel their contract was a mistake. Tianne appeared content enough with his response, moving on to discuss matters of the house with Everis. Lina continued pestering Sayra with questions and thankfully entertaining the one person he didn't want to converse with. Eating in silence, he was relieved to escape without further engagement, rising when he was satisfied with his meal.

Clearing his throat, Everis said to his back, "Sylven, we plan to commence our traditional celebration after lunch today. For the time being, would you perchance show Sayra around the manor while preparations are set?"

Stealing a deep breath, Sylven gestured to Sayra. "Would you care for a tour?"

Sylven knew he clearly conveyed his emotions through the bond they shared, letting her know what he desired in response, but for some damned reason, she took pleasure in his suffering. With a grin, Sayra excused herself from the table and took the lead toward the hall. "I would absolutely adore being graced with the opportunity to view your home," she announced, pointing in the direction of the staircase. "Shall we start at the bottom floor?"

"Yes," Sylven breathed, praying to the Goddess she grant him the patience to prevent him from strangling Sayra. It would be a close call.

Their steps were absorbed by the carpet, making their short walk abnormally quiet by the monastery's standards. There, you could hear anyone within a hundred meters with ease. The moment they descended the stairs, Sayra whispered, "We need to talk."

"No. I have no interest in discussing last night's ordeal any further, and if you have any semblance of common courtesy, you will drop the subject," Sylven growled, stopping once they reached the foyer.

He didn't need excuses. Valkyries weren't necessary when it came to encounters with the Horde. Sylven had held his own, a fact he was proud of. If he'd had his gauntlets, it would have been an easy feat to eliminate the daemon.

Sayra's face pinched together, but she nodded once, and the subject was dropped. "Well, in that case, you don't need to show me around. I figured you'd want an alibi to escape them for some time."

Sylven blinked once, then twice. That was perhaps the nicest thing anyone had done for him in quite some time. For a handful of seconds, he assessed her, surprised to find she wore leather trousers and what appeared to be a buttoned beige cloak cut off at the hips. It was an abnormal style of dressing but far more practical than the silly dresses most women in Acacea's polite society were swathed in nowadays. Another thing from her homeland, likely.

"I think I'll accept that." He sighed, dipping his chin in grudging thanks. While she was an unnecessary pest to his goals, Sayra was still a person first and foremost, even if a rather annoying one. "If you'd like, you may follow this hall…" He gestured to his right. "And exit out the side door at the end. You'll find our gardens there. It can be quite peaceful. As for me, I'll be in the library."

Without another word, Sylven departed, leaving Sayra to figure out her situation alone.

CHAPTER SEVEN

SAYRA

Sayra had few regrets in life. One forevermore would be her hesitation that night when she thought she'd fail yet another person in her life, leaving Sylven to die at the hands of the Horde. It shook her to the core when the scene replayed in her mind, the trauma immobilizing her when the daemon's claws were but inches from skewering Sylven's head. Except it wasn't Sylven she was seeing, nor the same daemon they had encountered. There were different builds to each of them. The one in her past...

Her brother...

Shaking the train of thought loose, Sayra grabbed her cobalt-shaded academy cloak and made for the gardens. After all, there wasn't much else to be done except harbor the culpability dragging her down. Sylven craved isolation, and quite frankly, she could use the time herself. Pulling the wool-lined fabric close, she trekked across the manor, a feat because of its massive size.

Before Droden overtook it all eleven years ago, her family owned land and riches. Her father ruled as an emperor of a tiny empire, and her family lived in an enormous castle with vast acreage. Faenda was far too rich for its own good, the mines producing far too much gold for their well-being. Droden was a greedy beast with an empty stomach, leaping on her people to satiate herself after they were bled dry of currency.

Now, her family lived in a manner not too different from Sylven's. A place fit for a duke, a title her father had sold himself and everyone around him to cling to.

Sunlight shone on her the moment she escaped the stone confines, the sound of birds chirping bringing a contented smile to her face. The path ahead was unobstructed. The staff at the Astor Manor had cleared it of snow. Sayra meandered along the serene trail until she discovered a gazebo amidst the snow-covered, towering hedges. The inside remained somewhat free from weather, and an effortless sweep of her hand made room for her to rest. Gathering her braid, she rested it over her shoulder and took in the beautiful craftsmanship, an array of angels dancing across the ceiling.

Sometimes, there was nothing as profound as enjoying the simplicity of nature, and while her impatience wouldn't guarantee she'd be capable of remaining for long, it was enjoyable to watch birds in flight and the dripping of melted snow falling from the hedges. Closing her eyes, Sayra breathed in the crisp air, all the while wondering where the contract with Sylven would lead. More than anything, she wanted to prove to him she'd make an excellent Valkyrie, one who wouldn't ever hesitate again.

Snapping her eyes open, Sayra leaped from the stone bench and made her way toward a commotion she'd picked up in the distance. Shouting sounded from the front of the manor, her feet quickening to a hasty sprint. Never, *never* would she freeze again. Even if she didn't like Sylven, Sayra would give her life if it meant saving him.

Her mind raced through several possibilities on the way. Did the wards fail? Were thieves breaking in? It took three minutes with her enhanced speed to reach the disturbance, the scene the last she'd ever expected.

Guards were ushering a carriage to the stables, Nes monitoring the scene with a scrutinizing eye as Prince Emrys spoke with the duke. The moment she rounded the corner, she met eyes with the prince, and her steps faltered. On the one hand, she was confused as to why they'd be there of all places. On the other hand, Sayra couldn't help but feel relieved. Questions had been nagging her during the journey to the manor, and she wondered if she'd be able to keep quiet until the next semester began. It seemed she'd have a chance to pester the prince until he fessed up.

While they were in a serious discussion, Prince Emrys managed to slip her a subtle nod before responding to one thing or another. Everis noted her arrival, beckoning her with a brief curl of his fingers. As Sayra approached, however, she noted the unusually grim air about Nes.

"Where is Sylven? Was he not with you to show you the grounds?" asked Everis, one bushed eyebrow raised in severity.

"Sylven wanted to retrieve a belonging before he did so," Sayra lied as she worked to send a warning to her Arcanist through their link. "He mentioned a novel pertaining to the manor in the library."

Nodding, the duke motioned to one of the servants. "Summon Sylven at once. He's likely in the library." He then turned to the prince. "Why don't you come in for refreshments? We'll also have a guest room prepared for you as well, should you choose to stay."

"That is most generous, Duke Everis. Thank you for your hospitality." Prince Emrys smiled, but even from the short distance, Sayra could discern it wasn't genuine. A smile born from etiquette only. It was passable, though, judging by the duke's pleased expression as they walked into the foyer.

The prince gave her a swift glance and an almost imperceptible look. One that warned her and made her recall their previous discussion.

Sayra lowered her chin, acting the part of a person paying their respects to royalty. It wasn't long before she felt Sylven's anger flare up, eliciting a wince the moment she knew he was notified. She then fell in step with Nes, quietly asking, "Is everything okay?"

"So long as Prince Emrys's guard lives," Nes said, her eyes shimmering with regret. "It all happened so fast. We traveled from the Rothlander duchy straight here, and in the unwarded zone, we were surprised by two daemons this morn."

Sayra's mind tracked the spot on a mental map. It was relatively close to where she and the Astors were attacked.

"They ambushed us the moment we were about to cross into safety. One guard took a surprise attack, and he's receiving treatment in the nearby city of Tern," Nes said.

Sayra's mouth fell in shock for a moment. "I'm relieved you're safe."

Such a thing happened occasionally where a daemon would sense majik and track it to a ward barrier only to lurk around until the Arcanist left. But for *four* to be within such close proximity of each other in such a short span of time was odd.

"It's only due to Prince Emrys," Nes confided, shaking her head.

They turned into the first-floor dining room, an enormous, sweeping table in the center lavishly adorned with a gold-and-maroon tablecloth and crystalline flowers with vines down the center. Candelabrums circled the room, graceful and elegant silver pieces accenting the table.

"What do you mean?" Sayra asked.

"He has exceptional magic. After the Horde's initial attack, he eliminated all of them," Nes explained, her voice in awe as she stared at her

Arcanist's back. "I didn't do much other than fend off an attack from the injured guard."

Blinking, Sayra felt a moment's worth of jealousy. Not due to the Arcanist's capabilities but rather the better match Nes and Prince Emrys had made. Sylven despised her, and it caused her to long for what they lacked. Boots sounded in the hall, the bane himself turning the corner into the dining room. Deep resentment echoed in her mind from Sylven as his hazel eyes met the prince's, his jaw clenched as he addressed the source.

"I'd like to speak with you, *Prince* Emrys."

The duke, hands prepared to pull out his seat, became disgruntled at the way his son addressed the prince. "Sylven—"

But Prince Emrys shook his head at the duke. "It's quite all right. We do have much to discuss, some of which is pertinent for urgency." He followed Sylven out into the hall and away from prying ears.

CHAPTER EIGHT

SYLVEN

Sylven paced in the snow, discussing matters outside of the gardens with Emrys. "So, you mean to tell me that there's an imperative reason I take on a Valkyrie, but the reason carries such importance that you decline to share it with me? This is a new type of reclusiveness, even for you, Emrys. Every plan you cook up in that head of yours you inevitably share with me. But not this one. The only one to permanently change my life, and you decide I'm incapable of knowing and handling the details. Have you ever thought once that things might be different if you had simply shared your plan, rather than throwing me to the wolves?"

Emrys's jaw worked, but otherwise, he stayed unnaturally still.

Sylven pointed an accusing hand at him. "You were like a brother to me, and if you had explained what was going through your mind, I might have gone along with it willingly. Have you ever thought about that? About the damage you've caused by taking this route?" He made a noise of disgust.

Emrys's eyes reflected Sylven's pain, his mouth opening to say one thing before his mind switched to another. "Sylven, I am truly sorry for how I handled things. Everything happened rapidly, and had I not stepped in the way I did, the chain of events would have been irrevocable and the fallout horrendous. It left me with no time to prepare for our conversation." The corners of his mouth tightened.

Staring at the ground, Sylven's fist trembled in his flurry of thundering emotions. "When will you learn that I am not something to handle? That I am more than a simple matter to be dealt with?" He raised his head, his eyes glistening with the sun's reflection. "Ever since we joined the academy, you have been slipping away, the distance between us making us less like brothers and more like acquaintances. I've tried—" But his voice caught, his head turning away from Emrys's dawning expression.

Gloved hands wrapped around his torso, Sylven tensing in shock at the hug. Emrys was as standoffish as they came, and while the embrace was incredibly awkward—likely for both parties—it meant more than words could convey. Sylven returned the gesture, but a stubborn part of him wanted to keep the anger alive.

"I will improve on that. You have my word and my sincerest apologies," Emrys said, breaking off the gesture with a face more in remembrance of the brother he used to have all those years ago. "I'm currently working on your situation, and I must receive permission before we can openly discuss that. Until then, I'm forbidden to even mention the subject further." Taking a breath, he added, "I'd like to be your brother again if you'll allow it."

Sylven was speechless.

Rys had never acted in such a manner. It was concerning, and it forced Sylven to worry about whatever was burdening him. It must have been enormous, something bigger than him, if Rys wasn't permitted to speak of it. And there were only two people who could hold such power over him. If Sylven's hunch was correct, then he was but a cog in the machinery along with Rys, neither of them pulling the strings behind the scenes.

Swallowing, Sylven folded his hands into his trouser pockets. "I accept your apology, and if we can go back to the way things were prior to the academy, I'd like that," he confessed, the air awkwardly hanging between them for a few seconds. He cleared his throat. "How are you handling the whole... contract aspect? Being unable to have privacy and all that?"

Amusement pulled at a corner of Rys's mouth. "You mean you don't know how to block the link? Everis never mentioned it?"

Dumbfounded, Sylven's jaw grew slack. "There's a way to block it?" In his head, he cursed at his father for neglecting such an important detail. His father refused to share anything about being an Arcanist. He wanted Sylven to learn everything from the academy, claiming it better than what he could offer.

Smirking, Rys explained, "Imagine a box around your mind, encasing it with steel. Once you have that visualized, lock it. It will take a lot of active management at first, but gradually it will become a subconscious process. The bond, after all, isn't meant to be invasive. It's a tool to use for communication, especially when confronted with a threat."

"Now that would have been great to know a day ago," Sylven said dryly, closing his eyes and giving it a shot. A breeze whispered through his hair as he steadied his breathing.

His mouth curled in a mischievous way.

It was time to pay back Sayra for her annoying tendencies.

Chapter Nine

SAYRA

Sayra felt tension ease from between her shoulder blades when Sylven's emotions turned from anger to forgiveness, her mind veritably hoping his dour demeanor would change. Nes was filling her in on their journey in the courtyard as the duke chastised his younger son inside the dining room for barreling through the staff rudely while practicing majik. Everything seemed to settle down. That is until she felt their bond begin to disappear.

It wasn't entirely muffled. She could still sense Sylven and his general direction, but the concern of something happening to him had her feet eating away at the distance before she could explain to Nes.

Nes—still dressed in armor—followed without a word, the silent understanding of urgency passing between them. They weren't far away, and as they rounded the corner and found both men staring at them in surprise, Sylven's emotions came barreling back through her head.

Glee sung through her mind, a smug beat that didn't originate from her.

"What was that?" Sayra asked, on edge and bewildered by the shared glances between the Arcanists.

Nes breathed heavily through her nose beside Sayra, head tilting at the prince as if they were silently communicating. "Prince Emrys was showing Sylven how to temporarily block the mental connection," she explained, posture straightening once she realized no threat was near. "Damn, Sayra, you scared me."

Defensiveness crept into Sayra's tone. "How did you know they were practicing this? I didn't know that's what this was." Crossing her arms, she glowered at all three of them.

They had covered the bare basics of the bond in their classes. Sayra didn't know that was what was going on. Her cheeks burned slightly, her brows lowering at Sylven's gleaming hazel eyes.

The prince spoke up first. "With the Old Covenant bond, two individuals are linked through their minds, creating the possibility of sharing emotions and thoughts. Both sides can learn to block their emotions and thoughts from emerging and being shared, but they cannot block their counterpart's. It's an old rite, ancient as bones themselves, but the nuances aren't fully taught until the Arcanist's second half of their fourth year of instruction."

Frowning, Sayra turned to Sylven. "You couldn't think to warn me?" she admonished, tapping her arm in thinly veiled irritation.

He just smirked down at her, making his face appear even more punchable.

"I informed him about this but only minutes ago." The prince sighed, giving Sylven a brief glance that said *at least try.*

"*Dra til Helvete.*" Sayra scowled at the smirking *dritt*, spinning on her heel and storming off to her assigned room.

Behind her, she could barely make out Sylven inquiring what that meant and Nes's loud, snarky reply as she followed Sayra. "Go to hell."

For the next few hours, Nes and Sayra chatted about their experiences thus far. For both, it was insane how much had transpired in such a short period of time. They settled into Nes's room once she changed into more suitable clothes, which for her entailed a close-fitted sapphire tunic and trousers. As they spoke, she brushed out her shoulder-length straight hair.

Sayra couldn't help but feel a pang every time Prince Emrys was mentioned. Nes was so animated throughout it all, though Sayra had nothing positive to share on her own behalf. Though she did note something interesting about Nes's Arcanist. Apparently, the prince had gone out of his way to journey there before heading home so he could right his wrongs with Sylven.

Just as lunch wrapped up, Sayra was notified to meet in the courtyard with her armor and weapon, much to her befuddlement. She did as requested, bringing along her sword, a serrated curved dagger, and the *spyd* wrapped beside her hip. The Faendan weapon was whip-like with several steel segments linked together. At one end, there was a leather-bound handle, her family crest engraved on the bottom. The other end linked a steel dagger, much like the tip of a sword but narrower.

Perfect for penetrating a daemon's hide or slicing deep with the velocity she could achieve with it.

When she arrived, Sayra was confused to find Korine dressed similarly, a stunning, quality hand-and-a-half sword at her hip. The entirety of the family was waiting—even the eight staff—silently observing from the sidelines. Her stomach knotted at the sight of Prince Emrys and Nes standing vigil.

"As tradition," Tianne began, nodding in her direction, "every Valkyrie must induct herself into our family by proving her worth in combat. Sayra von Lykken, you will face Korine Berndel in trial by sword to determine the honor of serving this house. It's a formality, but one we hold in high esteem."

Sayra's gut plummeted, begging her to turn tail and run from the embarrassment, but she refused to balk in the face of her imminent loss. Everyone had a weakness, and she acknowledged it was one of her many. Refusing would only give a false impression she was cowardly and incapable, two ideals she wasn't. So, she took a deep lungful of air and stepped down the cobblestone pathway into the field of shorn grass beyond which her opponent waited.

The Valkyrie Academy mandated the sword as the primary weapon to be trained with, even though Sayra wasn't the best with the lump of metal. With a hand on her hilt, she stood across from Korine, who shot her a warm smile. Sayra crooked her mouth in response, nodding once before awaiting further instruction. She couldn't help but think the whole ordeal ridiculous, but she wanted to prove she was worth more than her lowest graduate ranking implied.

With everyone gathered a suitable distance away, including the prince, much to her continued dismay, Everis clasped his hands behind his back. "This is a tradition dating back to my grandfather, a tradition I expect shall fall down to my great-great-grandson and beyond. It speaks of the reverence we hold for those who protect us and inducts a new member into our fold," he announced, Nes giving him a look behind his back as if he were crazy.

Sayra smiled at her blatant message. *Yeah, this is a bit silly,* she agreed.

Pulling her attention, Korine asked, "Do you accept this challenge?"

Sayra lowered her chin. "I do."

Before another word was spoken, Korine drew her blade, forcing Sayra to shadow her movements as she launched forward. Sayra deftly rolled beneath, careful to keep her blade away from her as she attempted to cut across the Achilles tendon. Korine hopped forward, correcting her stance to face Sayra. Both women circled each other, Sayra's eyes locked on Korine's. She was acutely aware her chest plates were loose from the daemon's damage. They shifted enough to distract her, but it was the only way to keep the dented steel from crushing her chest.

Korine exploited that the moment they reengaged. Knocking the sword away, she swiped at an angle aimed for Sayra's lower abdomen.

Right where the loose plating exposed her belly.

Gritting her teeth, Sayra knew she'd have to throw herself into a position of weakness to recover. Flipping backward, her knee connected with the handle, pushing it wide as she landed in a crouch. Korine was remarkable at recovering, not sparing a second to hammer down a powerful blow from above.

A stirring sensation roused in Sayra's chest, one familiar to her match with Netta. She recognized it as majik and vividly recalled the prince's warning to conceal it at all costs. Swallowing, she rolled to her side, a feat considering the sword she had to navigate. Going purely defensive, Sayra struggled to remain calm as the majik pushed on her chest, begging to be released. Her blocks became sloppy, and the momentum that drove Korine's force increased until one powerful blow knocked the sword clean from Sayra's hands. It resulted in a sharp point at her throat.

Embarrassment flickered in Sylven's mind, the emotion raising frustration in Sayra at her show of incompetence. The brief distraction from combat, however, was enough to suppress the majik. So much for the prince's confidence she wouldn't have to worry about it anytime soon.

"Well done." Sayra struggled to compliment Korine, her eyes not meeting anyone else's other than the Valkyrie's.

Korine's mouth twisted as she pulled back her blade, resuming her initial stance. Her amber eyes searched Sayra's before falling to the sword resting in the snow-dotted grass.

"Well, I suppose that's what you can expect from one graduating at the bottom of her class," Tianne said, a chuckle escaping her painted lips.

"I want a rematch," Korine said, taking up an offensive stance.

Shock coursed through Sayra, her stomach dropping at the thought. "I think we've seen enough of my sword work." She struggled to maintain her composure.

A small snort sounded from the duchess as her husband whispered to her to be quiet. It was one thing for Netta and the hags to constantly put her down as an acolyte. It was another to have nobles and a seasoned Valkyrie see her flounder in such a mortifying way. She didn't even last a minute.

"Your true skill isn't the blade, or am I wrong? I saw your unusual weapon during the Horde attack," Korine said.

Sayra's sight hovered on hers, deciphering why she'd lend such an olive branch. "My primary weapon is the *spyd* from my homeland."

"Then let us have an even match," Korine said, gesturing toward the weapon on Sayra's hip.

Without hesitation, Sayra removed her sheath, placed her sword within it, and passed it to Nes. Her friend's eyes were bright as Nes flashed her teeth in a grin. She ignored the mixed looks from the others, stretching the steel chain links between both of her hands. Taking her place across from Korine, Sayra nodded her readiness.

"Do you accept this challenge?"

"I do," Sayra said, excitement coursing through her veins at the prospect of using her true skill set for performance.

Once more, they circled each other, an eight-foot chain whipping in circles around Sayra. Korine advanced with caution, having no experience in that type of battle. Behind her, Sayra overheard her friend's voice.

Nes spoke loudly enough for Sylven's parents to hear her. "Sayra's expertise lies not with the blade but with her ability to move."

At that, Sayra darted forward. As fast as a snake and as lethal as a cheetah. The chain whipped around her torso, her leg flashing out to catch the end and redirect the sharp tip toward Korine. The Valkyrie's eyes flashed in surprise, and she leaped back, barely blocking the blow with her blade.

"She grew up in a dancer's studio, trained ruthlessly under the country's best instructor, and applied her agility and grace into the *spyd*—a weapon requiring mastery of the highest caliber to wield it," Nes continued, pride abundant in her words.

Sayra rolled her shoulders, withdrawing the daggered end and wrapping it across her arm as it lashed out, cutting in an upward arc. Her opponent blocked it partially, the chain wrapping around the sword and yanking back with Sayra's momentum.

Nes smiled. "There isn't a Valkyrie alive who could remotely dream of beating her when Sayra is in her element. She's an absolute terror when she's unleashed."

Korine barely held the blade as Sayra withdrew once more, slowing the geometric motion until she came to a standstill. Gripping the base in one hand and a portion of the chain in another, she hurled forward. Steel came arching sideways at her, the motion catching the chain. Rather than resisting and expending needless energy, Sayra flowed with the momentum, trapping the blade and hilt firmly within loops of metal. Using Korine's own force, Sayra ripped the sword from her grasp with an elegant twist.

"Not even her Faendan instructors could hold a candle to her flame," Nes finished.

A fist came flying toward Sayra's face, a chain wrapping neatly around the forearm behind it. Pulling down, Sayra flung her body over Korine's lowered frame. Her feet connected with the ground, and her body twisted in an expert maneuver. Everyone held their breath at the end, astounded to discover Korine entrapped in several loops of chain with the *spyd's* sharp end at her throat.

Sayra couldn't help but glance at her audience, hoping to see she impressed them. Relucent amazement shone from Sylven, and for the first time, Sayra felt some semblance of redemption from her low graduation status.

Korine laughed a wild thing. "Well done indeed!"

Smiling with gratitude, Sayra removed her chains and recoiled them. A metal-clad hand entered her field of vision once her *spyd* was clasped in place. Accepting the gesture, she couldn't help but feel warm from the seasoned Valkyrie's approval, though she had to refrain from throwing crude remarks Tianne's way to celebrate. It was no easy task.

"Thank you for the rematch," Sayra said, tone reflecting her genuine gratitude. Applause erupted from the bystanders, Nes's the loudest of all.

Winking, Korine retrieved her sword, dusting the snow from the sharp, gleaming blade. "I knew you had it in you. I felt it only fair that you fight an honest one. My advice?" The guardian looped an arm around her shoulders. "Don't allow anyone to push you toward the blade. You're no longer bound to train with it at the academy. Dispose of yours, and wear your *spyd* with pride."

My kind of woman.

"I think I'll do just that." Sayra grinned, facing Sylven with a spark of challenge in her eyes.

I am not worthless.

All she received was a trademark sour frown. Stealing a peek at Prince Emrys, she was delighted to discover a small smile there.

"What an incredible performance, if I can say so," Everis said, his face positively impressed by the match. "You are quite talented. Sylven is fortunate to have such a gifted Valkyrie at his side. Isn't that right, son?"

Sylven muttered, "Quite." His sourness nearly made her giddy with delight.

Regen stared at her, wide-eyed, perhaps for a minute or two too long. "That was amazing."

Lina was bouncing in place, grabbing Regen's arm and asking to play swords.

"Well then, let us be off to celebrate with a toast," Tianne announced, her eyes venomous as they daggered into hers.

"A splendid match," Prince Emrys complimented as Sayra passed, her spirits soaring ever higher.

She would have been lying if she thought the prince's words didn't affect her. Her lips curved just a tad further at the admiration she found in his eyes. For once, she felt worthy of her Valkyrie title.

Nes's face grinned at her, her voice animated throughout the entirety of the celebration. Through it all, the near-accidental use of majik remained forgotten in the maze of Sayra's mind.

CHAPTER TEN

SYLVEN

Rys and Nessika had departed ten days prior, the prince wanting to visit his family before returning for the upcoming semester. Thankfully, he had sent word of their safe arrival and their plans to return to Saint Highburn Monastery soon.

Sylven and Sayra loaded their trunks into the carriage as the sun crested the horizon, her trunk noticeably heavier than his.

"What's in there? A ton of bricks?" Sylven's brow lifted at Sayra as she brushed off her hands.

She shrugged. "A lady must always be prepared."

For what, Sylven hadn't the slightest idea. He rolled his eyes at her.

The day she beat Korine, he had noticed she tossed her sword the moment they returned to celebrate. Sylven wouldn't share he thought it never suited her anyway; her ego was already far too big.

He was relieved to finally be departing. The lectures on etiquette and how to properly fight in unison were exhausting. His father became more invested in Sylven's education after hiring a Valkyrie. Along with Korine, they were relentless, and Sayra basked in the attention. While she was on the irritated side when Rys and Nessika left, she quickly rebounded and hounded Sylven on his capabilities with light magic and his elemental affinity of wind. She was blown away by how he could switch positions of objects or beings, something she put to the test during their training.

While Sylven was still determined he didn't require a Valkyrie, he somewhat tolerated having company who cared about majik and the application of it. Sayra was devoted to learning what he could do, unlike many others.

The one matter Sylven found himself enjoying most was evenings with his father in the study. For once, they had meaningful discussions about his future and where he'd stand. It was a pleasant surprise to find Everis speaking passionately about Sylven's promise as a Sicarius, an Arcanist who wielded majik solely to eliminate the Horde. A Sicarius was a daemon slayer who roamed the lands freely with the noble purpose of seeking daemons before they could lash out against humanity.

While light magic such as protection spells or healing weren't traditionally useful in disposing of the Horde, Sylven had managed to overcome that disadvantage and hone his craft to the point where he posed a credible threat. He wasn't content with the notion of becoming a ward-worker or majik-smith, Arcanists who renewed wards or cast majik for human convenience. Once he graduated from Saint Highburn's Arcanist Academy, he'd apply to the Kingdom of Acacia's guard to train as a Sicarius and further amplify his deadliness when facing the Horde.

It felt like a slight burden had been eased from his shoulders to have his father's support at last.

Two bays snorted in impatience, itching to begin the journey. His parents were nowhere to be found, though his sister was speaking adamantly to Sayra. Those two caused all sorts of mischief for Sylven, and he learned to stay clear on day three of their visit to Astor Manor. Regen was currently practicing his warding around himself, not an easy task for a thirteen-year-old. He was to begin at the academy next year, a fact that seemed surreal to Sylven with each passing day.

"Okay. I think I—ow!" Regen protested, peeved Sylven was able to flick him on the forehead.

Shaking his head, Sylven explained, "When you say the word of power, you must also mean it. Intention is perhaps the most important aspect of majik. The word is only a guiding stone to help perfect the spell. Now, you've likely created a ward, but were you thinking of a physical barrier or a majikal one? You must concentrate and put the fulcrum of your intention on a physical one. Otherwise, you'll have a half-baked ward."

Regen rubbed his forehead, distractedly staring at Sayra out of the corner of his eye. The Valkyrie was adjusting her *spyd*.

"Focus!" Sylven said, huffing a breath.

Tianne and Everis emerged from the manor, both carrying paper-wrapped objects. His father's mouth curved as they met eyes, his voice calling out, "Would you and Sayra join us for a moment?"

They did so, pausing curiously before them. Everis handed his hefty gift to Sayra and Tianne a lighter one to Sylven.

"Please, open," his mother said, hands fidgeting more than usual when anxious.

Sayra tore into hers without hesitation, the paper protecting the gift within thrown down on their grassy lawn. The snow had finally melted the day prior, though the gray clouds above promised more soon to come. Sylven opened his gift as well, blinking in absolute shock at what he found.

A tailored and reinforced set of battle leathers sat within, the outfit of a Sicarius and one that could also be used in the *proelium*, a competition between pairs of Valkyrie-Arcanist *anima* within the Arcanist's final year at Saint Highburn. The victor of the monastery's competition could then go on to compete at the *Grand Proelium* between countries as their representative.

Gold stitching found the seams around the edges, his family's crest of the eagle over the heart. New boots were wrapped beneath the suit, perfect since his were wearing down. A striking pair of leather-based gauntlets lay on top, the appearance similar to gloves rather than the distasteful metal fashion others seemed to prefer. Everything suited him, and to receive such a gift meant more than he would have thought possible.

Beside him, Sayra was grinning from ear to ear at an elegantly crafted set of armor, similarly carved with the crest over her heart. A symbolic gesture that claimed her as an official Valkyrie of their esteemed house. What was more impressive was the shade of the armor, a hue between ivory and gold that appeared almost radiant. The detailing of obsidian vines gracing the edges of each piece was a stark contrast that made for stunning art. There were even holsters for her *spyd* and dagger, both crafted in black metal with tiny details of the goldish shade. A flexible set of black tights and long-sleeved shirts rested beneath. The material reinforced itself to help cushion blows without wearing quickly from the friction.

After taking in her gift, Sylven realized their sets were identical in terms of color schemes, his predominantly dark and hers light. The stitching in his was the exact shade of her armor, a detail so fine it amazed him how much thought had been poured into it. Both were given matching cloaks as well, simple cashmere and fur-lined pieces that guaranteed warmth on the chilliest of nights.

It made his stomach sink at how ironclad his parents' resolve was to the *anima* contract. It was going to be impossible to get rid of Sayra, and it sickened him to think of being stuck with the burden for decades.

Still, gratitude welled in both of them. They expressed their thanks in abundance as they said their heartfelt goodbyes to his family and Korine. Despite his quiet despair, Sylven knew it to be a boon they supported his desire to become a Sicarius.

Sayra was temporarily pulled aside by his mother, and a fleeting sentence passed between them before she joined him in the carriage. They departed Astor Manor, two hired guards leading the way on horseback through the winding forest. It was almost reminiscent of their journey there, how his nose had been buried in a book and Sayra fiddled with the lock mechanism on the door, questions flung his way every few moments. Sylven remained faithful to his devoted plan of ignoring her, bitterness encapsulating every thought at the predicament Rys forced him into.

This time around, however, Sylven kept his metal gauntlets clasped around his hands. The leather ones were perfect for formal competitions, but the metal gauntlets were far sturdier when dealing with daemons.

His mind was on edge as his eyes scanned beyond the towering trees. Nothing. Not when they passed charred remains where Rys must have burned daemons to a crisp, and not when they crossed into the sovereign territory of Saint Highburn. It was eerie hearing of two daemon attacks in such rapid succession, more so that each had more than one of the Horde.

It weighed heavily on him.

Late afternoon was upon them when they approached the mountain Saint Highburn Monastery was perched upon. Its grand spires rose high above the enormous swath of plateau it rested on within the mountains. The marble gleamed like a beacon, snow-covered pines dotting the surrounding terrain. Valkyries and guards alike patrolled the towering stone walls that encompassed the perimeter.

Crisp mountain air breezed past the carriage, heavy with the scent of pine as they rolled closer to the front gates. One of the horses snorted, the clomp of its feet growing louder as the path transitioned from dirt to cobblestone.

Sayra cleared her throat, a pointed curiosity emanating from their mental bond. "The monastery grounds are a collection point for all affinities of ley lines, right? There are only two places on the continent that have every element of majik overlapping in such a way."

Sylven ran his tongue across his teeth, debating whether to ignore her for a few minutes more or to indulge her for a brief time before he could escape to his dormitory. A twinge of guilt about how he had treated her convinced him to be nice. For the time being.

"Yes. It's the perfect location for any Arcanist to learn majik as every elemental ley line is readily available in the earth's veins far below," he said.

Thankfully for Sylven, a wind ley line ran close to the trail between the Astor duchy and Saint Highburn Monastery. So long as he wore his gauntlets, he'd always have access to majik.

The horses' breath was labored by the time they passed the small lake, doors already hauled open by the watchers. They gratefully accepted the nuns' aid in retrieving their belongings and moving back into their dormitories. Regrettably, Sayra's new Valkyrie dormitory was across from his, only a garden separating the two from her fourth-story room and his first.

Far too close for comfort.

"Looks like we get to be neighbors." Sayra winked, her spitefulness reaching him through their bond. "Have a good evening, Sylven."

The way she said it sent an icy chill down his spine. He grunted in response, departing for his room. The halls were busy with students returning from break, the common room irritatingly packed to the point where he had to push people out of the way. When he finally reached his room, he collapsed across his bed, embracing the peace and quiet.

Later, Waylen surprised him in the Arcanist dining hall, and they took the evening to catch up and share stories of their time visiting family. It felt easier to breathe when expectations weren't so high, and he wasn't constantly being sought by someone. While he ended up enjoying his break, it was reassuring to be back in a place he knew he belonged and to be right with Rys at last.

CHAPTER ELEVEN

SAYRA

Sayra couldn't be still, not when she had been so all day. She'd been restless lately, feeling as if her vow with the prince wasn't being considered seriously. He left for the capital of Acacea without sharing any of the details of her majik, only the promise they'd talk when he returned.

After unpacking, she threw on her training clothes. They were form-fitting and all black. In the Valkyrie's gymnasium, Sayra exercised until her arms gave out on dumbbell rows, her breathing labored and neck slick with sweat.

Thankfully, towels were provided for their convenience, so Sayra dried off and placed hers in the dirty basket before making her way into the corridor. The moment she rounded the corner, a fist shot out at her from the left, and a leg swept to catch her feet on the right. She twisted in the air, dodging the fist and returning a kick of her own into a padded chest.

Netta cursed while backpedaling to catch her balance, clutching the vest where Sayra's foot landed. Yevette, an orange-haired and heavily freckled member of the hags, rushed forward, one fist guarding her splotchy face and the other striking low.

Jumping in, Jayde threw a dirty punch to the back of her head, narrowly missing Sayra as she caught her wrist, pulling her forward to absorb Yevette's blow. Grunting, the tall brunette took a moment to retreat, carefully observing when to leap in.

And that's exactly what Netta did.

One hundred and ninety pounds of muscle and protective equipment barreled into Sayra's back, her dodge a second too late. Slammed into the ground, she had but seconds to recover, efficiently latching onto Yevette's leg and the doorsill to push out while spinning, sending the assailant tumbling to the ground where Sayra was moments before. Hopping back, she parried a blow from Jayde, then ducked low and thrusted her elbow firmly into her padded gut.

Cheaters.

She had a brief reprieve while the three Valkyries circled for their next move.

"Such a pity. The three of you had time to plan a surprise attack, with padded clothing for armor, yet you managed to screw that up too." Sayra sniggered with a savage grin on her face, her feet in motion and eyes flicking between the foes. She was being cautious of her blind spots. "You must have allowed Netta to lead the charge. I can't fathom why you'd do such a thing, considering she couldn't manage to graduate higher than the third tier."

With a roar, Netta lurched forward with a mean right hook, Yevette squirming behind her to knock out her legs once more. Several times, they jumped in pairs of two, Sayra struggling to gain any ground. Gritting her teeth, she watched as they silently communicated for a second, coming to an unspoken agreement. She knew it was only a matter of time before she lost. Three versus one never ended well, and the only advantage Sayra had was the small confines of the corridor and the opportunity to play them into each other.

The other Valkyries didn't practice this form of combat training like she and her cadre did. Sayra had trained relentlessly with Lynn, Nes, and Kimimari as acolytes for situations like this. With the amount of people itching for them to fail, it was only best to prepare for the inevitable.

As she dodged a high blow, another fist connected with Sayra's shoulder, spinning her momentum and sending her too close to Jayde. As she prepared to dodge, Netta's arms wrapped around her middle, taking her airborne and slamming her head into the ground.

Dazed and trapped, Sayra attempted to kick the others away but to no avail. Thoroughly pissed, she fought to escape Jayde's grappling that secured her legs. Yevette aided Netta in holding her down. She didn't stop fighting for a second—not when a fist drew the breath from her lungs and not when her rib cracked. Pain lanced through her body, instinct pulling her through to fight.

Netta idiotically drew close to her face, allowing a powerful headbutt to snap her nose with a satisfying crack. A maniacal laugh tore from Sayra's lips as blood spurted forth, Netta cursing as she signaled Jayde to hold. "You'll regret everything," she raged, her voice nasally and breathy. "Stop *laughing*!"

Kicking down on Sayra's femur, Netta delivered an excruciating blow to her thigh, likely fracturing the bone within. Sayra's neck strained as she bit back a scream, her eyes involuntarily tearing up.

A flicker of concern flashed through her bond with Sylven before being smothered. He probably didn't care. But footsteps raced down the hall, and for a split second, she thought maybe he'd come after all, sensing she was in trouble.

"C'mon, Netta, we need to go now," Jayde warned, releasing Sayra's legs and backing off with a jerk of her head.

Shaking with fury, Netta rose. "This isn't over, Sayra. You ruined my career, and I promise I'll ruin your life," she fumed, about to turn tail when Sayra managed to share a crude gesture with her right hand. Yevette pulled her back, giving her a stern look before Netta gave in and ran out the other corridor.

"Damn them," an unfamiliar Valkyrie said.

A ping of disappointment flung through Sayra's chest when she heard it wasn't Sylven. She had hoped he would show some semblance of compassion or remorse for his harsh words.

Kneeling beside her, the Valkyrie looked her up and down. "You good to move? I know someone who can patch you up without going to the healers and having to report this."

Good. The woman clearly knew the code and how things were between Sayra and those hags. They'd pay but only by her hands. It was a feud between them, a tradition of the Valkyries to handle from within.

"Yes," Sayra managed between breaths, every part of her alight with pain.

"Okay. The name's Breane. This is going to hurt," the blonde Valkyrie warned, her earthy eyes unflinching as she pulled Sayra to her feet.

Immediately, her right leg gave out, the pain too much to bear as her body sagged into Breane's. "*Dritt,*" Sayra hissed. She was pissed those three had managed to get the best of her.

"Can you make it to the end of the hall? Men aren't permitted entry, but my Arcanist can help you once we make it out into the main corridor linking the Valkyrie and Arcanist dormitories."

Nodding briskly, Sayra endured as they hobbled the final forty feet of the majikally lit corridor—half of the Valkyrie's gymnasium size. By the end of it, she felt as if she were hallucinating. She was in such mind-numbing pain that when she found a young man waiting in the main corridor who looked similar to Emrys—Prince Emrys, she corrected herself—she believed she was.

Helped into a half-slouched, half-sitting position, Sayra felt nausea rolling through her stomach, but she tried to hold herself together.

"Injured right leg and broken rib from the sound of her wheezing," Breane reported to the young man, his dark eyes assessing. Her blonde head dipped into Sayra's field of vision as she scanned her face. "And a concussion from the looks of it. Pupils are dilated irregularly."

"Noted," he said, crouching beside Sayra. "Do I have your permission to help?"

The question was directed at her, so she sluggishly dipped her head twice.

Stretching a gauntleted hand over her leg, he said, "*Sana.*"

Almost instantly, Sayra could feel relief in her thigh, helping to clear some of the pain-induced fog from her mind. His hand moved over her head, and the word of power was repeated. Blinking, she felt the world straighten, the edges of her vision no longer warping into abstract lines. Lastly, he moved toward her ribcage, the word ringing in her ears again.

"Thank you," Sayra said. Her shoulders dropped in relief as she rose. "I'm going to go chase their *ræva* down while they think they're safe."

Both of them looked astonished, the man bursting into deep laughter and Breane holding an arm in her way.

Frowning, Sayra stood her ground. "I'm serious," she protested, fists clenched and her mildly bruised body ready for the fight. "They only won because they prepared. Now, I'll have the advantage of surprise."

"No, I'm laughing because you're exactly how my brother described," he chuckled, catching his breath.

It clicked.

"You're Prince Vander," Sayra mused, giving the heir of Acacea a once-over. "You're much less intimidating than I expected."

Wearing a simple but well-made cream vest, a long-sleeved white shirt, and coal trousers, he appeared to be quite casual in contrast with his brother's serious persona. His onyx hair was longer, nose slightly upraised at the end. Whereas Prince Emrys was clean-shaven, Vander allowed stubble to grow along his jawline, making him appear older than his twenty years.

"Please, just Vander." He waved nonchalantly. "And you're Sayra von Lykken, once princess to the empire of Faenda. You know, I could make you a princess once more," Vander joked, waggling his brows.

Breane stared at the ceiling as if she were praying for patience.

"Har har," Sayra monotoned, a foot tapping with impatience. "Well, as much as I'd love to casually banter, I have some *dritts* to hunt down."

"You know, it's still vulgar and counts as cussing even if it's in another language," Vander pointed out. "Right, Breane?"

Just because Arcanists deemed themselves above it, especially within the walls of the monastery, Sayra held no such reservations. She rolled her eyes.

Breane folded her arms and made a face. "I'm staying out of this one."

But a feeling nagged at Sayra. She didn't like accepting help without knowing what to give in return. "What do I owe you for this? I don't make a habit of collecting debts."

"You Faendans and your debts." Vander chuckled, waving his hand. "How about this. Breane lost her sparring partner some time ago due to her accepting a position in a different country. The next time you're out there, Breane could use someone to train with."

Sayra glanced at Breane. "So long as you don't mind losing."

She coughed. "Says the Valkyrie who just got beaten black and blue."

"Touché." Sayra grinned.

"It's been a pleasure to formally make your acquaintance, Sayra. I'm confident we'll see each other again soon." Vander winked, jerking his thumb in the direction she came from. "If I were you, I'd save that beating for next year's *proelium*. Then, you can flounce your enemies in public with an entire audience rooting for you. I know I will be." Casting her a smile she got the distinct impression many ladies swooned over, he turned into the Arcanist dormitory.

"You must have your hands full with that one," Sayra said, shooting Breane a pitying look.

Shaking her head, Breane loosened a breath. "You don't know the half of it."

Same, thought Sayra. "Thanks again for your help."

"Don't worry about it. Do you want further assistance with them?" Breane asked.

Shaking her head again, Sayra said, "No. This is between me and them. Thanks though."

"Good hunting."

Sayra's teeth flashed, and she was off.

Chapter Twelve

SYLVEN

Sylven had wondered if he should be concerned, but when her mood shifted, he decided it wasn't his business. It was beginning to become a challenge to separate the girl from her position. Yes, he didn't want or need a Valkyrie. Yes, it was an enormous waste of resources and completely tarnished his happiness.

But...

Sylven was a human being. It was clear Sayra had suffered some sort of painful encounter, which led to injury. A tiny, almost insignificant part of him knew it was courtesy for Arcanists to be amicable hosts to their Valkyries. Though if he gave in, wouldn't that prove everyone right that he did need the Valkyrie and had accepted her in his life?

He was far too stubborn to relent.

The following morning, Sylven threw himself into his studies, and when afternoon came, he completed his paper on the founding of the Old Covenant and its historical impact. His upcoming semester schedule arrived an hour afterward, a curse slipping from his mouth when he read it.

Lecture 1: Advanced Principles of Wind Manipulation
Lecture 2: History of Anima

Lecture 3: Ethical and Moral Implications of the Arcane Arts
Lecture 4: Intermediate Light Majik
Lecture 5: Basic Applications of the Old Covenant
Lecture 6: Anima Combat and Survival Techniques

The last two classes he'd be sharing with Sayra every other day, meaning for two or three days out of every week escaping her would be impossible. Even worse, each class would be two dreadfully long hours, and the walk between them would give her plenty of time to talk his ear off. On the bright side, he was excited to begin new majik classes. It was always delightful to learn new words of power and different methods to manipulate them.

Knocking sounded at his door, pulling his attention from the parchment to the person intruding on his weekend. Grunting in annoyance, Sylven ran a hand through his hair and opened the door to discover Vander lazily leaning against the wall.

"Vander."

"Sylven." He nodded in the direction of his room. "May I?"

Widening the opening, Sylven gestured for him to enter. "What brings you here? Has Rys returned as well?"

"Rys returns on the morrow." Vander sauntered in, drawing the desk chair around to face where Sylven sat on his bed. Making himself comfortable, he took his time to reply, irking Sylven in the process. "Your Valkyrie sure got herself into trouble last night," Vander said at last, studying a seam along his forearm.

"She seems to have a knack for such things, much to my endless frustration." Sylven scowled, drawing his fists tight. Did Sayra not have any inclination that her actions could reflect poorly on him?

Vander's eyes glanced up, his hand still holding the inspected portion of fabric. "You seem to harbor a negative perspective regarding her."

"She and I are temporary. My intention was never to contract with anyone, much less a Valkyrie so bothersome and talkative." Sylven scoffed, taking in the freshly fallen snow outside his window. "Why do you inquire?"

Vander's face grew serious, almost wearing the expression Rys held every day. A rare thing from the crowned prince of Acacea. "It should have been you there last night to help her, not me."

Sylven's eyes sharpened, his body unnaturally still as he checked his annoyance at the crowned prince's audacity.

"Don't misunderstand me. I'm glad to have been of assistance. Breane arrived in the nick of time to prevent injuries far worse than a broken leg, concussion, and cracked rib. She was ambushed by three Valkyries."

Sylven clenched his jaw, remorse growing by the second. He didn't know the severity of her situation or that she sustained such injuries. But they were *her* situations, *her* problems to solve. He had been forced into his contract and didn't owe her anything beyond keeping her employed. Why was Vander, of all people, making a detour to criticize him? It made him wonder about his predicament and Rys's unwillingness to share information. The man across from him would never visit for any trivial matter.

Meaning...

"Sayra is important to your family somehow, isn't she? Both you and Rys have been dancing around her, impressing on me how dire it is to keep a Valkyrie, but it's more than that, isn't it? It's significant for me to keep *her* specifically as a Valkyrie, not just anyone," Sylven deduced, his breaths measured as he searched for any hint Vander might part with.

Standing, Vander smoothed out his sleeve, a near-cold expression twisting his face. "Sometimes life events are grander than just you or I, Sylven. I'm only here to ensure that all is well and that nothing regrettable occurs. I am, after all, to inherit the throne, and it is my duty to oversee such matters when they concern me." The warning was abundant in his words, even more so in the manner spoken. "There's more at play than you realize."

Vander mocked a bow of his head, turning to leave. An arrogance lifted his steps, a slight swagger that spoke of unearned confidence.

Sylven wanted nothing more than to yell at the circles being spun around him, almost as if a spider had cast a web that tightened with each passing second. It wasn't that he held no power in Acacea; he was set on inheriting the dukedom from his father one day. So, why was he being shut out by Rys and Vander? For Vander to have stepped in, there was something huge occurring, and Sylven had to get to the bottom of the situation. He mentioned Rys would be arriving at the monastery the next day, and Sylven fully intended to interrogate him.

The remainder of the day was spent digging through books in the library, a stunning three floors of massive shelves spanning the length of the building. Several rounded mahogany tables were clustered in the library's center, chandeliers hanging from the opening three stories high. Sylven flipped through one of the few books on Faenda, Sayra's homeland, trying to glean any pertinent information that could shed light on her importance. Other Arcanists, staff, and monastery guests passed by above, but thankfully, the noise was minimal. Occasional chatter would spout from the two second-year Arcanists across from him, a minor annoyance that peeved him more than it should have, but it was the *library* for Goddess's sake.

He found nothing.

The entire afternoon had been in vain, night falling with similar results. Sure, it was enlightening to learn about Faenda's spiritual worship of the earth itself rather than a goddess and their unusual fascination with anything in the arts industry, but nothing explicated Sayra's family in detail beyond her house being the four-centuries-old ruling family.

While Sylven would deny any who asked, he spent the better part of the following day stalking Sayra where he could. It started with her venture to the outdoor sparring ring for Valkyries. As she practiced with a muscular tattooed girl nearly as tall as him and an auburn-haired one just an inch taller than Sayra, he hid in the shadows. For an hour, he nearly forgot his original intention as Sayra maneuvered with her *spyd*. Her motions were graceful—not a single twitch of a muscle wasted or blow landed on her. If he were being honest, Sylven could discern an elegance in the way she flowed succinctly between offense and defense. It was mesmerizing to watch, almost as if she were carrying out an orchestrated performance on stage.

However, Rys and Vander couldn't be captivated by her weapon proficiency or her capability for dance. Was it her looks? Sylven could see that being the case for many Arcanists, but Rys wasn't the type to be remotely besotted by such a superficial trait. Vander, well, he chased every female who crossed his path.

Unoriginal and juvenile.

By afternoon, Sayra had returned to the sparring yard alone, stretching and moving into hand-to-hand combat with imagined enemies. Two other Valkyries had come and gone, and Sylven was despising himself for acting in such a manner. He excused himself solely because there was something to her story, and it was only a matter of time before he located a clue. But by four in the evening, Sylven had begun to question Sayra's sanity. It could not have been an everyday occurrence, the sheer number of hours poured into training surreal.

It did reassure him Sayra was well after what Vander had told him about her being ambushed. She must have healed fast, and it eased some of his culpability. When nothing happened, though, Sylven's patience wore thin. He nearly gave up on his mission when a new face appeared.

Breane.

Sylven's vision was hyper-focused, his ears straining to hear anything from his position behind a pillar. Unfortunately, he proved to be too far away and had no method of approaching further unless he wanted to reveal himself. His legs began cramping from the awkward positioning, but his eyes remained glued as Sayra volunteered her weapon to Vander's Valkyrie, the two eventually sparring with each other.

When they were at Astor Manor, Nessika hadn't been wrong when she detailed Sayra's capabilities. While exceptional and top of her class years ago, Breane was easily outmatched. Every attack was deflected with the sword-like end and any follow-up blocked with the clang of steel and redirected with the links. Whereas Breane's movements were powerful and bold, Sayra's were precise and ever shifting, her body never once slowing to a stop. If her hands were blocking, her feet were navigating to an advantageous position.

The sun had set before they were done, Sayra winded from the day of enduring exercise and Breane not far behind. Sylven—bored, rigid, and famished—gave up when Sayra finally coiled her *spyd* and made to depart. What a waste. Nothing gave him any insight, though in the end, he had to admit he didn't expect much to begin with. It was a shame he spent his last full day before classes being unproductive.

Sayra was a puzzle he couldn't solve. She was capable. The day had shown that much. Which only lead to more questions buzzing around his mind. Why had she hesitated that day with the daemon? Such longing filled him at the opportunity to out Sayra's misstep. Sylven would have been rid of her. He would have been free. Back then, his anger was too great to discuss the matter. Now, he didn't want to lend any misinter-preted olive branch toward her.

He'd have to figure it out himself.

Why did an otherwise unremarkable girl hold such interest from both princes, and what occurred behind closed doors for Rys to become so deceptive toward him? It had to be something grand since they hadn't ever had such a conflict between them. It couldn't simply be that Sayra wielded the dagger and chain contraption with captivating excellence. What was he missing?

⸺◈⸺

Dinner was a tedious affair, the small hall packed with navy-clad Arcan-ists of every year, gossiping about their breaks and upcoming classes. Six tables ran along its length, each representing a year's class of Arcanists, Sylven's the fourth year. Waylen was detailing his schedule, animatedly describing his eagerness to share lectures three, five, and six together.

"You know, I wish more than ever I had Emrys's dark majik arche-type." He sighed, stabbing a bite of caramel cheesecake with his fork. "Since my majik's elemental affinity is fire and all, I'd be able to do so much more with it."

Shrugging, Sylven drank deeply from his glass of water before reply-ing. "It's the hand dealt to those with light archetypes, being incapable of destruction and all. Every Arcanist can cast the same basic spells that adhere to their light or dark tendencies." He arched a brow at Waylen's downtrodden face. "Meaning all light archetypes can create protective barriers that a ball would bounce off if thrown at it. All dark archetypes can produce barriers that would obliterate the ball instead. Same inten-tion but a slightly different outcome."

Waylen frowned at him, not understanding what Sylven was getting at. "Yes, that's what we learned in our first year here. And?"

"Your majik has a light archetype but with the fire element. While you can't level a playing field with destructive flames as a dark archetype could, you are more than capable of incapacitating that very same field." Sylven lifted a square of cheesecake in front of his eyes, inspecting the caramel drizzle with a critical gaze.

Something looked off. He squinted.

Breathing heavily out of his nose, Waylen placed his silver fork and knife on his plate with a clatter. The noise was barely heard over the loud chatter of the dining hall.

Sylven glanced over at his friend, noting Waylen's furrowed face. Compared to the others of their year, Waylen appeared a year or two younger than his age.

"Think about it. If I, a wind-using Arcanist, had a dark archetype, I'd be capable of wielding tornado-force winds and could weaponize the air to cut through objects. Instead, I use my light archetype of wind majik to alter the speed of people or beings and displace them within the air."

A chair scooted back next to Sylven as an Arcanist sat beside him, speaking adamantly to another. His plate of balsamic chicken and lemon risotto wafted fragrant smells as it steamed.

Waylen's palms hit the table in excitement, his navy cuffs landing far too close to his dessert. "I see!"

Me too, Sylven thought as he spotted it at last. A small eyelash clung to the drizzle of caramel. He knew he saw something out of the corner of his vision.

"I need to expand my magikal light to flood the field and blind my opponent for a prolonged period. If I can hold it, I can use that time to maneuver."

Laying the cheesecake back on his plate, Sylven pushed it to the center of the table to remain uneaten. He wasn't much of a sweets person anyway. "I'd imagine, once you push through Advanced Physics of Optics, you may even devise a way to manipulate light to make images appear or disappear, similar to Arcanist Kenjar in chapter nine, section three of *A History of Arcanists*."

Waylen looked positively contemplative as he stabbed another bite of cheesecake, his brown eyes brightening. In general, light Arcanists weren't nearly as dangerous as dark ones, but with time and a crafty mindset, anything was possible.

If only an Arcanist could wield several elemental affinities or light and dark archetypes simultaneously. Sylven would pay any price if it meant he could be more lethal. He imagined he wouldn't share many classes with Rys because of his distinct dark archetype of fire majik, but whenever he arrived, Sylven was determined to inquire about his schedule.

As the night wore on, Rys still didn't turn up. While he knew it was unreasonable, Sylven worried himself enough to constantly check his room, but each knock was met with silence. Folding his hands in his pockets, he returned to his dorm with a frown and readied himself for sleep.

Chapter Thirteen

SAYRA

Sayra's body ached in a million places, the training wearing down her very bones. It was necessary, though, to prevent herself from slipping again. She had failed twice over a two-week span, once with Sylven in the face of the Horde and then when Netta managed to score that victory. Besides, it was calming to feel normal for once, even if it was fleeting. Sparring with Kimimari and Lynn was a great way to loosen the tense muscles in her shoulders. And Sayra had to admit, Breane was quickly becoming an individual she'd enjoy having as a friend.

She tossed her dirty clothes in a bin beside her restroom. A yawn escaped her as she glanced into her newly acquired mirror. Her acolyte dormitory came with the bare bones of housing necessities. Her new room was much more spacious, hosting extra amenities such as a turquoise tiled floor in the restroom and a showerhead with great water pressure.

Brushing her damp hair out, Sayra collected some stray strands and threw them in her waste bin beside the sink. She frowned as her hands ran through the bottom of her shirt. Her soft gray cotton top and pajama bottoms were starting to show signs of wear, a loose thread here and there and the potency of the color fading.

Time to visit the merchant shops. She sighed inwardly.

A small storm raged outside, clusters of snow circling in the wind beyond her large window. Opening a sizable trunk at the end of her bed, Sayra delicately folded her *slør* on top of the interior compartment elevated for jewelry and the like. Her new armor lay below it along with her holster for the *spyd* and her serrated, curved blade engraved with her name. Even with all of it, her trunk had room in spades. The old set of armor remained tucked under her bed, saved for the day she might need a set she wasn't afraid of ruining.

Closing the trunk, she groggily stood.

Stretching and yawning, Sayra reached for the ceiling, naturally falling short by many feet. She then tucked herself under her cream-colored sheets, sighing as she relaxed at last. Tomorrow would be a big day for her and Sylven, him starting classes and her joining an evening patrol with the guards along the walls. Whereas Arcanists focused solely on their studies, Valkyries only took two classes targeted at *anima*. Sayra would be with him during lectures five and six. The rest of their time they'd be training on their own accord and assigned patrols by the church.

If she was fortunate, perhaps Sayra would cross paths with some of the Horde while on duty. Of course, the wards hugged the castle walls tightly. She had her pride to redeem and a reputation to launch sky-high. She'd prove to Sylven she was a worthy Valkyrie, and she'd never make such a horrendous mistake again.

Smiling, she pictured a myriad of battles where she royally kicked Horde *ræva*, the images playing out in the dreams that followed. While it could have been minutes or hours that passed, Sayra's nose picked up an acrid scent. A man's voice murmured words outside her closed door.

Men weren't allowed in the Valkyrie dormitory, which only raised her hackles. Drawing her brows close, Sayra blinked at the sight before her.

Majik-borne, black-tinted flames consumed the entirety of her door, smoke already gathering at the apex of her room. Sayra flung herself from the bed and barreled toward the entrance to catch the culprit. Trying the handle, she found it stuck and immediately retracted it. She hissed at the mild burn her hand suffered.

Bracing her shoulder, Sayra prepared to break down the door. Sprinting forward, the side of her body charged straight into an invisible barrier, the majik flinging her back with equal force.

Her back hit the ground hard, the side of her head colliding with the wooden floor. Stars floated in her vision as she blinked to clear them. Sayra cursed at the majik, unsure of what to do next. The burn sizzled on her shoulder from where the barrier and flames touched her skin. Her cotton sleeve had a gaping hole, black edging around it.

Her heart beat uncontrollably in her chest, the sound of crackling flames growing.

The fire thoroughly charred the door, but the majik held it in place. Smoke clouded above her, increasing rapidly.

I need to do something.

Balling her fists, Sayra regained her footing. Her eyes locked on the large window beside her bed. She threw it open, hoping some fresh air from the snowstorm would find its way in. Still, her lungs burned from the heavy scent of smoke. Soot collected along her walls from the bright tongues of fire.

Grabbing a second pajama shirt, Sayra rushed to her sink and drenched the material, tying it around her face to create a barrier against the smoke. Grabbing her toothbrush container, she filled it with water and rushed to her door to figure out if that would have any effect.

The water sizzled before reaching the threshold, useless against the strength of the majik. Cursing yet again, Sayra had to rein in her growing panic at her predicament. Her eyes were wild. Every second that passed felt like a second closer to death.

Placing the holder down beside her desk, she paced to her window. She estimated the distance and determined it to be a potentially lethal jump from four stories high, even with her enhanced healing and sturdiness. Snow hadn't reached high enough to cushion her, and no one was out in the storm. Not a soul she could call out to or flag down from the Arcanist dorm.

Speaking of that, how had no one else noticed the fire? Surely, even with the thick stone walls, someone would hear, see, or smell it.

Sayra attempted to shout to anyone in the vicinity, banging the wall she shared with another Valkyrie.

Nothing. *Dritt.*

Running a hand across her sweating forehead, she marked the progression the fire had made thus far, already crawling across her walls and nearing her desk. Stone blackened in its majikal path, its smoke burning her eyes.

The only way she could see surviving was to overpower the majikal barrier with enough force, a determination that had her running forward and delivering a powerful spinning kick to the flames. Pain radiated from the burned ball of her foot, lending a slight limp to her step with nothing to show for it.

Flames continued to consume her room, her lungs crying for fresh air. Gathering herself once more, Sayra launched forward with a powerful right hook. Her knuckles blistered and cracked as she was thrown to the floor once again. Coughing in a small fit, she inched back from a flicker of flame that fell to the ground, stone beginning to crack along her walls.

It was then her fear must have truly reached Sylven, his own panic resounding in response.

Then it hit her.

Whoever thrust the majik upon her might have done so to harm him. It could be a way to remove her while some assassin targeted Sylven.

His emotions whirled unpredictably through their link—anger, frustration, and fear churning in her head. Clenching her fists, Sayra renewed her efforts against the door, the thought of Sylven being in danger emboldening her will to lash out. With each punch, her skin blistered further and oozed specks of blood. Each kick had her legs blackening and cracking as her limbs came in contact with the flames.

Tears stung Sayra's eyes. She gasped for air, coughing frantically as the corners of her vision began to blur. An icy chill knotted in her chest, and her heart pounded with the fear of failure and Sylven's own precarious situation.

Her movements became sloppy, her attacks weakening with each passing blow. Her body ached something fierce every time it slammed into the ground, piercing pain shooting through her veins. The lack of progress and the hopelessness that slowly sank into her bones was maddening, her thoughts fearing the worst.

Her teeth chattered as her mind reverently prayed for Sylven to be okay. With each new injury, Sayra's stress increased, and she debated a fall out the window.

A hacking cough doubled her over, the icy knot growing and striking her heart. As the fire spread across her floor, engulfing her desk and crawling around the exterior of her dresser, Sayra's mind felt fuzzy, and her lungs agonized as if burned themselves. Terror crossed the bond and leaked into her mind—Sylven's. Her own helplessness escalated, something within her very bones calling to the earth and pulling from the ley lines far below.

A deep chill rose bumps along her arms. It caressed her mind, a majik so wild and ancient it seemed to barely acquiesce to her base instinct. It was then the iciness lashed out, her consciousness wishing for the blazing firework of destructive majik to *go away.*

And away it did.

Not a heartbeat later, the fire whooshed out, the heat replaced with a gust of cold racing in from her window. Sayra's door was a black mass, her desk similarly toasted, and half of her dresser and floor were ash. But she was okay, and the thought brought her such deep relief she nearly collapsed into an aching heap.

Sayra refused to move. The pain renewed tenfold with even the slightest movement in any direction. Her muddled mind then remembered Sylven and his overwhelming terror. Her ears picked up an array of shouting voices in the hallway. Groaning, she creaked to her feet, stumbling to her door, which fell to ash the moment she reached for it.

What she saw horrified her.

Black-tinted flames spread from her door to the previously untouched rooms across the hall, slowly blackening and cracking the stone at an accelerated rate. Somehow, Sayra had managed to cast the fire outward and speed up its burn. She forced the other Valkyries into the same situation she had just escaped.

Voices became raised and urgent. Valkyries shouted throughout the hallway as they became aware of the fire and were unable to escape their rooms. One voice in particular snapped her out of the shock.

"Kimimari!" Sayra coughed frantically as she inched around a puddle of flame to her friend's door. Her elbow raced forward, rebounding just as her fists had against her own door.

No, no, no, no.

Sayra was nearly tossed into that patch of fire, the end of her elbow singed once more.

"Sayra!" Kimimari coughed, hitting the door to no avail.

"Please," Sayra whispered in desperation to the vacant power within her. Despite her efforts, it lay dormant and inaccessible. Over and over, she bashed her body against the door, hoping it would either give out or the power would spark once again.

She couldn't recall when the voices across the floor began to silence or when she last heard movement within the rooms. At some point, she recognized only the crackle of flames echoed in the marble and stone dormitory.

An agonized shout of anger escaped her mouth when the warded door threw her back again. It was absolutely petrifying to be incapable of rescuing her friend. Sayra's fists and feet left thin streaks of crimson across the stone floor. The shirt around her mouth was barely damp anymore, the moisture wicked from the boiling heat.

Her body trembled in desperation, and in her pain-addled mind, Sayra realized she had to make a decision.

Was Sylven in trouble? Should Sayra abandon her friend to save her Arcanist, the one she swore to protect? What if she left to search for Sylven only to find he was okay? Should she remain there, giving it everything she had to get Kimimari out of the flames?

A tear leaked from her eye as she straightened herself, her lips pressed into a quivering line. Sayra moved, her other shoulder clashing against the door. When her head hit the ground once more, her mind reached out for Sylven. While she felt his urgency, she didn't sense any pain.

That meant there was time, even if only a little, and Sayra could not give up on her friend so soon.

Repeatedly, she bashed herself into the fiery door's barrier, her mind and body losing themselves with the slowing strikes. No majik sparked in her, however.

"Kimimari, are you there?" she choked out, pleading with whatever higher force existed to help her burst through the door.

Everything swam around her. Her lungs felt as if they were collapsing within themselves. Her skin was blackened in numerous places, the pain excruciating.

"Kimimari!"

Around her, everything was falling apart, her mind memorizing every painstaking moment yet unable to comprehend the minutes passing that doomed her friend and everyone on the floor. It didn't seem real. It was like a cruel dream, plaguing her in the night. Her friend was dying or already dead. She felt as if she were falling into an impossibly deep pit of confusion, every sight and sound wringing the hope from her stuttering heart.

"Kimi—" Her hoarse voice relented to coughing once more. Sayra wanted it all to end, but that icy majik that previously filled her chest was empty, leaving her a useless husk when others needed her most.

It had become a devastating pattern that seemed to be woven into her very existence.

CHAPTER FOURTEEN

EMRYS

Emrys commanded the Arcanists to follow and Waylen to notify the monks to prepare for triage and evacuation aid. While he was certain they were already in action, it was imperative to cover every base when Sayra was involved, especially considering their instructors' quarters were distanced from that section of the monastery.

It didn't take more than three words from Sylven and the smoke billowing from a fourth-story window to veer him into hasty action.

Sayra's in danger.

Those three little words and Emrys didn't hesitate to drop the belongings he had begun to unpack from his long journey. He didn't waste a second in his sprint along with Sylven to ensure her safety.

Emrys alerted Nessika to clear the way for him when he arrived, receiving acknowledgment within seconds on her end, no questions asked. His Valkyrie instructed her peers to empty the northern stairwell.

Several monks arrived mere moments after Emrys did. Other Arcanists flowed in on his tailcoat, murmuring nervously amongst themselves as they huddled around the entrance. The monks split through the growing sea of Arcanists and evacuated Valkyries, following Emrys up the northern stairwell. When he bounded up the steps, Emrys permitted Sylven to take the lead and direct him toward Sayra.

As they raced along, the sixth sense he had for majik was going into overdrive. It felt slimy. Unnatural. Evil. Almost daemonic-like. The worst part was it called to him. A haunted melody that rung a familiar echo in Emrys's soul.

An old fear clutched his lungs, stealing his breath away. His face pulled into a faint snarl, forcing his majik to quiet as it rose to fight a force more sinister than even daemons.

Nefas majik.

It was the third, and last, archetype of majik forbidden from being used, else it cost an Arcanist their very soul.

His gut clenched when he saw it raging across the fourth floor where Sayra was. Black-tinged fire crawled across the rooftop, an evil spell with clever safeguards to keep those within from easily escaping or dismantling it.

As Emrys approached, he saw it was fragmented, a patchy work of majik that seemed to have been altered somehow. Those small holes became more prominent as other monks gifted with majik tore away at the spell.

Emrys faced the flame, his voice weaving through the strings of majik feeding on the fire ley line deep beneath the monastery. *"Abiit!"* He poured an obscene amount of majik into the destructive spell, its design to destroy the fragmented remnants of the *nefas* majik.

Like a gust of wind, the flames and smoke blew into the air, disintegrating and leaving a somber image before him. Once gray, the hall looked as if it had been licked with black tongues. Pebbled stone collected around the edges, and cracks spidered through the material. A single Valkyrie picked herself up from the floor, coughing forcefully into a charred and bruised hand. Her feet left footprints of splotched blood behind her as she drew herself to a door across the hall. Long, ash-covered strands fell around her waist, a black cloth around her face.

Even from the distance, even with never having seen her without a braid and that permanent defiant edge to her eyes, Emrys knew it to be Sayra. His majik responded to hers in a way he'd never experienced before. It thrilled him when she was near. Emrys felt that pull the moment the *nefas* majik between them dissipated.

All those years ago, when Emrys happened across Sayra as the acolytes sparred in their field, he knew she was something beyond remarkable. She was the one who would save their world from the Horde and those corrupting majik at its core. No matter the cost, he couldn't afford to lose her.

Emrys was given explicit instructions to avoid Sayra at all costs before she became a Valkyrie, but he cursed himself for his shortsightedness and vowed never to leave her defenseless again. *Never.*

Too many factions were at play, some already moving their pawns forward to begin the game that had been decades in the making. But it was too early. Sayra's majik was untested and underdeveloped. She wasn't ready to face her destiny. Emrys hoped some of the players remained oblivious, and the boards hadn't started the clock on their first move. He wasn't sure if he'd come out the victor. Wasn't sure if he'd lose everything in the process.

Together, he and Sylven rushed forward. Monks directed the other Arcanists to aid their own Valkyries.

"Sayra?" Sylven asked, apprehension lining his tormented tone, his face warring between guilt and relief as her head snapped toward him. "Thank the Goddess," he said under his breath, walking forward.

It struck Emrys to see that haunted dimness in her sight. For the first time, she looked... frail.

Emrys knew his mask was on the verge of crumbling, his breathing too quick and anger at himself too encompassing to contain. His boots thudded across the stone floor, his fists impossibly tight. An acrid, burning smell filled his nostrils. He should have been there, and that thought kept circling his mind as he followed her limping form into the room of her friend.

But...

Earlier in the day, a messenger had left his mark in the bell tower, a pinnacle of artistry and mirrored rays of spellbound light. Before Emrys had stepped onto the hallowed grounds of Saint Highburn Monastery, that light fluttered three times in a row. A specific number just as his network of allies relayed his approach to the gate. Without delay, Emrys went to retrieve the coded message hidden in a clever compartment within the enormous library.

After decoding it, relief loosened his shoulders. It was news from his father. News that set the next piece of the deadly game in motion. Finally, it was time.

But all he cared about now was getting Sayra out of there.

She slumped toward the door before her, the wood collapsing on itself as she brushed aside chunks of it. "Kimimari," Sayra whispered, kneeling beside an unnervingly still form on the floor. Her voice was scratchy from smoke inhalation, her shoulders quaking from another coughing fit as her hand prodded the Valkyrie.

Emrys could somehow feel her in the fabric of the majik that raged through the dormitory, a trace he'd never experienced from any other previous spell. It made sense, though. After all, she was vastly different from any other Arcanist, and it seemed only his majik begged to drink and revel in such details. When Sayra first used majik during her final trial, Emrys couldn't breathe. His own power tugged at him, all but forcing him to take notice of Sayra's. It was a bizarre connection, but it fascinated him all the same.

If Sayra had attempted to disarm the *nefas* majik with her own, that would explain the trace. But she failed. And if Sayra lost her friend, even with the slightest culpability of the Valkyrie's death or any others, it could break her. Emrys needed her in his fight against the Holy Family. More than that, it left a weight in his stomach to think of her enduring death a second time. Her brother's loss nearly took her with it—a bone-chilling story that made even his stomach curdle.

Regardless of his personal feelings, though, his family required her in good health. It was why Vander snooped around all those years, watching Emrys oversee Sayra's progression behind the scenes.

"Sylven, take Kimimari to the healers in the corridor," Emrys ordered, moving to kneel beside Sayra's doubled form. "Sayra..." His voice became gentle as he tried to reason with her. "We must depart with haste. These walls could collapse at any moment, and we must seek medical attention for you both."

Sylven bent to take Kimimari into his arms, nodding once at Emrys and entrusting him with Sayra's care. His hazel eyes darted to his Valkyrie's battered form before exiting the room, his reluctance to leave her clear from his torn face and slow steps.

"No!" Sayra dodged Emrys as she caught up to Sylven, barely avoiding Valkyries, Arcanists, and monks alike.

Emrys kept pace, his chest clenching at the crimson marks her feet left in her wake and the shaking hand reaching for Sylven's shoulder.

Sylven paused to look at Sayra, something passing between them before he dipped his chin. "Kimimari's alive. She's alive," he reassured her, adjusting his hold on the Valkyrie. "But she needs an Arcanist's healing, and the only ones capable are downstairs, okay? Let us take our leave before anything further occurs."

Sayra swallowed, stepping back and leaning against a scorched wall, her head lolling slightly. "I'm waiting for the others to clear first," Sayra insisted. She watched Sylven and Kimimari evacuate, a tinge of her old self fading each time an Arcanist or monk would emerge with an unconscious, or possibly dead, Valkyrie. Dread and fear plagued her face.

Emrys took a moment to further assess the majik's impact. It seemed to have expanded through the walls, forcing a sporadic barrier that prevented the other Valkyries from escaping. Smoke and flame did extensive damage throughout, but he surmised smoke inhalation seemed to be the root cause of many passing out.

All within the span of minutes. In a place they all thought safe. Emrys knew better, and one day, the others would as well—when the spell of secrecy placed on him permitted him to share.

Guilt tightened Emrys's jaw. He wished he could have taught her control sooner.

Despite his prompts, Sayra refused to move, stubbornly waiting until each room was cleared. Emrys moved out of the way but stuck to his promise not to abandon her. Throughout it all, he kept a monitoring eye on the structural integrity of the hall, mentally communicating with Nessika that Sayra would be okay. It didn't take long. There were only twenty-six rooms per floor, and the surge of volunteers efficiently searched every nook.

Emrys constantly checked his connection with his Valkyrie, ensuring his emotions and any stray thoughts hadn't escaped his notice. He should have been more conscious of it earlier, but unfortunately, he was completely thrown when everything began. Regardless, he knew he had chosen well. Nessika was as professional and capable as he'd hoped.

Naturally, her connection with Sayra was imperative as Emrys would have cast serious suspicion had he chosen Sayra as his Valkyrie. The strings he pulled had already turned the heads of a handful of individuals. Emrys knew he shouldn't get too close to Sayra. He should be more careful with his presence.

Nessika was as close as Emrys could get to her. *Should* get to her.

At last, Sayra breathed a heavy, guilt-ridden breath and progressed down the corridor. Monks waved them forward, a handful of skilled instructors surveying the damage and inspecting the area for clues. It was only a matter of time before they would want to speak with Sayra, and Emrys knew they had to have their discussion sooner rather than later. He shouldn't have postponed it for so long, but with the chain of events set in motion by her first use of majik at her trial, he had no freedom to deviate from his instructions. Already he had been chastised for stopping first at Astor Manor to check on her.

Emrys couldn't help it, though. Perhaps it wasn't wise, but he knew he cared more for her well-being than was proper. If his parents, the two rulers who knew exactly how Sayra's majik originated, knew about his public proximity...

Emrys's face tightened.

In his defense, none of what transpired was supposed to happen. Sayra's majik wasn't due to appear for another year. The fact that it did caused serious problems with their plan.

It was painfully slow going, but when they emerged from the dormitory into the corridor, Sayra began scanning all the Valkyries settled against the walls or spread across the floor, taking inventory to ensure they survived. The noise and environment quickly proved overwhelming, her face paling and shallow breaths quickening. She tore the fabric from her head to breathe easier.

"They're going to be—" Emrys started, placing a solitary hand on her back. But a snap of majik sizzled between them, and his hand jerked back as if she'd shocked him. He felt it then, a swarm of dark majik circling inside her and *pushing*. Sayra was resisting, but it was too powerful, her emotional state not in any way capable of smothering it before it escaped.

That was unexpected.

Emrys would need to investigate it further. While he hadn't shared his unusual connection to Sayra's majik with his family—since he knew they were withholding details from him as well—he had done his own independent research to no avail. Besides, Vander would certainly steal the opportunity to poke fun at his claim.

He also had no interest in sharing the oddity with anyone else. Holding his cards tightly to his chest only ensured further moves down the line when necessary, and for the time being, Emrys would adhere to the plan.

He would never forget the moment his parents told him.

King Ferdinand, a towering figure with broad shoulders and a commanding presence, settled into his plush mahogany chair. The intricate carvings on the armrests spoke of a regal history, while the deep-red velvet upholstery exuded an air of authority. The warm glow of the fireplace cast dancing shadows across the room, illuminating the ornate bookshelves that lined the walls.

Beside him, Queen Evangelina, a frail and ethereal beauty, carefully sank into her own mahogany chair. Its polished surface gleamed under the soft light, reflecting the elegance of the room. The delicate scent of lavender wafted through the air, mingling with the faint aroma of aged parchment and leather-bound books.

As they settled into their seats, a hushed silence enveloped the private study, broken only by the occasional crackling of the fire. The heavy curtains, drawn tightly shut, muffled the distant sounds of the bustling palace. The weight of their responsibilities seemed to hang in the air, filling the room with a sense of purpose and anticipation as Emrys and Vander sat in their respective chairs across from them, a circular rug of intricate making separating them.

"To continue our previous discussion, we don't want either of you involved until our informant has the opportunity to speak with Sayra. We must not draw any attention to the girl, not for some years. For the time being, keep constant communication with us. Report any findings you happen across, but do not search for them. Wait until the time comes to proceed, and then we may oust Sayra's abilities on a grand scale," Ferdinand said, his voice low, practically grumbling the words.

"Ahh." Vander rested his right arm over the armrest, leaning sideways. "Not only would this disprove the Holy Family's teachings about majik being Goddess-given, but it would send each country into a power-frenzy state for the source of majik beneath Saint Highburn Monastery that granted the ability to wield the power of ley lines."

Emrys nodded, connecting the pieces they'd thus far revealed. "Then, while chaos ensues, we'll destroy the majik source and use Sayra to close the daemon rifts for good."

His mother smiled, her pride coloring her expression. "When the time arrives, Sayra will be guided to close the rifts by the informant. This will end the control the Holy Family has clung to in each country by eliminating the very threat they brought to each land."

Emrys drew his hand over his chin. "Our kingdom would be free of the invisible strings that pulled control from you both. Acacea wouldn't be bled of its fortune any longer, and our laws would become free to bring back prosperity within its borders. Most of all, once daemonkind is wiped from the lands, we can restore the true faith of the Goddess. Not the false religion the Zefares preach."

"Indeed. For now, we watch and wait," his father said with a solemn face. "Anything short of patience will get us all killed, and I must insist that you both swear to keep to the plan."

And so they did.

Emrys desperately wished he knew everything his parents did but understood it could make him a liability should things ever go south. Gatekeeping the truth was crucial if Acacea was to succeed. When the day came, he'd have his own wealth of resources and cohort of allies to bring the Holy Family to its knees alongside his family.

Movement drew Emrys from the memory. Sayra looked to be sick as she pushed by him, making for the door that led to the gardens. Snow pelted them at a steep angle as they entered the storm, her lungs audibly gasping for air as she collapsed beside a tree, her frame shivering.

The wind chill bit Emrys's face as he watched Sayra wrap her arms around herself. Her unbound hair blew behind her, exposing angry, bleeding wounds scattered on her shoulders and arms. Emrys began removing his cloak to give to her.

"No," Sayra quavered, self-loathing abundant in her voice. "I don't deserve it. Just as I don't deserve to be healed for what I've done." Her body continued to shiver, both arms drawing her knees closer to her body.

Removing it anyway, Emrys wrapped the thick woolen material around her charred shoulders, uncaring if it became ruined by blood. He placed it carefully, trying to be gentle with her wounds. A hiss of pain escaped her lips, and her face remained downtrodden. Emrys sat beside her, a word of power, intended to keep their conversation private, leaving his lips.

"*Silentium.*"

He felt the majik settle in a bubble around them, unseen but strongly present. "I hate to ask, but I need to know what happened," Emrys said, his expression twitching in distaste at his own request. It was necessary, just poor timing.

Sayra steadied her majik, her head lifting just enough for those jade eyes to meet his. "I may not have caused it, but it's my fault," she wheezed, fighting a cough that escaped anyway. Her body huddled into the cloak further, her face reflecting the pain coursing through her from the many burns and cuts across her skin.

It brought Emrys some comfort when her hands gripped the ends of the fabric and folded them around her. He stretched out his legs, his impeccably polished boots dragging through the two inches of snow that accumulated over the grass.

"A man was outside my door when it started, but it was only intended for me, I think. I panicked. I lost control," she rasped, her eyes distant as she recalled the scene.

Emrys hung on her every word as a flake caressed her low cheekbones.

"I willed it away, and somehow the majik—*my* majik—spread the fire across the remainder of the hall instead." Her shoulders hunched further, making her seem even smaller.

Emrys clenched his jaw so tight it hurt. Never mind the snow that whitened his black frock coat or the chill that threatened to seep into his own bones without the thick woolen cloak. Pure, undulating rage nearly had him charging across the monastery to find the culprit of the unprecedented attack. For once, he found himself caught off guard. He could count on one hand how many people knew about Sayra's majik, and none of them had instigated the attack.

Was her selection as the target a fluke, or had a sixth player entered the board?

For the moment, he knew Sayra would be safe. Whoever attacked would need ample time to reconvene and prepare for another covert operation. Emrys had to help develop Sayra's majik in the meantime. Otherwise, she'd be worse off the next time around.

And Emrys knew there would be a next time.

Chapter Fifteen

SAYRA

Sayra didn't care to puzzle out Prince Emrys's mysterious motivations or vague expressions, not when she despised herself for every person she had gravely injured. Her ears listened to his assurances that it wasn't her fault, that she wasn't to blame for the dozens of burned and unconscious Valkyries that would have died if it weren't for him, but she didn't believe him. Not when that icy majik was still there, taunting her from within. Not when it threatened her control, teasing her by withdrawing before flooding through her veins once more.

"In the coming days," Prince Emrys finished, sharing a nod to confirm his promise.

Blinking, Sayra grimaced at him, her mind still muddled from the smoke. "What did you say?"

Seemingly unfazed, he repeated, "I will help you control the majik in the coming days. It'll only take a single spell."

Frustration and jealousy danced through her mind from Sylven, and Sayra glanced toward the corridor where he remained. Somewhat distracted, she became curious as to what was occurring in there to make him feel so. Frustration? That could be as simple as a cold draft passing by. The littlest inconveniences brought that out in him. But jealousy? That was a new emotion.

The prince shifted beside her, eyes scanning the windows of the Arcanist dormitory across from them. She belatedly realized he must have been freezing without his cloak. He had two layers beneath his navy frock coat, but with the wind, it couldn't have been enough. After all his procrastination with the impending discussion of majik, though, Sayra felt it was the least he owed her.

"Okay," she replied, still hating the guilt she felt at having his cloak, regardless of her opinion on the matter. It ate at her until she added, "Thank you, Prince Emrys, for the cloak."

Wincing, he shook his head. "Please. We don't need formalities. Emrys is just fine, and I only wish I could do more. I apologize for the delay in my explanation. I feel..." He trailed off, uncomfortable with being so forthright. "Responsible for what occurred tonight. I owe you more than an explanation at this point, and once you've received proper medical attention, we can have that discussion."

Scowling at him, Sayra gripped the material around her a tad tighter. "If you feel that way, then I believe it would be prudent to explain now."

A ghost of a smile played at his lips before quickly being smothered. "You are at risk of releasing majik more readily when you are injured. If you want to prevent something else from occurring, it'd be best to seek healing aid now," Emrys said, standing and offering a hand to help her up.

Sayra pulled her shoulders back, her regret and annoyance pushing her upward and casting his hand aside. "My life is not yours to toy with when convenient. I do not care for being *manipulated*," she lashed out, pent-up infuriation making her words harsher than they should have been.

At times, she cursed her gift for finding razor-sharp words that would wound deeply, and that day was no exception. Hurt flickered in Emrys's dark gray eyes as they turned away, his brows lowering under his wind-strewn hair. She despised the position of weakness she was in. Emrys had held all the answers over her head for nearly two weeks, forcing her to wait and then have her burns tended to despite her clear stance on the matter. But Sayra was far too stubborn to apologize, far too confused, pain-burdened, and vengeful to do anything but limp back into the corridor, leaving him to stand alone in the storm raging outside.

CHAPTER SIXTEEN

SYLVEN

The corridor was nearly vacant when Sayra emerged from the gardens, Sylven's gut clenching at the ebony cloak around her shoulders. The ends dragged half a foot of fabric on the ground, her stature dwarfed in the cloak. Half of him was relieved to see her eyes clearer than they were previously, but the other half struggled with the fact Sayra had been left to fend for herself the last time she was attacked. It was almost as if he felt obligated to care for her at that point, though every part of him revolted at the intrusive thought.

Sylven rose, unsettled as he waited for her to arrive. "How are you holding up?" he tried, nervously scratching the back of his collar where an annoying loose string hung.

"Fantastic," she growled, evidently in a poor mood.

Sylven hoped that wasn't how others perceived him the majority of the time. His eyes flicked to the door that remained closed behind her, curious as to what Rys said to piss Sayra off and why he wasn't returning to the building.

A healer neared them, requesting to attend to her injuries.

"I thought you should know that everyone is expected to make a full recovery," Sylven shared. He noticed those bright eyes of hers begin to relax.

She nodded her thanks, proceeding to remove the cloak. Agony contorted her face as the fabric dropped to the ground, and Sylven's stomach lurched at the extent of damage done to her shoulders, elbows, and pretty much every portion of her body. Even her left knee had a gaping hole in the cotton fabric, flesh peeling from a rounded burn.

Sylven wasn't sure any average human being could endure that type of torture, even if they had her resolve. Hell, most of the Valkyries didn't have half as many injuries as Sayra. Only Kimimari and another girl whose name he hadn't a clue.

"Can we talk for a minute?" Nessika quietly asked, her presence by his side undetected until then.

Sylven nearly leaped from his skin, which elicited a querying glace from Sayra. He nodded, trailing behind Nessika as she led him a couple dozen feet from the flurry of activity. A wariness had him folding his arms around the Valkyrie.

Nessika tucked some of her short, dark locks behind her ear. "How is Sayra doing?" A tense edge ate at the words.

"She's being healed and will be fine," he answered.

Rolling her eyes, Nessika propped a hand on her hip. "Aside from the *obvious*, Sylven." She pointed to her head where her thin brows peaked in exasperation.

Sylven grunted, hating the direction the conversation was headed. "Better," he said, staring at the wall opposite the one he leaned against.

"Man of many words," Nessika grumbled, standing in silence while Arcanist Warden, the Holy Family's head healer, worked on Sayra's knee with quiet words of power. Her voice pulled Sylven's attention back toward her. "What's up with Emrys? He's long gone now after rushing here so quickly. I would have thought he'd stick around a bit longer."

Sylven's eyes lowered to hers, his forehead pinching. "I would have thought you'd know whatever is going on between those two."

Nessika gestured for him to go on.

"I don't have anything more to say on the subject. Rys isn't being particularly open at the moment." It pained Sylven to admit that, but it was the truth. After everything that had happened, Sylven was certain there was something going on between them, and Vander somehow fit into the equation. It was a puzzle that only brought him a headache as he attempted to decipher it.

It bothered Sylven to be left out.

"Well, I don't have anything to contribute. He's very cautious and vigilant with his personal matters." Her icy blue eyes pinned his. "Why don't you ask Sayra?"

"We aren't close," Sylven said defensively, his hackles raising.

Nessika let out a short, incredulous laugh. "That much is clear. She signaled for me to keep you chatting while she slipped away."

His head snapped to the side to find Sayra gone, the Arcanist who healed her speaking to an overseeing monk. Searching the corridor for her, he came up with nothing. Cursing at his lack of attention, Sylven didn't bother responding to Nessika before he bound up the stairs, revisiting his earlier steps to her floor. Repairs were already in place, those Arcanists specializing in earth majik slowly progressing through the hallway. Sylven carefully passed them, turning into Sayra's room, which was currently a scorched mess with dried blood stained into the wooden floor.

Many words came to mind for him to share when he arrived, though all of them faded upon seeing Sayra kneeling on the floor. The cloak was once again around her healed shoulders. Her hands cupped something small, sorrow emanating from her. Sylven figured it was something precious that had been damaged in the fire, though he couldn't quite see beyond the silver flashing from a candle's light.

"What was it?" he inquired.

Her hands clutched the item close to her chest, and she rose from the ground to face him. Sylven couldn't shake how different she appeared with her hair straight down. It almost made her more feminine than just a guardian. It reminded him of that day he saw her in her final trial of strength, holding that sword against the other acolyte, the latter accusing Sayra of cheating. Sylven thought Sayra incapable of winning back then, better suited for the daily life of court than the life of a Valkyrie.

He saw it more than ever in her side profile. A face softer than she'd ever shown before. A gentleness in the way she cradled that item in her palms and the way Rys's royal cloak made her look like the princess she must have been.

Sayra projected the image of a warrior angel sent by the Goddess with ash and a smear of red across her sun-touched complexion. She was... enchanting, making Sylven's thoughts muddled for a moment before her words snapped him out of it.

"Something that is no more," Sayra hedged, tucking the item into the cloak's inner pocket to conceal it. "Why are you here?"

Bemused, Sylven waved at the fire damage. "Due diligence?"

"You didn't care the other night," Sayra shot back, her expression leaving no room for her usual banter. The words hit him with an impact that made him physically step back. "Nor did you care when you made it clear I am 'nothing to you but a major hindrance and inconvenience.'"

The words stung him deeply.

Sayra's eyes were cold and detached, but he could feel her suffering, lashing out as a cornered animal would. Perhaps he was finally receiving a taste of his own medicine after all these weeks, the thought making him feel even lower than he had previously.

Sylven straightened his back.

No, that wasn't entirely fair. He had been a jerk, possibly more than that, but he refused to allow her to guilt him any further when she'd been harboring some sort of secret with Rys. A true Valkyrie wouldn't harbor secrets, especially if they concerned her Arcanist.

"At least I have been clear about my motives from the beginning," Sylven said, stepping closer. His defensiveness encouraged him to deflect the blame, even though his chest constricted from his own faults. "You have something, some arrangement or deal with Rys that I've been left out of, even though I'm the only reason you're here." His voice rose in consternation, Sylven believing she was slightly hypocritical.

Something snapped in her eyes, and she bared her teeth at him. "Do you think I've had any choice in the matter about who picked me as their Valkyrie and the repercussions of events out of my control?" she asked, pointing an accusing finger at his face. The small smear of dried blood crinkled near her dangerously squinted eyes. "You. Know. *Nothing*!"

So Sylven wasn't the only one being played by Rys. Not that it mattered. He was still furious at the Valkyrie standing in front of him, even if a part of him knew he'd regret it later. Opening his mouth, he planned a smart retort that was promptly cut off by a female voice.

"We all have to wake up early in the morning. I think it best if we all return to sleep," Nessika announced, moving to stand beside her friend. "Sayra, I have room for your things if you'd like help packing. We can share my room until they can fix yours."

Without another word, Sylven stormed out of the dormitory, taking the corridor that branched into both buildings. He hastily prepared for sleep, taking care to wash the lingering smell of smoke from his body. Images kept forcefully flashing through his mind. The inferno he witnessed upon first arriving. The haunted and lost expression Sayra bore when they found her and the trail of blood left by her limping feet. Emrys's initial horror then his blatant relief when she was safe.

Nothing made sense. The images cycled through his mind whenever he'd fitfully awaken throughout the scant remaining hours before dawn. A new nightmare pestered him—Sayra dying in those dormitory flames.

When Sylven arrived at her floor, all he found was his Valkyrie's body laying lifeless between the flames. Her empty eyes stared blankly ahead as his sister, Jess, closed Sayra's eyelids. Her freckled face was angry at Sylven as her brown eyes rose to meet his.

"Yet again, an Arcanist failed to act for his Valkyrie. Sayra died because you didn't care enough to help. You let her get beat up by others and didn't bother to ask how she was afterward. You let her burn and die in this hallway because you didn't get here soon enough. Arcanists don't deserve Valkyries." Jess stalked toward him, her voice rising and lips snarling. "*You* don't deserve one."

Sylven flinched as the overwhelming guilt ate at his resolve.

"And Sayra knew it," she said.

Closing his eyes, Sylven couldn't handle his sister's words. The truth rang through him. Sayra didn't deserve his hatred, but some awful part of him clung to it anyway. If he didn't hate Valkyries and the Old Covenant bond between *anima*, then he'd fail Jess by becoming like the Arcanist that allowed her to die.

"I'm so sorry," Sylven said, falling to his knees beside Sayra's unmoving body. His eyes burned, his throat thick with emotion. "I never wanted this to happen."

"But didn't you?" Jess accused, her eyes full of the rage Sylven had for Jess's Arcanist when she died.

Sylven awoke in a cold sweat, his body heavy as he forced himself to move. It left him with dark circles under his eyes when he donned his Arcanist uniform, a fitted overcoat of navy lined with gold buttons down the center. Both the collar and cuffs were braided gold. He wore black trousers tucked into calf-length black boots and a simple long-sleeved white shirt. A golden cross held firm over his heart, representing the Goddess in her glory. All of it was tedious to put on that morning, his eyes and limbs leaden with exhaustion.

Class began without its usual fanfare, anxious words being tossed around about the rumored fiery attack from the anti-religion apostates of the Highlands. Eavesdropping, Sylven had to agree with some of their concerns. Never before had the apostates directly infiltrated the monastery, meaning they had a new recruit inside the walls, and it could be anyone. There had only been minor attacks on monasteries the Holy Family owned throughout the continent. For theirs to directly target an entire dormitory of Valkyries and nearly succeed, it spelled potential for disaster if the perpetrator wasn't caught.

The only two who didn't take part in the conversation were him and Nikolay, who sat uncomfortably beside Sylven at the two-person desk. He normally didn't partake in conversations that didn't pertain to him, the Zendiyan a quiet presence. Not a single suspicious eye was cast his way, not when they all blatantly knew the oligarchs were obsessed with their own internal power struggles and wouldn't ever risk a slip by taking a stance against the Holy Family and their monasteries.

Monk Miagu entered the class, a balding man with green eyes, and everyone silenced the second his foot touched the classroom floor. Stacks of paper rested gently on his moderately sized desk, his hand waving at the board behind him with an unintelligible murmur.

Words began writing themselves on the board, copied from his notes as he spoke aloud to the class. "Good morning to you all. We will begin by introducing my expectations for the semester and your first upcoming investigative assignment on combining forms of majik to create something with a fundamental alteration that strays from the basic foundation of wind. For now, please record my instructions, and we shall begin the lecture forthright."

Sylven did as he was told, listening intently as the monk described elemental alterations with one's base archetype, light or dark. It was a technique he was already acquainted with through his previous years of study, but he knew there was much room for improvement and other methods to create new spells. Options were as limitless as a person's imagination. So long as it didn't drain Arcanists of their majik and leave them without a heartbeat, of course.

Tapping the board, Monk Miagu stared at the class with a stern expression. "As always, remember to take precautions when exploring new spells and new takes on each. Start on a small scale close to yourself since larger works of majik farther away will cost exponentially more energy."

It reminded Sylven of the first time he transferred two twigs an inch from one another, both lightweight, a small distance between them, and within a half of a foot of his hands. At the time, that was fatiguing enough. It took years to graduate to larger objects and farther distances.

Monk Miagu crossed his arms, his head slowly turning as he addressed the class. "Individual spells are like muscles. The more you train them, the stronger and more easily managed they become."

Sylven could use his majik on large objects without a direct ley line of wind majik in the earth below but only once with his current majik capacity. After that, he'd need time for his body to regain energy or connect to a ley line.

"Arcanists rely on ley lines for enormous amounts of majik expenditure." The monk walked between the two-person desks. "It refills us as we utilize that majikal vein, but it's also taxing on our bodies to channel a ley line. Arcanists can harness their own stores of energy, but it isn't enough to work with on a grand scale and quickly becomes exhausting. It's safest to work with ley lines since we can wield majik to far greater and longer extents without our body's natural energy becoming fully drained."

Sylven's head was twisted over his shoulder to keep eyes on the monk as he began walking toward the front of the classroom.

"Be sure to have your gauntlets on during your experimental phase. The natural gemstones within them boost your body's ability to connect with nearby ley lines and can minimize the energy you expend while using majik. Please keep all this in mind with your upcoming project. It's not worth risking your life to forgo ley line usage and gauntlets."

By the end of class, Sylven had become excited about the upcoming assignment. Something *normal* to work on for a change.

History was as boring as ever, and Rys felt the same. There wasn't time or privacy to bring up important matters that needed to be discussed, not that Sylven wanted to anyway. He was far too cross at Sayra and by association Rys. Though it was unusual to catch Rys being distracted in class, there were several moments he'd observed the prince staring off blankly into the distance.

The complete polar opposite was Waylen during their third lecture, his friend goofing off when Monk Render wasn't facing the class. While Sylven despised learning ethics and morals, it was partially amusing to pass jokes between him and his friend.

Their instructor, a pale and serious man, tapped on the board with a piece of chalk. "Arcanists bear an enormous responsibility when wielding majik for the benefit of our people. Our wards keep daemons from invading our cities. Our Goddess-given majik can improve the outcome for crops. Our birthright can heal those who suffer physical harm. With such power comes the debt of knowing how to properly wield it to bring honor to the Goddess."

Monk Render circled three words on the board: wards, crops, and healing. His facial lines deepened as he grew thoughtful.

"We must endeavor to perfect a high-quality ward that can mesh with other wards. It would be unethical to pursue a career in warding if your quality of wardsmanship is subpar. There are lives on the line," Monk Render said, his face pinched. His hand pointed toward the written word *crop*. "As Arcanists, we must provide for our people. With warded land becoming scarcer, we have the moral obligation to make what little farming land we have prosper."

"My patience with this class is becoming scarcer," Waylen cackled beside Sylven, his body hunched over the desk in boredom.

Sylven covered the smile on his face with a casual hand just as the monk scanned the room.

Monk Render's abnormally thin mouth pressed into a line as his hand moved to the last circled word: healing. "Arcanists capable of healing have the responsibility of learning anatomy and physiology before laying their hands on a patient, lest they accidentally fuse a joint on a patient's elbow."

A snort escaped Waylen before he could suppress it. "I find that somewhat *humerus*."

Sylven worked hard to keep from snickering, but when the monk turned to find the voice behind the whispers, Waylen cracked. His shoulders shook with silent laughter as Monk Render's face glared at him disapprovingly.

"Arcanist Waylen, I'd like to see you later this afternoon for after-class detention. We can speak then about whatever aspect of this lesson you seem to find so funny."

Sylven glanced at Waylen's paling face with a look that read *I'm glad it's you and not me.*

By the end of the day, Sylven was already dreading tomorrow's lectures, knowing the last two would be with Sayra. He hadn't the slightest idea how to communicate with her after everything said between them, and he didn't even want to try. Instead, he focused on drawing up ideas for his Advanced Principles of Wind Manipulation class, irresponsibly ignoring his history research paper due at the end of the week.

The next morning, Intermediate Light Majik proved to be challenging for him. He'd never excelled at wards. During their first session, Monk Seru had everyone stand in a large circle.

"One by one, every student will come forward and produce their strongest ward against majik. Not to be confused with wards staving off physical attacks." Monk Seru's finger wagged above his ivory robes. "These wards are created with the sole intention of keeping majik from passing, and they require a much different focus when casting. Now, Arcanist Levon, come forward and produce your majik-defense ward."

Sylven bit into his tongue as he watched Arcanist after Arcanist produce varying levels of wards, each having practiced far more than he had.

"Arcanist Sylven, please come forward," Monk Seru finally said, his voice kinder than any other instructor. "Produce your ward."

Sylven muttered the word, feeling the majik spread around him in a thin shield.

"*Ventus!*" Monk Seru summoned a cutting gale, the wind arching forward into Sylven's shield.

A spiderweb of lines enveloped Sylven as his ward cracked and splintered, the translucent shield fading as his spell collapsed. Sylven frowned at the look of disappointment on his instructor's face.

"Perhaps work on this a bit more?" Monk Seru suggested, his eyes hopeful.

Sylven dipped his chin, his lack of practice with majikal wards abundantly clear. But he wouldn't start now. *There isn't much practicality to it unless I'm participating in the proelium, which I won't consider until next year*, Sylven thought with a sigh.

It was yet another medal to bear on one's chest if one won the competition, esteem Sylven held no regard for when his sole purpose was to hunt daemonkind. Granted, he was stuck with a Valkyrie for the moment and would be eligible to enter. His father would most likely prod him to enter next year to continue the family legacy of placing within the top three.

Though, it could be a great place to demonstrate his capabilities...

Reluctantly, Sylven made for the distant *anima* training facilities located near the western walls. Arcanists passed him on either side in the long stretch of corridor. Eventually, Valkyries mixed in once he neared the marbled classrooms. The moment he crossed the threshold, he spotted Sayra lounging with her feet crossed over an empty chair, her normal braid, *slør*, and black training leathers in place. A contemptuous smile greeted him as she patted the chair meant for him. Her back was to Rys. He and Nessika sat at the closest table. Waylen placed himself in the back, likely not wanting anything to do with whatever drama may unfold.

Wow, it felt claustrophobic in there.

Sylven took his seat beside Sayra, who elected to perch her feet on the top of his desk instead. Resigned, he groaned and stared at the ceiling until the instructor arrived. He was resentful of all the *anima* present who were chatting amongst themselves and passionate about beginning the class. Sylven couldn't be more repelled by the thought, his mood becoming irater by the second.

He tried looking at anything but his Valkyrie.

Beams of light shone from the arched windows on the left side of the classroom, snow piled at the edges of the sill. The marble floors had recently been shined, and a few banners hung on the walls with the Holy Family's crest.

Sayra's feet snapped off the table the moment the monk arrived. Most of the class straightened in their seats. Sylven shot her a contemptuous glare she shamelessly grinned at.

"Good morning, class." A monk he wasn't familiar with sighed, toppling a collection of notepads he carried onto his desk. Curly black hair edged his neck, his face in a permanent state of tiredness. With dark muscled arms under his robe and calloused hands, the monk could probably knock out anyone in a single punch. Leaning against the board, he lazily waved at the notepads. "All right, without a single word or movement, convey with your *anima* who will be the one to snag a notebook. One per pair, and if any rule is broken, you both will fail your first assignment." He smiled, seemingly entertained by the rigid students before him.

Before Sylven could even attempt to communicate, Rys was already rising and moving to secure a notebook. Arseny, one of the blond oligarchs from the tundra lands of Zendiya, was but a second behind. Sardonic amusement radiated from Sayra, who refused to acknowledge his questioning through their link. To his mortification, he couldn't identify whether she'd move first or sabotage his efforts if he selected to retrieve the notebook. Once, he attempted to convey his willingness, and she unabashedly denied it.

The audacity.

By now, a majority of the class had already taken their seats again. Sylven appeared more the fool as time passed. Desperate, he pleaded through their link, finally receiving her acceptance. Sylven placed his hands on the polished oak, rising from his seat just as a finger of hers shifted. With all the force he could muster, he thought at her, *Don't you dare.* Freezing, Sylven could feel her shock, that pinky stilling without further tormenting. He continued to the stack of notepads, receiving a commending nod from the unnamed monk. On his way back, Sayra gave him a haughty expression.

"It seems you've all managed to successfully acquire a notepad. I would hope so after two weeks of vacation," he said, walking down the center aisle between tables. "I am Monk Ibski, and during this semester, I will train each of you to become talented in proficient communication and fluid with the utilization of the Old Covenant."

Sylven could have sworn Sayra smirked at him out of the corner of his sight.

Goddess, help me, Sylven prayed.

Chapter Seventeen

SYLVEN

That being the first *anima* class Sylven ever had, he wasn't quite sure what to expect. The addition of Valkyries seemed to make the Arcanists somewhat more behaved. There were fewer jests thrown around and far more serious expressions as they straightened their navy-blue uniforms to perfection. The Valkyries were poised and focused in their black training leathers.

Except Sayra, of course.

She rested her chin on her hand, hunched over the desk, and stared at the monk in a curious fashion. Monk Ibski went on to detail the day's lesson, explaining how they would be communicating different topics through emotion and impressions *only*. He took the time to individually peer at both Rys and Arseny, who likely skipped far ahead and could communicate with words.

Sylven *would* have studied more in advance if he had intended to contract with a Valkyrie.

With the Valkyries scribbling a message on the notepad before mentally communicating it, Sylven watched as Sayra concocted hers. Her giddiness concerned him.

"Okay, done." She closed her eyes to relay her intention. Disgust and annoyance at his proximity showed, and the message made him frown at her.

"I do not smell," Sylven said crossly, perhaps a hair too loudly. Nessika's snickers could be heard on the other side of Sayra.

He sent yet another silent prayer to the Goddess to help him restrain his anger.

Arching her brows, Sayra sniffed in a dainty way and passed him the notebook. A frown crossed his face as he saw the stick figure with warped lines surrounding it.

Have it your way, he mentally challenged.

Picturing her with a sword, he knew he had conveyed his message when she snatched the notebook from his fingers, the drawing of a girl incorrectly wielding a sword irritating her.

Back and forth they went, sending cheap shots until the class concluded and the monk tasked them with practicing on their own as homework.

When they were released, Arcanists and Valkyries alike navigated to the indoor arena, formally called Saint Highburn Arena, beside the lecture hall. Students called it the dome. The hallway was filled with loud chatter and shuffling steps as they walked in clusters. Incense smoked from several ceramic angels distributed along the corridors, a pleasant aroma of cedarwood filling the air.

The arena's fifteen-foot, wood-carved doors stood wide open. It was a massive, dome-shaped marbled contraption that was excessive and expensive for no other reason than vanity. Grand arches spanned the ceiling, and enormous mosaic windows stood twenty feet tall. Sunlight gleamed through them, spilling an array of colors through the enormous space. Regular stone lined the floor, easily replaceable in case of damage.

It was said the entire building was warded to prevent damage, though too many spells and haywire strikes fell to the ground to adequately maintain them. Stadium bench seating encompassed the perimeter for any audience there might be during formal occasions. Three people currently lounged there, observing them from afar.

Sayra stood a ways in front of Sylven, flanked by Nessika and another Valkyrie whose teal *slør* matched hers.

Sylven scowled. *They're multiplying.*

All three Valkyries were speaking loudly, which aggravated him. Waylen and Rys were discussing non-verbal communication between *anima*. Sylven wanting nothing to do with any of it, he stood alone with his book bag until the class began. Minutes ticked uncomfortably by before a man and woman rose from the arena seating and came into focus. The third individual remained behind, still observing.

A Valkyrie and Arcanist but not just any. Catara and Jax Zefare, cousins in the Holy Kingdom of Eveline's lineage, were in the typical garb of monks, which was abnormal for a woman.

Why would part of the monastery's Holy Family be leading this class? Sylven questioned, suspicious of the anomaly.

The straw-haired man had the appearance of one who devoted time to physical and majikal training, an irregular combination for Arcanists. Tan and poised, Jax looked like a person who received the best of everything, whether it be a stylist for his gelled hair or a trainer to target his upper body (while failing to focus on the lower). Sylven got the distinct impression he was a ladies' man, and the scarily white-toothed grin he shared with Sayra's group only confirmed it. Sayra returned a charming smile, but to feel her revulsion of the holy man nearly had Sylven smiling like an idiot.

It was a relief to know those types didn't receive the interest they thought they garnered.

"Since today is your first in this lecture," Catara began, her hazel eyes sweeping the crowd, "we will forgive the lack of preparation on some of your behalf."

Confused murmurs shuffled through the crowd.

Jax raised a hand, picking up where his cousin left off. "Beginning with the next class, all Arcanists must wear durable clothing to be active in. Throughout our semester, expect to go through a few uniforms as we will be practicing both majikal and physical combat. All personal belongings must be secured in the male's locker room." He gestured to his left, where two sets of doors rested between the stadium seats. "Or the female's locker room." He then winked at the ladies, an actual giggle sounding from one of them behind him.

Disgusting.

They instructed the Arcanists to claim a locker for their belongings, Valkyries standing by as their counterparts slowly trickled back in. Once everyone had returned, Catara spoke.

"Don't mistake this class for some physical exercise class. It's not. It's a survival-based one. Once you leave these walls, your primary defense will be each other."

Everyone became serious at that, expressions shifting from humored to solemn.

"If you leave the monastery without becoming a cohesive unit, you will fail as many of your predecessors have. Does anyone know the survival rate of those who graduate in the lowest ten percent of the cumulative class?" she asked.

Doors opened behind their group as the question was posed, a chilled draft breezing by as two new individuals joined the class, the heir of the

Droden Empire, Kenji, and his twin sister Akira Haru. They sauntered in with a couldn't-care-less attitude about their tardiness.

"Sixty percent, if I'm not mistaken." Kenji lopsidedly grinned, his female version smiling beside him. They shared their black hair color, narrow and slanted autumn-gold eyes, and slightly shorter than average height, though Akira had a decidedly feminine slightness and innocence to her pale, delicate face. Unlike most of the girls present who wore their hair in a bun, hers was cut in a long bob.

The class was going to be pure hell.

Sylven was prepared to fake an injury at the first opportunity to escape. In addition to the others he had no desire to share company with, Akira was a two-faced nightmare. He could only recall a single incident where she visited from the eastern country—her studies conducted in Droden rather than the monastery—and she'd certainly left her mark. In addition to playing every male who would return her affections, she pitted them against each other with false rumors for her own entertainment. Thankfully, Rys warned him well in advance of her tactics, and her advances fell on deaf ears.

"Kenji," Catara replied, her expression a stern warning, "not even an heir can excuse tardiness. It is even more imperative that you arrive to class in a timely fashion."

"We are terribly sorry, *Sanctus* Catara and *Sanctus* Jax." Akira bowed, her sweet voice capable of smoothing even Catara's gruffness. The Holy Family's honorific surely had its own effect as well. "It will never occur again. I swear by it."

Catara exhaled a deep breath, waving them over. "See that it doesn't. Now, Valkyries have had extensive training to keep a noncombative individual alive. While we cannot mimic an actual Horde attack, we will amp up the challenge by pitting *anima* against *anima* to better acquaint each pair with each other's fighting styles and combat skills. Naturally, there are rules and limitations. To start..."

For twenty-six minutes—not that Sylven was counting—they learned rules of engagement and formalities they had to exercise during each mock-combat experience. Jax and Catara went around pairing two teams of *anima* against each other, Waylen and his Valkyrie, Jayde, to spar against them. They'd go in turn on their first day, different rounds for assessment and observation. Jax asked for volunteers, and before he even completed the sentence, Sayra's hand was up, her face an indifferent mask.

Inside, she was pissed, the strength of the emotion taking Sylven by surprise. It nearly masked his growing horror at the prospect of being on display before his peers.

A wide ring was formed around the perimeter, giving Sylven and Waylen plenty of space between them. Sayra and Jayde positioned themselves in front of their Arcanists, Jayde sweating nervously with a tinge of fear in her eyes. Sylven glanced between the two Valkyries, wondering what exactly the connection was there. A cold determination grew inside of Sayra, her savage excitement almost palpable.

Sylven stared at her back, wondering what sort of evil she was up to. When Catara gave the go, Sayra launched forward with her fists already clenched, not sparing a glance at Waylen. Balking, Jayde fell into a defensive stance as Waylen produced a ward around him, his large eyes locked on Sylven's. While his friend already appeared younger than his age, his anxiousness only enhanced the perception. He knew his friend better than anyone, which meant all his weaknesses were abundantly clear as well as the fact he had no offensive potential. Yet. He'd remain behind Jayde as long as possible, relying on her strength to defend him.

Regrettably, that meant Sylven had to ensure Sayra knocked out Jayde as quickly as possible.

"*Tardus*," Sylven grumbled, casting a spell to slow Jayde's movement.

Eyes wide, the tall brunette moved as if under deep water, unable to block a gut punch Sayra refused to hold back.

Sayra's entire body twisted into it, a manic grin sprouting across her face at the contact. Pure glee shimmered through his mind, and Sylven became concerned at the enjoyment Sayra took in violence.

What kind of monster did he contract with?

Waylen flinched, holding out his hand and producing a ward around Jayde before Sayra could snap forward again. Jayde roughly fell to the ground, Sayra's leg arching high in an elegant movement before bashing into the ward. It cracked, a thin wave of sputtering lines appearing before dematerializing.

Flipping forward, Jayde found her feet just as Sayra threw a mean hook, racing for the Valkyrie's desperate face.

"*Celler*," Sylven murmured, launching off his back-planted foot and racing forward with inhuman speed. The action caught Jayde's attention, her eyes wide as the moon at the blur racing toward her partner.

Sayra laughed a wild thing, deftly faking her attack and utilizing her momentum to flip over Jayde, her foot catching the failing ward as it broke. Jayde's jaw was viciously hit and gave an audible snap, her body flung back once more. Sayra dove to secure her victory with a deadly headlock.

Unsure of what to do, Waylen's hand shot out, and his eyes squeezed shut. "*Lux!*"

A brilliant flash of light blinded everyone, and the audience gasped in surprise. Sylven continued blind, eventually colliding with his friend's body and tumbling along with him. His fingers clutched his uniform, refusing to lose Waylen in his temporary blindness. His eyes couldn't adjust, but Sylven's hand balled into a fist firmly over Waylen's chest. The signal for victory.

Polite clapping sounded from the gathered grounds, Sylven's eyes finally making out Sayra's shape, her elbow digging deeply into Jayde's chest.

"All right. We have our first winning team," Jax announced, signaling for Sylven and Sayra to release their opponents.

Waylen accepted Sylven's hand as they stood. Sayra ensured she placed extra pressure on Jayde as she launched off her, and deep satisfaction rolled off her in waves.

"Everyone's performance will vary, depending on their majikal proficiencies. However, by the end of this semester, each one of you will become sufficient in combined combat," Jax's voice droned on.

Sayra retreated beside Sylven and Waylen, Jayde a few steps behind with a reddened face. Sylven felt guilty for the easy win, but in contrast to Waylen, he desired to have a career in combat, whereas Waylen planned to take over his family business of port trade in Acacea. It wasn't a fair match to begin with.

"Marvelous job, Sayra," congratulated Kenji when they merged into the ring of students.

Sayra beamed at the Droden heir, placing her hand on his outstretched one as he lifted it but inches from his face. It was a gesture of respect and courtesy for the opposite gender in Droden. "As always, Kenji, you are far too liberal with praise. I only performed as expected," she chided in familiarity, a temporary smugness emanating from her at Sylven's astonishment.

Beneath that moment of arrogance, Sylven felt a dark, spiraling revulsion slithering between their bond. It caught him off guard. Every physical feature she sported contrasted heavily with how she genuinely felt. Hatred triggered her boiling emotions, passing through their bond with reckless abandon. His curiosity was beginning to get the better of him as he searched between them, looking for any sign to clue him in on what was going on.

"Rumors are circulating that the culprit of Saint Highburn's great fire was perhaps none other than you," Kenji murmured softly enough for Sylven to overhear.

Sayra's polite smile slipped at that. Fear, icy and striking, raced through their bond. It gripped his chest with force, lungs freezing from the impact.

"Though, Sayra darling, you needn't worry over such tedious affairs. I've already assured the masses there is no other more devoutly dedicated to your people than yourself. Besides, the deranged Valkyrie who blamed her loss during the trial on your *majik* is already being outcasted. Her efforts to spread further lies are in fruitless taste." Kenji grinned, his emphasis on the word majik making it blatantly clear he too thought it was ridiculous.

Sayra blinked. "You have my gratitude." The words were a tad breathy, her mind racing with a storm of emotions.

Sylven's face softened at the back of her head when Sayra turned her attention to Catara. Not only had she dealt with an awful near-death experience, but Sylven understood how outrageous rumors could be. That others could be so cruel to further instigate needless torment.

Arcanists had hounded Sylven for years when he became adamant he didn't need a Valkyrie. He heard the occasional snicker at how two-faced he'd once been. Little did they know Sylven still stood firm in that belief, and his Valkyrie was simply an arrangement he was forced to oblige.

Everyone's attention returned to the next pair of combatants.

Sylven caught Kenji's lingering look at Sayra, a past connection linking the two of them somehow. He reasoned it out. Kenji's family currently ruled over her lands. Obviously, they shared a familiarity, meaning there was history enough between the two of them to openly joke and praise. Sayra *was* once a princess. Meaning...

Sylven moved beside her nonchalantly, his eyes pretending to take in the mock battle before him. "Were you two set to be engaged?" Sylven whispered. He received a quick elbow to his gut. Concealing his grunt of surprise, he shot her a *what-the-hell* look.

Sayra's cheeks grew pink. "Not anymore." Embarrassment and disgust shot through their bond, giving away more than Sayra likely cared to admit. "Don't speak of it again."

Sylven blinked. Then blinked again.

It wasn't commonplace for royals to marry. Despite the Holy Family having monasteries in nearly every country, there wasn't much intermingling beyond that of the faith and academies at Saint Highburn. Sylven supposed if Droden wanted an elite pairing, it would make sense for Kenji to marry Sayra. But obviously, things went awry.

Did it have something to do with Rys and Vander's strange interest in her?

If only Rys hadn't been sworn to secrecy.

Sylven's mouth pressed firmly into a line, his mind working to repress his annoyance in favor of patience.

Rys and Nessika were paired against Kenji and Akira, and everyone leaned on their toes in anticipation of the battle between two rivaling countries' princes. Even Sayra stilled, crossing her arms and watching in anticipation.

Catara's arm fell, releasing Akira and Nessika from their positions. The two made to collide, Akira tucking into a last-minute roll and lunging toward Rys.

"*Ignis*," Rys summoned, a circle of roaring flames erupting from the ground around him. "*Deinceps*." A snake of flame tunneled toward Akira, who barely managed to throw herself out of the way.

"*Vi*." Kenji smiled, leaping forward to engage Nessika with a confidence that made her almond eyes narrow.

Together, their fists collided, a whoosh of air passing by each of them with neither giving. They proceeded to engage in close-quarter combat, Kenji not as skilled but slightly stronger with his majik. Rys drew a cyclone of flame around Akira, her ward splintering as it closed on her.

It was brilliant, the power of the flames so intense Sylven could feel his face burning, and he was forty feet away. It ebbed and flowed around Rys, responding to his will.

A flicker of fear shot through Sylven, his eyes finding Sayra's closed before she repressed the emotion. In a way, he felt culpable. He hadn't responded quickly enough when the apostates had burned her dormitory. In the end, those minutes he waited could have meant a great deal for her and the others who nearly died, but Sylven was torn between hating the Valkyrie part of her on a fundamental level and starting to actually care for her as a person.

In the end, the latter won. How couldn't Sylven sympathize, being so close to fire after what Sayra had gone through? Even if he hoped she would despise him enough to terminate their contract, it seemed she might be more stubborn than him.

Sayra must have felt his sympathy. Resentfulness filled their link. She shot him a dirty look before refocusing on the match in front of them.

Concentrating, Sylven worked to block his own emotions from leaking, a task he'd take up when remembered. Her reaction didn't surprise him. After all, the animosity remained between them, intentionally on his behalf. But perhaps Sylven could *attempt* to be slightly nicer while she recovered from the apostate attack.

Wards shattered around Akira at last, her hand rising in defeat rather than allowing herself to be burned.

She moved out of the sparring ring.

Behind her, Nes backpedaled from a strong kick, the distance between her and the target allowing Rys to launch a fireball at Kenji. The ward flickered, several more balls of flame cracking it. Nes backed off, likely at Rys's command, watching his back as the two Arcanists dueled.

Sylven was glad Rys found himself happy with the contract between him and Nessika. He knew Rys would never mistreat her or intentionally leave her to fight daemons alone. They worked well together. Despite that, Sylven held firm in his ideals.

"*Confractus*," Rys said, his mask portraying indifference even though Sylven knew he was concentrated on the match.

Wards shattered around Kenji, the shock nearly bringing a smile to Sylven's face. Realizing he almost dropped the block on his link with Sayra, he reengaged his efforts to keep his mind private. She didn't bat an eye.

"*Tempestas*." Rys didn't move a muscle.

A rain of fiery shards fell upon Kenji, embers flicking from the gathered flames on the ground around him as if they were a puddle of water. Catara called the match then and there, Rys proving to be the victor when Kenji kneeled after being burned. That third observer finally departed the bench. A monk Sylven didn't know who was summoned by Kenji for healing. Much to his annoyance, Sylven could feel Sayra's enthrallment during the match at Rys's majikal display.

Other pairs came and went. Sayra cheered on her friend Lynn, who he learned also hailed from Faenda. The silver *slør* in her auburn hair was a dead giveaway. Her Arcanist was Casber, a boy talented with dark majik who hailed from the minor Kingdom of Yendire to the north. It was a country constantly under threat from Zendiya but never conquered due to the frequent infighting of the frosty oligarchy, their souls as icy as the land they lived in. Casber, an Arcanist with the dark archetype of water, constructed icy shards that tore into his opponent to secure their win.

At last, the final match concluded, and they were dismissed. Before the discussion of *how amazing* the class was began, Sylven attempted to depart, wanting nothing more than to escape his grievances and return to his homework.

"Arcanist Sylven, I'd like to speak with you," Jax said, his gelled hair glistening under the majik light fixtures.

Sylven refrained from showing his displeasure, though his eyes did stare longingly at the exit mere feet away before meeting Jax's curious expression. "Yes, Sanctus Jax?" He even managed a slight head bow out of respect for the member of the Holy Family. Something he wouldn't do for any other family but the royals of Acacea.

"I've been wondering what made you change your mind on hiring a Valkyrie," Jax said, pulling Sylven aside by the stadium seating. "You see, ever since we've established the academy, our aim has been to protect mankind from the Horde. The original Zefares established the monastery, setting some of the first wards around the perimeter that safeguarded the entire location."

Yes, we all learned that in our first year here, Sylven mused. He watched as others began filing out of the dome.

Jax clasped his hands behind his back. "Since then, we've received notice from other countries, namely Acacea and Droden, that they wanted to learn how we maintained such protection from daemons. That inspired my family to open an academy to teach about the Goddess and how she blessed our family with majik to reward our devoutness."

Sylven nodded along, pretending to be vested in the conversation. All the while, his eyes kept slinking back to Sayra across the hall. He felt a strange combination of fear and hatred sprout from her when Kenji approached, his face and words animated.

"As more men from both countries graced our halls, we began the tradition of blessing their people in the name of the Goddess, and she, in all of her glory, spread the gift of majik throughout the land. Soon thereafter, we opened the Arcanist Academy to teach everyone about wardcraft and other aspects of majik." Jax sat on the bench, waving for Sylven to follow suit.

He did, albeit unhappily.

"Years after my family expanded its reach throughout many countries, my great-great-grandfather had a dream inspired by the Goddess. The one where he learned to gift a symbol of majik to women. The one that created Valkyries as we know them." Jax's eyes grew distant as he looked at the floor, almost as if he were looking at something far below. "He knew to link them to Arcanists. That their prowess in battle against the Horde would be unparalleled. He was right, as always."

Kenji laid a hand on Sayra's elbow while laughing, and it shocked Sylven when Sayra's mind went numb, ceasing the river of horrid emotions that kept distracting him. He couldn't help the frown on his face as his gaze flicked between the two of them. There was something deeper there Sayra wasn't sharing. Something far more than a simple broken engagement.

Jax slapped his knees with his hands, looking out at the gathered Arcanists and Valkyries chatting in the dome. "Since the creation of the Old Covenant, we've relegated the amount of Arcanists lost to daemons to a minimal number, one that gives us hope we may yet survive the Horde."

At the expense of Valkyrie lives, Sylven darkly thought. *Plenty of traveling men are still hunted by daemons when out of the wards. No one but the rich and elite can afford to be blessed by the Goddess, leaving every other man to fend for himself.*

"You were always a curiosity when you declined to enter a Valkyrie contract," Jax said, the crooks of his mouth lifting. He leaned inward a bit, as if he were an old friend conversing with Sylven. "Every Arcanist is overeager to contract, but you seemed against it until the very last moment. Why?"

The pressing question hung in the air.

Sylven's mouth went dry. What was he supposed to say? Because he was forced to? That wasn't the right answer, and *I changed my mind* wasn't satisfactory.

Thinking fast, Sylven said, "Emrys changed my mind. He brought it to my attention that, as a future duke in his kingdom, I'll have to consider more than myself when it comes to the obligations I owe my people. While I still firmly believe I can remain independent, Emrys made an excellent point that it would bring peace of mind to all in the Astor duchy if I conformed with practical safety measures."

Something edged Jax's eyes at the revelation, the corners of his mouth drooping.

It isn't enough, the voice in Sylven's mind whispered. His gut instinct told him he needed to be more convincing. "Besides, my father has made it perfectly clear that I'm to continue the family legacy of placing high in Saint Highburn's *proelium*. For that, I require a Valkyrie."

"Ah, yes. We cannot disappoint our family now, can we?" Jax grinned, a carefree look entering his demeanor. Standing abruptly, he shook Sylven's hand. "It was a pleasure speaking with you, Arcanist Sylven. I look forward to seeing what heights the Astor lineage continue to achieve in our esteemed *proelium* competition."

"And you as well, Sanctus Jax." Sylven rose, feeling slightly disheveled at the conversation. Shaking it off, he exited the dome, though it seemed fate was tormenting him as a stocky figure moved to pace by his side.

"Sylven." Kenji greeted him amicably, shouldering a tote bag laden with hefty texts.

Sylven kept his voice even. "Kenji." Not stuttering a step, he persisted toward his dormitory, knowing any conversation would end once there. After chatting with Jax, his patience was at an end.

"You and Sayra made quite the impressive *anima* today," Kenji noted. An unidentifiable gleam filled his dark gaze, and Sylven had to work to refrain from snorting.

They were two separate entities in that mock brawl, and they each happened to win their respective duels.

"It's almost as if you were truly meant to have a Valkyrie all along," Kenji teased.

With a tight and very forced smile, Sylven replied, "Indeed." He couldn't say what was really on his mind. *You can have her and all the nonsense with it.* That simply wasn't an option when speaking to royalty of any country.

Unfortunately.

"Most curiously, I look forward to witnessing your progression as a team. Until next time..." Kenji winked, falling back in step with his twin.

Akira's narrow eyes twinkled, her red lips forming into a smile at Sylven's shock to find her lurking a matter of feet behind them all along.

A shiver traveled down his spine at just how easily Akira could have attacked him. Not that she would, but Sylven couldn't help but feel something was off with those two. Creases cut into his face, his mind uneasy with Kenji's unusual behavior and interest in speaking with him. Never in their previous years had the Droden heir made any attempt at such things.

So, why now?

CHAPTER EIGHTEEN

SAYRA

Sayra hadn't much time to prepare for her late afternoon patrol, and by the time she arrived at her station, her breathing hitched because of her swift efforts. Sylven's classes had ended slightly later than anticipated. Thankfully, she had minutes to spare as the Valkyrie overseeing Saint Highburn's defense, Aria, was in the midst of speaking to Catara.

Tower bells chimed thrice as Sayra lowered her head in greeting. Both pairs of eyes marked her approach. Jitters at being so close to a practical legend had her mentally assessing her own gait and confidence, especially when the Holy Family member moved to speak first.

"Valkyrie Sayra." Catara greeted her with a somber expression as she pulled her aside. The legend towered over her, easily reaching ten inches over five feet tall. Light highlighted her blonde eyebrows and the slight shadows under her prominent cheekbones.

"Sanctus Catara," Sayra answered, dipping her chin again in respect. "What can I do for you?" Nervous energy churned inside her as she stopped beside the stairwell. It reached toward the massive walls surrounding the monastery, another aspect that made her feel small at that moment.

Catara's keen gaze met Sayra's. Her ivory cape flowed lightly with the passing breeze. "I've read your report, along with every other Valkyries' statement, on the dormitory incident and decided to take further measures to ensure the well-being of our sisters myself. My family shall not rest until we determine the identity of the attacker and bring them to justice."

Sayra relaxed a bit, the wave of fear of discovery ebbing at Catara's words. They didn't suspect her, nor did they seem to take an interest in Netta's somewhat truthful rumor floating around the monastery grounds.

"Currently, the evidence points toward the Southern Democracy of Highlands and the apostates there acting against our Goddess. We believe we may have a cell within our walls," Catara said, her words heavy with anger as she crossed her arms. "I aim to check in with every Valkyrie on the floor where the attack occurred to see if there are any further details that might have been overlooked to determine how many were present." The edge to her words eased a fraction. "Is there anything else you may have remembered since then that could contribute toward a fuller picture?"

When a monk had gathered her statement in the morning, Sayra had been careful to mention nothing of note. She awoke to billowing smoke and flames just like any other. When she burst into the hallway, Sayra attempted to help Kimimari but ran into a majikal barrier preventing her from accessing the room. By the time the monks and Arcanists arrived, the other Valkyries had moved to assist others and retreat as far as possible from the flames. They had dispelled the majik, but Sayra couldn't leave her friend behind.

And that was that.

Shaking her head, Sayra regretfully said, "I wish I knew more. More than anything, I desire to bring the attackers to justice." That much was true. It rang in her very bones. A blend of anxiousness over the unknown faction and unbridled fury that the true culprits almost contributed to the death of Valkyries. But if she aimed to stay above suspicion, she couldn't divulge anything further.

A flicker of disappointment crossed Catara's face before resolve replaced it. Sayra felt regret for letting down the revered Valkyrie and doubted for a moment whether it was the right choice. She wanted nothing more than to confess everything. What greater force than the Holy Family was there, after all? She wasn't receiving answers from Emrys, despite his assurances that he would *eventually* give them. If anyone could help her, it would be another woman who strove for the same ideals Sayra did.

But Sayra would give the prince one last day, as he requested. If nothing amounted to his word, then she would decide what matters to take into her own hands.

"We shall. They will not find comfort in any crevice of this world while we hunt them to the edges of it." Catara frowned behind Sayra, other Valkyries arriving for their patrolling duties. "While I have you, do you happen to know anything of Valkyrie Netta's statement swearing you used majik twice, once during your exam and again starting this dormitory fire?" The question was coolly asked, a slight curve pulling down the corner of Catara's mouth as if she found the statement distasteful.

Dritt.

Sayra funneled every ounce of her self-control toward not showing her panic. Frowning in sincerity, she kept her voice calm. "Valkyrie Netta and I have... a rivalry of sorts. It is regrettable that she chose to spread lies, but they are completely unfounded." Sayra feared her racing heartbeat would give her away, but she held firm in her stance.

A guard nodded respectfully at Catara as he passed by and headed up the stairwell. The Valkyrie dipped her chin in return.

"Indeed, it is quite unseemly." Catara sighed, her lips pursing before she continued. "She will be spoken with on this matter. If she doesn't take heed, we may remove her from duty."

Sayra only nodded, not trusting herself to speak. Netta had it coming.

A crinkle pulled at Catara's light eyes. "I once had a rival in my days at the academy. Though, we treaded similar paths in the beginning. We sharpened each other in every way that mattered to Valkyries, becoming two of the most lethal guardians in our class." A heavy pause had her closing her eyes for a breath. "My advice is to make it exactly that so she does not sabotage your future."

A rival. Curiosity got the better of Sayra. "What happened in the end?"

A faraway expression overtook Catara's sun-kissed face. "Something that led to ruin. In modern day, we harbor numerous adversaries that threaten our very way of life and that of the Goddess's touch on our people. We absolutely must do everything in our power to prevent the greatest evil from overtaking our land."

Something had sharpened her focus, her demeanor shifting into what Sayra expected from one of the greatest Valkyries of all time. That resonated with Sayra, who had a similar drive within her, fueling her desire for something greater than her previous life. Ultimately, rivalries were trivial in comparison to the might of the Horde, and she took Catara's wisdom to heart.

"Know this, Sayra. History is written by those the Goddess bestows her favor on. What is asked of us, *demanded* of us, can exceed the bounds of humanity."

Sayra hung on her every word, her intuition insisting there was an underlying importance to her lesson.

"We bloody our swords so others survive. So they can plant gardens, dance in celebration of our Goddess's solstice, marry the love of their lives, and bear children for the next generation to carry on our will and faith. We carry that weight, knowing the alternative is far worse than anyone could predict. Should we falter, humankind will perish. Wear the daemon blood you shed with pride, and never stray from the path the Goddess has set for us all. If we may be so fortunate, perhaps it will be within our generation that we see the end of the threat against our people." Catara murmured that last part, her emotion genuine with every word.

While Sayra didn't believe some goddess was to thank for what humans accomplished, she had faith in the meaning behind the Valkyrie's words. They were inspiring. She could easily see what made Catara so remarkable, and Sayra hoped to wield such unwavering conviction once she better understood her majik's origin and purpose.

If she could make a difference in the Horde's collective end, Sayra wouldn't balk.

"Thank you, Sanctus Catara, for your words. I take them to heart and will bring honor to our sisterhood," Sayra said, bowing her head.

With a pleased acknowledgment, Catara left Sayra to Aria's management and went to question another Valkyrie who arrived about the fire incident.

Tuesday's patrol was rather boring and uneventful, but walking around the eastern castle walls provided a beautiful view of the pointed church spires and steep mountains located higher up on the ridge. Marble walls gleamed across both academies the monastery hosted, step rooftops giving way to meticulously kept gardens and corridors linking every main building to the church at the far end. A small town was nested near the entrance to the monastery where guests could reside and staff lived. The marketplace thrived with people shopping for wares. The sweeping valley on the other side opened northward, and there wasn't a daemon in sight during her entire patrol.

By the time the moon had begun its ascent, she had returned to her dorm with a note given to her by Nes. The Valkyrie worried over her well-being before Sayra managed to glance at it. After reading it, she cursed Emrys's princely *ræva* and prepared for some weightlifting. Nes gave her a questioning look, but Sayra simply shook her head, refusing to speak of it.

Much to Sayra's surprise, Breane arrived at the Valkyrie's weight room shortly after that, making the evening slightly better with a training partner. However, Emrys managed to occupy her mind throughout the night, much to her displeasure. The note, which was in ashes in the drain, had read:

Sayra,

I must apologize for delaying our conversation once more. Unfortunately, a matter has interrupted my evening, and I can no longer meet tonight. I will ensure it is promptly dealt with, and in two nights, we shall discuss what we've verbally spoken about. Meet me at seven o'clock in room six at the Arcanist dormitory.

Jeg husker løftet.

Yours truly,

Emrys

Jeg husker løftet.

I remember the promise.

Sayra grumbled aloud, "My *ræva* he does."

After leaving the gymnasium, she checked on Kimimari in Lynn's quarters to find all was well, much to her relief. Lynn was nowhere to be found, having left her second-story room alone. It was strange how often Lynn mysteriously disappeared. Sayra took notice since they all had to share rooms as repairs were being made to the fourth floor.

That night, she awoke with clammy skin, a chilling trundle of majik constricting her chest. Her hands gripped the sheets, lungs tight with the fear of releasing deadly energy once again. Beside her, Nessika didn't so much as stir as Sayra panicked. Hours passed, her muscles aching from the tension her body held. Eventually, the knot of icy majik receded. Only much later did Sayra dare to relax, falling into a somewhat fitful sleep.

That made three nights in a row. It seemed she'd never rest well again.

The following day, Sayra made an interesting discovery over breakfast with Nes, Kimimari, and Lynn. Stray auburn curls were practically bouncing around Lynn's shoulder-length braid when she placed her tray beside Kimimari. Her face glowed as if... Well, Sayra couldn't ever recall her appearing so euphoric.

Though her mouth watered at the smell of the freshly made pancakes untouched in front of her, she couldn't take the suspense anymore. "Lynn, where have you been the last few days? I was told you arrived back from winter break some time ago, but I couldn't seem to find you." A handful of seasoned Valkyries spoke loudly at the buffet line near them, causing Sayra to lean toward Lynn.

Nes and Kimimari paused while eating their pancakes, wondering the same thing.

A bashful grin split Lynn's face, her slight freckles crinkling. "Will you keep secret with me?" she asked the girls, Nes, for once, not correcting her grammar.

They nodded in confirmation, eagerly awaiting the news.

Her voice was quiet, just loud enough to hear over the clink of silverware and chatter. "I am dating," Lynn beamed, toying with a blueberry on the edge of her fork.

Sayra's jaw slackened, and Kimimari's brows shot up in shock. A skeptical edge crossed Nes's face, her back leaning away from the table.

She needed to know *now*. "Who?" Sayra whispered, her neck extended further.

"Casber." Lynn obliviously smiled, not catching Kimimari's outright horror beside her.

A stone sunk in Sayra's stomach, her curiosity morphing into concern. Dating, *dritt*, even marriage wasn't forbidden between *anima*, but it could become disgraceful, especially in early contracts. Generally, it was frowned upon since Valkyries weren't trained for such things, and if one were to have a baby, that duration off duty would be a liability for the Arcanist. Some retired when they were ready to have children and settle down. That was a more respectable exit.

For those who broke up the relationship, a majority of the time it caused reassignment. It also brought dishonor to the Valkyrie for leaving her Arcanist and abandoning her vows. The scant occasion where the two would stay together regardless of fracturing the relationship, it resulted in an awkward team dynamic.

The third option wasn't bad. The Valkyrie could become a wife, and while many marriages between *anima* were successful, they still had a liability issue during the childbearing process and tension if the Arcanist hired another Valkyrie instead.

Then there was the fourth option. The Valkyrie became a concubine or, in some cases, a second wife. The practice began a century ago when the male population started to dwindle. Countries legalized a second or third wife for men in hopes that humanity would prosper once more. It wasn't widely accepted by the public, but nowadays, it was prevalent. It was the most common alternative seen in Valkyrie-Arcanist relationships due to the bond heightening communication and compatibility.

Despite it all, almost all Valkyries remained professional in their duties, those training into the profession strongly dissuaded from the notion of ever dating their Arcanist.

Nes shook her head gently, her face sorrowful as strands of dark hair swayed alongside her chin. "Lynn, you have to be careful." She placed a hand over Lynn's paler one. Her words were full of warning. "Do you know him well enough?"

Whipping her hand back, Lynn glared at Nes, her demeanor shifting so quickly Sayra felt she had whiplash. "I knew acceptance you would not have," Lynn puffed, angrily stabbing two more blueberries.

"Lynn, you know the statistics as well as we do. We're just surprised. If you genuinely like him, we'd like to know more. We trust your judgment," Sayra said, even though the weight heavy in her gut doubted the situation.

The last thing she wanted was Lynn to be isolated during such a crucial time. If things went south, they wanted to be there with her every step of the way. Besides, if it was recent, there might be hope to undo the damage.

Lynn peaked through her light lashes at the three of them. Nes nodded once in agreement, but Kimimari was careful to keep her expression neutral.

"Okay." Lynn hesitated, chewing on her lip before continuing. "Casber is..." She hunted for the word. "Thoughtful. He cares about the thoughts I think and the commonalities we share. Kind, intelligent, and..." Blushing, Lynn lowered her voice an octave. "Strong."

Two Valkyries walked by, their expressions worn, likely from overnight patrols.

"I'd like to meet him one of these days, Lynn. He sounds like a nice guy." Sayra forced a smile. She genuinely cared to meet him to ensure he didn't have ulterior motives. Lynn was like a sister to her, after all. They both had sacrificed much to get there, and they'd both lost a brother as children.

They still couldn't speak of it nearly a decade later.

"Where have you two spent your time?" Nes asked, taking a large bite of her croissant.

Perking up, Lynn said, "I met him at winter break. He's funny and friendly. Since we arrived here, we will exercise at Arcanist gymnasium, walk around, and so."

Sayra smirked. "And so, huh?"

Nes rested the back of her hand on her chin. "You two have been in his room alone, haven't you?"

Reddening, Lynn shook her head. "Not that! Yes, but not that." Her hands frantically crossed in the air. Settling down after some mild laughter, she said, "I'd like you all meeting him. Weekend lunch?"

"That'd work for me. He better be fine," Nes purred, peeling her orange. Lynn laughed at that. Nes's eyes flicked toward Kimimari with a pointed message.

"And me," Kimimari said, albeit reluctantly.

Sayra gave a devilish grin. "The guys have all the homework. I have all the time in the world this weekend."

"Amen to that!" Nes cheered, clinking their water glasses together.

Lyn smiled in contentment all the while. "I've wanted to share for some time," she admitted, fiddling with her own glass, her loose curls partially obscuring her face. "I was ashamed to admit but relieved for your understanding."

The grin slipped, Sayra's face smoothing. "Lynn, I've known you for thirteen years. Our mothers were friends. I'll never abandon you over a guy, and that I swear." Earnest notes rang in her words.

"Thank you," Lynn said, a mischievous sparkle in her eye. "And you have an interest in one?"

Grimacing, Sayra shook her head, noting Nes's probing eyes and the intensity directed at her. "No. Sylven and I both hate each other, and that's that." Sayra pushed her half-full plate away. "Though, for once, it's completely the other person's fault and not mine." She cut off Kimimari's response, the tall Valkyrie raising a doubtful eye. Sayra simply stuck her tongue out.

"I think Prince Emrys has a fling," Nes said, carefully not making eye contact with anyone. The way she picked up her fork was far too casual. "Though he's sworn me to silence on sharing anything."

Sayra's chest constricted, her worst fear coming true. To Nes, perhaps to Sylven as well, their relationship could easily be misread as a fling. The secrecy in conversations, the condemning note Emrys sent with Nes, and... wait.

Nes sounded almost jealous. Did she have a crush on her Arcanist?

Sayra supposed Nes could have fallen for him; after all, he was the mysterious, handsome, and dark sort. He likely had dozens of suitors waiting for him in Acacea's capital, regardless of the fact he was a second son. The thought didn't help Sayra's clammy palms, her mind wanting nothing more than to clear the air, but without sharing the true reason, it just wasn't possible.

"Aww, no details further?" Lynn complained, sullenness decorating her heart-shaped face.

Shrugging, Nes finished her last bite of orange. "Secrets are secrets, after all," she somewhat apologized, still refusing to glance Sayra's way.

Ouch. That one hurt.

Tomorrow night, if Sayra finally conversed with Emrys, she'd ask him to fill Nes in on the situation. The last thing Sayra needed was tension she couldn't fix, and besides, she didn't want Nes thinking she was involved in something that clandestine.

Kimimari sighed, standing and organizing her tray. She easily stood a head taller than Lynn and Sayra as they followed suit, though Nes was only a few inches shorter. "I have patrol duty today. Have a good one, all."

Nes grabbed her plate, a beat behind and with a shadow clinging to the surrounding air.

After a chorus of goodbyes, the three separated and went their own ways, Sayra avoiding any further discussion with Nes by spending some time at the gymnasium.

All the while, guilt gnawed at her for withholding secrets from her friends.

CHAPTER NINETEEN

SAYRA

The rest of the day she lifted weights, taking a break for lunch with Breane and then practicing with weapons afterward. That night, Nes had patrol duty, and Sayra, thankfully, managed to avoid crossing paths with her.

The next day, after an easy stretching-and-resistance training session, it was onward to her first lecture with Sylven. It wasn't nearly as bad as she thought it would be, though she shouldn't have antagonized him further. It just brought her so much joy, and he *did* deserve it.

The combat class was fantastic; everything about it was right in her zone. Sayra hoped to be doing some one-on-one combat with Sylven one day. Maybe knock him out once or twice. Now that would be amazing.

A girl could dream.

Throughout the lecture, she kept shooting daggers at Emrys. She couldn't help but feel impressed by his performance during their combat training. Sayra got the distinct impression he showed off a tad more than necessary. After the class convened, she wanted nothing more than to chew his head off for postponing their conversation another day, but the last thing Sayra needed was to draw Nes's attention at that moment. Just in case she believed Sayra was the one Emrys liked.

The only thing that derailed her was the incident with Sylven discovering a portion of her and Kenji's past. It was never her will to be promised to him. The thought was like a collar around her neck growing up. Her only escape from that life was to turn toward the church, signing her life away to its cause and becoming one with their Goddess by receiving the mark upon her nape. Sayra was no longer beholden to Droden, and Kenji never seemed to have any hard feelings during the number of times they crossed paths over the years.

Sylven needn't know any more of it. Certainly not when he asked about it again that day.

Sayra watched as Lynn and Casber frolicked off to his dormitory after combat class ended. Sylven stormed off as if someone had peed in his cereal, and Nes shadowed Emrys with a meandering look toward Sayra. The royal Droden twins cast off with a quick wink at her, leaving Sayra to explore the monastery out of boredom until she neared the cathedral perched at the top of the city-like complex.

It was a reminder to the Holy Family and all visitors that the Goddess was above all, a sentiment Sayra naturally didn't share but respected all the same.

The only word to describe the masterpiece was breathtaking. Sharp spires, seventy-two in all, ranging in size from her height to twenty feet, lanced across the roof, holy guards patrolling along pathways at the top in five-minute intervals. A diamond-shaped, stained-glass window depicting the Goddess beckoned worshipers in over the mighty bronze-formed doors, inscriptions written within concealed crevasses, and vine-shaped irons locking the doors in place.

Statues of saints and their stories were tucked away in occasional alcoves on the cream-and-black-layered marble exterior, circular columns sprouting from the ground and arching upward to merge with the building, a network of vined arches connecting each. The entryway was a staggering hundred steps up from where she stood. Grand arches linked the entirety of the ascension.

The sight alone made her want to worship something, but she'd leave that for those who believed in faith.

Bells rang as a worship session began, angelic voices reverberating through the open doors leading inward. A few nuns, staff members, and guests hurried inside, two nuns closing the enormous doors behind them.

Wrinkling her nose, Sayra turned away and walked to the gymnasium. The only bad Valkyrie was a dead one in the field after all.

She passed several Arcanists of every year, a few Valkyries talking amongst themselves in the corridors. Another nun stood beside an incense fixture, lighting a new smell that wafted through the hall. To Sayra, the semi-burned scent reminded her of wood. It sent a chill through her limbs. Images of fire raging through her dormitory flung through her mind, her skin aching in the areas it had burned her.

By the time she got to the gymnasium, she had repressed those memories. Hours passed, and her muscles fatigued from the high intensity and weight she focused on during the session. One of these days, she'd pack on some more muscle. Sayra didn't feel comfortable being around Nes—not yet—so she showered and changed there into some casual attire. Semi-loose trousers tucked into brown boots and her high-collared, ivory buttoned top.

There was something to be said for fuzzy clothes. The inside material was incredibly soft. Braiding her still-wet hair and tying a seafoam *slør* around it, Sayra was finally ready to confront the *djevel*.

Devil.

Hastily dropping her things in a locker, Sayra marched over to the Arcanist dormitory, surprised to find a lounging figure with a woman draped suggestively beside him in the common room.

She pouted her lips. "Busy night?" Sayra asked, her voice layered with sarcasm.

Reluctantly, Vander broke the deep kiss he was sharing with the woman and glanced at the intruding Valkyrie. "Whatever would give you that inclination?"

The woman shot a nasty look Sayra's way when he whispered something into her ear, her red curls bouncing around her slip of a dress as she brushed past Sayra to climb up the stairwell beside her. Sayra didn't think much of it. Just another rumor confirmed to be true about the eccentricities of the prince before her.

Growing serious, Vander rubbed the stubble of his chin. "How do you fare after the fire?" Light from the nearby fireplace flickered across the panes of his face, the crackle of a log splitting filling the space.

It was only the sincerity in his voice that had Sayra bothering to respond at all. "A little burned out at the moment."

Raising a brow, his fingers stilled where they rested against his jaw. "Even after that ordeal, you manage to still flaunt your sardonic tendencies. Impressive, truly." A corner of his mouth curved suggestively when she didn't react, both eyes gleaming with something she couldn't identify. "What brings you to the Arcanist dormitory? Were you seeking my company intentionally?"

Sayra snorted.

Sprawling into the thick cushions of the navy loveseat, Vander draped an arm across the headrest where the woman had previously been. "It seems I have room for another."

She had no such desire.

"If I were you, I wouldn't keep your lady waiting," Sayra said with a judgmental glance, moving to pass him by before the conversation extended further outside her comfort zone.

"Careful, Sayra." Vander chuckled, his fingers tapping along the mahogany wood lining the furniture. "You nearly sound envious."

Tilting her head at him as she passed, Sayra only breathed, "Not a chance, *Prince* Vander."

Quiet laughter sounded as she pressed down the hall, pausing to knock at the sixth room on the left. Not two seconds passed before Emrys opened the door, for once appearing... casual? No, that wasn't the word. Comfortable? Maybe. He sported his normal black trousers, though he wore a loosely fitted gray top with his collar unbuttoned and matching socks.

"Good evening," Emrys tried, appearing slightly off-kilter for the first time since she'd met him.

Sayra glowered at him as she passed through, catching Vander's winking face out of the corner of her eye as he moved toward the stairwell down the hall. With a huff, she removed her boots beside the door and placed them next to Emrys's before stepping onto his burgundy rug and making herself at home on one of his plush ebony chairs. Closing the door, Emrys placed himself across his mahogany desk, a small leather notebook in front of him.

Those dark gray eyes of his were wary as he pulled out an object from his pocket, placing it gently beside the notebook before rescinding his hand. Sayra pressed her lips into a fine line upon seeing the item, once half-burned but restored to its former glory. A beautiful and delicate gold chain with a dove's side profile of flight hanging at the end.

It had always been slightly misshapen, the tiny peak more curved and wings longer than were proportional, but it was entirely precious with meaning. A gift handmade by her mother, imperfectly perfect.

"How?" Sayra asked, her throat working at the memory of receiving it.

Emrys wouldn't tear his eyes from the notebook, his mind in another place. Another time. "Nessika returned the cloak Monday morning, and I found it in the pocket. You were correct when stating that I owed you. In fact, I owe you more than you are aware of. It was the least I could do," he reasoned, his chest barely rising as if he were restraining himself.

"It was the last gift my mother ever gave me," Sayra said, grasping the pendant and pushing the recollection back, back. It was a time she didn't want to remember. "Thank you." She meant it, but the bitterness of being dragged through the mud for weeks tainted her heartfelt words, even if it stirred something in her chest that Emrys had gone to such lengths.

He nodded as she pocketed it.

Sayra cut to the chase, leaning forward and resting her elbow on the table. "You mentioned you felt responsible for that fire incident. Before that, you said you had a hand in the reason I'm in this whole situation. Why did you say that?" Her eyes flicked between his, waiting for some sort of response, verbal or not.

Emrys ran a stressed hand behind his ear and sighed before at last meeting her eyes. Sayra felt as if she were seeing him for the first time. No guard. No pretense. Just an overburdened twenty-year-old man, and for some reason, seeing that side of him dropped her own hackles.

"Shall I begin at the start of this tale?" he asked. "Yours, that is?"

Sayra gestured for him to do so.

"Nineteen years, ten months, and one day ago, you were gifted with majik, not through some Goddess or higher power but by a woman who stole a majik-granting relic while working with my parents to undermine the Holy Family's regime," said Emrys. The line sounded rehearsed, as if he had spent the evening perfecting the simple pitch that would catch her, hook, line, and sinker.

Well, holy *dritt*. It sure did.

He stood and sat across from her at the small table, so clean not even a speck of dust dare floated on it. Sayra's expression bounced between confusion, annoyance, and disbelief.

"You were chosen to become the progenitor female Arcanist who would sow seeds of dissidence into the oblivious people of the continent, eventually cracking the foundation of the church's power by proving false their testimonies," Emrys explained, his features slowly turning grave as he leaned back into his seat.

The information was overwhelming, so naturally, Sayra handled it as any average person would. "Well, splendid job if I do say so myself! Yes, quite the maverick I've become," she said, flipping her braid over her shoulder. "A role model for all young girls out there, if I dare say, nearly killing an entire floor of Valkyries due to a lack of information and help from the people who did this to me."

Her temper rose fast and hot. Placing both palms face down on the table beside her, Sayra leaned across it and met Emrys's regretful expression. Despite her reaction, his convictions remained firm.

"I would have stepped in sooner, if possible," Emrys said, quietly but not weakly. "I'm bound by majik to not reveal anything I'm not permitted to. My family is rather cautious. Many resources and bridges between contacts were sacrificed over the years to obtain insider knowledge within the Holy Family's circle, even more to gift you majik and the anonymity to keep you above suspicion."

"But why has it taken nearly nineteen years for anyone to tell me this?" Sayra's voice trembled with ferocity. The anger was molten and bitter inside her chest. It was near impossible to get to where she was today as a Valkyrie. Where was the help years ago—before she lost her brother?

"If I'm not given the freedom to decide my own path, then the least I am owed is more than I was given! For weeks, I could feel this majik crawling inside of me, eating away at my sanity at night when the chill would stretch to my limbs. Other times, I'd burn from the inside out, every ounce of willpower I could muster required to contain it."

Closing her eyes in pain, her nails dug into the table and her head hung low. "Every day it's worsening, randomly waking me in the middle of the night, threatening to expose me during the day. I don't want it. Not to mention all I have sacrificed, yet I'm expected to keep giving." Her voice broke into a whisper during the last sentence, her anger draining into exhaustion.

She was trying. Trying so hard for her brother.

And now? Was she supposed to forget about him and Lynn's sibling—their sacrifice? The countless hours of training didn't mitigate the threat of her majik, the lack of sleep only wearing down her durability in the face of it.

"A binding spell was placed on you to suppress your majik until the time came for you to learn about it. That time wasn't supposed to come for another year. The reason I had to postpone our discussion was because of that exact predicament. I didn't want to not have the answers you were waiting for," Emrys explained.

Sayra peered up at that.

Emrys's voice lightened when he saw her interest. "I had to meet with some contacts away from the monastery to puzzle out why you were in this situation. The most concise conclusion is that the binding spell is weakening, but from what is unknown."

She realized then his haggard appearance stemmed from his lack of sleep the night before. Evidently, he had just cause to push back their meeting after all—beyond being a prick. Some of her anger ebbed.

"I've been ordered to renew the binding spell so you aren't at risk of leaking majik until you've had a chance to meet with my parents," he informed her.

The king and queen of Acacea.

Her stomach was in knots. Sayra didn't want anything to do with royalty ever again. She didn't trust those with total power over a country, and she certainly didn't trust Emrys's parents. Why not teach her how to use the majik instead of placing a bandage over the problem? That was a temporary solution that would need to be removed at some point. What would happen next year?

So many questions buzzed in Sayra's brain she had to lean back to take them all in. There was no doubt she had majik, and if the church was somehow capable of granting it, then that explained how she possessed it despite it being a Goddess-given gift. Her people believed it to be a natural blessing from the earth. Both were wrong, yet she wanted to hear more on the *how*.

"Before I agree to anything," Sayra said slowly, her mind spinning with hundreds of thoughts, "I need to know about the Holy Family and how they select who gets majik. Also, why is it so bad that they do?"

Emrys considered her question. "Fair demands. I promise I'll do my best to ensure I can right any wrongs. I agree you should have been informed long ago, but as I previously said, I was bound to an oath I couldn't break. I've only recently received clearance to have this discussion at all," he said.

Sayra's lips formed a line at the admittance.

Emrys's parents had clearly played a role in preventing Emrys, and most likely Vander, from divulging any secrets. Though she understood that, she swore to give Vander a piece of her mind the next time they crossed paths.

"From an outsider's perspective, the Holy Family does no wrong." His face contorted in disgust. "But they are truly the most despicable lineage to grace the lands. Corruption is only the tip of the iceberg. Manipulating entire nations is their pastime, granting majik with the Grand Priest's supposed blessing and brainwashing governments through their education systems. Each king, emperor, oligarch, and elected leader has been tainted and indirectly controlled by the Holy Family when they passed through these walls."

Sayra's body tensed. Her father had once walked these halls as an Arcanist. Had he too been manipulated to surrender his throne and betray his people?

"They redistribute wealth through trade agreements, political treaties, and foreign exchanges and thereby instill their claws into each leader's mind. Majik can be granted freely to any person; gender is not an issue, only age." Emrys shook his head in sorrow. "If given to humans older than a babe, they become a daemon. Babes are pure, untouched by the world's sin, but as we age, we lose that innocence, allowing corruption from majik to be incorporated into our very cells. Every daemon originated from human flesh and bone."

Sayra's eyes widened with horror. The realization came swiftly, her hands shaking ever so slightly. Those two daemons who attacked her and the Astors used to be living, breathing people. "I've helped kill... a person?"

"Yes," Emrys confirmed, his eyes empathetic yet tired, worn down from the knowledge and having to eliminate the Horde in his travels. "Unfortunately, we haven't reached the worst part. Those who receive the so-called 'blessing of the Goddess' to become a Valkyrie either merge with the curse like you have or momentarily die, losing their minds and bodies to majik and forming into a daemon. Their soul is gone, but the majik reforms their flesh, twisting it into unspeakable atrocities. Have you ever wondered why the Horde mainly targets majik-users?"

Sayra was going to be sick. Her arms curled around her middle, her mind flying as it made new connections. "Abominations target abominations. Majik was never meant to be taken from ley lines, was it?" she asked, afraid to hear the answer.

"Never," Emrys said, an underlying anger bringing a chill to her arms. "Centuries ago, a founding member of the Holy Family discovered a relic, embedded with a runic language more complex than any ever written. The widely accepted explanation was that it hailed from an ancient civilization, one destroyed by the greed of its own people, a fate we must alter for our own, or we'll be the true death of humanity."

"This is..." Sayra's mouth wouldn't work, her legs rising to pace across his carpet. "Insane."

"There's more."

"Of course, there is," Sayra muttered, resuming her trek back and forth with her hands on her hips as if recovering from a race.

After a deep breath, Emrys resumed, "The Holy Family conducts experiments on the Valkyries and acolytes that are deemed unnecessary. Those who don't graduate are selected."

Feet freezing mid-stride, Sayra's blood ran cold. The memory came back in a flash. The day before they graduated. Catara and dozens of monks observed the acolytes who didn't graduate, a grim air about them. It disturbed Sayra then, the off-putting feeling.

Catara had given her that weird look, almost as if she regretted what she was about to do.

"I fell into that category," she monotoned, her mouth suddenly dry and knees threatening to buckle. One of her hands reached toward the small cross imprinted on the back of her neck, the vivid memory of receiving it flashing in her mind.

Every acolyte, one at a time, filed into the Holy Family's private chapel to be blessed with the mark. The Grand Priest himself murmured words of power above Sayra. The experience was short but excruciating since the majik altered her very being. Afterward, as nuns ushered her out of the right exit, she felt an indescribable change in every fiber of her body. Strength. Power. Speed. Her mind felt sharper and capable of anything.

But while she celebrated with her cadre of friends, other acolytes who they thought were dead had morphed into daemons below the very stone they walked on.

The Grand Priest had reassured them each consecrated body would receive the highest righteousness in their burial, and the Goddess herself would be on the other side, welcoming them into the afterlife. Sayra didn't think twice about the private ritual they claimed to have held for each of them beneath that chapel. She didn't do much except grieve for those who lost their lives in such an honorable pursuit and for the families who would receive a letter of condolence. As the living acolytes held vigil for their fallen sisters, those tortured souls lost every semblance of what made them human.

At the time, Sayra didn't think much beyond the oddity of the haste each failed acolyte had been moved out of the dormitory on that fateful day Emrys saved her. She should have reflected more on the morbid air the classroom held when the acolytes deemed fit for graduation departed. The defensive stances each instructor took upon themselves as if they were to fight the leftovers. What became of them?

When Sayra started at Saint Highburn's Valkyrie Academy, the instructors claimed they passed every candidate. It wasn't until their last semester the instructors regretfully shared they would hold back a select number of the lowest-scoring candidates from graduation. They instilled competitiveness in each acolyte and said some may be returned to their homeland or given bottom-of-the-barrel assignments. Never did they explicate further. Never did Sayra or the others question if such a thing had happened before. They all believed it when the Holy Family shared their reports of the program's previous successes.

How terribly naïve.

The death rates were high for low-scoring Valkyries, and Sayra suddenly knew why. They simply fixed the numbers, writing off the failed acolytes as dead when they secretly ushered them into their very own experimental program. When she stated her assumptions aloud, Emrys nodded in confirmation.

What made Sayra nauseous, though, was how close she came to divulging all she knew to Catara just the day before and the warning Catara gave to Sayra to tread the right path. She said Netta would be removed, as so many other Valkyries had been, if she continued to bring dishonor to the sisterhood.

Emrys stood, moving across the room to place a hand on her shoulder. "I would never have allowed that to happen to you," he swore, his face fierce and alive with his resolve. His eyes, normally so elusive, were radiant with passion—a stark contrast to how she used to perceive them.

In that moment, Sayra realized what he had endured for her sake. From lying about her majik to the monk to forcing Sylven to accept her as his Valkyrie to searching for answers to her majikal dilemma... it was more than anyone had done on her behalf, and she criticized him every step of the way.

The whole situation was overwhelming.

"How do they remain unaware of the fact that I am—that I have—" she corrected, a buzz sounding in her ears, "majik? Beyond that of my majik being suppressed."

His voice sounded odd to her as she listened to him say, "From my knowledge, they still believe the woman who stole the relic to have fled to another continent. Trails of breadcrumbs were scattered in various directions, but one was carefully crafted to ensnare their attention. One that guaranteed they wouldn't suspect you or anyone within my family or network."

Unsteadiness made the floor shift below her feet, and minuscule beads of sweat formed around her brow.

"Sayra?" Emrys sounded concerned, and his hand gripped her shoulder tighter. "I need to renew the binding spell. Your majik is reacting unpredictably. I don't know what could happen next if I don't fix it."

Her face pinched, a strange disconnect between her mind and body budding. "I want a choice," she insisted, her eyes fierce. "Everything thus far has been done *to* me, but this time, I want to decide. Remove the binding spell." The buzz rang louder in her ears, and she felt the blood rush from her face. Something cold crawled into her head, sapping her thoughts and threatening to burst from her.

Another hand gripped her other shoulder, a man's words echoing in her head. "If I remove it, it will only place you in more danger if you expose your majik."

That very majik a strange woman forced into her body thundered through her veins. Sayra's lungs felt full of fluid, a weight being pressed against her chest and affecting her ability to breathe.

Pulling herself from his hands, she sat against the end of his bed, not trusting her consciousness to remain for long. Trying to force the majik to retreat, her calming breaths weren't quite working the way they used to.

Emrys was beside her, kneeling in a picture of concern. His mouth moved, but his words weren't reaching her ears. Indecision flickered across his lined face, a hand balling at his side before he closed his eyes, engulfing her smaller hand in his. Mouth still moving, he released multiple words of power, and Sayra's vision flickered.

Deep down, she willed the majik away. She couldn't suppress it, so maybe getting it out of her would work. Suddenly, a shock raced through them both, the release of her majik's constraints freeing her mind. It wove between them, strands of shimmering translucent energy materialized, leaving her hand and swarming around the darker whispers of Emrys's emerged majik.

At first, they both stared in bewilderment and awe, never having seen the physical form of majik. And then Sayra felt it. A weak thread between them. Her majik was drawn to his, and his reciprocated in kind. It was as if it wanted to meld into one force.

The fear in Sayra's mind of losing control shattered the mystery of the moment. Her majik continued to leave her, the subconscious thought of wishing it away disrupting the fragile link and pushing it toward Emrys. Slowly, her heart grew weaker, skipping beats and leaving her pale.

Realizing what was happening, Emrys tried to force his hand from hers and disconnect the threads of majik. Failing, he panicked. "Sayra, you have to stop," he cautioned, his voice urgent as her eyelids fluttered.

"It's not working," she gasped. Black spots appeared across her vision.

"*Claudicare.*" Emrys tried to cast a spell, the majik not working. "Sayra, say that word with the intention that your majik stop draining out."

"*Claudicare,*" she repeated faintly, which halted the transference.

Emrys withdrew his hand as if he were burned, keeping a safe distance from her. Shaking his head, he said, "You have to recall your majik. You've nearly given me all of yours somehow."

Closing her eyes, Sayra said, "I don't know how. Do you?" On one side of the spectrum, she felt incredibly feeble, more so than she ever had before. Speaking was an effort, drawing breath challenging. But otherwise, she felt at peace, a faint buzz in her veins she'd previously lacked. It was exhilarating to feel the thrum of majik, its presence no longer overbearing and threatening but rather a tamed energy she could finally use at will. Blinking, she turned her head toward him.

"A few days ago, I didn't even know it was possible." Emrys grimaced. "The first time you did it was when we were in the corridor after I wiped the majik attacking your dormitory."

She shrugged her shoulders. The effort proved taxing. "I wanted it gone." Her lids shut of their own volition, fatigue sweeping her into a comforting lull.

"You could try to reverse it with..." Emrys's voice drifted off, the sentence lost to her memory.

CHAPTER TWENTY

SYLVEN

"Let me get this straight." Sylven spoke slowly at first, his arms folded across his chest. "You want to spend the night at my place because Sayra fell asleep in yours? Why not just poke her awake like a normal person and send her off? Why was she even in your room to begin with?" He flung his arms wide.

"We were conversing about matters I'm forbidden to discuss outside of her and my family. She fell asleep," Rys said, obviously lost as to how to explain his predicament. He dropped an extra pillow and blanket on the royal-blue carpet beside Sylven's bed.

"Unbelievable." Sylven groaned, wanting nothing more than to tug his own hair out. "I can't keep this charade up any longer, Rys. I'm at my limit. With her. With this contract. If I don't receive answers soon, I'm considering negating it." Sylven ran his hand through his hair, his desk chair supporting his back as he leaned into it.

Rys went unnaturally still, a glint of fear unlike any Sylven had seen before entering his eyes. "Sylven, please," he reasoned. He held his palm between them. "If you do that..." His mouth floundered for a moment, frustration warping it. "I can't say it."

Scoffing, Sylven stood and walked to his window. Placing his hands on the chilled sill, he stared out at the flakes of snow lazily floating down from the night sky. "Of course."

"I've taken a blood oath," Rys said, the words difficult to emerge from his mouth.

Tensing, Sylven banged his forehead against the window. *Of course, Rys did. And of course, I'm expected to let things go because it's the right thing to do when Rys is majik-bound to protect this secret. But why must it be so hard and so incredibly taxing?*

Then a thought struck him like a nail being hammered into his head. "Has Sayra taken an oath?"

"No." The reply was swift, Rys clearly wanting to divulge what knowledge he could depart with.

Sylven would seek answers from her then. But first... "Is this situation because of a romance between the two of you?"

Rys gave an incredulous huff. "Do you think I'd be here if it was?"

A short barking laugh escaped his lips, and Sylven turned at last. There was an anxious edge to Rys's demeanor, one that wore down the rough edges of Sylven's frustration. "Fine. Stay here. For your awareness, however, I fully intend to drag answers from her. I hope that won't be an issue between us," Sylven warned, not willing to except any answer other than what he wanted.

"It won't," Rys promised. A relieved expression crossed his face. "I sincerely hope you're given answers." He sat back in the cherry wood-carved chair, a deep breath releasing from his broad chest. The tension easing from his friend's shoulders was visible.

Sylven nodded in response, flopping onto his bed with his feet dangling off. An earlier situation floated through his mind. "By any chance, do you know what went on between her and Kenji?" he asked, half expecting a response along the lines of *I can't say.*

"To summarize, her father arranged a deal with the Droden emperor to retain power after the absorption of Faenda by marrying them. Sayra, being Sayra..." Sylven snorted at that. "Fled and swore herself to the church to remain autonomous from her family and Kenji," Rys explained, the wooden chair shifting.

A tiny kernel of appreciation grew in Sylven upon learning of her background. It was impossible for some people to overcome the politics of royalty and nobility. It explained her complete and utter dedication toward her duty as a Valkyrie.

In this world, a man's life was worth troves of gold while a woman's life equated to as little as the value of fodder. There were far too many women in comparison to men, and many spent a lifetime never marrying. While Sayra was an exception, Sylven wouldn't want to marry Kenji either. The man was just... disgusting.

As soon as that thought came, it was trampled by pain. It reminded Sylven far too much of his own sister Jess and the near-ludicrous dedication she had toward her cause.

It struck him then. Sayra and Jess were far too alike for his comfort. The bickering Jess and Sylven always engaged in. The way Sayra and Jess carried themselves with a smug confidence. How they refused traditional roles. Their absolute dedication to fight for what was right even at the cost of their lives. It was inevitable Sayra would have the same fate as Jess. Sylven didn't want to bear that responsibility.

He couldn't bear it if Sayra died too.

Clearing his throat, Sylven redirected his thoughts. "Interesting. They seem on good enough terms. Though I thought it strange when

Kenji cornered me today, suddenly taking an interest in having me as a friend."

Rys shifted in his seat. "And you think it might pertain to Sayra?"

Rolling his eyes, Sylven drawled, "What doesn't?" Grunting, he sat up, perching himself against the wall his bed ran across. "Between you, him, and Vander..."

Rys's eyes narrowed, a muscle tightening above his jawline. "What were Vander's words?"

"Oh, you know, him having the gall to criticize me for not kneeling at Sayra's every whim." At Rys's frown, Sylven inhaled deeply and restarted. "He gave it away there was something between your family and her, saying there was more at play than I realize."

Silence hung between them.

At last, Rys spoke up. "Vander is dangerous, Sylven. If there's one request I can make beyond that of retaining Sayra as your Valkyrie, it would be to avoid him. Both of you."

Tipping his head, Sylven gave him a disbelieving face. "Vander? Dangerous? Stop. You'll make me die of laughter." The most the princeling could do was perhaps date every female of age. He was simply a womanizer, his only focus revolving around his next conquest. Both grades and his attitude reflected that.

"Vander means well but makes devastating, careless mistakes. I think he's up to something. He's poking around more than he ought to be," Rys mused, his expression returning to brooding seriousness.

"What?" Sylven couldn't comprehend the logic behind that, but he wouldn't discount Rys's worries. He was rarely off when making judgements. It was the only reason Sylven continued to play nice-ish with Sayra.

Rys shook his head, turning to stare out the window. "You'll connect the dots when you hear from Sayra. Vander and I share the same blood. He wields the same logic but has a vastly different way of manipulating it. While I'm on the path of sensibility, Vander aims to, one day, expedite everything through his own methodology." He rested his elbow on the desk.

"I can't trust him not to interfere. My parents share similar sentiments, which is the only reason he hasn't lent his aid. Though you can rest assured he's been picking at every mistake I've made. It's his only method around the blood oath, and one that serves his particular need to be *right* about everything." Rys's annoyance leaked through his words.

Struggling with the notion Vander actually had a brain, Sylven wondered, "What about his marks on his lectures? He never scores high. He's always firmly in the middle of his class. How can a mastermind achieve marks that low?"

"Perhaps it takes a mastermind to skillfully achieve such consistent marks, always remaining right in the center so everything else around him will be targeted first," Rys said, wrinkling his nose.

"This is a lot to swallow," Sylven said, shifting slightly as one of his legs began to fall asleep. His face screwed up. "I suppose it will all make sense once I talk with Sayra."

Emrys agreed.

Sylven knew he loved his brother dearly but was endlessly at odds with Vander's idiosyncrasies. With an annoyed groan, Sylven stared at the ceiling as his wooden wall clock ticked in the silence. Finally, he gathered his resolve and reached for his shelves, grabbing a particularly thick *History of Anima* textbook. He braced it open. Flipping through the pages, he eyed the title of chapter three. "Unfortunately, I'm going to need tonight to work on our history paper, if you don't mind. I think a distraction is exactly what I need."

Blanching, Rys looked toward Sylven's door. "May I borrow some paper? I left mine in my room..."

The rest remained unsaid between them, Sylven smirking in response. Sharing his textbook and a notebook, they wrote the night away on their origin paper of *anima*, Sylven for once feeling as if things were normal. It was a feeling he longed for more than he knew, reminiscent of their old days, where all three of them, Sylven, Rys, and Waylen, would do homework throughout the evening. Together, they shared every eve and every meal. Perhaps that reality could be theirs again.

Chapter Twenty-One

EMRYS

Emrys ensured he left a thorough note behind for Sayra, detailing the importance that she remain silent about her majik. He issued an apology for his brief departure, but he wanted to give her privacy, and he indicated he'd be staying down the hall with Sylven in room ten if his presence was needed.

It shocked Emrys how heavy Sayra was. For a small Valkyrie, no taller than five feet, four inches by his estimate, she had packed on quite the muscle. He left her on his bed, the note on the nightstand table, and spelled a trap for any intruder should they break in. In the end, it proved fruitless. When he returned after class, he found her sound asleep.

For once, Emrys wasn't sure what to do. It was obvious carrying her out or requesting Nessika to do so would be regarded badly. Too much explaining. He didn't need any monks or nuns bringing word back to the Holy Family she had been passed out in his quarters. That would raise suspicion without doubt.

Vander didn't need to know either. His only goal was to begin their parents' plan. He was trying to prove himself capable of the title of crowned prince. That much Emrys could surmise. Despite the need to wait another year, Vander must have thought it important to begin asserting his superiority as soon as he could, trying to wrest control from Emrys with every communication he sent to their parents. It was absurd.

Emrys had no intention of displacing his elder brother, but words fell on deaf ears when the matter was concerned. He debated sharing his insights with his parents, but it would be juvenile to stab his brother in the back in such a manner. Emrys would simply parry any attempts Vander tried while working to maintain their own withering bond. Family was paramount to him, and Emrys knew if his parents became involved in Vander's childish actions, his brother would harbor a vindictive grudge. Vander struggled to let go of slights, especially when his sore spot, Emrys, was brought up. It didn't please Emrys to think such thoughts, but he knew Vander was envious of his closeness with their parents.

He was determined to handle the situation, though he hadn't planned on disobeying his parents and removing the seal on Sayra's majik. Initially, he had intended to follow through with their order for him to renew the seal, but her words had struck him.

Everything thus far has been done to me, but this time, I want to decide.

There was a devastated undertone to her words that gave him pause. She was right. Unknown to her, others had planned out her entire life. Once the world knew her truth, there was a very real possibility they would hunt her down. No one asked her if they could use her life for their own ends. The only other person who tried to give Sayra some semblance of normalcy was the one person who forced his family to wait until her twenty-first birthday before using Sayra to change their world.

They weren't allowed to speak with her or control her life in any way. Ultimately, Emrys had to step in, but only because Sayra's life was in danger otherwise.

I want to decide.

Emrys gave her the control she longed for, defying his parents and the one who gave her the majik. There may be consequences to pay for it, but he knew Sayra was worth it.

If only she would wake up.

The majikal dilemma was unexpected. He had imagined every possible scenario of something going wrong. What if Sayra still had majikal buildup and kept using it in public? What would the Holy Family do if they found out he was teaching her majik? Sylven hadn't returned yet and—

"Nessika?" Sayra asked sleepily, her face half-planted into his down-filled comforter.

Heaving a relieved sigh, Emrys closed the door behind him just as another Arcanist opened his door down the hall. He sent a quick prayer of thanks to the Goddess that Sayra was awake, and even more so they'd been sly enough not to gather attention at the odd hour Sayra visited.

He murmured a noise-disrupting spell, his dark majik inclined to destroy any vibrations in the air that noise cast when it tried to pass the translucent walls of his barrier. "No," he said, "though she did inquire after you. I informed her you were sleeping here while I stayed in Sylven's room and to keep that between us three."

Sayra snapped up, eyes wide and escaped hairs from her braid encompassing her dismayed face. "I stayed here overnight? Oh no. Oh no," she said, brushing strands out of her face and quickly removing herself from the bed. A slight blush crossed her cheekbones, her frazzled state endearing to Emrys. "Nes is going to assume—"

"Nessika won't," Emrys interrupted. "I promised her otherwise and informed her I was staying with Sylven for the time being. She believed me."

Sayra's face relaxed at that.

"Since we haven't discussed the matter..." He put his book bag down beside his desk. "Nessika cannot know about your majik. The smaller the group aware of it, the more secure you'll be until you are proficient enough with it."

Smoothing out her sleeves, Sayra raised a brow. "Just for now?"

"Just for now," Emrys said, giving her a purposeful look. "Though if you want to share with Sylven, by all means."

Sayra's face scrunched up. "No way. He's insufferable."

Emrys did feel somewhat culpable for his friend's poor relationship with Sayra. Sylven was incredibly loyal, always sticking to Emrys's side growing up and challenging his majik to greater heights. They shared a goal of mastering their power for the greater good. While Sylven could come off as rude, sullen, and abrasive to others, Emrys knew it wasn't always so.

After Sylven's sister passed away so horribly, about the same time they started at Saint Highburn's Arcanist Academy, Emrys was there when a deep-rooted anger skewed Sylven's outlook on life. For weeks, Emrys postponed important meetings, plans, and studies to be there for his friend. That light Sylven harbored for his passion twisted in those weeks, rekindled in a darker version of himself much later on.

Emrys understood his desire to be without a Valkyrie. In a way, it was his tribute to a lost sibling Sylven was incredibly close to. It hurt him to watch Sylven grow into an isolated shell of himself, one where he placed his anger on society and did everything to contradict what his sister died for. Emrys tried to reason with him, but nothing could fix the enormous gap in Sylven's heart. So, Emrys strove to be there for everything. It was his way of showing Sylven he wasn't alone. To some, Sylven came across as intolerable, but at his core, Emrys knew he was a man worth the effort.

"He saved your life by keeping you as his Valkyrie without being informed of the entire situation," Emrys pointed out, resuming his seat from the previous night.

Pressing her lips into a line, Sayra didn't respond until she sat across from him, her fingers drumming on the mahogany table. "I'll consider it," she reluctantly decided, those green eyes of hers distant as they stared at his desk.

"Thank you," he said, his relief palpable.

A few Arcanists walked by outside of the dorm room, laughing as they joked with each other. The noise soon faded.

Emrys pushed his small notebook across the table toward her. "This is a comprehensive list of words of power, words you'll need to learn in order to survive."

"But no pressure, right?" Sayra half-heartedly joked, taking the pocket-sized notebook and peering at the first page. Her eyes met his. "Thank you. For this and for everything. I apologize for my previous frustration, and while I wish I would have been informed sooner, I recognize the fault lies not with you."

A smile turned the corners of his mouth. "I appreciate your words. I'm honestly surprised you've handled it as well as you have."

"You expected worse?"

"Yes," he said honestly.

A laugh burst out of Sayra, a lighthearted thing that loosened the muscles knotting his shoulders. He couldn't help but chuckle himself, the sound bringing a mocking gasp from Sayra.

"So, you do laugh!" Her eyes were amused, both hands resting on the notebook in front of her.

"Rarely and in between," Emrys acquiesced, eyes admiring the way her face shifted when enjoying herself.

It was challenging not to feel that way after years of watching over her. Sayra was mesmerizing to him, a former princess who gave everything to spite her obligations. A young woman striving to overcome impossible odds as an acolyte. A Valkyrie who stuck firm to her beliefs despite wielding majik, and one willing to devote herself to a cause grander than ever imagined. Sayra was resilient but human. She wasn't perfect, making several mistakes along the way. It was how she came back from them that caught his interest. She owned up to them, carrying them as scars for all to see as she built herself up even stronger.

It was dangerous to view her with such admiration, but Emrys couldn't ignore the way he felt around her. He worked to hide it among the masses under the mask of a prince, especially when relaying his reports to his father.

Recentering himself, Emrys knew he had to focus on her training. As much as he enjoyed the lightheartedness, someone within the monastery was preparing their next big move, and time was not on their side.

"Regrettably, we must return to business. First, we need to discover what your majik archetypes are. It's clear you have a light archetype as you're capable of sharing majik."

Growing serious, that soft edge hardening, she straightened her back. "Sadly, my education in these matters is lacking. What makes that clear?" Sayra asked, her eyes inquisitive.

"Light is not capable of anything that inherently causes danger," Emrys informed her, pointing to the notebook. "I have basic words listed under each affinity. I wasn't sure which you'd be proficient in."

"How can I learn?" Her eyes bored into the leather.

A corner of his mouth turned down. "Without access to the church's resources and without being able to test in a safer location, trying out different elements provides the third best option."

Sayra picked up and opened the book again, scanning the pages as she flipped.

Emrys continued, "Naturally, you'll want to begin with a small and easy—"

"This one," she interrupted. Her face was set, her mind made up.

Calor. Heat. A fire-affinity spell.

For a moment, Emrys hesitated. It wasn't an element he wanted to test with her, not so soon after the inferno she had been stuck in. It nearly killed her and others. The resolve in her gaze, however, said it all. She wanted to overcome that which she couldn't control.

"Let us begin then," Emrys said, handing her a book from his nearby shelf, last year's edition of *The Founding of Saint Highburn Monastery.*

Confused, Sayra gripped the hefty brown text. "I just say the word and intend for it to happen, and it should warm up?" she asked with skepticism.

Emrys nodded in confirmation, eager to see the results.

"*Calor,*" she summoned, willing the fire element into the book. Flames erupted from the text, making Sayra hastily drop the book onto the table and leap out of the chair. She leaned against Emrys's bed in shock.

Waving a hand at the burning text, he ordered, "*Abiit!*"

"That was me?" Sayra breathed, holding a hand over her pounding heart.

Emrys took a moment to analyze the situation. He was thoroughly bewildered. Only light majik allowed transference between Arcanists. Sayra had summoned light majik when she slowed Netta in her final trial. Conjuring destructive fire was dark majik of the fire ley line. Summoning it wouldn't be possible if Sayra had a light majik archetype, and it was impossible for any Arcanist to wield both light and dark. What she achieved didn't obey the laws of majik.

Transference wasn't a published spell within the Arcanist Academy's texts, so perhaps he was somehow misinterpreting which archetype—light or dark—was required. Maybe it was a dark archetype spell only expert majik-wielders were competent in within a more advanced course of study. A type Arcanists possibly learned at the Sicarius level of talent. However, that didn't explain the speed spell Sayra cast on Netta.

And both she had cast without an incantation, which in itself was unheard of.

There was only one solution that could prove, without a doubt, the situation.

"Let's try this spell. *Corporis custodia*. When you cast, imagine a bubble encompassing you to protect you from physical interference," Emrys instructed, practically hanging on the edge of his seat.

Stealing a moment for a reassuring breath, Sayra repeated after him. Emrys rose, sensing the rise of majik from the earth once more. He held his breath in awe before his hand even met resistance from the invisible shield produced around her. Fingers outstretched, his skin pressed against the thin barrier. Sayra observed, without fully comprehending, the gift she wielded, appearing somewhat impatient for him to deliver the verdict. But Emrys couldn't stop there. He had to test the endurance. If there was a reality where a person could wield both light and dark archetypes, then perhaps their strength would be similarly unparalleled.

Without an explanation, Emrys swung around, lashing out with his elbow and breaking the spell with ease.

Well then, average spell-producing capabilities.

Sayra sighed, leaning against the wooden edge of his bed with a bitter expression. "That was disappointingly weak. What's the point if I'm not any good?"

"Humor me," Emrys coaxed, withdrawing a small letter opener from a drawer in his desk. Before Sayra could protest, he stabbed the meat of his palm, just under the thumb. The pain was sharp, and his lungs froze as it radiated outward.

"Nes is going to kill me," Sayra stressed, rubbing her forehead.

Amused, Emrys drew close and held the hand out to her. "*Sana* is the word to heal."

Blood began to trail down onto the floor, the puncture deep enough to require at least two stitches. Without further delay, she held a hand over his and murmured the word. His skin sewed back together, the blood the only trace of any injury ever present. Emrys wasn't surprised. His earlier theory was confirmed. Though he still wanted to clear the other two options.

"Next, say *aura*. Focus on a gentle breeze, mind you. I don't feel like cleaning my room again this week," Emrys joked, excitement buzzing through his veins.

A small breeze whistled through his hair at her word, the wind curling between them before dissipating. Sayra smiled at the spell, intrigued by the majikal display.

It was odd for Emrys, feeling her majik and his responding to it. It felt almost as if it had a personality of its own and itched to be used alongside hers, though he refrained from even thinking along those lines. Any majikal unknown was potentially unsafe to explore until they knew her limitations and abilities.

"Last one. Place your hand over this stone." Emrys pointed at one beside his window. "Then, say *fissura*. Be careful to focus on a small crack. Otherwise, you could utilize too much majik and put your life in danger." Almost as an afterthought, he added, "And mine too."

Placing her hand on the stone, Sayra concentrated on forming a tiny fracture. "*Fissura*."

An inch-long crack webbed through the stone, amazement similarly cracking through Emrys's concentrated demeanor. Her eyes gazed into his, waiting to hear his thoughts on the tests.

"You know, I really hope this was worth it. You lost a book cover, and now you have a cracked stone," Sayra remarked, draping an arm across the windowsill. "I feel like there had to be a less destructive method."

"You've been gifted each element with proficiencies for both light and dark archetypes," Emrys revealed, plans shifting and whirling in his mind.

Cocking her head, Sayra grinned. "What I'm hearing is that I can easily out-majik Sylven." Her eyes raised to the ceiling as if imagining how the scene would play out. "This is going to be absolutely hilarious when he finds out."

A single corner of his mouth twitched. "Not quite yet," he said. Her grin shrunk into a frown.

"You'll be required to train with each affinity and archetype in order to make each spell powerful. That will take time," he warned, sitting back beside the table. "You'll need to memorize the words and repeat each spell for many months before you'll be somewhat of a match. Although your flexibility of element usage will give you an enormous advantage."

"Do I have time for this?" Sayra asked, carefully taking her seat across from him. A flicker of apprehension crossed her face at the thought of another situation similar to the fire occurring.

Emrys responded with a shake of his head, his right foot tapping the burgundy rug as he puzzled out potential solutions. One kept rising to the forefront of his mind. One that could help her improve if she knew what circumstances gave her such unparalleled ability. When Sayra had shared her majik with him, it had been more than he had ever wielded in one sitting. His majik was still bursting at the seams. Already she possessed a larger capacity, which would lend itself well in combat when it came to that. If he could only figure out the how...

His foot stilled, eyes rising to meet her intrigued ones. "I have an idea. Next weekend, we will journey out to see a friend of mine in Acacea. We will seek answers there, but for now, I'd recommend practicing every second you can spare. There aren't many Arcanists gifted with the sense of other's majik, but the Holy Family is bound to have a few in their arsenal, which is why I request that you train only here so I can conceal its use. As I said all those weeks ago, your life will be forfeit if they find out."

In disbelief, Sayra murmured, "I can't believe they'd assassinate me."

He could hear the note of wariness in her tone and understood her position. After all, she hadn't a shred of proof beyond what she experienced majik-wise and his explanations.

"They wouldn't hesitate," Emrys pressed, leaning forward with both elbows on the table, hands tightly clasped. "You threaten their control over the masses. Your very existence and knowledge would undermine the lies they've shared for generations. The plan is to wait until you are powerful enough to defend yourself against them, until we can properly expose your talents in a large gathering of every nation."

"It would be public knowledge. Proof being shown to every witness so that rumors couldn't be snuffed before it reaches everyone's ears," Sayra mused, chewing on her lip before it clicked. "Your parents want me to participate in the *Grand Proelium*, the *anima* competition between every country."

Emrys gave her an approving nod. "You must. The most abundant population will be present to witness the championship match."

"One year and five months away. Okay. So, Sylven must agree to participate in the Saint Highburn *proelium* next year and win alongside me. We then have to be chosen to represent the monastery in the *Grand Proelium*." She hesitated, her mind struggling to wrap itself around the enormity of what they were asking from her. "And the church? You have evidence of such crimes? Will my role in this be enough to make the other countries revolt?"

"It will be enough to make them question, and from there, we will provide our witness, the informant you'll soon meet with if I can track her whereabouts. We have a handful of people on the inside, but none as credible or as knowledgeable as the woman who gave you majik. When the nations agree to investigate, the church will be forced to permit them access to their underground chambers where they conduct the experiments, women are tortured, and daemons are created. They hold hundreds of people down there, Sayra," he murmured, face pained as he relayed the importance of the undertaking.

"Some have never seen the sun since being born there. Others are half-human, half-daemon hybrids, women torn apart and stitched back together with daemonic limbs. It's gruesome what they are experiment-ing with, a violation of everything my kingdom stands for, and many others once they discover this. Our informant witnessed the atrocities several times and proved it to my parents at the cost of several lives. A story they themselves will explain in detail when you meet them."

Sayra's face contorted in horror and disbelief, her throat working to respond. "I realize this is a lot to ask, but would it be possible to see any of this myself? It's... hard to believe. If I'm to devote my life to this cause,

I'd like to be certain of what I'm standing against when it comes time to sway others to our side."

Her eyes begged for him to understand, and even though Emrys couldn't help but feel a tiny flicker of hurt at her doubt, he couldn't argue her request made sense. Who'd give up everything based on abstract promises with only the guarantee of words? Perhaps a love-struck fool, but Sayra was anything but. Emrys approached life prioritizing a logical pathway, and fortunately, he had already predicted she might make such a request of him.

"My parents have one insider left within the Holy Family's circle. The rest have been purged. I understand how impossible it is to go against everything you've been told is truth, but once you meet our informant, you'll receive the very proof you desire. My parents are pushing up their timelines as it is since you know about your majik. I only ask for your patience until we can arrange a meeting, and your willingness to work with us." Begrudging the fact he couldn't give her answers that would convince her otherwise, he said, "For now, though, I'd be willing to offer a blood oath to solidify my honesty."

Emrys saw the flicker of a shadow deep within her gaze and wished more than anything he could say more. Alas, a blood oath was unbreakable, and all he could do was wait as Sayra blinked away the momentary lapse. Emrys knew she had no reason to trust him. Everything he'd done up until that point could have been a clever ploy with ulterior motives.

In part, it felt like it was. Emrys was beholden to his parents and country. There was much he knew he couldn't share. Not yet. Even though he wanted nothing more than to do so.

There was something between them like a trundle of majik that always seemed to pull Emrys toward her. He wondered if she felt it too.

That connection. Wondered if that was the reason Sayra's countenance changed, her face softening.

"I will take the oath if you swear that all you've shared is not deceitful in any way," Sayra said, her heavy words contradicting her soft tone.

Without hesitation, Emrys drew on his majik, swiftly giving Sayra instructions on the process. He used a small knife to poke the meat of their thumbs, a tiny bead of blood blooming in response. Together, they clasped hands, both bleeding thumbs pressed together. Sayra's hand was lightly calloused, sure and steady.

With a deep breath, she prepared herself. "Do you swear by *juramentum* that all you've shared today with me is true?"

Without hesitation, Emrys said, "I swear by *juramentum* that all I've shared today is true." His expression was deadly serious. "I haven't lied to you. I never will." That part of the oath was freely given. Emrys meant it and would live by it.

Majik snapped between them, a chill-like feeling lacing down his spine. A blood oath was bound by their very blood and impossible to break. In time, they could release the majik from both sides to end the oath, but until then, he was beholden to it. Many would think Emrys reckless, but he'd do it again for Sayra in a heartbeat.

Finally, she rested both hands over his, much to his surprise, and lowered her face until her eyes peered up at him. "I trust in your promise. We will bring the Holy Family down and make them pay for their atrocities. I swear my *spyd* to your cause," she vowed.

In that moment, Emrys wanted to freeze time, the ferocity of Sayra's face captivating him in a way he'd never experienced. Before then, before all the weeks in her presence, he idolized the symbol of her, one that would drastically alter their reality and make her a living legend. Now he had felt drawn to her as if compelled. Every time he neared her, his majik responded as if they were two magnets of opposite poles. Sayra was the only person rivaling his own gift of majik, and somehow, the force sensed it on a fundamental level.

But it was more than even that. She carried herself as if no obstacle could prove troublesome in her path. She acted as if her will would overcome the direst of circumstances. Sayra proved time and time again she would not allow the death in her childhood to squander her spirit. It only forged her into a sharper blade. The world around her seemed to conspire and twist her destiny as they saw fit, but she sat in front of him, unfazed and unyielding as the world tried to melt her down, unaware she would shape it in her own image.

Sayra would conquer all, and Emrys wanted nothing more than to bear witness to her incomparable power. One day, he envisioned those captivating eyes being the last thing the Holy Family saw before they were wiped from the earth.

It meant more than anything Sayra placed her trust in him.

CHAPTER TWENTY-TWO

EMRYS

Emrys found a lead at long last, and as fortune would have it, he could act on it immediately. It had been nearly a week since Sayra had learned all he could share, and her majik already showed signs of improving from the long hours she dedicated to it.

In those first few days, Emrys wanted to unravel the basics of majik with her, spending a minimum of five hours per day practicing. While it left him with scant minutes to find the perpetrator of the dormitory fire, he wasn't willing to leave Sayra in a vulnerable state until she could cast basic defense spells and become more confident in her majik. While he was in class and she was free, he maintained barriers around his room to create a safe place for her to practice minor spells without him. Skipping his classes would have only cast suspicion on himself. But today, Emrys would pursue his lead.

When he began his first year at Saint Highburn's Arcanist Academy, he envisioned the need for insiders. From Vander, he gleaned there were occasional women who snuck in on the arms of individuals with money. Whether it be an Arcanist hailing from a position of power or a high-ranking monk, debauchery seemed to be present in everyone. From his own instructors, Emrys was shown where traveling merchants presented their wares in the Market Hall beside the resident sector of monks, nuns, and other serving staff. From his parents, Emrys was introduced to the expansive network of information thieves who would be at the monastery.

Within months, and after a fateful encounter in the nearby town of Tern, Emrys founded Ophelia Majik Co, a separate entity neither his brother nor parents were aware of to prevent overlap should anyone be exposed. It consisted of three branches. Each division head—Ty of the thieves, Kent of the merchants, and Madam Cassandra of the working women—had valuable intel, summarized from each echelon of society across the globe. The compilation of information their own people gathered and trickled up the chain never ceased to amaze him along with how they managed to worm their way into the Holy Family's business.

Not in-depth, of course. That would take years more, but the surface-level intelligence was worth its weight in pure gold.

For instance, one of Cassandra's ladies overheard a fifth-year Arcanist bragging about a complex mesh spell he pulled off with a third year one night. It was such an impressive feat of majik he couldn't help but share it with her, hoping it would lead to something between them. Little did he know she was in the employ of a spy network, and Emrys was a hound on a trail with the slightest of clues.

Meshing majikal spells between Arcanists was extremely challenging, requiring a mastery of the base spell and control of every aspect of the intention behind it. The fire that consumed Sayra's dormitory wasn't natural, couldn't be tamed by water, and burned at an abnormal rate. A classic dark archetype of majik. The barrier preventing her from escaping was a work of a light-archetype Arcanist, and for it to hold while another's flames burned around it revealed a meshing of intention between the two Arcanists performing each bit of majik.

The last element of the spell casting contained *nefas* majik, otherwise known as forbidden majik. One of those two Arcanists must have used it, causing the spell to be much harder to disarm. That Arcanist was likely dead by now, trading a part of his soul just to make his majik stronger. It left the one surviving Arcanist who spoke with one of Cassandra's working women.

A criminal feat apparently worth sharing at the cost of getting lucky one night.

After his sixth lecture concluded for the afternoon, Emrys hastily departed before anyone could interfere. He despised that both Jax and Catara Zefare saw it fit to lead the *anima* combative class and held a slight suspicion they were watching that particular group with abnormal interest. He wondered at that often, taking extra care when visiting the library to receive coded messages from the staff his parents had in their network, or when visiting the market stalls for fresh quills and other supplies, or when meeting with one particular unnamed Arcanist who happened to have his Valkyrie travel to Tern often to receive and send messages from Ty through their linked bond.

Emrys didn't dare establish any sort of relationship outside of that arrangement. He wouldn't even think of the Arcanist's name to prevent any sort of familiarity between them. Likewise, the other Arcanist was indifferent to Emrys. It may have come across too drastic to some, but to Emrys, every precaution was worth the risk if it meant it would make a difference in the endgame.

Emrys played it all so carefully.

Even then, as he strode down the corridors of the monastery, he maintained his demeanor, Arcanists and staff alike parting around him the moment they saw his sweeping black cloak. While Emrys thought it was silly they paid such respects to him, it did prove convenient when moving around the grounds. He kept to an intentional routine, always visiting the library and market on the same days and times. Plenty of eyes marked his every move, giving his actions the normalcy he required to stay out of the Holy Family's notice.

Ascending the stairwell of his dormitory, Emrys casually rested his book bag on top of the side table in the second-floor common room. Two other Arcanists chatted amicably across from him, barely sparing a glance as Emrys unfolded a notebook to reflect on the day's studies. Leaning back into the velvet cushions, he began his vigil.

He waited. Ten minutes, then twenty. Thirty slowly ebbed into forty. Still, Emrys flipped through his notes.

When fifty minutes had passed, the two other Arcanists retreated into their respective rooms, leaving Emrys to wait alone. Only a few minutes later, he picked up the incoming sound of footsteps, taking care to maintain his composure as a freckled, light-toned Arcanist named Tanner jubilantly whistled by.

The Arcanist never saw Emrys place his notebook into his bag and never heard his steps trailing behind him. Not when he unlocked his room just feet from where Emrys had waited, and certainly not when Emrys set a sound barrier around it.

With a fluid motion, Emrys caught the edge of Tanner's door with the toe of his boot, pushing into the Arcanist's room with ease because of the element of surprise.

"What the f—" Tanner cut himself off, turning as white as a sheet when he saw who locked the door behind him.

That was all Emrys needed.

He dropped his bag, roughly grabbing the collar of Tanner's white long-sleeved academy uniform. With his height and strength, Emrys had no trouble throwing the Arcanist into the wall, then leaning toward him with the calmest expression he could manage. Inside, he wasn't even a semblance of the sort.

"Who put you up to the dormitory fire?" Emrys asked, his reputation threatening enough to the terrified Arcanist before him. There was something in the recesses of his mind that lurked, a darkness that urged him to kill the man where he stood. It whispered to Emrys that Sayra would never be safe with Tanner walking the monastery grounds. It would be all too easy to arrange an unfortunate accident. The thought narrowed his eyes.

The shorter man's fists clenched, his eyes wildly flicking between Emrys's. "You can't hurt me. It will ruin you," Tanner hissed.

A grim smile curved a single side of his mouth. "You gravely misunderstand me. I'm a second son, one who will forever walk in the shadow of my brother." His lips curved further. "The thing about shadows is that we blend into the darkness, obscuring the deeds we must commit for the greater good."

Without uttering a word, Emrys lifted his free hand, tongues of flame licking his fingers.

It was a power move, one that seemed so trivial to any non-majikal person. Any true Arcanist knew what fear that inspired in another lesser user of the arcane arts. Only those with exceptional mastery over an affinity could wield majik without a verbal word of power to guide it. Rather, the caster recited it in his mind. It was typically seen in those ranking within the elite echelons of Arcanists. Even then, it was rarely used due to the wildness such a spell could result in.

Emrys took care to keep the element under tamed perimeters, only using it in the most basic spell he could conjure. What Tanner didn't know was it was a bluff of sorts. The spell was a gamble as he made his move, a high-stakes bet Tanner would believe Emrys's capabilities were far superior.

Yes, Emrys was above the fifth year in capability, but that was the extent of his mastery of unspoken majik. Judging by the raw fear flickering in response to the play, however, Tanner lost.

"You know I can't tell you," Tanner spluttered. His eyes darted toward Emrys's raised hand and the cold detachment in his attacker's eyes.

Emrys evaluated the situation, concluding the Arcanist's words may be truthful if he were sworn to a blood oath. Still, the darkness in the back of his mind urged him to burn Tanner where he stood.

"Take me to the person who ordered you to do it, and I suggest you move with haste, lest I lose my patience." Emrys's brows lowered just so. "But understand if you try anything, I know where your family lives in the Rendevar Coalition."

Tanner's face slackened at the blunt threat.

A brutal edge entered his voice, one Emrys didn't fake. "If you lead me astray, remember the last summer you spent with your ill mother and betrothed sister. If you run or refuse, recall your grandmother, who still runs her weaving shop to support your flagging mother." Pushing off the Arcanist, Emrys waved away the fire. "For they will be your last memories of them."

For a split second, Emrys truly thought the man would run, but when Tanner worked his jaw and nodded once, he saw the defeated resolution in his eyes. Emrys stepped away, unwilling to show the man his back, but when his hand stretched for the doorknob, Emrys didn't foresee what came next.

Tanner bolted but not for the door. His legs carried him swiftly to the back of his room, eliciting a curse from Emrys. He couldn't use majik to stop Tanner. It would be a terrible mistake to leave traces of it. That would lead to an investigation, which Emrys had to avoid at all costs if he wanted to stay low. There wasn't a chance Emrys would scramble after him for naught.

He frowned as Tanner launched himself headfirst out of the second-story window, peeved he'd have to make another visit once the Arcanist was healed.

If he survived. Emrys gave him a fifty-fifty chance that Tanner didn't snap his neck at that angle.

A thud sounded, and by the scream outside, the situation wasn't too pleasant for Tanner. Breathing out his anger, Emrys quickly grabbed his book bag and left the room before any witness could place him there.

He forcibly relaxed his shoulders, smoldering the boiling anger that had threatened his control. With long strides, he crossed the hallway and moved to descend the stairwell with haste.

"Ah, little brother." Vander grinned at him as he halted in front of the entryway. "You know, I've been meaning to touch base after Sylven's acceptance of his circumstances." An amused light shone in his dark eyes.

Keeping from reacting in any manner that could later be used against him, Emrys nodded. "Everything is as it should be."

Clapping his hands together once, Vander appeared pleased. "Excellent. I've grown quite fond of our little spitfire."

Sayra.

Emrys allowed some of his irritation to leak through his expression. "Such commentary is rather inappropriate, don't you think?"

Huffing a laugh, Vander ran a hand up the stairwell railing, his other pocketed into his black trousers. "Oh, you absolutely must loosen up, brother. You appear as if you're about two twists from snapping. May I suggest enjoying some of the delights of the world for once?" He appeared to Emrys as if he had no intention of leaving him be.

"If only I had the time," Emrys replied dryly, moving in such a way that showed his clear inclination to exit.

Vander didn't budge.

"I'm curious. Were you coming to visit me?" His room was further down the hall, but Vander knew very well Emrys wasn't.

He pointedly said, "I'm following up on anything that clues us in to who may be behind certain matters."

"And?"

Emrys took a moment to assess their conversation. Something felt... amiss. "I found nothing," he replied. "Is there something you happen to be concealing?"

Vander mocked a gasp. "How did you know? I kept my rendezvous with Nun Ilia quite secret this afternoon."

Releasing a breath, Emrys just shook his head. Vander was Vander after all. Despite having his own agenda, his elder brother was simple in that sole regard. "If you hear anything of use, please share it at your earliest convenience." He then moved forward, even if it meant colliding with his brother.

Vander sidestepped, passing Emrys with a sly smile. "You know I will. I'm investigating various informants now. It does seem that every nun I explore happens to amount to nothing beyond a good time." Then, as if speaking to himself, he added, "Perchance I should begin to renew my efforts with the kitchen staff. One particular lady is especially attractive."

Shaking his head again, Emrys prayed to the Goddess that for once Vander would pull his weight. It seemed Emrys had to carry it most times.

Even though he was incredibly intelligent, Vander wasted much of his potential on frivolous activities. He was dangerous because he too easily let crucial details slip to the women he wooed or anyone he thought was interesting. One day, Emrys was convinced Vander would ruin all their parents' hard work by accidentally revealing their plans to the wrong person. Or even by trying to have Sayra's timeline moved up. He was as impatient as he was a womanizer.

By the time Emrys arrived at the library—just in the nick of time—he decided he'd further pursue his efforts with Tanner after his upcoming trip to Tern. It was time to prove what more he could to Sayra while the guards in his father's pocket resumed duty on the weekend shifts. Ophelia Majik Co. was the perfect location to start. Upon their return to Saint Highburn Monastery, Tanner, if alive, would be ready for another confrontation. Perhaps the time away would make him sweat more, making him more receptive to telling the truth.

Emrys acknowledged he had lost his composure with Tanner, but the man nearly killed Sayra. That was all the justification he needed.

Chapter Twenty-Three

SYLVEN

Sylven was indeed proud of how he was progressing by blocking his emotions from leaking out. He only wished Sayra would do the same. Concentrating day and night on his studies proved challenging when she'd grow exceedingly frustrated at something or another, her temper varying from exasperated to downright furious as the night passed on. Sure, she was improving but not fast enough for his liking.

From his dorm room, he could sense her proximity, meaning she was likely in Rys's room. Sylven couldn't fathom why he imagined Rys falling for her. She was a torch floating in a pool of lantern fuel, one strike away from lashing out with that abhorrent tongue of hers at all times. When she was constantly becoming irate at whatever it was they were doing, it helped solidify his nonromantic conclusion.

After two more days of enduring Rys and Sayra's clandestine activities, the weekend finally arrived. With his homework turned in, Sylven planned to insist on addressing the matter. Not that he hadn't attempted to do so in the many days that passed. He made a valiant effort that was shrugged off by Sayra's knowing smirks and coy hair flips just to vex him. The Valkyrie was unbearable to the point where it drove him insane.

His only escape was his assignments, so Sylven dove into them headfirst, occasionally with Waylen at his side.

Sayra was, once again, in Rys's room when he returned from his ethics lecture. Knocking on the door, Sylven impatiently tapped his foot. A scuffle sounded from inside before the door cracked open, a long-lashed green eye peering out at him from the small opening.

"Oh, it's just you," Sayra huffed in annoyance, retreating to Rys's table and shutting a small leather-bound notebook. One of Rys's trademark ones. She pretended to fix the sleeve of her heather-colored half-cloak shirt, taking care to not meet his eyes.

It peeved him she pretended to not know it was him. Sylven knew the Old Covenant bond worked both ways, and he sensed where she was at any given time. *Patience*, he told himself.

Closing the door behind him, Sylven searched the room. "Where's Rys?"

Shrugging, Sayra decided not to elaborate. Rather, she tapped her nails in an annoying rhythm on the tabletop.

"Why are you here?" Sylven scowled, praying for the exuberant amount of stamina required to deal with her.

Raising her nose at him, Sayra retorted, "Waiting for Emrys."

Throwing his hands to either side, Sylven barked out, "And why are you waiting for him?" His navy cloak fell to his sides.

"Wouldn't you like to know?" Sayra hummed, the sound of her nails clinking making him want to chuck her out the window. It didn't help that she was excruciating to be around.

"I would actually. Yes," he countered, crossing his arms and glaring at her with every bit of fury he could muster.

Since their second day of classes, Sayra chose to make every interaction with him as tedious as possible. They practiced communication during his fifth lecture, every message from her focused on some negative personality trait of his. So what if he did the same? Sayra had started it. During their combative lecture, she even intentionally allowed the other Valkyrie to whack him.

Hard.

"Say please," Sayra cooed, her expression delighting in his suffering as she lounged with predatory grace across the furniture.

Sylven could have sworn even his ears were red. "Please," he gave in, knowing he couldn't tolerate things for a day more much less a semester. The smugness emanating from Sayra nearly had him storming from the room.

But.

He needed answers for Rys's behavior, not to mention Vander's. The elder brother crossed paths with him in the hall earlier that morn, giving Sylven a chilling smile that left him mulling over just how cunning he could be. If what Rys divulged was true, and he had no reason to assume otherwise, then Vander might continue to lord the information over him as well.

"I can use majik," Sayra informed him, observing her nails nonchalantly.

Taking a steadying breath, Sylven blew out his nose, his last string of tolerance taunt and fraying. "Seriously, Sayra. Rys said you'd be willing to tell me." He stretched the truth just a tad.

Staring at him with a deadpan edge, she held out a palm, face up. "*Flamma.*"

A tiny flicker of flame rose from her hand. It was only two inches high but enough for him to lose his cool. "What. The. *Hell,*" he blurted, dropping into the chair across the table and moving his head up and down to see if there was some device producing the fire.

Negative.

Flame extinguished, Sayra returned to pick at her nails. "I can use majik," she repeated.

"Yeah, no kidding," Sylven exploded, a hand hitting the table as he leaned forward, forcing her to look at him. "What's going on here? Why do you have it? How is that possible?"

He felt like his head was going to burst. Rys's interest in her suddenly made sense. Though that also meant Vander knew, along with his parents, if Rys's oath told him anything.

Sayra explained everything Rys had shared with her, demonstrating her wind affinity when he didn't believe her capable of multiple elemental usage.

"So yeah." Sayra shrugged, but Sylven could feel bitterness radiating through their mental link. "After years of being left in the dark, now I know that I could wield majik all along, that I've been prohibited from doing so until it was convenient for others, and that I've finally been given a modicum of respect since Emrys let me keep the ability to wield majik instead of renewing the seal to block it."

Sylven could barely breathe.

Leaning to one side, Sayra rested the side of her face into her palm. "And now, I have to figure out how I'm going to give up everything I hoped to achieve to fit my future nice and neat into the mold your kingdom's leadership expects of me. All because the Holy Family is manipulating every country around them and torturing acolytes beneath the monastery. They created the evil that's killing off humanity in order to gain wealth and power."

Horror, disgust, and panic rendered Sylven speechless.

Her green eyes bored into his, a knowing glint in them. "Fantastic, isn't it?"

Swallowing, Sylven struggled to prevent his emotions from reaching her. What he had just learned... It defied everything he knew and believed, and it left him questioning himself and his religion. Was it that the Holy Family had twisted the faith, or the Goddess was nonexistent? It couldn't be the latter, not when there was a higher purpose for life and the unseen force that shaped the fabric of their universe into reality.

Right...?

Suddenly, the motive for him to have Sayra as his Valkyrie made sense. She would have been murdered by the Holy Family for failing, which only pissed him off more.

If Rys, or either of his parents, had included him in their plans, then he would have willingly joined forces with them. Hell, he'd have never chewed Sayra out that first day or gone to such lengths to distance himself. Everything he stood for went against partnering with a Valkyrie, yet he would have sacrificed his values and personal beliefs if he had been included.

Then, there were the horrors of the church to face.

Knowing everything made him disgusted at being a student at the academy. The thought of attending classes made him sick. Did all the staff willingly partake in their collective criminal activities, or was it solely the Holy Family and their most trusted inner circle?

He couldn't imagine a criminal ring that horrific being expansive, lest their secret be spilled. Although it seemed whoever the informant was who stole the relic managed to sneak in and gain their trust, leaving with more than just her life. Did he truly want to be a part of that? What would become of his family if they were unsuccessful, or what if the church preemptively discovered their motives and eliminated them?

Sylven could never place them in danger.

After minutes of mulling, Sayra studying her notes all the while, Sylven managed to determine his stance on one matter.

"I won't contest our contract," Sylven managed.

Sayra noted the subtle shift in tone and raised her eyes to meet his. Her narrow shoulders drooped as she leaned back, a hand still holding the binding of Rys's notebook open.

"But I want nothing to do with any of this right now. I don't know what to believe. I just… need time." Sylven backed off a step, holding up his hands. He wanted to hit something, to shout and rage against the unfairness of it all. He knew Sayra could feel everything, but he wasn't in a state to contain it any longer.

Sayra gave him a sympathetic look, which bordered on worry, as he left in a rush. A chair scooted back as the door shut, giving him the impression she was going to follow, but that was exactly what he didn't want. Before she had the opportunity, before Rys walked down the hall, Sylven hastily left the building, searching for anywhere else to go.

His feet brought him to the Arcanist training center. He burst through the doors and turned right. Majik lights flickered on as he strode through the narrow hallway, banners of every noble family who attended the academy lining the long walkway. Blood thudded in his head, and his jaw clenched so tightly he thought a tooth might break.

Sylven's navy cloak, unclasped in the front, billowed around him like a dark gust of wind as he stepped into the empty training room designated for wind affinity Arcanists. The room buzzed with the soft hum of the whirling breeze. It carried the faint scent of ozone and the invigorating freshness of an impending storm. The air seemed to caress his skin, whispering promises of power and freedom. But right then, he wanted none of it.

Inside his trouser pockets, Sylven's hands fished out two pieces of metal.

He slipped on his gauntlets, the metal and fiery rubies flashing on the back of his hands. His eyes took in the circular room. A dome of sapphire crystals scattered a kaleidoscope of refracted majikal light. Runic symbols were etched into the walls to anchor the spell of the wind gently flowing through the space. The runes were in the same language used for majik casting. The Old Language. The runes constructing it made spells semipermanent, similar to the ones used on Valkyries' necks to enhance their abilities.

In the center, a raised dais allowed dark archetype majik-users to train with concentric circles of silver to channel through. Vents were wrapped around the walls and the space above his head. There were logs and metals in a far corner to practice sawing through with wind.

For light archetype wind users, there were dilation fields to practice speeding or slowing objects. Catapults allowed for the teleportation of objects mid-movement, while several ramps and dispersed walkways along the walls let those who could manipulate an object's weight to defy gravity. Suspended dummies were hung throughout as targets. One section hosted a vast array of runic pedestals that held objects of varying sizes. Some were light as a feather, though the heaviest of metal objects weighed over a ton.

There.

"*Commutatio!*" he shouted, throwing his gauntleted hands out toward two columns on either side of himself, each resting a three-hundred-pound metal ball on their curved tops. The impact was immediate, each ball switching locations with little fanfare.

Over and over, Sylven moved heavier objects, every one of them colliding in their new location with a booming *thud*. Sweat dripped along the sides of his face. Still, his rage boiled inside, needing more to satiate it.

"*Celler.*"

Sylven's body moved fast toward the elevated platforms.

"*Pondus amittere.*"

His vision flickered. He became nearly weightless, his left foot pushing from the ground as he bounded between different levels of height. Sylven spun his body, lifting his leg for a roundhouse kick that hit a sandbag dummy squarely in the chest.

Gravity reclaimed him as he leaped back to the cushioned floor. His lungs gasped for air, his knees giving out for a second as his hands released the clasp of his cloak. The material fell to the floor as he forced himself to face the airborne obstacle course once more.

The spells wore off, but with three words, he activated them again. The second time, Sylven rotated his body in the air, landing a devastating blow to the dummy's shoulder. He'd been aiming for its head. By the time he hit the ground, his weight had reclaimed itself more swiftly. Both ankles shot with pain as he landed, his body wobbling. Sylven's vision swam, his hands shaking when he turned toward the obstacle course once more.

His ire hadn't lessened.

"*Celler.*" Sylven sprinted toward the first platform to jump. "*Pondus amittere!*" he yelled, shooting himself off the podium fifteen feet into the air.

The last of his energy gave out, the spell collapsing before he reached the second platform. Sylven's hand darted out, grasping the ledge while his feet connected with the support beam under it. He barely noticed his fingers slipping from the stone as his body fell to the ground.

His back hit the floor hard, his head whipping afterward.

Then, blackness.

Sylven dreamed of being carried through a black mist, words spoken in the distance. He strained to hear them, unable to make heads or tails of the meaning. Breathing in, his head felt as if it were slowly splitting open.

"It was so long ago," someone whispered to him in sorrow. "But it haunts me to this day."

What does? he wanted to ask the voice, one so quiet he strained to listen. But he couldn't form the words.

"When we were attacked by the first daemon. When you stood in front of our carriage, I thought you were safe. But when I turned to see a second daemon racing at you, I put everything I had into getting there first." The woman's voice caught with emotion.

Sylven's chest tightened as he vividly remembered the daemon's claws reaching for his head.

"I wasn't going to make it. I thought you were dead. When you cast that spell and moved out of harm's way, I didn't see you anymore. Instead, I saw the body of my brother getting ripped to shreds in front of me just seconds after he pushed me back into the safety of the wards. He shouted that everything was okay, but as the daemon tore his entrails from his body, I couldn't do anything but watch as the worst, blood-curdling scream sounded from him. Then his friend." Her voice broke.

That sorrow resonated in him, the pain a familiar one.

"It wasn't okay." Something tiny hit his face, trailing down the side. "And it wasn't okay that I failed you either. I thought I lost you. I thought I was watching as another person died because of me."

Something inside of Sylven cracked at that.

The woman's voice was torn as she said at last, "For that, I'm not worthy of being your Valkyrie."

Sylven wanted to reach out, to say something. But all he could see was utter darkness.

"But I'll be damned if I ever let you die. I swear, Sylven, I'll make it up to you, and the two I failed before you. Even if this majik has a different path set for me, I won't abandon my duty to you. Even if it takes the rest of my days and my hell-bound soul afterward."

Blinking, Sylven awoke to a sterile white room.

Angel statues sat in hollow sections of the wall across from where he lay on a plush white cot. His cloak was neatly folded beside him and a partition sheet pulled for privacy on either side of the bed.

Sitting up, Sylven furrowed his brows at the cloak, struggling to reconcile everything that happened.

"Oh! Arcanist Sylven, you're awake." Healer Cheryl smiled as she stopped in front of his bed. In her hands, she carried fresh linens, the white blending with her robes. "I'm glad to see it. Unfortunately, I wasn't able to rid the bloodstains from your shirt collar, but I think some of the staff could bleach them out when they come through to collect laundry. Just leave them a note to let the nuns know."

The fall. The force in which his head hit the ground. Even cushioned, it had hurt like crazy.

Nodding, Sylven said, "Thank you, Healer Cheryl. I must express my gratitude, and please pass my thanks to Arcanist Warden for speeding my recovery." He was the Arcanist who healed students innumerable times when they ran to the infirmary for help.

The elderly woman nodded. "You're fortunate to have such a reliable Valkyrie." She started walking off. "Take care now." Her kind voice disappeared as she began her chores.

Sayra had helped him. That was her voice that spoke in his dreams. But they weren't dreams at all, he realized.

Looking down, Sylven pulled his collar forward, his eyes raking the pool of red that stained the fabric. Slowly, he lowered his hand, picking up his cloak instead with a white-knuckled grip. He swallowed hard, closing his eyes tightly as Sayra's words repeated through his head.

Never had he felt so low in his entire life.

CHAPTER TWENTY-FOUR

SAYRA

The expanse of steel-fortified, forty-foot stone walls surrounding Saint Highburn Monastery was an incredible sight from afar. They safeguarded a sizable plateau hosting the majority of the monastery grounds, weaving up and down mountainsides with dozens of towers and spires rising far above its confines. Low-hanging clouds often concealed the top-most levels of the cathedral itself, an elaborately carved marble mastery positioned at the ground's highest point. Sayra eyed the dozens of hollowed-out sections of the cathedral wall, which contained statues of angels, and she raised her sights to the peal of bells high above in a tower.

Twinkling stars shed scant light over the monastery, a full moon providing much detail to the surrounding snow-clad forest far below. It was in those moments Sayra truly appreciated the serenity of the surrounding lands. They were breathtaking. A gorgeous feast to look at for any who cherished nature.

Several hours had passed into her shift with Kimimari, and she found herself reflecting on her time in Faenda. "Do you miss it? Droden?" she asked, her boots lightly clanking across the stone. Majik lighting radiated from metal fixtures along the wall, recently renewed in strength from a monk's spell.

Out of the corner of her eye, Sayra caught her friend shrugging. The metal gleamed on Kimimari's shoulders, her long black hair wound tightly into a bun. "Not much. I send a sizable portion of our monthly pay back there to help Tori and Huya cover expenses for the others." At Sayra's inquisitive expression, she sighed. "Even though they are awful adoptive parents, I want the others to have better options than I did."

A corner of Sayra's mouth rose as she lightly shook her head. Kimimari was too good for those people. None of her family were blood-related, and none of them bothered to pretend. While blood certainly didn't make a family, as proven by Sayra's cadre of sisters in all but blood, it was pathetic how little Kimimari's family tried when she was growing up. Her parents all but ignored her, and the siblings outcasted her due to their stark differences in personality. All four of the others were the outgoing sort. The second eldest, Lunri, sought prestige and wealth and eventually found a position as an assistant to a Droden political figure.

Sayra snickered many a time that Lunri likely found many suggestive positions with her superiors.

The others weren't as conniving, but they also sought greater heights than their low status permitted in the poor sector of the empire. The two brothers wanted to pursue academia, while the last sister desired to open a pastry shop and currently practiced at home whenever coin could be spared. Despite years of barely being spoken to, years of getting leftover necessities after her siblings were cared for first, and years of sacrificing so the others could stand a chance, Kimimari wanted her siblings to succeed. Sayra wasn't too surprised her friend shared what extra coin she had with them.

Out of their cadre, Kimimari was the most forgiving and selfless. Within their first week as acolytes, Sayra had been severely lacking in the strength category and maintained a distance from the others in her class. Only Lynn clung with her during meals and downtime. Lynn was incredibly social, however, eventually making strides to chat with others. After a particularly brutal combative class, Sayra skulked to the back of their dining hall and violently stabbed every vegetable on her plate.

Mere minutes later, Kimimari lowered her dinner beside hers, and a quiet voice asked if she'd like to train after-hours. Sayra despised losing, and it wasn't long before Kimimari's weight training improved her physical capabilities. They worked tirelessly. And without her help, Sayra wouldn't have been patrolling with Kimimari that evening. The thought caused her to frown, a chill racing down her spine at the alternative. Knowing what lay beneath the monastery, and what her failure would have led to, Sayra owed Kimimari her life.

"They are fortunate to have you," Sayra said, a rare smile crossing Kimimari's face at her comment. "As am I."

Sayra meant it. With every fiber of her being.

"Don't go soft on me now," Kimimari replied, though her face was pleased.

They continued in silence, a normal practice between the two of them. Even with the truth of the Holy Family lording over Sayra every day, she couldn't help but feel a sliver of peace. No matter what happened, she was grateful to have her sister-in-arms there with her. From Lynn's contagious cheerfulness, Ness's unwavering convictions, and Kimimari's endeavoring perseverance, Sayra knew they could face anything. When the day came Sayra could finally share everything, she knew without a shadow of doubt they'd fight alongside her.

What had Sayra done to earn such people in her life? Whatever it was, she was eternally grateful.

Metal clanked upward in the stairwell mere meters from them, a platinum bun surfacing as the Valkyrie crested the wall. Sayra's heart stilled in her chest at the sight of who was once her revered role model. Her fingertips dug into the leather over her palm as she forced a respectful bow. "Sanctus Catara."

Beside her, Kimimari did the same but with light in her eyes. Reverence.

Just a week ago, Sayra shone with that same reverence for Catara. But she couldn't help but feel a fool. The Holy Family had come across as idealistic to all. When established, they single-handedly united almost every country against the Horde and constructed a way to combat them with Valkyries and Arcanists alike when all else crumbled. Acacea and Droden had been in frequent skirmishes along their border, while Zendiya had a civil war tearing the fabric of their country apart at the seams. The southern countries were divided between taking sides, peace a foreign concept to all. But when Sayra saw Catara turn her attention to them, all she could think about were the lies they had founded their principles on. She lived under her enemy's roof and worked alongside them.

"Valkyrie Sayra, Valkyrie Kimimari," Catara greeted, a hand resting casually on the hilt of her artfully carved sword. "How go your patrols?"

"Smooth and uneventful, Sanctus Catara," Kimimari informed her.

It was different for Sayra, being close to one of the Holy Family outside of her joint combative class with Sylven. There, she wasn't required to interact directly with them and could act normal. Her nerves felt jumpy while out on patrol, heart beating into a frantic rhythm. Logically, Sayra knew Catara didn't know about her majik. If the Valkyrie did,

Sayra would have since disappeared, along with all the others who had fallen prey to their nefarious deeds.

Still. What if Sayra gave something away? What if Catara was feeling out a tentative suspicion?

"Bless the Goddess," Catara said, eyeing them both with a polite smile before resuming her rounds.

A slow breath escaped Sayra's nose, her feet flagging as Kimimari resumed their path. As they continued, though, Sayra felt as if they were being watched. It was an eerie prickling on her neck. Perhaps it was idiotic, but she turned to see if her intuition was correct.

All she saw was a confident figure striding away from them, indifferent to Sayra's internal anxiety. Shaking her head, she caught up with Kimimari, waving away the look of curiosity her friend shared.

As the patrol concluded, Sayra felt relieved at the notion of sleep. It was entirely possible she'd been devoting too much time to training and was over-exhausted. By the time they turned into their dormitory, Sayra couldn't help the fatigued daze that clouded her mind. Somehow, she made it into her guest bed in Nessika's room, barely discarding her armor before falling fast asleep.

⁕

The next morning—hardly a handful of hours later—Sayra was relieved when restorations had been completed on her floor, finally moving her belongings back with the help of Nes the minute a nun alerted the Valkyries. It was unusually tense between them, a feeling Sayra was unaccustomed to from her friend. It wasn't until her trunk was snuggly secured beside her bed's end that she turned to address the assumptions Nes garnered from Sayra's days and nights of sneaking around with

Emrys. As Nes turned to leave without a word, Sayra's hand on her shoulder halted her exit.

"Nes, please. Can we talk about this?" Sayra sighed, stepping back when Nes turned to face her. It killed her she couldn't be honest, but there had to be something she could do in the meantime to mend things.

Nes raised her head. "About what?" She wasn't going to make things easy.

"Emrys," Sayra said, the one word conveying it all. "I know it appears bad. But I promise, Nes, there isn't anything going on between us romantically."

Nes's face went slack, and Sayra recognized the telltale sign of her impending explosion.

Quickly, Sayra continued, "I respect that vow we made all those years ago, and I haven't betrayed it. I know what it is I stand for, and I am true to that."

And Sayra was. When their inner circle grew, so did their dedication. With each other. With their cause. Sayra would never forget that summer night when they discovered their classmate, Vena, had been cast from the Valkyrie Academy under dishonorable circumstances. Rumors circled swiftly, ranging from her poor performance and grades to her flippant disregard for authority. Their instructors clarified she'd had clandestine meetings with an Arcanist. Such deviances disgraced the very foundation Valkyries were ingrained with. Granted, they said it in a much more polite way, saying she strayed from the morals and values Valkyries were supposed to uphold, but the acolytes all got the point.

It never crossed any of their minds to break curfew and try to flirt with the boys. Even so, when Nes had been disturbed by the whole ordeal, Sayra swore they would hold each other accountable and never date a guy. Their sole purpose was for the greater good, and neither would allow such impulses to muddy their Goddess-given duty. Though Sayra still didn't harbor a shred of religious faith, the vow was kept close to her heart all the same.

Scoffing, Nes smiled in a malicious way. "You're lying. How would I know, you think?" She angrily propped a hand at her waist, a single finger held from the others. "There has only been one time, Sayra. *One time* when I ever felt Emrys's emotions through our link."

Bewildered and frustrated at her friend's lack of belief in her motives, Sayra folded her arms and prepared to weather the storm.

"That night of the dormitory fire, I felt everything crystal clear from the moment he discovered you were in danger and let his block slip. No one, especially not a prince in another country's government, would care that much for another Arcanist's Valkyrie if he weren't head over heels," Nes bellowed, her voice passionate with her belief in her friend's betrayal.

At those words, Sayra went still, the realization dawning belatedly.

"He was *terrified*. A prince, who hardly reacts to anything, scrambled here and dispelled the majik for *you*. Rather than helping anyone else, he ran to retrieve *you*, letting Sylven care for Kimimari." Nes laughed, her hand running through her short strands. "When you were safe, his only care was for your well-being, even after all the self-loathing from your words that night."

Sayra's chest hurt, and her lips pressed into a thin line.

"Tell me, why else would he devote every night to you? To go as far as to ensure I knew there was nothing clandestine?" Nes questioned.

Sayra completely understood her disbelief, her frustrations. But even the answer Sayra wanted to share, the one barely hanging on the tip of her tongue and ready to spill, wouldn't have fully satisfied Nes. Once Sayra could have justified it all. There wasn't any emotional aspect of their arrangement. However, knowing what Nes had felt brought a different perspective to the situation. One where Emrys had likely kindled an emotional attachment beyond that of an interested party looking out for her general welfare.

And Sayra couldn't explain it, but there was something—a thread between them—that pulled her to trust and confide in Emrys. It wasn't entirely romantic in nature, but something *more* caused her to gravitate in his direction when he was around. It was a sixth sense that prodded her when he was nearby, and that bizarre connection was a huge reason she felt compelled to place her faith in his motives.

She couldn't deny there was a flicker of something like butterflies in her stomach at Nes's words. Emrys seemed to have feelings for her, and as juvenile as it sounded, Sayra couldn't help but realize she might return the sentiment. There were moments his features stilled in such a serious way when he wasn't looking at her. She had stolen many a glance to admire that face, wondering what thoughts would cast such burdens upon him.

He'd given her his cloak that night of the dormitory fire, something she couldn't help but be grateful for. The smell of juniper and traces of vetiver had masked some of the smoke-tinged air and stuck with her the following day.

Emrys had disobeyed his parents, the king and queen of Acacea, to allow her to practice her majik. And when he had laughed with her, the sound completely stole her attention.

No. What was she thinking? She was a Valkyrie for *dritt's* sake. Sayra couldn't be thinking such thoughts, and she had to assure her friend of that.

She shook her head, her body suddenly feeling the lack of many nights of sleep. "If he truly feels that way, Nes, it's unrequited." After returning from majik training, Sayra had focused solely on her physical workouts, always making it a priority to upkeep her strength and stamina. She regretted it, not feeling emotionally up to par for the conversation or where it might lead.

"Every single night you leave early and come back late, Sayra. Why then?" Nes interrogated, her head jutting forward. Shadows lined her high cheekbones and narrow jaw. "Emrys is silent on the matter, and I can't fathom any reason why you'd be with him."

Sayra played with her braid, attempting to figure out some way to explain things but coming up woefully empty. "Nes, I swore I wouldn't share the reason. It's beyond me, but can't you take my word that it isn't romantic in nature?" Her heart was no longer in the right place to continue the discussion.

Nes backtracked, swinging Sayra's door wide. "Maybe not on your end, maybe not yet, but Emrys certainly feels that way." The door started closing before she paused, pushing it wide once more to face Sayra. "I don't understand when we started to withhold secrets from one another. At least Lynn had the guts to tell everyone." Her icy, accusatory eyes struck deep before they departed.

Sayra wanted nothing more than to curl up in her bed and forget her training for the day. If it was only her own pathetic life she had to be concerned with, she wouldn't hesitate. Her eyes clenched closed under tightened brows, stinging from the burden on her shoulders and the debt she owed. The life she lived was because of her brother's death and the death of Lynn's brother so many years ago. The way she threw herself into her training with reckless abandon was because she had to, for them, become worthy of their sacrifice. She held a whole continent's future on her shoulders.

Would her friends also be sacrificed along the way? Would they ally with the church as they were instructed to, betraying her in the process?

And how would she manage everything given there was more to Emrys's mentorship than she originally thought?

Nes's claim wasn't entirely unfounded. Sayra was forced to acknowledge that when the traitorous corner of her mind whispered she cared for Emrys in a similar manner. It was awkward thinking of it, but mainly because Sayra knew she couldn't address it with Emrys without revealing her kindred thoughts.

She squared her shoulders, wiping away her concerns with the mindset that one who owed so much could not dwell on selfish inhibitions. With that in mind, she left for Emrys's room to endure yet another day's worth of majik training and night of weight training.

A familiar face left another room the moment Sayra was passing, and her decency got the better of her. "Netta," Sayra acknowledged, her eyes marking the arm the Valkyrie held at an odd angle.

She planned on doing the right thing, but it didn't staunch the pure joy Sayra had felt after cleverly enacting swift revenge outside the very same gymnasium where Netta and her friends had ambushed her. Granted it was only Netta who had been present, Sayra had managed to twist her arm and lock her into a chokehold. While it wasn't nearly as brutal as the hurting Netta and her hags inflicted on Sayra, it was enough for what little time Sayra had to work with. Once it was over, Netta had passed out in a heap, and Sayra swaggered back to her dormitory.

The burley Valkyrie blanched for a moment, her uninjured arm flinching before her body grew stiff. Netta's tilted ebony eyes were uncertain, weighing Sayra's presence to see if she was there for another round. "Sayra," she grumbled, looking back to the room she came from.

While Sayra reveled in the sight, a grimmer, more pressing matter had her mind reluctantly casting away the childish revenge. Albeit reluctantly. "This feud must end," she said, meeting her longtime adversary square in the face. Despite the years of being bullied by the woman, years of verbal threats and excessive physical force during training, Sayra didn't want the brutality of what lurked below the monastery for Netta. She wouldn't wish that on anyone.

Silence hung between them, Netta's mouth slipping into a slight scowl. "Yevette and Jayde have been avoiding me because of you." Her eyes narrowed down at Sayra, a hint of anger tracing the severe lines of her square face.

Another Valkyrie named Imani took a single step out of her room before realizing there was a standoff before her. Without hesitation, she turned back and closed the door behind her, wanting nothing to do with them.

Understandable.

Sayra knew she had a newfound reputation among the Valkyries. After flouncing Netta and her posse one by one, the trio since suspiciously quiet, it went without saying Netta's rumor of Sayra starting the fire was conjecture. A handful of other rumors warned students to remain firmly in Sayra's good graces. Despite that, Sayra knew Netta would cling onto any slight made against her.

Sayra really should have brought the feud to blows much sooner to end their petty rivalry. It brought her a plethora of cathartic emotions to hear how isolated Netta had become after everyone learned of her lies. Which, ironically, were all true or partially true, but she needn't share that.

It sucked having to be the bigger person.

"You threatened my life," Sayra said matter-of-factly. "Any other person would have likely done more, but I'm prepared to put all of that behind us so we can perform as expected as Valkyries. We are acolytes no more, Netta. We owe what fight we have in us to the greater good."

A rough laugh escaped her twisted lips, Netta's expression becoming distant as her face turned away. "I hate you for that. For this. I hate that you're right, and I hate that you had the gall to say it first." Her fists clenched. "When we arrived at the Valkyrie Academy as acolytes, I knew if I had any chance to make a name for myself, I'd have to take down the greatest threat to my position." Her cold eyes met Sayra's. "You. You're a legacy, your mother being a legendary Valkyrie and all. Out of our entire class, you were the only one with that advantage."

That was what it was all about? All the years of endless backstabbing and undermining? And what did that say about Sayra that she didn't question Netta's motives before then? That she concluded the woman to be a simple *dritt*? It seemed Sayra underestimated the hulking brute before her, even if only a smidge.

"Growing up, my parents demanded that I let nothing stand in my way, and I learned that removing whatever obstacle tried to stop me turned out to be highly effective. For years, it worked. I was almost first in our class. In the end, I lost to your entitlement. Whatever bargain you made with the Holy Family, whatever strings they pulled to see you succeed, it worked. It seems I'll never overcome something out of my control," Netta said, a hand plucking at the fabric of her black training uniform.

For the first time, Sayra felt a tiny pool of empathy for the Valkyrie before her. Netta had no idea of the scope of things or just how out of her league she was. She didn't understand that by ending the feud, Sayra was saving her life. But there was a grudging comprehension growing in Sayra of just who Netta was, and she wasn't terribly different from herself.

"Don't misunderstand me, Sayra," Netta growled, a large finger jutting out with promise. "I hate you still. I hate your privilege and how others crawl at your feet. I will never be one of them, and one of these days, I'll beat you fairly. The only regret I have is stooping lower than my title allows. Everyone will see that I'm the better Valkyrie one day."

Sayra lowered her chin, her eyes shining with the challenge. On Netta's surface, she found the reflection of herself staring back at her. When Netta moved to leave, Sayra didn't bother to go after her.

A deep voice echoed from down the hallway. "Until that day comes, don't you dare die to some measly daemons. I have a name to make for myself."

Sayra watched as Netta slunk away, stunned by the admission of the scorned Valkyrie. She felt something resolve inside her chest. Something deep. Inhaling, she also felt accomplishment, knowing Netta was out of harm's way. Not hers by any means but out of Catara's. Sayra simply had to be on her best behavior.

Chapter Twenty-Five

SAYRA

Returning to Emrys's room, Sayra found the Arcanist absent. She trusted in his promise it was safe to practice majik within his walls and set to it as the hours passed. Later that night, she nearly left to search for Sylven, but she stopped herself due to his clear distaste of her.

He wanted time to himself, and she would respect that so long as he stayed out of any more trouble. It was quite the amount of dire information for him to learn in a handful of minutes, and she'd be lying if she said she wasn't concerned. Especially since he went and injured himself so badly after learning about it all.

Sayra looked down at the notebook spread across Emrys's table without really seeing any of the words. Her fingertips curled on her lap.

The accident had terrified her.

Sylven blocked out most of his emotional turmoil until the very end. When Sayra felt it, she went searching for him, but by then, he had fallen. Sayra felt his pain and then... nothing. She practically broke down the doors, and when she saw his head bleeding so profusely, she didn't hesitate to rush him to the infirmary.

She cast basic healing spells to close up the worst gash, but her majik was far too weak to heal any internal damage. Besides, she couldn't very well explain the blood if she had healed him too well.

It pissed her off how reckless he'd been, but even more so that Sayra felt like she couldn't do anything right when it came to Sylven. The words of apology had spilled from her. Thankfully, he was out cold and would never know about that moment of weakness. Sylven needed a strong Valkyrie, not some emotional wreck.

In the end, she was relieved when the Arcanist who healed Sylven said all would be fine. So, she folded his cloak beside him and left before bothering him any further.

Emrys made his appearance as she attempted to study. Sayra brushed off the notion of his affection and concentrated on her work. She could only focus on maintaining the facade, which meant gluing her sights to the words, lest she give away she knew more than she should. But it took a monumental effort. Over and over, Sayra cast every spell Emrys listed within a small protective bubble. It was pitiful just how weak they were from her wards to her flickering candlelit flames. But Emrys swore it took repetition and practice to cast specific spells and increase their effectiveness.

A majority of Arcanists only began practicing within short, heavily regulated bursts at Saint Highburn's Arcanist Academy. Their first year was exceedingly slow, focused on theory and core curriculum. They were given one class to practice basic majik. Much to Sayra's dismay, it would take months of concurrent and tedious spellcasting to catch up to a suitable degree of proficiency.

The next morning was much the same. Scant hours of sleep, majikal practice, and ignoring all other matters that tried to impose on her concentration. It wasn't until noon she remembered she had plans, completely scattering her attention and sending her into a guilt spiral.

"I completely forgot I had a matter to attend to with my friends," Sayra said, shooting up from Emrys's table and pocketing the notebook.

He held out a stilling hand. "We must depart by one o'clock if we are to make it there by nightfall. It's in the Astor duchy, fairly close to the border of Droden. You'll meet me at the front gate by then?" he asked, lifting his head from a paper he was currently working on.

"Shouldn't be a problem," Sayra said with a nod of confirmation. "Did you inform Nes already?"

They'd be traveling without her friend to be less conspicuous since Sylven had no interest in tagging along. With just the two of them, they wouldn't need a carriage for such a short turnaround, and they'd make excellent time. But Sayra could only imagine what Nes must have thought.

"Yes," Emrys said in that solemn way of his. "She knows to keep it in confidence. I'll remind Sylven of our departure."

Declining her head in response, Sayra left and hastily made her way to Lynn's room, the corridor surprisingly alive with Arcanists and Valkyries traversing the halls during the weekend break. Words flew by, some pertaining to assigned patrols and others about which monk was the most challenging to learn from. By the time she arrived, everyone was already laughing and chatting away inside her friend's room, her knock answered by Lynn squealing out her name excitedly.

Stepping in, Sayra immediately felt Nes's burning stare. She acted as if things were normal between them and gave her a brief smile. A trying feat. "Sorry I'm a bit late," she apologized, happily returning Lynn's bear hug before she was yanked in the direction of a free seat beside Kimimari.

Lynn had recently moved a rectangular floral-clothed table into the center of her room, just over a soft, rose-colored rug. Nes and two empty seats sat across from her and Kimimari.

"Please don't worry!" Lynn grinned, her eyes shining more than usual, and her feet practically bouncing toward Casber.

Kimimari shot her a knowing look, her own face slightly uneasy. Sayra felt bad for her friend, the Valkyrie never having been comfortable in the presence of guys and always a tad on the awkward side. Much like Sayra's upbringing, it was either marriage or pursuing the Valkyrie title for Kimimari. On the fortunate side of things, at least the ratio was in her favor to not have to marry.

The walls were decorated with dried floral arrangements, Lynn's hobby on full display above her dresser, around her bed, and beside her window. It was all similarly structured to Sayra's own room. A cherry-blossom candle flickered on her dresser, the smell making Sayra take a deep breath.

Casber appeared out of place, constantly repositioning his feet and twitching his hands. He had an overcompensating propensity to smile or laugh at everything. Still, it was endearing for Sayra to see similarities between him and Lynn in the sense they both wanted others to like them but also feared they'd be automatically shunned. At first glance, they seemed to mesh well.

He was of average height, Sayra noted, and his wide smile was genuine. Between his longer-than-usual, wavy honey-brown hair, similarly shaded eyes, and rounded jawline, he had a face that could get him out of tricky situations. Sayra wondered if he'd be willing to help her pull a not-so-terribly-harmless prank on Netta.

"Sayra, meet Casber." Lynn held a hand toward him.

Sayra smiled politely, still imagining ways she could work him into her mischievous plans. "It's nice to meet you."

Pulling a chair back, Casber sat. Lynn draped her arms around his shoulders from behind his seat. "It's been great meeting everyone," he beamed, winking in Lynn's direction when she moved to kiss his cheek.

Kimimari winced, but no one else seemed to notice.

"You were telling us about your homeland," prompted Lynn, still hugging her man.

Even Sayra was a tad uncomfortable.

"Yendire is quite small, much like Faenda," Casber resumed, his cherub face lighting up. "Though the monarchy there is quite loose. It's more of a constitutional one where the parliament holds petitioning power. The landscape is remarkably flat and windy on the best of days."

As Casber continued his descriptions of the tiny kingdom and its economic proficiencies with the mining industry, Sayra hated to admit it, but her mind kept wandering. Kimimari asked a polite question, inciting further explanations on what manner of ore they mined. Nes ignored Sayra's presence the entire time, but Lynn and Casber more than compensated. She was pleasantly surprised at his interest, perhaps even a tad flattered, when he brought up her renowned skill with the *spyd*.

Sayra decided to return the favor after all the flattery. "I've noticed your skill during our combined combative class. You and Lynn make a great team," she said, somewhat wistful but happy for the two of them. It made her long for easier days, the majority where her primary focus was being a Valkyrie and not a clandestine Arcanist. Since she was both, what did that technically make her?

A mess probably.

"Thanks, Sayra." Lynn smiled, plopping into her chair beside Casber and holding his hand dotingly.

"We spend extra time outside of lectures practicing," Casber said, jerking his thumb toward the combative field. "Speaking of, did you get that scar from your training here? I've heard rumors of how intense it can be."

Beside her, Kimimari gave Sayra a reassuring sideways glance.

Sayra knew he meant well, and it wasn't a jab, but regardless, an inner part of her always recoiled when it was mentioned. While her friends knew its origin, it wasn't a tale she shared lightly. By that, she meant only three people outside of her family were aware. Even Lynn gave her an apprehensive glance, an apology flickering in her eyes at his candor. Which meant she hadn't shared the day they both lost someone with Casber, prompting Sayra to wonder just how deep their relationship went.

Nes only pursed her lips at Sayra.

"Something like that," she deflected, rising from her seat upon seeing the clock. "I'm sorry to spend such a short time here, but I have something important I must take care of." Casber's eyes grew wide, understanding he broached a personal subject, but Sayra quickly put his mind at ease. "You haven't offended me in the least, Casber. So long as you take good care of Lynn, you and I are good in my book."

Relieved, he shook her offered hand as goodbyes were exchanged, and Sayra departed for the monastery's gate. Nes's farewell was neutral, the slight sending a pang through Sayra's chest. She couldn't comprehend why Emrys wouldn't permit the information to be shared with his own Valkyrie. Did he not trust her? The prince sure didn't seem the type to let many in.

In public, he was stoic and quiet, his presence not detected by sound but rather by the inherent confidence he exerted. Even then, standing beside one midnight-black steed and a bay, the guards gave him deferential nods as they passed, the stableboy respecting the distance between them. But when they were together, just the two of them, the shift was prominent. Relaxed was the best word to describe Emrys; he smiled and even permitted a slight slouch as he diligently worked on his papers. Sayra knew it wasn't a side he shared with many other people.

She wouldn't ever repeat the words out loud, but he fascinated her in a new way. Whereas many saw him as a second prince, she knew him as someone who cared deeply about his passions. There was a night when Emrys completed his studies for the evening, just one where Sayra declined his assistance for spell work afterward. A part of her wanted those short moments where he neared, her nose picking up the complex traces of his scent. An intricate balance of juniper, black pepper, and vetiver, it was something she had begun to associate with the two locations on his body where she knew he applied it. One at the base of his neck, and another near his left wrist. Both places conveniently close to well-built muscle. Places she didn't dare let her eyes linger on. Sayra was a Valkyrie after all and had to be above noticing such things.

But the other part of her desired to see what exactly it was the dark prince, known as Emrys Navarre, did in his spare time, and she wasn't disappointed.

Days prior, Sayra had watched as Emrys withdrew a thick leather-bound notebook from a desk drawer, a metal clasp secured around its middle. Sayra paused in her incantation, eyeing the newfound development with profound interest as he carefully unfolded it across the polished wood of his desk. In it, various sketches of incredibly elaborate contraptions were artfully displayed, lines of worded descriptions and other notes sprawled across the margins.

Inventions.

At least, that's what Emrys revealed when he noticed her prolonged staring. He shared that one day he'd like to create new methods of living for those who didn't have the resources of majik at their disposal. Products that allowed for light beyond the wick and wax of a candle or a majikal spell. Before Sayra could begin her barrage of questions, Emrys reminded her she required focus for her own studies. It was one of those rare moments where his lips curved just so, the slight tilt of his head casting shadows across the strong panes of his face. Reluctantly, she returned back to her spell work, but occasionally she snuck a glance at the latest swipe of his penmanship.

Sayra knew she shouldn't be recalling those memories, especially when they were about to embark on a journey together. But thinking of it all just made her realize how she subconsciously had begun to harbor feelings for him. She'd been so blind.

When Emrys's eyes shot to hers, she saw the darkness in them lighten, his posture relaxing a hair under his thick cloak as he offered a hand to help her mount. Sayra raised a brow at that, a teasing take on her upturned mouth.

"I daresay I've had more riding experience than you, but out of courtesy and my undying admiration for the prince of Acacea, I shall accept your hand with a maidenly curtsy." Sayra gave him a mischievous smile, dipping low into a graceful bow and taking his gauntleted hand with her leather-gloved one. It was much easier to work the *spyd* with leather over metal.

"'Undying admiration'? I didn't know I garnered such sentiments," Emrys mused, eyes crinkling slightly.

Mounted, Sayra adjusted her hood, already pulled low, so none of the patrolling guards would notice it was a blonde Valkyrie leaving with the prince instead of his own. The cloak covered the Astor family crest on her armor.

If a Valkyrie was with an Arcanist, most guards didn't mind if they left to visit the nearby city of Tern on weekends. It was an easy distance to make during the daytime. Safe so long as people were prepared. If anyone died, it would have to have been out of sheer stupidity.

It also helped that the current guards on duty were all in with Emrys's family.

Sayra mocked a look of surprise. "The flocks of ladies don't express such things as they fall at your feet?" Their steeds exited through the massive gates, the guards closing them as they trailed down the snow-slicked pathway to the valley below. The afternoon sun shone brightly on her white cloak, her new set of armor occasionally reflecting a glimmer of light when she loosened the cloak to be comfortable. "Or is it that you don't notice such tedious gestures?"

Emrys smiled slyly as his eyes scanned the forest below. His expression told her he was very much aware of the nuns, staff, and even a handful of Valkyries who paid him more than his fair share of attention.

When they reached the main path, Emrys began his usual training lectures on majik. They directed their horses when the trail split in a handful of directions, though each was clearly labeled. Travel was much swifter without a carriage. After hours of passing undulating hills, they would eventually give way to the flats near Sylven's family lands if they turned off the main trail.

They passed over the duchy wards next. The city walls of Tern rose soon thereafter, and they met no resistance except for the occasional chilled wind. Slowing, Emrys signaled for Sayra to draw near, his hood remaining tucked over his head.

"When we pass through the security gate, strive for an inconspicuous persona. I don't have any guards here under my parents' allegiance to keep our travel secret. If someone outside of those we intend to interact with remembers us at a future time, we've failed," Emrys said, his inflection serious. Onyx eyes drifted toward her face. "Keep your hair tucked and face down if you're able. You'll stand out without a doubt here."

He gave her a smirk.

"Do they not have people with lighter eyes and hair? Faendans aren't the only ones with such traits," Sayra asserted with a challenging tilt of her head.

Emrys faced the oncoming gateway, his expression concealed from her as he quietly said, "That's not what makes you stand out from the others."

A warm tingle buzzed through her as she took in his silhouette in earnest, hating to admit it but finding him... attractive. Emrys always had been, but it was never a detail she strove to pay mind to. It was terrifying to confess to herself because it was the last complication she ever wished for.

Sayra was a Valkyrie regardless of the fact she possessed the capacity to summon majik from the earth's lines of power. She had a duty to focus solely on Sylven and not be distracted by one of his friends and his robust shoulders, clever intellect, and carved facial features. Not to mention the feeling of his hand on hers earlier...

Taking a deep breath, Sayra dashed the intrusive thoughts from her mind, pulling her hood low as Emrys requested. That night, she'd allow herself to forgive those thoughts. She meant what she told Nes the other day, and she had no intention of backtracking just because she learned of his affection for her. Certainly not because Sayra felt she *might* return the sentiment.

Guards flagged them forward, seemingly uncaring of who was entering their sizable city during the peacetime between nations. War hadn't prevailed for decades, the treaty afterward permitting free travel throughout the continent. Only Zendiya was reluctant to the notion, their culture a secretive and wary one. Currently, the only threat posed to the union of countries beyond daemonkind was the eastern continent of Thapula, a lawless land of machinery devoid of the Goddess's blessing. Though Sayra recognized that was the Holy Family's doing with their harvest and distribution of stolen majik.

A small amount of coin passed between Emrys and the town's horsekeeper, extra gold pressed firmly into the owner's hand to ensure their privacy. One nod confirmed their deal, and the reins passed from Sayra's leather-clad to his calloused hands. A nagging thought reoccurred in her mind as they trekked down the main street, her armor sticking out like a sore thumb. Emrys had assured her earlier it wouldn't be the case. Every city paid a yearly fee to the church for Valkyrie protection. The higher the sum, the greater amount of Valkyries present. Given the close distance to the monastery, Valkyries traveled through Tern frequently, especially considering supply and trade lines ran through the area from Droden before branching off into Acacea and vice versa. It was the only comforting thought as her metal boots passed through the thin layer of snow, occasionally reflecting a glare of light.

Double-storied cobblestone buildings created narrow alleyways between them, but a single wide street ran through the city center. Lanterns were already lit, citizens milling under them as flecks of snow dwindled from the heavens. Businesses were calling out their wares, and some evocative women beckoned from the shadows of tavern signs, heavily made up with scandalous clothing peeking out from folds and twists of fabric. Sayra accidentally made eye contact with one suggestively smiling at her.

"We service women too," the harlot catcalled. An appreciative whistle sounded as they passed.

Disgusted, Sayra's face remained locked to the ground behind Emrys's feet, careful not to trip over any protruding stones. A few men and many women clinked ales within warmly lit but rowdy taverns, women dressed in tight-fitted frocks whisking away empty mugs and returning with ones foaming over the top to cheering customers. A few merchant shops remained active along the strip, those that were serving a late-night meal or selling antique wares. Occasionally, they'd pass a staggering drunk or a group of partying youths, the world vastly different than the monastery.

Clotheslines hung between buildings, and smaller shops' signs were draped along the winding alleys. Sayra's awareness was on full alert throughout it all, every crunch of snow drawing her attention and every step of a passing person measured in case they suddenly swerved their way. Even though she wasn't contracted with Emrys, she felt duty-bound to ensure his safety as they banked left down a shady alleyway, her mind acutely aware of the knife and *spyd* on her hips. They zigzagged in the hopes of losing a tail that may never have been trailing them in the first place, but precaution was necessary when secrecy was paramount. Further and further they went, past smoking residents and other wanderers, until Emrys suddenly stopped and knocked on an artifact shop's door. The sign read Ophelia Majik Co.

A swaggering man opened the door. He looked to be about Emrys's age but with a permanent mischievous tilt to his mouth and muddy eyes, his nose slightly upturned at the end.

"Well, well, well. Look what the night brought in." The man grinned, beckoning them in.

Emrys entered with Sayra on his heels, following behind the shopkeeper as they snaked around several tables displaying what appeared to be instruments for fake majik. The prince's voice spoke in a familiar, friendly tone, "Thank you for meeting us, Kent."

Kent shot them another grin over his shoulder, descending down a flight of stairs behind the merchant's desk where Sayra assumed excess inventory would be held. "No worries about it, my man. Gangs all together for this one."

Boxes were strewn everywhere, and a hulking shelf of financial documents and folders cracked open to reveal yet another staircase. Kent sealed the false shelf behind them, the handle looking easy to operate—much to Sayra's relief in case the situation turned sour. Blinking, she had to admit she was impressed with the secrecy as they entered a new, spacious cellar far beneath the first floor. Two others were gathered, sitting and playing a game of cards across a circular pine table. A music box spun an upbeat melody Sayra couldn't place, which livened the stone room. Drawings of popular musicians clung to one of the walls, but that was where any festivities ended.

An in-depth map with elevated landmarks was spread across a back rectangular table, every country on their continent noted along with those surrounding them across vast oceans. Portraits of the Holy Family and others Sayra didn't recognize hung across the wall above it, descriptions and notes pinned beneath each.

Sayra's brows rose at the tiny devil horns drawn over the Grand Priest's face.

On the short wall to her immediate right of the doorway, a heavily inked map of their continent, emphasis around the monastery, dangled.

Shelves of tomes and notebooks bound with labels covered the last free wall, the space clearly meant as some sort of war room.

Incense on their meeting table burned a leathery scent, smoke wafting into the air in lazy curves.

Sayra turned to ask Emrys what was going on when a curse slipped out of a small black-haired female, her electric-blue eyes pissed as they fell on her. "Kent, what is a *Valkyrie* doing here?" she spit out, the word sounding dirty.

The curly-haired man across from her tossed a card across the table. His skin was a shade darker than Nes's, and his cheekbones were nearly as high. "Cass, if she's with Emrys, and Kent allowed her in, then obviously she is not the enemy." He leaned back, folding his leather-clad, muscled arms behind his head.

"Thank you, Ty, for being the voice of reason," Kent quipped, moving to stand beside the female and patting her on the head once before she ruefully swatted his hand away.

"Everyone, this is Sayra," Emrys introduced before pulling his hood down. Sayra moved to mimic his actions. "Sayra, this is Kent."

Kent gave her a cheeky grin, dimples denting either side of his mouth.

"That's Ty," Emrys said, pointing to the slightly older man who dipped his chin in greeting. His appearance was unquestionably similar to an assassin's, which only further confused Sayra about the small club of warmongers.

"And Cassandra," Emrys finished. The female pouted, her cleft chin momentarily prominent before angry words escaped her.

"Okay, well, cool. So, I guess we have another girl in the club," she huffed, cross she wasn't made aware of Sayra's arrival in advance.

The getup Cassandra wore was interesting. An elegant cream cloak over a revealing dress of lace and silk. It spoke of the nightlife a businesswoman could run, giving Sayra the distinct impression she may have been a madame at a nearby establishment. The rouge, eyeshadow, and natural lipstick weren't nearly abundant enough to make her a worker.

Sayra was sure they got business, especially considering how close Tern was to the monastery. There was a high population of men there, and the town was a crucial safe point for any traveler.

Wearing the typical garb of a merchant, Kent appeared the most ordinary out of the collective group, with his finely fitted forest-green tunic falling just below the hips and old-style black trousers. It was puzzling to take in such a mash-up of random individuals, and Sayra was distinctly aware an Arcanist prince and a Valkyrie only added to the oddity.

Emrys addressed the group. "I promised you all information on how we devise the Holy Family's downfall." He turned to her. "Sayra, these are my primary contacts for intelligence gathering. We all aim to achieve the same goal, perhaps for different reasons but to the same end. They aren't associated with the crown. Would you mind explaining your part on my behalf?" His eyes were pointed, and Sayra knew he was referring to her unique situation.

Ty observed from the corner of his eye while a haughty Cassandra waited beside Kent.

Somewhat irked, Sayra's lips pressed tight as she stared at him. "I'm to share this with people I've never met, but I cannot even hint at it with Nes?" she protested, scowling at Cassandra when the young woman rolled her eyes.

"We don't bite," Kent joked, giving Cassandra a second look. "Well, the men don't." The amendment caused him a swift elbow to his gut, pained chuckles sounding from his doubled-over torso.

Emrys faced her, understanding flashing in his eyes. It underlaid his determination for Sayra to speak the words he couldn't share. "Nes will be told when we can afford others to be brought in. First, we need to make contact with the informant who started all this. *They* are the ones who can help us find her," he promised, gesturing toward the unusual trio.

Breathing out her nose, Sayra performed the spell that delivered her message well. "*Flamma*," she enunciated clearly, loud enough for each member to hear and know she summoned the flame that flicked across her raised palm. While it was quite enjoyable to see Cassandra's face morph into disbelief, a fact that brought smugness to Sayra's, it was annoying to be demonstrating as if she were an animal performing tricks.

Ty's head snapped toward her, a sharp glint in those dark eyes.

Clapping, Kent walked over to give Emrys's shoulder a friendly shake. "This is brilliant!"

"Yes, yes, yes." Sayra sighed, ending the spell and folding her arms across her chest. "We need to search for the woman who gave me the ability to harness majik because she stole some sacred worship relic and ran off into a desolate corner of the continent to remain incognito. There are questions she must answer that pertain to everyone going forward with the king and queen of Acacea's plan to expose the church. It goes along the lines of me making some grand reveal to the masses and then the information of how I came to wield majik being released." Her chin inclined. "Which, of course, you all already know, the sole exception being the tidbit pertaining to a female with majik capabilities."

It was purposeful, her intention to murk the details in her irritation. Sayra felt they knew more than she did about the plan, and she had no desire to explain away what was already known. Their maps exposed that. A particularly detailed one of the church outlined underground passages on the wall. Another detailed a distinct scarlet circle in the northwest territories of Acacea. That circle must have been where she currently resided, the portrait of an ambiguous woman pinned above.

Kent spoke up, his eyes alight with approval. "Clever one, isn't she? What are you doing with a gal like her, Emrys?"

"That was of their own volition when they discovered the informant who betrayed the Holy Family. Ty had been the one to ensure her escape after all," Emrys explained, not flinching from the sour glance Sayra sent him. He gave her a look, pointedly not taking Kent's bait. "She never shared all the information to either my family or Ophelia Majik Co and was wise not to for her own safety and yours." He gestured in the direction of the trio. "As I'm bound by oath, and my family unaware of this location and the people running the ring, only you were able to make the connection between both parties."

"How are you here if both entities were to remain separate by the woman's wishes?" Sayra challenged, ignoring the shuffle of cards Cassandra fiddled with.

Stepping in, Kent said, "Happenstance, actually. Emrys is quite the digger himself with many off-the-grid contacts. One led to us, and now we are all the best of friends."

Another deck of cards was shuffled. Loudly.

"I see," Sayra remarked in a dry tone.

"Tyyy," Cassandra whined, placing the cards down and cupping her chin with a well-kept hand. "Do you think I can get majik too?"

"I doubt she has any left from the relic she stole," Ty replied, standing to an intimidating height and assessing Sayra as he did. The attention was bizarre, being far too curious for too little reason. Unless there was something he knew that Sayra didn't.

"Does she not have a name?" Sayra asked.

Emrys shook his head. "No. She remained quite clear we were forbidden from mentioning it, going as far as to bind any person to the oath who knew her. Part of the reason she survived all these years with the church on her tail." Something in his eyes caught Sayra's notice, an almost deceptive edge, as if he were concealing some detail of import.

That question she hadn't yet asked rose to the surface of her mind, teasing her with the new bits of information. Even when a new idea clicked, it didn't quite sit right with her. Sayra tried anyway.

"This woman knew my mother then," she stated with a shrug. "There's no other explanation I can fathom as to why I was chosen."

Cassandra hit the table with the bottom of her cards, a slight smirk on her painted lips.

"Another topic I cannot broach, I'm afraid," Emrys said.

Grinding her teeth, Sayra remained silent, not having another word to share. Her mind recalled her mother's funeral so vividly. There were hundreds of faces there, almost none of which Sayra had recognized at her young age. Besides, she had been so consumed by the deathly pale face of her mother in that casket to have noticed much else. The informant could have been any of the blurred faces present that day, leading to a dead end.

It wasn't anyone in her immediate family. Her father guarded his last son jealously, both despising Sayra for getting her eldest brother, Brevn, killed. Her younger sister, just by one year, still fought to have a relationship with her. Beyond them, Sayra didn't have anyone close enough to her family who could be a lead.

Ty's hulking frame gathered beside the portrait wall, his finger tapping the drawing of an unidentifiable woman. "Let's get on with the planning." He decided for the group, everyone collectively taking seats alongside the table to prepare for the discussion.

As it began, Sayra couldn't help but anguish over the fact that all the puzzle pieces of the female informant were present in the room, each piece guarded by a different person unwilling or incapable of sharing where it lay. Though slowly, achingly so, Sayra gathered the ones available, the image forming before her to reveal a figure who'd prove more questionable than heartening.

CHAPTER TWENTY-SIX

SYLVEN

Sylven spent the weekend morning in silence, staring at the off-white painted ceiling from the top of his navy sheets. His thoughts were like the trunk of a tree, always branching off in different directions but stemming from the same root. The truth of what Sayra told him was the core of every thought and how he'd proceed to that latest development the resulting branches. The thoughts then trailed to how Rys purposefully avoided him after Sayra confessed their secret and how he knew Rys well enough to know his intention with that slight.

Rys was giving him time to sort just where he'd lay his allegiance without any persuasion on his behalf. A kind gesture. A thoughtful one, especially when he left him a brief letter sharing the sentiment and outlining his plans for the weekend. But still...

Sylven wanted Rys to fight for him for once rather than carefully navigating the field, awaiting his opponent's move before responding in kind. The distance he maintained stung, almost bringing Sylven to decide not to assist their cause out of spite. Juvenile, of course, and he knew it. He took many calming breaths before he regained his senses, knowing rash action would never be the correct decision. He'd come to regret it, as Sylven already did for much of what he had said and done.

Rys was always the type to silently support him, and he'd been there through everything for Sylven. It was selfish of him to feel as if Rys had to do more on his behalf, but he couldn't help that lurking feeling of jealousy at how close his best friend had grown to Sayra.

To think of him leaving alone with her that weekend was odd. It almost felt as if Sayra had replaced him in some sort of manner as Rys's closest friend. Sylven knew that wasn't true, but he couldn't shake the haunting feeling.

Dumb. So incredibly dumb to feel this way.

Why couldn't he be a better person and stop making excuses for his behavior? Why couldn't he just let things go? It hurt his head to circle around those questions to no avail. He felt... lost.

Pointless brooding would do him no good, he determined, rising from his bed in one fluid motion and grabbing the tossed-aside cloak on his nightstand. He recalled Waylen mentioning practice at the sparring hall with his Valkyrie. Perhaps he could escape himself for some time and enjoy the company.

He didn't want to think about those words Sayra shared with him. She likely didn't realize he heard them anyway.

Within minutes, Sylven wound through the maze of bustling corridors, refusing to be brushed aside when a gaggle of third-year Arcanists clogged the hall in their thoughtlessness. He brushed shoulders with an oblivious one, earning a nasty glare as he passed without caring. It peeved Sylven to watch their faces light up when Valkyries would pass, their own childish dreams of acquiring a contract the most exciting topic for their upcoming year.

How annoying and naïve.

Despite his thoughts, he felt guilt clinging to him like a second skin for his actions.

Not being able to stand the absurd number of underclassmen flocking through the hall, Sylven decided instead to detour through a courtyard brushed with frozen snowfall. It was a matter of steps until he heard the squeal of the heavy door opening behind him, and he knew he had company. An overeager third year wanting his account of having a Valkyrie perhaps? He lined up a few harsh words to send the youth off with and spun around on the slippery cobblestone pathway. Those same words died, however, the moment he spied his two stalkers.

A sickly sweet smile graced the lips of Akira while Kenji dipped his boxed chin in greeting as they neared him. Sylven hadn't the faintest clue as to what they'd chased him down for. In silence, he waited for them to make the first move.

Steps away, Kenji halted, his burgundy cloak fluttering to a stop around him. His twin posed beside him flirtatiously as she ran her eyes along his cloaked body.

Yeah. He was going to need a shower to wash that off.

"Greetings, old friend." Kenji grinned, already off on the wrong foot with Sylven. They were nothing of the sort, and his deadpan expression conveyed that to the princeling. "Oh, come now. After three and a half years of comradery, I believe we can call each other so."

Sylven said nothing. He didn't so much as blink in response. His distrust of the Droden heir ran deeper than his dislike of Valkyries, which was quite impressive in hindsight.

"I'd like to further acquaint myself with you, Sylven. I fear that many Arcanists here are losing sight of what matters. After all, Tanner nearly killed himself out of depression." Kenji shook his head as if sorrowful. "The poor man quit the academy to work on his mental well-being back at home."

That shocked Sylven. He'd never heard of an Arcanist leaving the academy so late into schooling.

"To that end, I believe I have been neglecting our friendship and would care to retrace what could be the start of it," Kenji said, easygoing with his attitude as if speaking to Cage, his *actual* friend.

Akira padded forward in a cloak matching her brother's, a white-gloved hand caressing his bicep as she tilted her face upward to meet his disdainful gaze with a hopeful one of her own. "We'd absolutely love the opportunity to dine with you and Sayra this evening," she said coyly, her hand grazing his elbow. "Perhaps we'll all get the opportunity to grow closer thanks to the Holy Family. They have been quite acquiescing. Especially considering they've bestowed the Goddess's mark on me since our families have ties. It's given me quite the advantage, and whatever lucky man I elect to court."

Firstly, *disgusting.*

He'd never date anyone from Droden, Acacea's long-standing rival country. Especially someone so forward. Yes, she was beautiful by Droden's standards with raven hair, diamond shaping to her face, and porcelain skin, but her personality was another massive thing he despised about her.

Recentering his mind, Sylven focused on the main problem. With all he knew, what did that make the Droden twins to the Holy Family? Droden was the first country to pair with the Holy Family and allow them to establish satellite monasteries throughout their territory. Perhaps because of that tie, Akira was granted the favor of the Zefare family.

Interesting.

But why go to such lengths to arrange a private evening with him and Sayra? Such an opportunity would be coveted by many, the chance to win the favor of a future emperor remarkably fortunate. Was Kenji aware of her majikal capabilities, or was that simply a coincidence?

Sylven eyed him for a split second before determining otherwise. There wasn't the slightest chance Rys or his family had shared such valuable information, especially considering even Sylven hadn't been privy to it until recently. Kenji had to be aware Sylven would never betray Rys, and he never gave anyone a reason to believe he'd ever commit such a deed. The only logical deduction was Kenji's desire to grow closer to Sayra.

"Regrettably, we will not be able to dine with you this eve," Sylven said in his least apologetic tone, removing himself from Akira's proximity and turning to leave.

"Tomorrow night then?" Kenji rocked back on his heels.

Exhaling, Sylven knew he had to tread carefully. The Astors held a prominent role in Acacea's court, his father being King Navarre's right-hand diplomat and all. It could reflect poorly if Sylven continued to refuse arrangements with Kenji should he complain about it to Emperor Haru and word reach Everis's ears. While Sylven didn't give a damn about his own reputation—he wanted nothing to do with that position anyway—he would be guilted if his father fell into a troubling situation because of him.

His face must have given away his answer. When he faced the princeling once more, Kenji's expression was pleased with what he found.

"Sayra has prior commitments this weekend that will take up her time considerably," Sylven explained, his words as polite as he could bear to make them.

A crease appeared between Kenji's brow, and Akira shared a secretive, sultry quirk of her mouth as her eyes roamed once more.

"Perhaps next weekend might work best with our conflicting schedules," Sylven suggested.

"We'll make the time for you," Akira simpered, her short bangs swaying with her head movement.

A tightness pinched Kenji's eyes, though his smile remained persistent. "Friday evening, then, at seven. I shall reserve the formal dining hall for our occasion." When Sylven nodded in acquiescence, he said, "Dress appropriately, Sylven. I'd hate for you to feel displaced." He gave an amiable wink before gesturing for his sister to retreat back into the warmth of the corridor, the latter departing with a twirl of her hair before the door shut behind them.

Grunting in annoyance, Sylven resumed his earlier route, his mind set on confronting Sayra on the finer details of what that dinner would allude to and just what Akira had meant. He waved his left arm in repugnance, wishing the memory of Akira's hand trailing down his arm would vanish along with the feeling. It took every ounce of self-control to not push her away, even more so not to gag at her unseemly expressions.

At last, he entered the dome where his *anima* combative class was held. Sylven spotted two lone figures practicing hand-to-hand combat, Waylen's lacking in comparison to the expertise of his Valkyrie's. All the same, he commended his friend for the effort and will to learn what most Arcanists neglected in their own training.

Waylen's Valkyrie—Jayde, he believed—delivered a cutting blow to his abdomen, a clear weak spot he overlooked guarding when attempting a left hook.

"Rough," Sylven commented, trying for a small smile when Waylen gave him a grimace and waved.

"Didn't expect to see you here," Waylen wheezed, righting himself and moving to greet him with clasped hands.

Shrugging, he replied, "I needed some air." He then noticed a perceptible limp to Jayde's leg. "You managed to get a shot in?"

Snorting, Jayde shook her head. "He's improving but not at that rate." She cast a sideways glance at the recovering Arcanist. "No offense." A bitter edge tilted her lips. "Another Valkyrie ambushed me in the night in response to a decision of mine."

Narrowing his sight on her, Sylven had a sinking feeling. "You're one of the three who ganged up on Sayra."

"Yeah."

Waylen looked mortified. "You did what?"

Jayde chewed on her lip, hiking a single shoulder. "All I'll say is that the payback was deserved. I accept that. Sayra's damn good at what she does. Minus swordsmanship. It just took me a while to figure that out," she reluctantly admitted, shaking out her limbs.

Sylven hadn't moved an inch.

"What happened?" Waylen asked, glancing apologetically at Sylven before growing stern in her direction.

Jayde stretched her arms behind her back. "Another Valkyrie, Netta, had a grudge against her throughout our academy years. Netta believes Sayra cheated in a fight against her and wanted revenge. We won, three people against Sayra, and solely because we had the element of surprise and planned accordingly."

Waylen's face became furious. "That's not honorable."

Rolling her eyes, Jayde said, "Don't worry. She hunted us down and individually pummeled us. She sucks with swords, but she did train harder at hand-to-hand combat than any of us. I'd say we're more than equal at this point in time. Even Netta is lying low. It's Valkyrie business, Waylen. Just as we stay out of Arcanist drama, Valkyries handle their own."

The force of his emotions caught Sylven by surprise. Vindictiveness rolled through him at the admittance, and a dark, cold part of him reveled in the fact Sayra came back swinging at them all. Even knowing that, however, he couldn't quell the guilt for his non-action at the time and the contempt he felt toward the nonchalant Valkyrie in front of him.

Sayra didn't once complain to him about any of it, and that gnawed at his very core. Sure, the Valkyrie drove him utterly insane at times, and yes, she most certainly sent barbed comments his way solely to peeve him, but did he not deserve it?

Sylven had to admit he should have done far better to separate the idea of a Valkyrie from the infuriating lady he knew as Sayra. He allowed his hatred for one to bleed into the other, tarnishing his interactions with her from the very beginning. The day it happened, Sylven should have been there to help Sayra when she was ambushed.

Regret and fury reached a boiling point inside him. So much so his fist connected harshly with Jayde's jaw, making her stagger back a step before she regained her balance. Sylven felt pain shoot through his knuckles. It felt as if he'd punched a sturdy tree. Due to the modifications Valkyries had, he wasn't concerned about permanent harm, but damn, it felt good to finally act.

Not on his behalf but Sayra's.

He took too long to realize what he should have been doing all along.

Jayde worked her jaw, a deep breath escaping her chest. "I deserved that one," she said, her amber eyes rising to meet Sylven's. "But if you ever try that again, I won't let you hit me and will retaliate." And she meant it, her gaze unwavering as she delivered the statement.

Sylven flexed his aching hand, steel in his expression. "We're even."

"Even," she confirmed.

Waylen stood there in disbelief, confused as to whether he should have intervened. Luckily, it seemed the situation worked itself out. "Well then," he said, eyes flicking between the two. "Would you care to join us in sparring?"

Chapter Twenty-Seven

EMRYS

E mrys was careful to maintain his composure around the presence of the Ophelia Majik Co members, a task normally subconscious for him, but it proved challenging in Sayra's presence. He'd grown accustomed to letting his countenance relax around her, the entire duration of their journey spent in observation and majikal discussion.

In just a few weeks, he already felt more at ease speaking with her than nearly any other. He was impressed with her progression in the arcane arts, her memory unparalleled and the strength behind her spells slowly increasing. She'd finally perfected the concealment spell, which permitted her to practice the arts whenever convenient. It was the dark archetype Emrys could wield that eliminated any traces of majik being used outside the confines of her set boundaries. It cloaked low-level majik.

Emrys knew it would speed up her training, but he was wistful over the loss of their shared sessions.

Emrys surmised the informant would disclose further information on Sayra's potential skillset when the time came. It intrigued him how extensive it was thus far. Often, he wondered about her limitations. Whereas a typical Arcanist required at least a day's rest after extensive spell work, Sayra required only a few hours. She could cast spells without verbalizing them, an achievement only the best Arcanists could hope to master after years of practice. Granted, it proved dangerous to her in the past when she pushed that fire majik throughout her dormitory, but it also revealed countless possibilities.

Impatience flickered in his mind. He worked to bury it, knowing the informant had her reasons for postponing answers for such a drastic period of time. As they delved into plans years in the making, it was a relief to see things unfold at long last and somewhat successfully. He'd already sent a coded missive to his parents, acknowledging he renewed Sayra's majik seal. The lie was hard for him to commit to, but he believed they were wrong for withholding it given that Sayra knew. Not even Vander would be told she could openly wield majik.

In the end, Emrys was glad Sayra insisted on learning it. For one, she was better protected. He was also relieved to hear his parents were shortening the timeline in response to Sayra learning about her majik. They were reaching out to the informant to see if she'd meet with Sayra and Emrys in two months. Then, Sayra would learn everything he withheld and more.

Two months.

Until then, he had to ensure no one else discovered Sayra's abilities, and the wrong people didn't sniff out the ploy. Emrys also had to refrain from spilling the last player on her board, the one who would drastically alter her life. Unfortunately, only she could deliver the final, crucial elements necessary to defeat the church and the Horde.

The intel the informant had gathered was a safety net to ensure her own independence in the creation of the rifts. There were two scoring deep into the continent, one far in the northern tundra lands of Zendiya, and the second low between the sandy dunes of Kevsha and the vast plains of the Rendevar Coalition. They were both unfathomably deep. Rumors had been proven true about how they could kill people with fear if one came too close. Countless lives were lost in the pursuit of discovery and exploration but all for naught. Each person's heart would give within the last hundred meters of the rift. At night, a crimson hue could be seen from miles away, the entire site an unholy shade of horror that produced screams of the damned. They'd wail at all hours, endlessly tortured without a second of relief.

The Horde emerged from them, assumed to be fallen humans who rose from the combined forces of hell and majik. The southern rift appeared around four years ago, spreading terror across the lands as the population of daemons increased.

Before then, the Holy Family had a trade route linking each country encompassed by wards. Each country had guards and Arcanists patrolling daily to ensure integrity. People traveled freely between lands until the second rift cracked open. Daemons wore the wards down too fast after that to be replenished.

The night the routes fell was one of infamy with nearly a thousand people dying in a matter of hours. The warded routes were an endeavor that could never be replicated. No one knew when the next rift would emerge, and the thought terrified everyone.

One person had the answers. Yet she refused to deliver them until her chosen one, Sayra, was prepared and past the age of twenty—an age deemed appropriate for the impending information that would be departed.

Emrys could not share that with Sayra, and it weighed heavily on his soul along with every other secret he kept from her and the others. It pulled at him constantly, the cumulation of knowledge he wielded and was forbidden to disclose. One day, he swore to himself, it would pay in spades. The Holy Family's king would be checked, and the restoration of the lands would commence. Without the rifts, without the temptation of the so-called holy relics to further create daemons, the world would never have to fear the Horde again. It would take a decade to clear every square inch of land and sea from the monstrosities, but the results would be unparalleled.

All of that ran through his head as they concluded their meeting, Sayra's occasional glances piercing through his very mind as if she knew he withheld such information. The Valkyrie had a knack for reading others, a gift he admired and respected, even if it made the situation tedious at times.

"Zendiya is currently in a deep power struggle, each oligarch family prodding each other's weaknesses and flaunting their own blood-gained advantages. Newcomers to wealth and power there are also attempting to gain entry into the three allotted spaces for ruling families by trying to eliminate one currently in place," Kent said, using a stick to tap the northern country's location.

If Emrys had to hope for one family to prevail and remain in power, it would be Arseny Barcov's. He was the most malleable from the feelers Emrys put out for their cause, his family the most distrusting of the church's presence.

Moving the stick southwest, Kent said, "Droden is prepared to coronate Kenji upon his upcoming twentieth birthday, making him the youngest emperor in history. Regrettably, his father's health has further deteriorated in recent months, making his son's escalation inevitable."

Since women were prohibited from ruling due to their old-fashioned laws—unless there wasn't a current male heir—it left approximately half a year until Kenji ruled. The revelation drew Emrys's face tight.

Kent rapped the small territory on the northeast corner of Droden. "Faenda's latest uprising is being quelled by the Droden soldiers."

The update made Sayra's face pale, her hands slowly splaying across her legs as if the strength left them. After spending her entire duration of training at the monastery, Emrys knew she hadn't returned due to the vast distance. She was oblivious to the unrest and harsh restrictions placed on the Faendans.

Emrys would gather updates on the territory regularly. Sayra's father rolled over in a disgraceful manner whenever Emperor Haru would impose new laws upon their people; his only desire was to remain in power and maintain wealth.

"Faenda has been rebelling against Droden's rule for a few months now," Emrys murmured Sayra's way.

Ty glanced at them, assessing before returning to face Kent as he spoke.

Sayra soaked in the information, her eyes unreadable for a few seconds before she nodded.

"Droden has placed harsher restrictions on the lower and middle classes in Faenda's territory, including rationing food and water supplies, curfews, and public punishments for those who defy them."

It weighed heavily on Emrys's shoulders to see such distraught in her eyes, occasionally peeking through the neutrality she strove for. Emrys almost called the meeting then and there had the next report not threatened to still his heart.

"Thapula is acting," Kent noted with a grim expression. The stick poked the edge of a vast land in the far east of Thapula's continent. "Dozens of corroborated reports have streamed in from the western lands, all indicating another player has entered the room. War ships are being built over the vast expanse of ocean, the small isles between them being occupied by militant forces. All for what?"

A hint of unease surfaced on Ty's face, and Cassandra shot him a more obvious look of worry.

"They want to explore our continent for the infamous rumors of majik," Emrys distantly said. He knew that didn't bode well for his family's efforts. The foreigners would likely flood their land with sheer numbers until they grasped the Holy Family's source. He doubted they'd back off willingly, especially when they weren't aware of and wouldn't believe in the devastation majik brought. They were complete, idiotic fools coming to a new land in search of a new source of wealth.

The forces and technology the Thapulans wielded were vastly superior, and while Emrys worked diligently with Kent to begin their own advances, they would never compare to those of the enormous empire. With their population untouched by daemonkind, they held no disadvantages. Not when men there had never been hunted by the Horde. Unless Thapulans engaged directly with daemons, they wouldn't have to bear the fear an Arcanist would since they didn't wield majik.

"If rumors of our majik are spreading to the Thapulan people, that means the upper echelons have likely known about it for some time." Emrys's thumb tapped his other one on top of the table, his mind whirling.

"Thapula would start sending spies, which has likely already occurred." Emrys's eyes lifted to the enormous map. "Perhaps next they'd try emissaries before sending warships, seeing if they could acquire the Goddess's blessing of majik. When all goes south, they'd fight for the land, believing it to be the source that's granting power to people."

Cassandra sulked in her chair, her arms crossed over her chest.

"All of this could happen within the span of months. If my kingdom is lucky, years." Emrys sighed. The weight of that knowledge bent his spine a fraction more.

Kent set his mouth in a grim line before returning to the map. His stick wacked a few other locations. "Nothing to report from the other minor lands, each functioning normally and with its own oddities, namely the rumors of majikal canines."

Emrys paid that no heed. Such dumb whispers circulated through cities when people grew bored. However, Sayra was quite enthralled by the prospect, naming off potential uses for such an advancement. It took several minutes for her to begrudgingly return to topic, much to Cassandra's annoyance. Emrys was sure Sayra did it out of spite for the woman's rudeness, the Valkyrie going so far as returning her mocking expressions. It would have amused Emrys to witness had his mind not been planning how to proceed with the intelligence updates.

"One last topic I feel I should mention." Kent leaned tiredly into his chair. "For one reason or another, or potentially even by pure coincidence, the Horde have begun coordinating attacks in greater numbers."

With a sharp edge to her voice, Sayra asked, "What do you mean by greater numbers? Are they collaborating?" A sarcastic inflection entered the last word.

Emrys waited, his arms patiently crossed. Cassandra never seemed to stop fidgeting across from him.

"That's exactly it," Kent replied, his chin lowering. "The intelligent classes of daemons have been banding together. I only have four reported cases, but it's something to be wary of."

"Perhaps they've realized their strength in numbers rather than barbarically tearing each other apart," Emrys hypothesized. "Let us hope it's not widespread and isn't an exponential increase." He knew nothing was coincidence, however. Another matter to keep tabs on.

Sayra's fist slowly closed on top of the table, her shoulders leaning forward. "What do you mean by 'intelligent classes'? There aren't any such things." Her eyes swept the table, skipping Cassandra's and going right to Emrys's.

A giggle sounded from Cassandra, and Ty shot her an annoyed look as he kicked his heels on top of the table.

Kent clasped his hands behind his head, one finger tapping. "Recently, we've begun to notice similarities between different forms of daemons. Depending on their size and appearance, we've begun to classify their... traits, if you will. Some are more aggressive toward non-magic males, and some are cleverer than to charge straight into a sword."

Sayra's face tensed as if remembering. "I see. It makes sense to categorize them. After all, I've seen differences between the three I've come face-to-face with."

That wiped the expression from Cassandra's face, her hands stilling at last. She was deathly afraid of daemons. She never left the city if she could help it.

"We have some charts, but they are underwhelming at the moment." Emrys's face creased. "Right now, we are gathering reports on daemon activities and behaviors to better assess them, but it's slow going."

Sayra's face turned appreciative. "That could make a huge difference in determining how to best bring down the daemon you encounter."

Emrys signaled for Kent to share the file.

Opening a folder, Kent pushed a report across the table. "Here's what we have so far."

Without delay, Sayra dove in while Kent continued to rattle off information.

A glum air clung about them all, the night's reports grimmer than the usual affair. It was unsaid amongst the group, but they were well aware they were in for a horrendous storm's worth of destruction before any of it cleared.

CHAPTER TWENTY-EIGHT

SAYRA

Sayra woke up the next morning refreshed, the wonders of a full night's rest rejuvenating. Together, she and Emrys convened on the bottom floor of the bed and breakfast for a quick meal of eggs, fruit, and bread before departing. Just as Sayra was about to pay for her stay, the woman shook her head.

"Your balance was already covered, dear."

Frowning, Sayra cocked her head at Emrys. "I can pay for my room and board."

Holding the door open for her, Emrys's eyes scanned the street for any signs of threats. Her job.

"I'm well aware. It wouldn't be proper if I dragged you all the way here and made you pay, though, would it?" When Sayra opened her mouth to object, Emrys gave her a look. The one where a tiny corner of his mouth hiked up just so and his eyes a slight mischievous. "Allow me to be a gentleman."

Dritt. There went that warm, nervous energy in her stomach again.

He lowered his hood to the level of his eyes after closing the door behind Sayra.

During the sunny day, the city was positively alive and flowing with people going every which way in the market, each stall dealing with customers or calling out prices to passersby. Some haggled, others outright forked over the coin, while a select few enjoyed viewing the wares on display.

Walking behind Emrys, Sayra noticed a stark change in the way people looked at them. By them, she primarily meant Emrys. Even fully cloaked, they commanded attention. People detected the glint of armor beneath hers, making the connection the man she guarded was an Arcanist. Stares marked their progression, but the chatter and liveliness didn't halt one bit.

Then Sayra's instincts kicked in. Maneuvering forward, she deftly caught a large object in her hand before it slammed into the side of Emrys's head.

Everyone seemed to draw a breath.

"I'm so sorry, misses," a young girl, no older than eight, called out. Her round eyes were wide, more than a flicker of anxiousness crossing them.

Keeping her face beneath her hood, Sayra reassured her, "No harm done." She then gently rolled the kickball back to her, and the market relaxed as they continued onward.

"My hero," Emrys said, his tone amused.

Sayra smiled. She couldn't help it. "I strive to impress."

The clopping of hooves signaled the arrival of their steeds from the stables, both appearing similarly rested and nourished for the journey ahead. The minute they were out of earshot from the village, she insisted upon continuing her majik training, switching between different affinities as they traveled between varying ley lines. It was exhausting work, but for one reason or another, her majik replenished exceedingly quickly—much to Emrys's surprise.

Even more shocking, though, was her capability to forgo gauntlets. Other learning Arcanists relied on them to enhance their connection to ley lines, but Sayra felt them as clear as day. They hummed far beneath her, some further away calling to her majik. Out in those lands, though, it was more like the touch of a breeze to her majikal senses. At the monastery, where every major ley line passed through each other, it was a melody of energy singing to her.

Granted, gauntlets still amplified the majik she could wield. She experimented once at Emrys's insistence. His gauntlets were much too large for her hands, but the difference was drastic.

A thought crossed her mind. "Are there locations without ley lines?"

He gave her a solemn nod. "They are called dead zones, rare and in between, but every Arcanist is made aware of their locations across a generic map. It's not precise, but it helped our ancestors create routes around them to avoid that complication. The majority of routes run along three lines, which explains the sometimes-erratic pattern they can appear in."

"Is that another secret I'm not permitted to know?" Sayra smirked at him, her mount giving a convenient snort as she did. "Even my horse agrees the notion is ridiculous."

Emrys rolled his eyes at her, his mouth upturned.

She mocked a gasp, clutching her armored chest with a hand. "How very unprincely of you to roll your eyes! Whatever would your people think of you?"

"Evidently, I'm a charlatan of the worst sort," he joked back, a tiny corner of his mouth rising further.

"A charlatan indeed." Sayra sighed, shaking her head scornfully. "However will you return with your head held high?"

Shrugging, Emrys said, "If I am to be a charlatan, then I'll return with another at my side."

Blinking, Sayra notched a brow at him. "Careful, Emrys. I do believe I am beginning to rub off on you. If you're too careless, you'll end up a rowdy sort."

"Would that be so terrible?" he playfully challenged, his eyes raking through the surrounding trees.

"It depends on what you're going for." Sayra smiled, still observing him from the corner of her vision. "If you'd prefer the persona of the enigmatic and elusive prince, I'm afraid you've gone too far. You'll have to overcompensate on the broodiness aspect, almost to Sylven's level." A chuckle sounded from Emrys, the smile growing wider on her own face in response. "On the other side, if you care to—"

Stiffening, Sayra's head swiveled to their left, her hands instinctively tightening on the horse's reins as the animal halted itself. Emrys mimicked her, noting the growing fear that tightened their chests. Pulling off her cloak, Sayra draped it across the horse and released her *spyd* from its holster.

The horses refused to move, their eyes wildly rolling in their sockets.

"*Corporis custodia,*" she murmured, draping a physical barrier over them both and receiving a grateful nod from Emrys.

Her majik was weak. She knew it, and so did Emrys, but she was a Valkyrie first and foremost. Even the slight boost of majik would only enhance her skills, despite not having enough time to train with it. It wasn't much, but when Emrys rose his own barriers against them, Sayra knew it was much better than nothing.

Energy pinged in her veins, majik, adrenaline, and fear all coursing through and electrifying her body. Heart pounding, Sayra gestured for Emrys to remain mounted, a deal they'd already agreed to, but one she felt the need to enforce to ensure his safety.

Sayra would never lose another Arcanist. It wasn't an option, no matter the cost.

She recalled the daemon that attacked her long ago. It played with her and her brother, seeming to enjoy eliciting as much fear and pain as it could from its victims. The daemons that recently attacked the Astors were straightforward. Bloodthirsty. They were similar in terms of the fear majik they had but night and day when it came to the way they attacked.

The approaching evil differed from either of those past times. Sayra could feel that innately.

For the most part, daemons remained asleep during the daylight hours. Only those with more strength were capable of resisting that urge and could somewhat lumber through the land in moments of dawn or dusk. Gripping her *spyd*, her eyes staked the general spot it was approaching from.

"This one wasn't on your list of aberrant daemons," Sayra called out, her voice grim.

Emrys clucked his tongue, encouraging the horse to move closer to Sayra's. "No. No it wasn't." He pulled off his hood, his face severe.

It distracted Sayra that she couldn't *feel* Emrys's condition. The need to glance over her shoulder to check on his well-being was overwhelming. She was the only Valkyrie present. No guards. No one else to provide physical support. Should she falter and Emrys not summon majik swiftly enough, he'd be as good as dead.

She couldn't afford to freeze.

They both remained silent, their fear growing steadily as the monstrosity closed in on their scent. *Have faith*, Sayra told herself. Faith is what combated a daemon's fear, and Sayra knew if she strayed from her confidence, the Horde's menace would overcome her mind. Ravens scattered from a tree behind them, Sayra spinning as the leaves shook upon their branches.

Emrys shouted, "*Sphera!*"

Balls of flame darted forward, leaving a fading trail in their wake from Emrys's position facing the lumbering daemon. Shadowing them, Sayra rushed onward toward the spiky four-legged monster. With each step, the scene moved slowly, in an almost surreal way, her chest growing tighter with every inch gained. Her mind screamed at her to run, her legs threatening to betray her as the distance closed.

Focus.

It was all a façade, the emotion brought on from the presence of the daemon. A fact Sayra wasn't quick to forget as she pushed past the veil it attempted to capture its prey with. They *would* survive.

With each step, more details struck her. The smattering of human blood dripping down its hunched back, spikes curling from its spine. A half-chewed arm still being crunched in three rows of dulled, mold-infested teeth. A rotten, bloodcurdling stench wafting from its gore-smeared shell of a head. Ravenous scarlet eyes locked on her from the fifty-foot distance between them.

This was once a human, she thought.

A flap of decomposed flesh opened on its hind legs as it leaped forward straight into the flames aiming for it. A screech had her covering her ears as the daemon fell on its side, mouth charred to the point where all that remained was human bones in place of its split tongue, black leaking from the internal burns it bore.

It began laughing, and the sound sent an ominous chill down her spine as it echoed around them. It cackled like a deranged human.

Sayra looked back at the swaying forest, searching for something that set off alarm bells in her head. Her confidence was wavering, a sure sign that another daemon approached. She steadied her stance, bracing a foot back as an echo of laughter emanated from the distance.

Then her eyes went wide, her heart shuddering at what she saw.

Two others emerged from the twisted pathway ahead, and the laughter grew louder, as did the thundering in her chest at the portentous, hopeless sight unfolding before her.

The others were of the same physique, similarly blood-smeared around their decomposing, blackened maws. Their meal looked recent from the fresh glimmer of crimson there. The fear they radiated compromised her thoughts, her own fear irrationally amplified beyond what any average human being could bear.

Three enormous daemons of the Horde.

The furthest away still carried a half-connected body in its wicked grinning mouth, a young boy of eight at the most. Empty eyes stared at the sky, blood escaping a corner of his grayed mouth. The daemon ground its lower jaw against its prey, bones cracking and flesh shredding. Some of it hung from the height of the daemon's maw. With the grace of alpha predators, the Horde closed in as if they held all the time in the world to hunt, eliminate, and torture. And they did. The net of fear they cast between the three of them was incapacitating.

Sayra's faith was crumbling faster than an avalanche off a shear mountainside, raw disbelief and doom clawing at that final string holding her rationality in place. Her mouth shook as if refraining from crying.

With a terrified glance, Sayra saw Emrys hunched over his unaffected steed, head resting against the base of its neck. With an aching twist, he barely managed to move his face toward her, a picture of despair in his contorted features.

Even the dark prince fell prey to the overwhelming force the Horde exuded, his body inhibited by such deeply ingrained terror that every function was disabled. His mouth struggled to form a single, dreadful word. A word that hit her harder than she'd ever imagined.

RUN.

Sayra's knees trembled, the gravity around her feeling as if it were pulling her to the ground. Near her, the first daemon rose, swallowing the bones it carried as its mouth began healing from the infected burn.

Despite every pleading thought that begged her to escape, Sayra couldn't. Wouldn't. She swore herself to this cause and would never forgive herself if she didn't fight till her last breath.

"I am Sayra von Lykken." It started as a wordless prayer of sorts, her mouth barely moving. "I am the firstborn daughter of Arene von Lykken, slayer of thirty-seven of the Horde." It became a whisper to herself, a noise that a gentle breeze wasn't strong enough to carry to anyone else. "I'm sworn to my cause. My faith is unwavering." Her voice became less constricted. "I am a Valkyrie, bringer of death to daemonkind. Fear *me* because I'll be the last you'll ever see."

Sayra threw every fiber that wove the tapestry of her soul into the fray.

A single step toward the healing daemon left her breathless, the twist of her arm nearly impossible. Her *spyd* swung forward, catching the daemon straight in the eye with a spear point, black liquid pouring from the wound. It screamed a wild laugh, shaking its head violently as Sayra recalled her weapon.

Faen, she inwardly cursed, hating the fear-induced weakness that slowed her.

Somewhere far in front of them, she felt a man's anxiety for her and Sylven reaching through their link. It wasn't the time, however. Even though they could communicate through vast distances, Sayra required every ounce of her concentration.

"*Celer*," Sayra commanded, feeling the wind majik through her limbs. "*Vi*." Earth strengthened her frame, making the next movement she made manageable.

With a shout of fury, she sped forward with every ounce of power she could muster while the two others closed in on Emrys's immobilized form. Yanking the chain, her *spyd* ripped across the monster's face, tearing the other eye in the process with a disgusting squelch. The chilling cackle still escaped its mouth, unafraid of a pesky thing like her.

The majik wore off quickly, her hands shaking from the raw panic wearing down her resolve. Staggering, Sayra moved toward Emrys. The daemons were only thirty feet from him and closing in.

They knew they would win.

"*Celer. Vi.*" Sayra shot forward, grabbing the bottom of the dagger-like portion of her *spyd*.

The daemons didn't bother looking at her, not when Emrys was so close to them.

Leaping, Sayra gracefully fell into a somersault, slashing out at the closest daemon's Achilles tendon. An audible snap met her ears as she regained her footing, the beast collapsing on its injured leg. The second daemon screeched as it swiveled to her. Leather skin flapped in several places, the smell eye-watering.

With a speed that belied its size, the daemon swept a thick, spiked leg toward her. Holding out the chain of her *spyd*, Sayra barely managed to connect the steel between two spikes, her boots dragging in the muddy snow. Her arms shook, the majik wearing off once again.

Thinking fast, she got out, "*Rima.*"

A small crevice in the earth split in front of her, around the other daemon's forefoot. Its laughter cut off as the beast fell forward, and its body hit the ground with a loud boom.

"*Claudere!*" she cried.

The earth then abruptly sewed itself together, trapping the daemon in place. As her knees began to buckle, the other daemon chortled.

I need to finish one of them off, otherwise the fear will continue to debilitate me.

Readying her *spyd*, Sayra renewed the speed and strength spells as she lurched forward to finish the job. The daemon with the injured foot spun, throwing out one spiked leg toward her unprotected side. She barely adjusted her *spyd* as it crashed into her, sending her body flying backward.

Over and over, she tumbled through the trampled snow. Her hand flung out, stabbing the daggered end of her weapon into the frozen dirt beneath. It caught, though her shoulder ached from the force. Gasping for air, Sayra kneeled.

The two daemons returned to focus on Emrys, though one was attempting to pull its leg from the earth in vain.

The ground shook then, a sinister laugh erupting from behind her.

The third daemon.

Eyes wide, Sayra swiveled just in time to meet the enormous maw with her weapon. The sharp end dug into the tender flesh above its top row of teeth. Several inches sunk deep into its skull, penetrating the rotten core.

Her arms shook as she withdrew the *spyd* with a violent pull, the daemon collapsing before her. Breathing hard, she turned back to the others. Once more, she repeated the majik words and stepped forward.

They all laughed in unison, but the thing that made her very bones crawl was the chuckle that sprouted behind her.

No, I killed it!

Her head swiveled to see the daemon slowly rising again. A loud crack sounded in the other direction, and Sayra looked to find the other one freeing itself from the earth. And it went straight for Emrys.

His eyes were wide, pleading for Sayra to obey his order to run. There was a resigned look on his face that cracked something in her resolve. Something fundamental. Something that made her throat thicken with emotion.

His mouth formed another word.

BACK.

The spells evaporated, leaving her a trembling husk as she fell to her knees. Her hands shook as they braced her body above the snow. Raising her head, Sayra saw the daemon she killed sway toward her.

Only seven feet away.

She would die and Emrys with her.

The thought fractured her composure further, her wrath drawing her majik in a dark, twisted way from her body. Words escaped her as the majik took shape, molding to her will alone.

It was cool as it ran through her soul, the darkness billowing through her like a cloud, feeding and growing from her ire at the Horde and the helplessness of the situation. Even with her current spells, her strength wasn't holding, the speed ebbing as the fear majik of three daemons pelted her down.

Her lack of experience and majikal proficiency was dooming both of them, but Sayra *couldn't* lose Emrys.

For the last time, she took in his face on her right side. That expression, such crushing horror and agony on a face that always had withstood anything thrown its way, shocked her. For him to be brought to such a state amplified by the Horde, one with such a gift as his, it likely meant a death sentence for them both. Before, Sayra would fight solely to redeem herself, to compensate for her lack of previous strength, but she felt the shift as clear as day. A new drive willing her to live and to save her companion.

It was glorious. Her majik warped the energy buzzing through her, her desperation willing it to empower her strength. Sayra's mind recoiled at the oiliness the newly tainted majik contained, but it was quickly shushed and repressed.

Oh, Sayra would certainly bring about the end of the Horde's control over the continent and the corruption of the church with their evil experimentation, but she'd only do it if Emrys was there alongside her, and those she'd grown to care about could see the light that emerged from the freedom thereafter. So, she allowed that curling blackness to edge her spell. It could corrupt her soul if need be. Anything to save Emrys and keep those precious to her safe. And to avenge that innocent child slaughtered at the Horde's hands and all those before him.

In a second, the laughter stopped. The majik ebbed through her body as she stood, and something strangely beautiful happened to the daemon. Its pointed, scaly skin shifted as if there were snakes squirming beneath it. The daemon folded in on itself, a bloodcurdling scream numbing her ears as a stretch of skin exploded, blackness gushing from the monster in spades.

Sayra felt a warm drop of something running from her nose above the splitting grin on her face. Her eyes flashed in sweet retaliation. The monster then writhed upon the snowy grass, every capillary bursting before venules followed, torturously working to the larger veins and arteries until each was wrecked, the heart giving way in a surge of majik that shredded it beyond recovery. Sayra's ears rang as the daemon collapsed, its brethren deathly quiet ahead on the trail as they reassessed their situation.

Breathing heavily, Sayra forced her shaky legs to carry her, propelling her forward. Her hands quavered as the drop of blood caressed her jaw and dipped below her armor.

Body heaving, Emrys gripped the saddle's horn, his head rising marginally from a third of the fear being extinguished. His features were still contorted in pain, but those wide onyx-gray eyes were just a shade clearer than before as they took in the splattered mess of the daemon beside her. Disbelief crossed his face, something deeper running through him before he fought to rise against the oncoming Horde.

The daemon in the lead hissed, grittily releasing an echo of words across the stretch of trail. "Hell summoner," it beckoned to Sayra, challenging her with its ire-laden sights. The words scraped against her ears, the noise akin to the scratch of metal against metal. "You die first."

Sayra cocked her head. *Daemons talk?* Something in her bones ached, the edges of her vision fuzzy. She shared an obscene gesture, fully conveying her thoughts on the matter, though a part of her reveled in the strange title.

It exuded supremacy.

Without restraint, the monsters sprung forward, hastily eating the ground away rather than stalking their dangerous foe. The Horde knew her capabilities and wouldn't spare a second more to end her life so they could enjoy taking Emrys's.

"*Infundibulum!*" Emrys roared, thrusting a clenched hand toward her oncoming adversaries. A stunning tunnel of flame circled from his palm, crossing fifty feet as it enlarged into a raging, funneling storm that barreled into the Horde. The heat forced Sayra to squint, a shaking hand uselessly raised to protect her face from the burning onslaught.

Both daemons screeched when it encompassed them, flakes of flesh rising with the flames until they crested the funnel, dissolving into fine ash. Their hatred propelled them forward, noticeably flagging as the flame progressed.

The seconds ticked by, sweat beading on Emrys's forehead as his brows lowered in painstaking concentration. A nicker sounded from Sayra's horse. Although trained alongside majik and untouched by the presence of daemons, the animal was still wary of the situation before her. Both daemons pulled themselves forward with razor-sharp claws, closing in on Sayra regardless of the barrage of majik burning their charred husks to a crisp.

Licking her lips, Sayra thrust that lingering smolder of mist within her at the Horde, willing her power to amplify the heat to damn those daemons to *helvete*. It was thrilling the way her majik blended with Emrys's, blackness leaking through his flames like ink in water. Sayra's majik seemed eager to overlap his, consuming every ounce of flame. Waves of burning heat became nearly unbearable as the fire blackened, instantly turning its contents into a pile of ash below.

The release of fear was instant. Sayra felt like she was floating.

Emrys gritted his teeth, pulling back his hand as the dark flames raced toward him through his own majik. The spell was cut on his behalf, but Sayra's overlapping spell raged toward him, enveloping the flames as they disappeared mere feet in front of him.

Jaw slackening, Sayra could only watch as a bystander as the flames consumed the last inch of his spell, barely inches from his face.

"*Abiit,*" Emrys ordered, fatigue lacing his words as he leaned back into the saddle.

The dark flames remained, unaffected by his command to be rid of them.

Suddenly, a hysterical laugh bubbled out of Sayra, and Emrys's eyes darted to her in dawning alarm. Delight made her smile at the deadly, stunning majik, and her hand reached out in a cupping motion. The majik followed her control, her darkening will swirling it through the sky and weaving it down through the trees and the first fallen daemon. Satisfaction twisted her face as it burned, burned, burned, her mind imagining the screams it would cry if the soul still remained present.

Her head tilted again, observing as flecks of ash floated through the slight breeze, her enemies demolished before her. Nothing could compare to the rush and the knowledge she could overpower any foe.

A devilish desire entered her mind, the power corrupting her dreams and ideals. Sayra wouldn't hide her delicious ability any longer. It would be ridiculous to take such a meaningless course of action, especially considering she could easily fell the Holy Family with the flame alone. Why wait? Sayra didn't need the public's approval, the politics of many countries, and their idiotic fumbling of the situation thus far. They had blundered in circles, content with their own cages and the semblance of power they believed they exerted over their people.

Was it not their fault to begin with?

The fools permitted the church to manipulate them to such extremes they believed an immense gift hailed from a *Goddess* when it was and could be so much more. Perhaps Sayra should raze them all from the earth. She could start anew, the raw power of the hidden ley line in the center of the earth feeding her pursuit.

No, she thought. *That isn't quite right.* Her skill came from something far more powerful, a different world than the one she resided in. A silly ley line could never hope to contain such might, such potential to alter the fabric of reality.

Sayra laughed for a different reason, her glee exhilarating from the gorgeous thought of killing each person in her reformation. Was it some sort of madness?

A small part of her questioned it, immediately repressed by the surge of majik clouding her mind. Madness it could have been, but only true madness could achieve the change the paltry world needed. Was she truly mad if she was the only person to realize it? If anything, it only proved she was the sole enlightened one, and they'd grow to worship her as such.

Flames engulfed the forest around her, trees collapsing into ash in the black majik's trail. The horses became skittish, snorting at the wildfire that began ravaging the icy trees.

"Beautiful," Sayra admired with an awed expression. Another steady trickle of warmth ran from her nose.

A hand twisted her arm, turning her attention to the prince before her. Sayra couldn't fathom why he bore such a dreadful take to his features. She eliminated their foes, after all. The pale skin around his eyes was pulled taut, his jaw clenched so tightly his muscles feathered on one side. A tender hand was placed against the side of her head, his thumb tracing her cheekbone.

"Sayra, please," Emrys said calmly. His apprehension leaked through and intertwined with his tone. "Release your majik. It isn't natural. It twists your mind into something unrecognizable if abused."

She gave him an arrogant smile. "Now, why would I do that? My power is unparalleled. I can bring down both of our enemies without batting an eye," she sang, summoning the flames to circle their bodies to prove her point. "I believe any *sane* person would keep it."

"I can't lose you to this majik, Sayra," Emrys implored, his eyes searching for her humanity. His brows drew close together when he found none, his dark eyes widening with a new kind of fear.

Heat rose around them, loose strands of her hair rising in the inferno. Sayra felt like a goddess, all her power electrifying into a tingle along her skin. With every inhale, the flames closed a fraction. With every exhale, they relaxed, widening the diameter between the walls.

Her blood was alive, dancing within her to the rhythm of her heartbeat, everything about the new divine blessing intoxicating. Including Emrys. He appeared magnificent with her writhing flames behind him, his black locks shifting from the draft. Every corner of his face danced with the shadows of her fire.

"Remember Sylven?" he asked, his tone urgent. "You are sworn to protect him. And what about Nessika? Your other friends? Will you leave them behind too?"

It was inexplicable, but Sayra could feel herself being drawn to his majik and him responding with an eagerness. His majik was stirring when hers grew close, a feeling Sayra hadn't noticed before when she practiced near him. She tilted her head, searching his eyes and wondering if he similarly wielded the new force.

His eyes were growing desperate, his brows narrowing the longer his majik struggled to be expelled and to rise and meet her own. Emrys stole a step toward her, his palms up to show he meant no harm. "If you allow this majik to rule you, Brevn's sacrifice, your brother's life, would have meant *nothing*."

Sayra blinked at that. Something deep within her mind tugged at her, but she immediately cast it aside.

"Sarya, this will kill you," Emrys swore, taking another step toward her.

"Nothing can—"

Emrys marched forward and, before she knew it, swept her into a passionate kiss. Placing his gauntleted hand on the small of her back, he trailed the side of her face with his thumb. Sayra forgot everything; those dark thoughts pushed to the recesses of her mind as her body responded to him.

Closing her eyes, she lost herself in his touch, her hand drawing him closer by the shoulder. It was everything she'd ever imagined a kiss to be and so much *more* since it was with Emrys. Her lungs took in a breath, reveling in his alluring cologne. A spark she'd felt between them ignited, their majiks teasing each other at the pads of their fingers, lightly tingling the skin under layers of fabric and metal.

Then she remembered her vow. Her duty.

It happened so fast, everything around her imploding at once. Hands lashing out, Sayra pushed Emrys away with an ounce of too much strength, sending him stumbling backward. Her vision tunneled around her, a cold so piercing it shivered through her empty husk.

The flames were gone. They disappeared when Emrys moved in.

Sayra had broken her vow. She had lost control. Their surroundings were in ruins.

Hundreds of trees were gone along with the bodies of the Horde that had attacked them. Yes, they were daemons, but they had once been human beings. And that poor little boy. He didn't deserve to burn.

What was she doing?

Sayra covered her mouth with a gloved hand, her head reeling from the loss of the majik and the gruesome display they had witnessed. That was when she noticed black flecks of blood across her gloves, gained when she exploded the daemon from the inside out. Her own was smeared against the palm. Tearing them off, Sayra felt nauseous, immediately turning to vomit on top of the charred earth. Earth she burned when she lost control of the majik once more, nearly killing Emrys in the process.

Would she always cause others to be put in harm's way?

Sayra heard the gloves being picked up beside her, her hung head refusing to meet Emrys's gaze as she struggled to stand, knees locking to prevent her from collapsing. Only protocol had her feet stiffly moving, the next steps firmly ingrained into her mind. Everything threatened to rock her from her feet.

Emrys seemed to understand she couldn't function, her only drive to maintain her obligations as a Valkyrie. He promptly whistled to summon their mounts.

Retrieving her cloak, Sayra swiped off as much blood as she could manage, neglecting the dried black spots on the rest of her armor before wrapping it back around her hollow frame. That would have to be cleaned when they returned. But the stain Sayra left on her brother's sacrifice could never be removed.

It's okay, Sayra.

The words haunted her with an edge of disgust.

Everything was too quiet when Emrys handed her the thrown gloves, Sayra slipping them back on her hands. He had wiped them through grass and snow, clearing the blood from each. They started on the trail, the air between them heavy.

Not a single thought crossed her mind, for Sayra knew it would be her undoing.

Sylven was right to want to be rid of her.

Chapter Twenty-Nine

EMRYS

Emrys checked his mental shield against Nessika, knowing fully well it slipped again when he helplessly watched as Sayra threw herself at one of the three daemons. Every bit of concentration he could muster at the time was forced to spell out that one word. Run. A single word Sayra ignored to fruitlessly save them both. Even as fear threatened his consciousness, Emrys felt horror overtake him as her majik failed her. He couldn't bear witness to her death. It was a fate worse than torture by Horde.

But when she fell to *nefas* majik, Emrys became stricken.

Past historians created well-documented accounts of those who delved into and committed to the *nefas* arts. After one taste, the beckoning of corruption would always linger. Only those with exceedingly powerful connections to majik could summon it, normally resulting in a crazed death as it ate them from the inside out.

Emrys had fallen into it once long, long ago.

A billowing cloud passed over the sun, blanketing the ground below with shade. He dared a glance in Sayra's direction, finding her gaze empty as she stared ahead. A dried line of blood ran down her face, smeared from when she swiped her skin with her gloved hand earlier.

A picture was ingrained in his mind of flames of the darkest color raging around her, loose blonde strands of hair rising with the flow of air. That tinge of madness raged in her captivating eyes, such raw power emanating from within. Sayra was the picture of an avenging goddess, her majik drawn forth to smite the sin from the earth itself. It was beautiful, but only in the way a dying person captured an ethereal view above a cliff before falling down it.

Emrys never wanted Sayra to harbor that darkness again, lest it fully claimed her soul.

Hell summoner.

Tension pulled at his shoulder blades, Emrys's mouth drawing into a tight line. Never in the history of Acacea or any known country on the continent had anyone heard any spoken word from the Horde.

It didn't bode well.

There were hundreds of ways everything could go wrong, and between *nefas* majik and speaking daemons that attacked during broad daylight, it only complicated matters further. If the true people who were behind the dormitory fire so much as prodded Sayra at the wrong time, or if a daemon approached Saint Highburn Monastery's wards while she was on patrol...

His teeth clenched painfully tight. Emrys hadn't the faintest inkling of what was going on. Not a single idea.

Hell summoner.

Perhaps it was in relation to her exceeding majikal capabilities. Sayra was possibly a beacon of majikal light to them, whereas any average Arcanist could only hold a candle to her roaring flame. That trail of thought made Emrys ponder every happenstance Sayra had with the Horde. One instance reappeared in his mind as he filtered through every encounter, and that was at Astor Manor.

Not two but *four* daemons had pursued Sayra and the entourage. The straggling two were agitated when Emrys discovered them prowling outside the wards of the Astor duchy. Sayra's majik must have beckoned those daemons within a certain radius as the seal on her majik was failing to conceal the radiance of her power. It could be the daemons' primary drive was to eliminate her, thus responding to her presence.

And that seal was currently gone.

It awoke daemons during broad daylight to seek her. The piece didn't fit firmly into the puzzle, but Emrys couldn't deduce a sturdier conclusion without further evidence. For now, it would have to suffice.

The clomping of hoofs against dirt drew Emrys back to their surroundings. Sayra still hadn't budged. Her gaze was hollow as they passed a broken carriage. The horse leading it was long gone, and Emrys spent several minutes scouring the area to see if anyone remained behind.

He found nothing except one section of path that led into the forest where a streak of fresh scarlet was dragged into the tree line. With a sickened stomach, Emrys concluded that was the young boy's family who traveled in the destroyed carriage. They must have all perished by daemons from the looks of the monstrous footprints throughout the snow.

The next hour was trying. He couldn't help thinking of the fate that fell upon those travelers, one that almost claimed him and Sayra too. Beside him, Sayra pulled the hood of her cloak lower, as if she couldn't bear the thought of him seeing her face.

Such concern for Sayra's well-being weighed him down, but he wasn't the type to press matters when others weren't prepared for it. He held out for years for Sylven, and if Sayra needed a silent friend, then that was what Emrys would be. Unassuming but present for when she needed him.

She had kissed him back, however.

Emrys tried to repress the memory of her arms circling him. The incomparable rush when she deepened her kiss. He wrote it off as *nefas majik* controlling her mind, but his thoughts couldn't help but counter with the logic the kiss had broken the hold darkness had over her. Ultimately, was it genuine, or was it the remnants of an altered version of herself reciprocating in kind? He didn't know.

Shaking his head, Emrys blew heavily from his nose. He couldn't lose focus. He needed every bit of concentration and help he could garner in the coming weeks until Sayra's twentieth birthday. Until the informant could lay out the answers on a silver platter.

It was time to enlist Sylven, if he was willing. Perhaps Waylen could be entrusted with basic details, though it would be a gamble since he was by far the most devout of them all. Emrys required every ally he could muster beyond the handful of monks, nuns, and guards under his father's secret employ within the monastery. At last, the rebellion was beginning to take shape, and the thought of endless repercussions flitted through his head from what he was tasked to do next. Nothing would ever be the same. One thing was certain, however, and that was the impending fight of their lifetime.

A slight breeze whistled through the glen around them, Emrys stealing another look at Sayra. For her and for his kingdom, Emrys wouldn't hesitate.

Chapter Thirty

SYLVEN

Damn Sayra and damn Rys and their obscure journey to a place they deemed important enough to risk their necks on. Damn the hellish contract that sent him over the edge to insanity. Sylven couldn't stop pacing in his room, nearly pulling his hair out when Sayra's overwhelming fear flooded their link, meaning only one thing. Their lives were in danger.

Why did he insist on staying behind?

It wasn't until Nessika came banging on his door, livid and terrified, that it really struck him how severe the situation must have been for her to have felt a slip by Rys.

She let herself in, slamming the door behind her. "Where did they go?" she demanded, fists clenched beside her hips.

Of course, Sylven knew the city they'd traveled to and the route they'd take, but he was sworn to secrecy by Rys, making him wonder about the last communication and trust he had with his Valkyrie.

"If Rys didn't inform you, I am in no position to contradict that." Sylven helplessly shook his head. He monitored the bond, noting a bizarre blend of emotions before he felt the situation resolve. "Besides, Sayra seems fine now, and if she is, then Rys is too."

Nessika's face relaxed for a moment, her eyes glassy, as if her mind were in a distant place. A minute ticked by, Sylven wringing his hands behind his neck and waiting for the verdict. He needed to learn how to verbally communicate with the bond as soon as possible. Blinking fast, the Valkyrie let out a breath, her muscles beneath her training gear loosening a smidge.

"And?" he prompted, brows raised as his foot tapped the royal-blue carpet.

Jaw ticking to the side, Nessika allowed her shoulders to drop an inch. "They're fine. Three daemons ambushed them, Sayra and Emrys managing to defeat them once they arrived in the area. They are in route, fatigued but unharmed otherwise."

He could tell she was at the end of her patience—a feeling he was well acquainted with.

Sylven ungracefully plopped into his desk chair, his stress easing by a margin. "Thank the Goddess." His eyes were glued to the ceiling. "Those two are going to be the death of me."

Rounding the table, Nessika placed herself a mere two feet away from him and crossly planted a hand on his desk. "You know what's going on with them, don't you?" she asked, those icy eyes sending a chill down his back at the unspoken threat in her voice.

Whereas Sayra was a storm to be weathered, Nessika was an earthquake that would stop at nothing to topple any objects or people in her way—a force he truly did not want to piss off any further.

"I do, but I'm in no position to share that. Ask Rys to be upfront. Or Sayra."

"This is manic!" Nessika fumed, pushing off the table and flexing her fists. "I'm not some outsider, yet I'm treated that way by Emrys. Sayra is one of my best friends, and she lies to my face." An accusing glare burned into his chin, Sylven's face still tactfully raised to the ceiling. "But for one reason or another, *you* know."

When he said nothing, she growled, "Sylven, they almost died. And for what? A honeymoon?"

That caught his attention, his eyes regrettably shifting to hers before he could help himself.

Bitter victory shone in her eyes, and her face pulled in disgust. "I knew it," Nessika murmured, her mouth drawing back. "They are together. I don't understand why he didn't simply contract with her instead."

Because it would have been too conspicuous if he contracted with her. But Sylven didn't say that aloud.

Snorting, he rolled his eyes at her. "C'mon, really? You think they would endanger themselves over something that trivial?"

"What else could it be?"

"Something bigger than you or me," Sylven said glumly, slouching forward.

Nessika's hands unfolded, her thin brows drawing close. "What do you mean by that? Are they arranging diplomatic ties between Droden and Acacea? Sayra isn't royalty any longer."

"It has absolutely nothing to do with romance," Sylven monotoned, giving her an expression that read *I'm very over this conspiracy.*

Shoulders sagging, Nessika leaned against the edge of his desk, eyes closed and face downturned. "Please, Sylven. I swear I'd never tell another soul, but I can't keep doing this while they risk their lives pursuing... whatever this is. I just want to be there for Sayra and to fulfill my duty toward Emrys. It kills me to see Sayra so exhausted all the time, to watch her coming back in the early hours of each morning from the gym with the weight still on her back." Her long lashes slowly opened. "I've been a poor excuse of a friend to her of late. If it isn't romantic in nature, I've said some unfoundedly harsh things to her."

A semblance of empathy emerged in Sylven at that, having been in her exact situation for nearly the same timeframe. They were two sides of a coin, both left out and left guessing in the dark. None of it made any comprehensible sense to Sylven before Sayra revealed the truth. Consequently, Sylven wasn't convinced he wanted to know that truth. His entire life shifted beneath his feet, his rock-solid plans for the future crumbling before him.

While being away from the two of them gave him time to ponder, Sylven was still stressing about how the world-churning information would affect his family. The only thing he knew without a doubt was he'd never allow them to face such circumstances alone again.

Didn't Nessika deserve the same options he was given to decide whether she'd pursue the path beside them or ask for reassignment to another Arcanist?

"Swear you'll never tell another soul," Sylven warned, gripping each knee as his decision was made. There would be consequences. Rys and Sayra could be furious, but Nessika deserved to know and to decide her own fate.

Her expression morphed into shock, her full lips parting slightly. Recovering quickly, she promised, "Of course. I'd never tell a soul outside of us four. Thank you, Sylven. I can't mean that enough."

Her earnestness caught him off guard, though he should have expected no less from a guardian Emrys vetted himself before selecting. "Before I share, understand that Rys was sworn to secrecy by a majikal oath; therefore, he's completely unable to share any details with you. As for Sayra, understand that she's been burdened greatly, and Rys requested that she not share her tale with you or the others for her own safety."

Sylven waited for her confirmation before resuming. "Sayra was unfairly given the short end of every stick. Right now, I think more than ever, she needs you in her corner."

Hell must have frozen over for me to say that, he thought.

Frowning, the Valkyrie's brows upturned in the middle. "I feel like crap now, but that makes more sense already."

Leaning back, Sylven recounted all he had gleaned from Sayra, Nessika remaining silent through it all. Her nostrils flared when he recounted the carnage committed in the Holy Family's name. To her credit, she didn't call him an outright liar, much like he would have done if the roles had been reversed.

Like he did with Sayra.

"Even I don't know everything, only what Sayra could share with me directly," Sylven confessed, somewhat relieved to unburden the weight on someone else. Perhaps it was selfish, but he needed another person to speak freely with who wasn't Rys or Sayra. Neither of them understood his stance. "Honestly, I don't know where I stand in all of this. It's..." His hands helplessly gestured.

"There isn't any room for question, Sylven. The Holy Family must be brought to justice for their crimes, and we have to help Emrys and Sayra where we can," Nessika decided, her voice strong and expression determined.

Sylven was speechless. Just like that, the Valkyrie made a decision, whereas Sylven remained unconvinced. What did that say of him? It baffled Sylven that she did so quickly, as if it were painfully obvious what the correct decision was. Not to mention she believed everything he shared without evidence.

"Aren't you frustrated in the least by the secrecy?" he asked.

A smirk crossed her face at that. "No. In fact, I've been a complete jerk to Sayra, and I'll readily admit that. Sure, I can try to excuse myself all day and say that this is all inconceivable, but the reality of the matter is my mind was so fixated on it being something scandalous between the two of them that I became narrow-minded."

Sylven admired her bluntness.

"What am I supposed to do?" He vocalized the question swirling in his head, the answer still alluding him.

Snorting, Nessika gave him a look. "You're supposed to get off your butt and stop mulling about in self-pity. Have they asked anything ridiculous of you?" At his silence, she nodded. "That's what I thought. Continue being there for them, and when the time comes, if they need assistance, you'll know your answer before they ask."

He huffed, annoyed she had called him out and annoyed she was right.

"You're unfazed by this? Isn't it insane to try and topple a power greater than what you wield?" he grumbled, flicking yet another balled-up paper across his desk, observing it as it rebounded against the wall.

"It's insane to allow this to continue. If we go along with the perception that we as individuals have no power to inflect change in the grander scheme of things, then we'll become complacent with the way the world is and complain about how society allowed this to happen," Nessika countered, her eyes crackling with passion. "What we must do is rise up before it's too late. I'd rather die knowing I started the change than contributed to the continuance of corruption. Then, at least, I'd pass away in peace, knowing I had lived a significant life—one to be proud of when I reach the Goddess's heaven."

The Valkyrie's words struck Sylven, his face twisting away as he pondered the impact of them. The world was on the precipice of a life-altering event, the dominos already falling in place in a seemingly endless chain. Sylven didn't think he could bear the bystander's guilt when it came, and in one of the coming days, it inevitably would. Whether it might be the preventable loss of his friends—Sylven consciously included Sayra in that growing list, a very questionable addition but due to her importance in the grand scheme of things—or his family, it would crush him.

Which was worse to lose—family or friends? In the end, Sylven supposed it would come to an ultimatum should his family side with the Holy Family. Only then would he have to decide. But for now, for now...

"We should be there when they arrive." Sylven changed the subject, only willing to further mull things over in private. "Until then, would you kindly allow me to have some semblance of privacy?"

"Boy, you aren't going to have that anymore," Nessika told him, but thankfully she steered herself toward the door, giving him the space he craved.

Didn't he know it.

Maybe he was crazy, or maybe he was so lost he didn't know the difference, but something propelled him to step toward Nessika and say, "Wait."

She paused just a foot from his door. Turning her head, she gave him a quizzical glance.

"You still believe then?" He waved a hand. "In the Goddess and her will? Even after everything you've learned?"

Nessika's forehead pinched. "Of course. She is real despite what the Holy Family may have twisted her words to be."

Shame clouded Sylven's eyes, his jaw working side to side. He wished he was as steadfast as the Valkyrie before him. "Then why is it this happened? *This* is her will?"

Compassion softened Nessika's face. "Her will is for ours to be free. It's our greatest gift from her, but for those who reject what the Goddess stands for, it becomes our greatest bane. This evil and the pain from it are a cost we must endure to persevere. We will expose the Holy Family."

"But we are *nothing* compared to them." Sylven braced a hand against his chair. "How would this realistically end well?"

"Don't be ridiculous. We have all we need now." She gestured to her chest, then Sylven's. "The Goddess gave us each other, and together, we will find the way. I know it." Before he could process it all, Nessika left his room.

⸻◈⸻

The hours dragged by painstakingly slow, Sylven's mind far too distracted to continue his pointless studies. At long last, he felt Sayra near, his feet guiding him to the guarded gateway between the monastery's grounds and the wild beyond. Tucked away in a corner, a cloaked Valkyrie already awaited their arrival with a book held between her polished nails. The gates were being cranked open by two guards on either side, Nessika flipping a page across from him.

Sylven had no desire to engage in another conversation, so he tucked his hands into his trouser pockets and stood as a slight breeze pulled at his navy cloak. Strands of hair flicked across his forehead, his sight firmly locked on the two frothy-mouthed horses trotting his way. A cloaked woman, Sayra, rode upon the lighter of the two steeds, her face tucked under a hood. Beside her, tense and unusually grim, was Rys.

Sylven felt nothing from Sayra, their link unblocked but empty as if she were numb. His hand fiddled with a coin under his cloak.

Rys looked at Sylven, gesturing to meet them in the stables where Nessika waited just outside. Nodding, Sylven's boots crunched over snow as he and Nessika filed in behind. The stable boy came by to take the horses and care for them.

The woman leaned a gloved hand against the wood of the stable for a moment before looking up toward him. Sayra's eyes were heavy-lidded and her face lined with exhaustion.

But what really struck him was the way she seemed to look *through* him.

A deliberate and commanding voice pulled Sylven's attention from the Valkyrie. "We need to move before the guards switch. Their shifts overlap within the hour, and I'd rather not have our arrival be notated in the books." Guards sealed the gate as Rys nodded in greeting to Sylven.

Without hesitation, Nessika charged forward toward Sayra, Sylven feeling her dread increase as the Valkyrie neared.

Sayra started slowly, her words faint before cutting off. "Nes, I—"

Hands enveloped Sayra's cloak, Nessika pulling her into the deep embrace of one who almost lost someone they loved. Furrowing her brows, Sayra carefully returned the hug.

Words were whispered from Nessika, and Sayra's face changed into stark relief, so much so her eyes glistened under bunched brows, her hands gripping Nessika's a hair tighter. Sylven felt the wave of emotion, nearly making his own eyes water in the process.

He felt how much it had weighed on his guardian to withhold such burdensome secrets, to be ridiculed and have to bear it when her friend confronted her time and time again. He felt no regret at all for his actions, for the truth to have been revealed from his lips to Nessika. Everyone needed another at their lowest points, and it brought Sylven some peace of mind that there would be less friction between their group at last.

His nose wrinkled at that. Since when did he become such a softie?

Redirecting his thoughts, Sylven approached Rys as he wrapped up his discussion with one of the stableboys. The glint of coins caught his eye as Rys passed them to the young man. The two stableboys retreated with the horses, a long rest in store for each of them. Always the busybody, Rys debriefed key points of the attack to Sylven and Nessika, Sylven's gut churning as the tale was recapped.

Sayra and Nessika turned to depart for the dormitory, leaving Sylven restless and confused at whether he should say anything to Sayra. For him, it was difficult to decipher the conundrum she was and what her situation entailed for him. Was she truly his Valkyrie if she meant to deviate from her course and become a leading figure in a rebellion? If that were the case, Sylven owed her nothing, and they'd trek their respective own paths, though it was obvious Rys wasn't going to leave her be, making it inevitable Sylven would have some sort of interaction with her in the future. Knowing it wouldn't be the typical, detested Arcanist-Valkyrie contract eased his mind, though.

"Sayra," Sylven called out, watching in apprehension as her haunted gaze found him. Nessika's brow inclined. "I'm glad you've returned safely. You and Rys, that is," he quickly added, pinching the bridge of his nose in slight awkwardness.

No longer did he have to stoke his resentment toward her. Sylven was too exhausted from bearing that grudge. He had the opportunity to start anew in that aspect, and while he hadn't decided where his cards lay, it would have been pointless to continue detesting her after all he knew.

A nod, a flicker of gratitude through their link, and she resumed her path. It was enough to convey her response, one acknowledged by Sylven as he twisted his head to the person stepping in beside him.

"What really happened out there?" Sylven asked, his face pinched in concern.

The story was barely passable. One Arcanist and Valkyrie taking on three daemons? Never mind the fact that Rys was a dark-majik user with an abnormally strong capability for the fire affinity, the fear the three daemons would have caused should have been incapacitating. Not to mention the strange flux of emotions Sayra had during that time. Sylven had felt it all, except for a minute when something dark blurred their bond.

Shaking his head, Rys murmured, "Not here. Let's return to my room, and we can speak freely."

In silence, the two wound through the entry hall and skirted around the packed marketplace stalls that thrived on weekends. Selling goods from all countries, merchants pocketed a fair amount of coin from the students and staff at the monastery. It was an affair many chatted about in the evenings in the common room with others in their class, a nice reminder of home during their long duration at Saint Highburn Monastery. Some students stayed there year-round, not having seen their families for almost four years.

To Sylven, it was needless spending and ogling at overpriced merchandise, the time better spent with one's nose in a book.

The corridors were noticeably emptier as they progressed away from the monastery's entryway, Rys leading the way without a single glance in Sylven's direction. Sylven noted the abnormal vacantness hovering about Rys, the way it took him a second longer to register an oncoming person and nod when greeted.

That trip must have taken its toll.

Rys's cloak twisted around him as he turned to open the door, allowing Sylven to enter in front of him. Sylven made himself at home at the table, silently waiting for Rys to engage in the conversation after a whispered word of power floated between them, masking noise others could overhear beyond the confines of the room. Carefully folding his dark cloak, Rys placed it in his laundry basket in his bathroom before sitting across from Sylven, his cutaway navy frock coat wrinkling at the waist. He smoothed out his white collar half-heartedly.

"We were as good as dead," Rys murmured, his eyes distant and directed at the wall behind Sylven.

Sylven's stomach lurched at that, the regret of him not joining their journey further gnawing at him.

Rys sighed, resting an arm across the tabletop. "As you probably surmised, the three Horde should have overpowered us, and they did. That is, until Sayra used *nefas* majik."

A majik insanely strong at the cost of sanity.

Gray eyes marked Sylven's shock, Rys's chin declining in response. "She was nearly claimed by it, but fortune had it she was able to come back. Hopefully, in two months' time, we'll be able to meet with someone who can give the answers we all need."

"By the Goddess." Sylven felt the blood drain from his face. "I'll never forget almost losing you to it when our families had traveled from the capital to my family's manor."

Rys slouched over his table, a hand massaging his temple. "A terrible mistake made by a child who thought he needed to help four Valkyries and ten guards take out a single daemon. I nearly killed Korine trying to protect everyone. If it weren't for your dad sealing my majik temporarily..." Rys closed his eyes.

"How did Sayra recover from that?" Sylven couldn't fathom it, recalling the abnormal feelings from Sayra tingling through his mind. A hint of madness was all he felt before it went fuzzy. The thought chilled him.

"I..." Rys hesitated, some new emotion crossing his face Sylven had difficulty deciphering. He blinked his eyes open.

Was it embarrassment that dragged Rys's gaze toward any point in the room but him?

Finally, Rys sent a hand through his straight locks, scattering them as he mustered his next words. "I kissed her."

Sylven's jaw slackened, then rounded in question before clenching shut. He didn't know where to begin or how to address that declaration. His mind circled around the fact Rys had previously assured him the relationship between him and Sayra wasn't romantic in nature, but Sylven couldn't help but question the reality of the situation. How was it not romantic if Rys saw fit to kiss her, if he determined the only method to salvage Sayra's soul was to do what he did? It had to have meant something to her to restore her consciousness. Otherwise, it would have been as ineffective as they were when Rys used forbidden majik. Rys's mom begged him to stop in the carriage that night to no avail.

Maybe Nessika was right about their romance, and Rys simply hid it from him all along. Sylven was certain there wasn't any convenient blood oath to stop him from sharing that.

Rys assured him it was platonic. He *lied*.

For some reason, Sylven felt his mind shift into irrationality, some instinct wanting him to return the blow Rys had just landed. His jaw ticked to the side. "I informed Nessika about Sayra." With a deep breath, he repressed everything else he wanted to say. Even in his anger, he knew it was beyond childish. But he was *furious*.

Rys's countenance grew cold, any trace of that embarrassment evaporating at Sylven's words. A muscle worked in the prince's jaw. His appearance was eerily similar to the king's when his wrath was provoked. "Why?"

It was one word, one word that contained such underlying anger and authority Sylven nearly confessed then and there before reminding himself Rys was the cause of the problem.

"You know why. Don't make my words redundant." Sylven scowled, a fist balling on his thigh.

Rys closed every barrier around his face. Anything Sylven could glean from his expression had been cloaked thoroughly. "I said once before that my partnership with Sayra wasn't romantic, and I hadn't lied to you. Never have I lied to you, Sylven." Even his words lacked emotion, each of them falling flat the moment they left his mouth.

"Then why…" Sylven threw his hands at his side. "You know what? It doesn't matter. I informed Nessika because she deserves to know. Don't worry, she won't tell anyone else, nor will I. Waylen doesn't need to be dragged through the dirt like I've been. He's been pleasantly out of this entire ordeal."

"Evidently, it does matter. I assure you, I am making every effort to keep matters professional. I had no choice but to do something shocking that would completely redirect her focus, and I don't regret for a second I did that to ensure she repressed the *nefas majik*," Rys clipped, his body taking on that ethereal stillness he showed when nearing the limit of his patience.

But something in his wording caught Sylven's attention.

"Making every effort, are you?" Sylven queried, raising his brows and leaning back in his chair with an incredulous tilt of his mouth. "When did you start having feelings for her in such a way?"

Rys's nostrils flared as he inhaled, a hand slamming into the table as he rose and passed Sylven. Drawing a leather-bound book from his nightstand, Rys opened it to a half-filled page with written notes. Grasping a pen, he inked several words, his voice so low Sylven barely registered it.

"You may leave now."

Sylven was being dismissed, and not by his friend but by the authority of the prince of his homeland. It struck him harder than he thought possible, the blow feeling physical on his chest. Biting his tongue to refrain from shouting, Sylven slowly rose, eyeing Rys all the while to give him time to change his mind.

He didn't.

Without another word, Sylven left the room.

CHAPTER THIRTY-ONE

EMRYS

Not long after Sylven left, Emrys heard the sound of paper sliding under his door. Without delay, he threw aside his notebook and picked up the scribbled communication. Taking a breath to calm himself, he lit the note on fire with a quick spell and set off to the library.

His parents had a new message waiting for him.

The timing was urgent since they sent it out of the blue. After he snuck the paper that had been left in the tiny compartment, Emrys only stalled for a half hour, pretending to study. The moment he was back in his room, he decoded the message, which he thought he had misread.

After two more attempts, he leaned back in his chair. A new energy buzzed through his veins. The informant, upon learning of the majik Sayra accidentally used during her final trial as an acolyte, decided it was time to act.

The informant had begun her trek to meet Sayra long ago. She was arriving Monday and fully expected Emrys to bring Sayra to a meet-up spot that wasn't priorly approved. Being the independent entity she was, Emrys's parents told him grudgingly to do as the woman requested.

Hope kindled in Emrys's mind.

It was what Sayra needed, and he couldn't have wished for a better time.

Chapter Thirty-Two

SAYRA

Nessika lent a shoulder as Sayra all but collapsed into her desk chair, sluggishly removing her armor piece by piece. The walk there was arduous, and deep-rooted exhaustion had grown through every cell in her body. She didn't care that her armor fell to the stone below or that she appeared every bit the wreck she felt like.

All that mattered right then was Nessika finally knew the truth, and she promised to be at her side to help her through things. The apology still rang through her ears. Nessika's concern thawed the lingering chill in Sayra's veins from the day's chain of events. She hollowly recounted how they had defeated the Horde, skimming over the fact that Emrys kissed her, and she may have liked it.

More than liked it.

All the while, Nessika helped her clean the metal to a shine, Sayra rinsing the blood from her skin in the restroom and emerging somewhat refreshed in gray pajamas. The last of her armor was polished to perfection, resting inside her trunk beside her pristine *spyd*.

Sayra exhaled, her legs giving out as she flopped on top of her bedsheets. "Thank you, Nes. For believing."

Nes flashed her teeth. "What kind of friend would I be otherwise?" Growing serious, she added, "I swear I will help where I can. I won't allow Emrys to sideline me anymore, especially not when I can be of use."

"You can choose not to be involved still. It's asking a lot," Sayra mumbled, her eyes involuntarily closing as her hand fumbled for the corner of her comforter.

Barking a laugh, Nes shook her head. "No way am I dissing you a second time. You're stuck with me. Talk later?"

A small smile spread across Sayra's face, gratitude making her heart swell as she pulled the down-filled fabric over her chest. Her response died on her lips, sleep sweeping over her like an ocean's wave. Dreams of Faenda graced her deep slumber, the warm sands she used to play in beside the crystal-clear waters of the western coastline. It was a paradise during summer months, people across the empire flocking to the lukewarm waves for relaxing vacations. It was one of the few locations in her homeland that was still warded outside of homesteads, a haven for all to gather and celebrate life.

Sayra would never forget the last summer she spent with her siblings and parents before her mother and brother died. Such a fierce part of her longed for them and wished the daemons never tore them from her life.

Knocking at her door disturbed the reminiscent dream, her heart panging at the familiar faces that were no more. Sayra's body ached something fierce as she reluctantly rose, slipping on her plush navy slippers before trudging to the door. Sunlight filtered through her window, her sleep assumedly cut short by her latest guest.

Nes stood in full training leathers and a black cloak, her arms casually crossed.

Raising her brows, Sayra blearily asked, "Do you have a patrol today?"

Blue eyes sparkled as Nes let herself in. Sayra rubbed her eyes, closing the door with an elbow.

"Even better."

Biting her lip, Sayra's mind ran through their schedules, drawing a blank. "I'm not forgetting about something, am I?"

Nes's hands clasped Sayra's shoulders, shaking them lightly. "Emrys told me the informant is here to meet you."

Huh?

"She's going to meet us in an hour. You have to get ready! I figured I'd let you sleep in as much as possible."

Confused, Sayra peered out the window. Her eyes snapped wide. The sunlight was from the setting sun. She'd nearly slept an entire day away.

"Holy *dritt*," Sayra whispered, her mind processing everything. "Holy *dritt*!"

Nes's grin almost split her face.

"Wait. Emrys told you?" Sayra froze, a small smile cornering her mouth.

Inclining her chin, Nes went to Sayra's closest. "Yep. And we are all going."

"Sylven too?" That raised her brows.

"Yep."

His change of heart confused Sayra, but she'd be lying if she said it annoyed her. Maybe Sylven was becoming less of a *næva*. Turning, Sayra plucked out training leathers and closed the bathroom door behind her.

"Sooo, how is it with having you-know-what?" Nes casually asked, a small bump sounding as she presumably leaned against the wall.

Tugging on her last sock, Sayra quickly spelled a barrier around their room for privacy. "We can talk freely now." Opening the door, she moved to work on braiding her hair. "It's... strange. I love using majik. It's freeing. Amazing. But I'd trade it in a heartbeat if it meant the Holy Family wasn't corrupt, and I could continue living my life as a normal Valkyrie." She couldn't keep the hollowness from her voice.

Understanding flooded Nes's face. "Think about it like this. If they weren't corrupt, then daemons wouldn't exist. Arcanists wouldn't be here. Nor would Valkyries."

Sayra caught her meaning. With a forced smile, she tied off the end of her braid. "I'm grateful to have you guys. I really am. It's selfish, but I don't want to be in some grand coup or have to navigate the very real possibility we may not succeed."

That last part hurt her chest.

Lowering her gaze, Sayra reached for a black *slør* to match her leathers.

"At least, no matter what happens, none of us will be alone," Nes said, quietly resting her head against the wall. "Together, we stand the best chance of winning. And if the Goddess will have it, we may just see a future where the Horde is defeated."

"I hope so," Sayra murmured, not allowing herself to get that far ahead. Pushing back her anxiousness, she set her sights on Nes. "Let's do this."

They arrived at the gardens, a meticulously maintained oasis nestled at the heart of the monastery. Towering evergreens adorned the landscape, their branches delicately frosted, glistening like crystals. Ornate benches, thoughtfully placed, encircled ethereal fountains, their angelic sculptures emanating tranquility. Lush beds of flowers burst with resilient winter blossoms, painting the space with varying shades of violet and peach. Lampposts arched overhead, casting a warm and inviting ambiance onto the walkways. As darkness settled upon the sky, the garden pathways embraced a gentle glow, courtesy of lanterns enchanted with magic. They swayed with the passing breeze.

Emrys and Sylven stood across from each other beneath a copse of trees. Sayra would have missed them if it wasn't for Emrys stepping out to beckon them. She caught Sylven's broody face glancing at her. Assessing.

"This way," Emrys said, ushering them down a slanted path. "The gardens have one water drainage location in the center to prevent flooding, and it's just around these trees."

With majik, Emrys ensured no one could hear them as they collectively removed the steel lid, opening a narrow tunnel with ladder rings going far, far down.

"Pleasant," Sylven grumbled, his eyes taking in the dirty rungs. He scratched a spot on the top of his head, his walnut locks scattering in slight waves.

Without delay, Sayra dropped into the tunnel first, surprised it went down nearly thirty feet before she touched the ground. Her hands felt the chill of the stone as she moved some distance to let the others in, careful with her footing in the pitch black.

Wait. She had majik.

"*Sphera*." Sayra watched as a small ball of flame hovered over her left hand, lighting the narrow tunnel. A deep gutter ran in front of her, making her vastly grateful she didn't walk in that direction.

Nes went last, closing the lid and locking them in.

Sylven stared at the fire in her hands, his hazel eyes flickering. "I'll never get used to that."

Shrugging, Sayra moved to the side so Emrys could take the lead. He conjured his own flame, one remarkably brighter than hers. Then, they walked. The slope tapered downward, weaving through many tunnels, all conjoining and splitting in dizzying ways. Without hesitation, Emrys would bank right randomly only to make two consecutive lefts afterward.

They were deadly silent, knowing well the area was restricted.

It wasn't until they reached a section that was caved in that Emrys stilled. Turning, the flames flickered close to his profile, casting shades of yellow and orange across his face. "What I'm about to show you isn't a place we'll ever go again. I do this so that we may all go forward without any doubt, and only because I've since realized my parents' plan failed to take into account these recent changes to their original methods."

His eyes met Sayra's, an involuntary tingle racing down her spine. Her mind instantly went to the kiss they shared and to the warmth of his face against hers. Then, she immediately repressed it. Guilt tore at her stomach for the betrayal of her and Nes's oath to avoid romantic entanglements. One betrayal she had yet to admit to Nes, but one she hoped to recover from before it was too late.

Sayra closed off the line of thought, not wanting to raise suspicion from Sylven with the influx of emotions.

"I'm going to show you just a fraction of what the Holy Family does beneath the monastery before we meet the informant. You all deserve to know and see with your own eyes," Emrys said.

Sayra swallowed at that.

Emrys's sight left Sayra's in a begrudging way, as if he didn't want to take his eyes off her. To Sylven, he lowered his chin. "You were right."

Beside Sayra, Sylven shuffled, his hands tucked into his pockets. There was a conflict waging war in his expression, but ultimately, he settled for a brief nod.

"I'll cloak any noise we may make, but I ask that you try to be as stealthy as possible. Sayra." Emrys faced her. "When I dispel my fire, rid yours as well. Hold on to each other's shoulders for balance and guidance."

"Easy enough." Sayra's nerves ate at her. The danger they placed themselves in left an impact on any bravado she could muster.

Scanning them all, Emrys's face was deadly serious. "Do not touch the wall at the end of this particular tunnel. Do not get too close."

Sayra could barely breathe.

"And whatever you do, don't get spotted," he added.

Nes's hands moved in a nervous pattern at her sides.

"There will be one crack in the wall between stones that will let you see one section. We get in. You look. You do not react. We leave to meet the informant. Any questions will have to wait for later. Agreed?"

They all nodded in unison.

Without further fanfare, Emrys walked through the clogged hallway as if the rubble blocking it didn't exist. Eyes bulging, Sayra followed, Nes and Sylven trailing behind. First, it elevated upward several feet before steeply spiraling down. Further down the tunnel it turned from stone into a dirt pathway with wooden support beams. Sayra could have sworn they could all hear her racing heart. Beneath her gloves, her palms felt clammy. It seemed like forever before Emrys glanced over his shoulder, sharing a look and then extinguishing the fire.

Sayra's flames disappeared with a word, her hand reaching for him in the dark. At first, she connected with the side of his arm. She bit her tongue, suddenly feeling nervous for an entirely different reason. Warm fingers found hers, pulling her hand up to his left shoulder. Sayra couldn't breathe as the hand lingered for seconds longer than it should have. Then, Emrys removed it, leaving her cold.

Her face burned, and Sayra was very grateful for the darkness they stood in.

Sylven's hand found her shoulder, and they began their descent beneath the monastery. The path was narrow, Sayra's elbows occasionally grazing either side. All she heard was their shuffling steps and the sound of faint breathing.

Something sounded far ahead when they completed another turn, something that echoed in their tunnel. A shudder raced through her as a stream of majikal fear teased her mind. The sound grew until she realized it was the familiar laugh of daemons. It circled her mind, hastening her breathing.

They were close.

A tiny light grew in front of them. Sayra blinked, trying to see if she was seeing something or if it was real. But as they slowly walked forward, she knew they had arrived.

It startled Sayra when Emrys grasped her hand again, her focus on the horrific scene that was about to unfold. He carefully guided her forward until her face was inches from a carved-out section that revealed an open crevice. The widest point was the size of a coin. Perfect for her eye.

Taking a deep breath, Sayra took in the sight before her. The hole was just below the level of the roof, giving a clear oversight of several cells in each direction.

She couldn't breathe, and the daemons seemed to know it, their laughter echoing a fraction louder as she stared down at an acolyte she recognized. One who didn't graduate with her. One whose room was being cleared out by nuns when Sayra told her friends she graduated.

Xena.

Her body sat listlessly against a bare stone wall save for two cuffs chaining her arms above her head. Both empty eyes stared across from her pale, bloodstained body. Brown rags covered her torso down to her thighs, where they had been cut off. In lieu of human legs, back-bent, decaying daemon legs grew.

Even from where Sayra stood, she could smell a putrid odor and see Xena was no longer. There were several others around her in various states of experimentation, but on the far side, Sayra saw a tranquilized daemon the size of a donkey, smaller than any she'd encountered.

It could have been her, and that thought kept circling her mind.

Nausea rose from her stomach at the sickening display of cruelty. Xena's cell neighbor was the only one untouched by daemon flesh, and she rocked herself against the wall as her head twitched wildly in every direction. Her face was frantic, searching for something. A clang resonated from down the hall, footsteps approaching. Sayra watched as Jax Zefare whistled down the center, his face cheerful as his eyes honed in on the other Valkyrie.

Her name was Ralla. Another failed acolyte.

She began screaming, her body seizing as if sickness had struck her.

Jax pointed for two monks to unchain and grab her, which they did without question. Sayra could only watch in abject horror as they dragged her weak body from the cell, disappearing into the other side.

It could have been her.

Sayra's head spun, her mouth dryer than she'd ever felt before. A voice in the back of her mind caressed her worries, whispering that just a touch of *nefas* majik could wipe them all out there and now. It itched under her skin, compelling her to call upon it again.

Breathe, a voice in her head reassuringly told her. It sounded distant and muddled, but when Sylven's hand squeezed her shoulder, she knew it was him.

Inhaling deeply, Sayra struggled to regain her sensibilities. She couldn't use that majik again. Not when it risked her sanity and her friends' lives. Emrys had warned her on their long trek back to the monastery it would happen. She had to take care to repel the invasive thoughts.

Sayra backed away, Emrys's second hand guiding the small of her back toward his other side. Sylven took the spying hole, but that tiny sliver of light that shone through it highlighted the contours of his face. Concern had his eyes searching in her direction before he peered through the despicable crevice.

Within seconds, Sylven's block on their bond slipped, and his shock and revulsion poured through her head. He didn't linger, swiftly allowing Emrys to guide him beside Sayra. As Nes took the spot next, Sayra rested a tentative hand on Sylven's upper arm. Just in a moment of solidarity. Hatred, disgust, despair, and so much more ran through their heads. For once, Sayra was thankful Sylven was there, and the sentiment was reflected through his side of the link.

Emrys regained control of their exit, everyone linking up and trekking back. Sayra felt something fundamental shift within her, something that had her swearing to destroy every single member of the Holy Family and those who partook in that despicable place.

Even as a tear fell down her cheek, Sayra swore to end them all.

Chapter Thirty-Three

SAYRA

R ys took the lead in front of her, a summoned flame lighting the gray walls they carefully picked their way through. None of them had uttered a word. There weren't any to be had. A draft had Sayra pulling her cloak tight, the sense of the impending unknown setting her nerves on their finest edge. First the dungeons and next some unknown person who might further destroy the world she knew.

Her mind was frayed, and Sayra didn't know how much more she could take.

Only a few scant feet cleared her head in the drainage tunnel. At some point, her breath fogged, the air becoming moist around them. Rivulets streamed by their feet, moisture collecting into fine droplets above. An uncanny echo sounded from every clash of boots against stone, the drip of water into puddles. Sayra couldn't sense what was ahead or how far they had yet to go.

As if sensing her unease, Rys murmured, "Almost there."

Great. Because she sure wasn't a fan of the environment. Being that far underground... It felt more like a crypt than a place to adventure.

Sayra held her fire to the side, somewhat comforted by the warmth and light. Nes walked in front of her. When they first summoned fire after seeing the dungeons, Sayra would never forget the glance they shared. Her friend's face was murderous, the response reflected in Sayra's heart. With just that look, they both agreed to bring those culpable to their knees.

A shuffle sounded ahead, catching Sayra's attention. She caught the step of another just around the bend of a side tunnel. Light weakly flickered, giving her the distinct impression they were about to meet the mystery woman herself. Emrys inclined his head as he looked back at them, confirming her perception.

Heart pounding, Sayra's eyes ate up every inch as they rounded the corner. A figure leaned against a wall with a torch in hand. She was strapped with a variety of fabrics, concealed by a thick, fur-lined, mulberry-wool hood. A great sword was attached to her hip, plain and lacking in any specialized embellishments.

The woman's voice rang out. "Sayra?"

Freezing, Sayra locked into place, Emrys twisting his face away from hers. She gave no mind to his reaction but rather the voice she hadn't heard since she was eight.

"You can't be," Sayra said, her voice low and her heart clenching in pain. The woman sounded just like her mother, Arene, but that was impossible. She perished against the Horde, defending one of the Holy Family. There wasn't even the slightest chance she could have survived.

Removing her hood, the woman's features came to light. Eyes as green as hers, hair a handful of shades darker, and features near delicate as her own.

It was her mother's face.

Sayra couldn't grasp her emotions, the tidal wave drowned out by the riptide threatening to pull her under. Her mother was alive, but how? The Holy Family must have lied about her passing, the last eleven years of her life spent in misery for the loss of the two people she cherished most.

But one of those ghosts stood in front of her, an aged replica of the mother who used to braid her hair and guide her wooden version of a toy sword in her hands. The woman who departed most of her wisdom before returning to her duty each year. The moments were brief whenever she'd visit. Heavenly days. They were too sparse, though, and the last nine months of her mother's life were spent at the monastery away from Sayra and her brother.

If she had been alive all those years, why had she never once visited Sayra? Especially after Brevn passed. Sayra had lived in torment, blaming herself for running away on the evening of her birthday. Another one her mother had missed, though that time the excuse was death.

Everything could have been vastly different had her mother made a single appearance to reassure Sayra of her survival, even if Sayra had to keep the secret. Her mother knew of her betrothal to Kenji, yet she never once interfered, even though she was well aware of his abhorrent temperament and his father's. Had it not been for Sayra secretly enrolling in the Valkyrie Academy, going as far as to sign the binding papers in a clandestine manner, she'd never have left Droden. She would have been locked away in a castle, kept as a prize without the faintest inkling of freedom.

"Are you okay?" Sylven murmured, moving in close to her side.

Sayra barely got out, "No. My mother is alive, and I'm about to kill her."

"That's not—"

Sayra ignored his words, electing instead to clench her fists and rush the woman. "How!" she shouted. Her voice trembled with fury as her arm lashed out, quickly blocked with a grim expression and muscled arm. "Dare!" Twisting, she swooped low to attempt an elbow to the gut. Her mother swung her leg, the knee connecting in the nick of time. "You!"

Swiveling and rising, Sayra attempted a mean uppercut to her jaw, Arene's leg spinning out in unison. Her fist almost connected the moment the boot took her own out from under her. Sayra caught her upper body with two precisely placed palms, flashes of past brawling sessions with her mom clouding her mind. Flipping back, she regained her footing and searched for another opening.

Sayra never won any of their practice brawls, and it seemed time hadn't dulled her mother's capabilities.

Regret lined Arene's sun-kissed face. "I deserve it all and worse. I know. Let me explain myself, Sayra."

The prince knew her intention before even Sayra did. "Stop," Emrys commanded, the authority causing a second's hesitation before Sayra lurched forward once more.

The Acacean prince wasn't hers, after all.

But the damned Arcanist threw himself in her path, her curled fists nearly colliding with his shoulder. The only problem was at that close a range, Sayra couldn't spare the space to stop her momentum. The force was already there, driving her forward, and there was only one rather unfortunate path that wouldn't completely shatter his unreinforced bones.

Speeding up her spin, Sayra lowered her trajectory, pushing her shoulder out further so it would impact first. It hit his chest, lacking the force that thrusted her hand into the stone beside his waist. Slammed into the wall, Emrys let out a grunt as his head connected, his gray eyes narrowing in pain. Breathing hard out of her nose, Sayra's chin rose at him.

"*Fy faen*! What were you thinking?" Sayra seethed, pushing back from the wall and, not completely unnoticed, his chest. Gesturing toward the stone next to him, only a foot away from her silently observing mother, a spiderweb of caved-in rock formed where she had hit it. "I could have killed you!"

Her hands were shaking, right fist smarting from the impact.

Emrys didn't even balk, not sparing a single twitch of the eyes to track the location where her fist found purchase. At the fatal mark that could have imploded the entirety of his left torso. Sayra felt it then, the rising of his majik, as if he were summoning it in preparation to cast. Her brows lowered dangerously further, her own majik rising subconsciously to challenge his.

"We haven't long. I can buy us some time to venture out. Soon, our absence will not go unnoticed. Nessika has a patrol duty coming up," Emrys argued, a hint of frustration pulling his face taunt. "We require the information she has to bring about the downfall of the Holy Family and the Horde. Without it, nothing will change."

His voice didn't rise, but the urgency behind his tone gave Sayra pause. It was a new tenor she'd never heard.

Grinding her teeth, Sayra repressed the energy in her veins, pushing it away to clear her mind of the potential for its use. Emrys could sense it, his shoulders visibly lowering as he removed himself from the wall.

Sayra's eyes locked onto the ones mirroring hers, her temper barely reined in. "Get on with it. Tell me how you decided to sacrifice your own child for the greater good, abandoned her to the sharks of Droden and then to the viper's den of Lykken," she mocked, relishing the flinch in those large, emerald eyes. "To be married to an abusive *ræva* and endure years of my father's hatred. To be the cause of my brother's death. All because I couldn't bear the fact my own mother had passed."

Raw, undiluted shock emanated from Sayra's mental link with Sylven. She belatedly realized what she had exposed, but at that moment, she couldn't regret it. Not when it had the impact she wanted on her mother's face.

Nes was stunned. For the first time, she was unsure of what to do as she stood beside Sylven. The latter's face was drawn, but he didn't move to interfere.

Pain etched into every bit of her mother's appearance, her mouth pressed into a drawn line. Sayra then decided to throw the final dagger into her mother's cruel heart.

"In the end, you're the cause of Brevn's passing. Of this," Sayra said, pointing to the scar across the bridge of her nose. Giving a hateful laugh, she shook her head. "You never cared enough to be around then, so I don't know why another eleven years would matter to you."

Her mother, Arene von Lykken, guardian of the holy Grand Priest himself, legend of the Valkyries and vanquisher of thirty-seven of the Horde, became misty-eyed. A single tear budded beside her eye.

An ounce of remorse clung to Sayra's stomach, knowing full well her mother had cared for her during those scant visits. She truly valued each and every one. The anger was unreasonable, sprouting from her hurt over discovering her mother had abandoned her.

"Sayra," Arene began, her voice choking. Clearing her throat, the woman straightened her shoulders, becoming a Valkyrie rather than a mother. Sayra had seen the shift every time she departed to return to her guardianship. Whenever matters became serious.

Currently, it was to confront her own daughter.

"I was entrusted with the Holy Family's darkest, most closely kept secret. The true way Arcanists were made, not born, and what really happened to girls who never made it to the status of Valkyrie. My honor demanded I act rather than remain silent, turning me to my distant relative's husband, a man in the Acacean court."

Suddenly dried, Arene's eyes became solemn. "They were the only court known to contradict the church in the past, and I held hope that they'd hear out my words and act as I had been driven to."

Emrys folded his arms beside Sayra, enraptured by the story spun by her mother. Sayra simply looked on with disdain.

"The timing was unfortunate. I was pregnant with you and Queen Evangelina similarly indisposed. They waited for far too long to act, thus enticing me to look elsewhere for aid. I made many contacts during those months, discerning new allies and spreading the truth about what exactly was held under those marble floors. We concocted a bold, insane plan, elaborate to the finest grain of detail, and we rehearsed to the bone."

Sayra despised admitting it, but she wanted to know every element of the supposed heist.

Arene gathered her breath before resuming. Her eyes were only for her daughter. "Inside the deepest chamber, the only vault heavily guarded by Valkyries of the highest confidence, was a relic as old as mankind, engraved with a language far beyond our understanding. It's been said it belonged to a superior race before ours, one that fell to the force we ignorantly toy with now. Majik."

Arene's face tightened. "There are four separate pieces, all capable of puzzling together. Whenever a male baby is born, do you know what occurs?"

Flaring her nostrils, Sayra narrowed her eyes. "An archbishop blesses the boy for good fortune with the Goddess's touch. Those babies who don't receive the blessing don't receive majik, which leads me to presume that the archbishop conducts the ceremony with a piece of that relic, infusing the majik when young and only when young. If they waited until an older age, the child or adult would become corrupt and merge into the form of a daemon."

Impressed, her mother gave her an appraising look. "Correct."

"And so?" Sayra asked.

"I stole two of those pieces," Arene announced.

A small gasp came from Nes, somewhere behind Sayra. Sayra could feel Sylven's shock and unease through their bond before he wrapped his emotions away.

Sayra gaped at her mother. She couldn't help herself. It seemed mad. If her mother owned two, then wouldn't their presence be enough to convince the people? Why had they needed to "gift" her majik? Even Emrys's gaze widened in surprise, one of the few times he'd been caught off guard.

"One I broke down, learning the hard way that they can be used not only to open a pathway for humans to use majik but also as a source of majik themselves." Her hands moved to bundle up the fabric on her left leg, Sayra staring in befuddlement until it was high enough. A metal cylinder ending in a strange hook shape took place of her lower leg. "I was fortunate to know a Thapulan inventor who created this replacement when I accidentally set fire to a building with myself in it." She allowed the fabric to fall from her grasp. "Using the relic as a source of majik caused it to crack. I knew then either the relics somehow expired outside of the monastery or that using them created instability."

Sayra stared at the fabric surrounding the fake leg.

"The latter is impossible. They wouldn't exist any longer after years of granting majik to babes," Emrys countered, awaiting her reasoning.

"Exactly. At that time, I was well into my journey to convene with your parents, Prince Emrys," Arene agreed. "I knew I only had a matter of weeks with the relics. It was not long enough to reveal their purpose to the world before they decayed. My days were numbered before the Holy Family discovered my deceit. I knew they'd send an indefinite number of enemies on my tail."

Swallowing, Arene looked Sayra squarely in the eye. "I did the only thing I could think of to protect you. I used the remainder of the first relic to incorporate the second into you."

"The relic… is in me?" Sayra slowly asked, hardly believing the words. The impulse to start patting down her arms was overwhelming.

"I used *nefas* majik with the first relic to merge the essence into your bones. It's a sustainable source of majik for the duration of your life. You'd be capable of protecting yourself, and possibly many more, depending on what effects it had on your abilities," Arene explained, a glint of curiosity emerging in her eyes.

Snorting, Sayra couldn't help but shake her head at the wall she had punched. "And you did this not knowing whether I'd die, have terrible side effects, show no presence of majik at all, or be some incredible majikal prodigy?"

"Queen Navarre gave me her blessing to test it first on another subject in her presence, so we investigated a safe portion and its effects on Prince Emrys. He was the only male baby in the city limits at the time, and he was similarly merged with a small piece of relic."

"What?" Sylven blurted out, staring at Emrys as if he had grown a second head.

Sayra's neck snapped toward the prince, his eyes wider than ever before. He looked flabbergasted. It made sense to Sayra then—his sensitivity toward identifying majik and the bizarre way theirs interacted.

They shared a similar source.

"Your parents never told you?" Sayra asked, raising a brow at him.

Emrys just frowned at her, a crinkle appearing in his forehead.

"Join the club." Turning to her mother, she said, "Well, you're in luck, Mother Dearest. I'm miraculously alive and capable of wielding every ley line. What a stroke of luck!"

"We need to know how to close the rifts," Emrys abruptly cut in, which truly was a shame because Sayra was just getting started.

She expressed such sentiments with a glower. "Wait, wait." Sayra waved her hand. "If she used *nefas* majik, how did she not fall to it?"

Sylven whispered something in Nes's ear. Something Sayra chalked up to him explaining what *nefas* majik was. They were never taught such a thing during their years at the academy.

"Your mother didn't use it. The relic acted as the source. It wouldn't have affected her as it wasn't *her* majik." But there was a wariness in Emrys's voice.

Sayra huffed, crossing her arms and returning to glare at her mother. "Well, then."

Shifting her weight to her good leg, Arene responded to Emrys's question. "Rifts are made and closed in the same way—with the relics. From what I gathered one night from the Holy Family's drunkenness, only a single portion is required. Other than that, I haven't the slightest idea. Given that one is in front of us, I believe Sayra will be more than sufficient to restore the earth."

That left her with a million questions, most prominent of all: how would she know when the time came?

"Why wait all of this time to tell me?" Sayra protested, feeling the weight of her responsibilities bear down on her at once. "You've had years to reveal yourself. You've had years to help me." That last sentence held more than a note of anguish, the undercurrent roiling below finally surfacing.

Such sympathetic sorrow stole away the Valkyrie façade from Arene, replacing the woman in front of her with her mother. The shift could have given Sayra whiplash.

"For years after I secured your future, I was taking second glances over my shoulder, never sure when the other foot would drop. I was so incredibly blessed to have those years with you, but when a mole ratted me out, I had no choice but to run. The Holy Family lied to cover their tails, and as for me? I wanted you to have time to enjoy life without knowing any of this," she explained.

Sayra's heart clenched painfully in her chest. Each beat sent another stab into it.

"I'm only here now because I caught wind that the seal on your majik waned. I surmised that the relic was capable of eating away spells cast on you, and since you knew the truth, I decided it was time to meet," Arene said.

"If it weren't for Emrys and Sylven, the Arcanist I contracted with, I'd be dead right now," Sayra informed her flatly.

Her mother closed her eyes with such a pained look that her chin fell low.

Nes stepped to Sayra's side, concern etched in her gaze.

"Don't worry, I'll stick with the plan. We'll work together but not as mother and daughter. My mother died years ago," Sayra said. Her throat was thick with emotion as she turned. "Anything further you'd like to discuss, take it up with Emrys. I can't stand the sight of you any longer."

And with that, she left her mother behind as she did all those years ago. Of course, this time Arene's remains weren't in the dirt. They stared back at her, a silent sob escaping from her living corpse.

THE END

If you have enjoyed Shield of Ruin, please leave a review. I enjoy hearing back from you, even if it's a kind word or two. Feedback inspires me to continue writing the next book. Keep turning those pages for a sneak peek into a new series!

AUTHOR NOTES

S. H. BLODGETT

Firstly, thank you SO much for reading *Shield of Ruin*! It's been a dream of mine to write a book since I was in middle school. I never thought I'd accomplish this feat, and I'm so thankful for your support in reading this first published work of mine. My first book was written in 2020, and since then, I've been enjoying every moment of my writing career. *Shield of Ruin* was written in the beginning of 2022, and since then, has undergone the journey to where it is today. It will be the first in a line of many books to come!

When I'm not lost in my writing world, you can find me hanging out with my amazing husband and our super lively 4-year-old German Shepherd. They are my world! My husband currently serves in the Army, making me a Milspouse of six years. What a wild time it has been! We've moved on average once per year since we got married in 2019. I read far too many books, love diving into video games, and enjoy a good hike. Especially in some stunning places! I've recently moved to Washington state, and let me tell you, it's gorgeous out here. So, that's me living life, enjoying the journey, and hoping my stories find a little corner in your world too.

I'm thrilled to share that the sequel, Sword of Ruin, is out! If you'd like sneak peak chapters and other fun updates along the way for the rest of the series, join my mailing list to stay in touch. If you have any comments or questions, feel free to reach out via my email bookinit @shblodgett.com. I try to respond to every person! In the meantime, please write a review on Amazon. Every review helps boost my book and extends the reach to new potential readers. Plus, it lets me know you want a sequel!

I'm so grateful and appreciative of your support. I hope to share my next story with you soon! If you'd like to explore more about my work, connect with me on social media, join my Discord community, or find direct links to my books and website, check out my Linktree below.

https://linktr.ee/s.h.blodgett

I
LEGACY OF THE DRAGON
BLOOD
AND
BETRAYAL
S. H. BLODGETT

A Sneak Peak into Blood and Betrayal

Book One in the Legacy of the Dragon Series

Rancorous cheering sounded behind Caenrya as she descended from the arena's battlefield. Her feet moved on their own accord as she repressed the wave of disgust and hatred she harbored for the patrons of the underground fighting ring. Revealing even a hint of weakness in her bearing would lead to repercussions for her sister, should her actions reflect poorly on their daimyo. Only a nod from her masked handler reassured her they'd survive another day as she passed through the tunnel. Her bruised fist loosened a hair by the time she was guided into the holding cell.

A metal grate clunked to the floor behind Caenrya. Her black leathers rested against the chilled stone of the room as she was left waiting—always waiting—at the daimyo's beck and call. The daimyo was a calculating man of vast power and wealth, a lord in his own right within a lawless land where no true ruler maintained structure.

Caenrya's final match concluded the evening, and the other fighters lined the endless hallway around her. Only one fighter rebelled in their holding chamber when he refused to obey his handler's order to stay silent. One Caenrya knew to be new. No seasoned fighter would dare the whip, and the sound of the lash almost made her flinch.

Don't react, she recited, suppressing the wave of fear and forcing that indifferent mask to remain locked in place.

Caenrya's handler stood like a statue beside her cell, waiting for their daimyo to collect them after his gambling business concluded.

Once more, the hall fell silent to footsteps. A thundering of them reverberated through the ceiling. She knew then it would only be a matter of minutes before her daimyo collected his winnings for the evening's bets. It was only natural there was much for him to gain. After all, Caenrya was the most profitable fighter in his collection. Having never lost a match in the underground fighting rings, her victories were assured, just as her cooperation was with her younger sister held hostage back at Shikei—the nightmarish bunker where she, and the daimyo's other fighters, were imprisoned. Their sole purpose in life was to earn money for a lord who'd kill them when they proved useless.

It was only a matter of time before she, too, wasn't a financial asset.

One by one, the fighters were claimed by their owners, a handful traded to a new lord or lady through clandestine deals shaken upon over a glass of sake. More than a few jewel-clad people gawked at her in appreciation. Some with outright jealousy that they didn't own her. Caenrya ignored them all and pushed her exhausted frame from the wall when a man's obscenely elaborate silk kimono shone in the minimal lighting of her cell. Without glancing at his face, she knew his up-swept eyes spoke of permanent superiority as he hailed his handler to unlock the steel grate between them and Caenrya.

They were eyes she learned the hard way never to meet.

Without a word, Caenrya fell in behind her daimyo, an intimidating man of extraordinary wealth with a penchant for seeking priceless treasures. His armored guard of four divided themselves to escort their charges through the underground exit. Their emergence garnered reverent whispers as they passed through the exit into the forested mountain range beyond. The daimyo signaled for her to fall in step, and her stomach curled inward as she listened.

"Upon the commencement of the following week, you are to embark on another contract at the behest of the contested lands." The daimyo's deep voice lacked the emotional depth any normal person had.

It was a voice that never ceased to chill her to the bone.

Caenrya distracted herself by wondering which faction she'd be aligning with this go-around within their disputed land. Who was next on her list to assassinate. Her daimyo's loyalties lay with whoever produced the most coin.

The daimyo's silken hair swayed across his lower back as they passed the dense line of pines, the pathway worn by the influx of visitors the arena received every other full moon. "I need not remind you of our arrangement."

Nodding in response, Caenrya wouldn't speak without explicit permission.

The daimyo signaled their departure with a flick of two fingers. They collectively pooled their taiji—a mystical inner energy that ran through their veins—and bounded toward the river weaving throughout the valley. Caenrya once used to relish the harmony of energy that allowed all beings to interact with the earth's natural taiji. Balancing hers against the ground gave her a spring-like mechanic, allowing her to bound vast distances with speed rivaling that of a mountain cat. It made journeys much more tolerable.

Now, though, Caenrya felt indifferent to it as they flew beside the rippling water and only visualized it as another tool of survival.

One day. Caenrya dreamed of a day when she and Verina could escape their soul-crushing lives. Perhaps Caenrya could find a way out, taking Verina with her, and return to the home they were stolen from. Only the faintest of impressions remained in her mind from their life before their capture, but Caenrya adamantly believed it was a better life than they could find here. Every day was spent fighting to survive. Possibly a foolish hope, but it was everything to her.

Even if it meant damning her soul in the meantime.

A clear sky twinkled overhead. Two full moons graced the center of it all with a pearlescent hue. The scuffle of nocturnal animals caught her ears, and the slight scattering of dirt with each leap filled the air as the distance passed in the blink of an eye. Each of the four ronin—the hired guards of the daimyo—kept on high alert. Their eyes searched at a constant pace, and their heads swiveled toward any movement in their perimeter. Weapons of varying types littered their crimson lacquer-dipped plates. Silk cord tied them into a fine mesh of the highest caliber.

Everything about the masked ronin put Caenrya on edge. Especially knowing they'd turn on her the instant she attempted anything deviating from her orders.

Hours passed on their trek back to Shikei before the air tangibly changed. Her shoulders tensed, and her skin tingled at the feeling of being watched. The towering trees around them seemed to lean over her. The ronin leading them slowed, and their group condensed around the daimyo as they stilled beside a copse of pines. One held out a palm, warning them to be quiet and still.

Every internal alarm was blaring with abandon, raising goosebumps along her arms. Her fatigued limbs groaned at the thought of an impending battle. Her reserves were close to being depleted after the countless matches Caenrya had to endure, and it brought a grim edge to her mouth at the thought of an ambush. Truly, it was—

A kunai shot from across the banks of the river. Only a flash of moonlight caught her attention before her body reacted instinctively to the airborne double-sided knife. Caenrya threw herself forward, taking the sharp blade to her shoulder to protect the daimyo. Pain lanced from the deep-rooted injury, and her teeth gritted as the ronin leaped into action.

The lead pulled the furious daimyo into the safety of the overflowing foliage, and the others engaged with emerging black-clad figures. In mere seconds, the sound of clashing metal overtook her surroundings.

Having no weapons put Caenrya at a distinct disadvantage. Her near-empty stores of taiji downright guaranteed anything but a fair fight.

However, it didn't prevent her from joining the fray.

Mid-air, Caenrya felt the shift in her blood as her right hand created the *zen* hand seal—a unique hand movement that activated the taiji in her body. At the same time, she recited an incantation in her mind.

Her taiji's nature shifted, and her body thrummed with a power unique to her bloodline. Pale blue taiji formed a crackling blade around each hand. Her shoulder sung with pain as she blocked the barrage of katana-borne blows one assailant greeted her with. The slightly curved blade sliced through the air, sizzling when it met the resistance of Caenrya's taiji blade.

It took but seconds to determine these opponents were vastly different from those she triumphed over in the ring, even those she felled in war zones.

It was the lack of shock that widened her enemies' eyes at her ability, the grace in which her current ones flowed in unison between attacks within their tag-teamed pairs. And the fact that she was steadily losing ground and being corralled toward where her daimyo had been pushed into hiding.

Her breaths became ragged gasps as she parried between well-timed blows, her footing almost catching on a protruding root.

These enemies were faster. More precise and brutal than nearly any she'd encountered before. Sparks flew as she blocked a nasty blow racing for her healthy shoulder. A grunt escaped her from the angry flare of agony radiating from it.

Minutes passed. Caenrya knew she wouldn't last through the duration of the skirmish. Two of her daimyo's ronin had already fallen, only one remaining at her back to repel the onslaught of four attackers.

Out of the corner of her eye, she caught the flash of flame summoned, a fiery tornado erupting from an enemy's taiji attack around the last of the ronin. His shrieks cut off within seconds. Seconds where she was forced to navigate herself toward the river amid dodging several blows to avoid being caught in the flame.

Caenrya's feet balanced on top of the flowing water, and her movements were purely defensive as they circled her. It wasn't long before a katana cut into her leg, and her taiji faltered.

A distant part of her hoped the death would be fast. That the enormity of her duty would at last be over. She was a shell of a being while working for the daimyo. Only the rare moments she could visit Verina ever brought any semblance of genuine emotion back to her otherwise darkened heart.

But now... Now she'd be ashamed to admit she willingly released her hold on the taiji flowing through her limbs. Ashamed to confess she wanted nothing more than the end of the horrific life she led. She didn't deserve it anyway. Not when a dreadful part of her wished to be rid of the burden of her sister, knowing Caenrya could have fought her way out and escaped ages ago.

When a powerful blow connected with the back of her skull—her vision blacking out—Caenrya's body slackened. A ghost of a smile graced her lips.

She knew then a split second of true contention, an emotion found not in piles of gold coin or a lover's returned smile. Rather, it was within the knowledge her time spent suffering was at its bitter end, her burdens shedding like a snake's skin.

Though it was dampened by a lingering memory of her sister. In that moment, all those years ago, Verina's pleading face made her promise everything was going to be okay.

Deep down, Caenrya knew it never would be, but she would die trying to make it so.

***

Drifting in complete darkness proved to be rather soothing. Such silence made her feel at ease. Caenrya couldn't remember the last time she could let her guard down in such a way. To do so was death, but now that she had fallen to it, it was...

Lonely.

Until a strange presence wormed its way to the edge of her consciousness. It prodded at her steel-clad mind. Caenrya's curiosity allowed her defenses to crumble at the effort the foreign presence put forth. It was then she heard a voice—one unmistakably alive.

"I'm in," a man said. His words echoed in the recesses of her mind. "I'm searching now."

A flash of memory crossed Caenrya's void, a time she'd repressed violently and refused to recall. She knew then she had survived. Not even death would rescue her from the daimyo.

Of *course*.

But a piece of her was relieved. There was still that last thread she clung to, one that whispered she could still save her sister.

Now, though, it was threatened by the man using his taiji to invade her subconscious.

Growling in rage, Caenrya grabbed that vine-like probe with ferocity. Her fist drew it close as she whispered, "I'll enjoy ripping your mind to shreds."

The man's fear leaked through, and his voice was urgent as he shouted at someone to wake the captive. Her. The thought made her grimly laugh at the irony. The invader's consciousness squirmed as her mind struck back, his own mind easily falling apart at her efforts.

From her years of training, Caenrya knew the mind and soul were fragile things. When a person used their taiji to attack with their intangible spirit, they were in their weakest state. Only if a person was assured they were more powerful than their foe could they engage in such an attack.

She was being underestimated.

And. It. Pissed. Her. Off.

A rush of adrenaline laced through her body, and her lungs gasped for air while her eyes snapped open.

Details flooded her sight, from a dreary concrete bunker to an entire company of panicked adults circling the room in a hurry. A balding man was slumped at her left, his glazed eyes unseeing as they faced her pinned form. Liquid rushed through a tube into her arm, metal wound around her leaden limbs. Blaring white lights shone, making the finer details of the white-coated forms and the weapon-clad ronin blurred.

Blinking, Caenrya spotted a bizarre insignia on their person. Some had it over their hearts; others wore it on their shoulders. Six people total.

These weren't ronin. Ronin didn't affiliate themselves with any organization. They were worse.

Shinobi.

By the appearance of their insignia, these warriors belonged to a clan, a crucial and disturbing distinction. As her eyes grew accustomed to the lighting, she picked out the black uniforms identical to those who had ambushed her. She saw emblems of jagged wings over their right shoulders.

Only one figure remained calm at the end of Caenrya's cot, and his stance said more than the set of his face would have. Unflinching with a confidence that spoke volumes. Formal silk attire with royal hues of blue and silver, a cape draping over his left shoulder with the emblem of a jagged wing clasping it to his uniform. The same emblem as on the others. With another blink, Caenrya made out the stern set of his expression, warring on a face that appeared naturally kind.

She ignored the flurry of a white-garbed medical shinobi analyzing the slumped man beside her. "You're wasting your time. My obligations are to another, and no number of honeyed promises or veiled threats will persuade me to fight for you."

For a clan.

There were five sections of divided land on their continent, four of them belonging to individual clans. The section she lived in was the only rogue territory where everyone fought each other to rule. Clans had an established hierarchy, but that didn't make them any better for it.

They certainly never helped the innocent in her territory.

A second passed. Her brows furrowed when the man's steel-gray eyes analyzed her without reaction. His bronze hair was mostly tied in a wrapped topknot up high, a gold wing pinned through the middle. The lower half of his hair fell straight to his shoulders, a neatly trimmed beard wrapping around his jawline. A regal countenance.

A white-garbed woman shook her head, brunette curls bouncing around her heart-shaped jawline. Her voice was urgent as she reported to her lord, "Shogun Arundel, Shinobi Aaric's taiji is too far distressed for me to neutralize. The girl's Kū nature is superior to mine."

Kū nature, one of the five elements of taiji: the mind. Caenrya's strongest affinity.

A pacing black-clad shinobi behind her appeared as if he might launch at Caenrya at a moment's notice. His tanned jaw was locked as he faced the shogun.

A flicker of confusion crossed Caenrya's eyes. Why was she in the presence of a shogun? *This man is the leader of the clan*, she thought grimly. With that morsel of information, the dynamic shifted.

The shogun marked her lapse, folding his arms across his chest as his eyes assessed her.

Tucking away that information, her mind reevaluated the situation.

Caenrya hadn't ever crossed a clan leader's path, hadn't thought them involved with the illicit dealings of the war-torn territory they intruded. In fact, none of the people in the room blended with her perception of the average criminal.

What was their goal in ambushing them? Caenrya had misjudged them. At first, she thought her ambushers wanted her as their fighter in the rings. But there was more to it. Were the clans now vying for the contested land along with all the other warlords? That would make sense since they had targeted her daimyo, who was one of the many figures of power there.

"You're not a member of the Kriv Clan." A statement, not a question, asked by the shogun.

Caenrya blinked, her brow pinching. Kriv Clan? She knew little of their land's history, but that name had never been whispered to her ears. She greedily clutched to her chest every bit she could glean of the unknown world and would have remembered the clan's name.

Knowledge garnered power, after all.

And right now, she was powerless.

Understanding lit the shogun's eyes. "We refer to the contested lands by the clan that used to rule it. The Kriv. There are enough members from the Kriv Clan remaining among the warring lords, thus it remains titled as such."

An incredulous laugh escaped her before Caenrya could suppress the noise. There wasn't an ounce of humor in it. "I have no clan. I don't belong to any Kriv Clan lord. I thought you knew who you were slaughtering before you ambushed us," she accused with more than a hint of venom in her tone. Caenrya despised losing to *them*. It hadn't been a fair fight. Now what would become of her?

"She's obviously lying," snapped the pacing shinobi, his hand reaching for a tanto blade slung across his black trousers. His ebony eyes blazed with raw anger, and his unbound hair waved about his broad shoulders with each step.

The length of the blade was a third of a katana's, something Caenrya subconsciously noted as her mind devised ways to combat it.

"Rainer." A black-clad shinobi slapped Rainer's hand, her thin mouth a fine line. "If she dies, Aaric has no hope of regaining his mind." The man who tried to probe Caenrya's mind. "Do you wish to make his daughter, Owena, an orphan?" Her auburn head tilted at him with a grim look.

Closing her eyes, Caenrya attempted to focus her taiji.

"It'll do no good," the shogun said, his calm voice drawing closer. "The surrounding graphite-imbued metal prevents the use of taiji."

Her eyes snapped open. Caenrya glared at his squared face in response, her mind circling a method to escape. It appeared she wouldn't be able to rely on her power. "How about this? Release me, and I'll release your friend here. I don't particularly have any fondness for the ronin your people have killed. There won't be any hard feelings on my end."

The shogun gripped a bar on the side of her cot with calloused hands. "Are you a hired ronin?"

Drawing a deep breath, Caenrya tuned out the deadly stares she accumulated around the room. "No," she finally said, a hint of acrimony stretching the word.

"We acquired intelligence that a ring of black-market trading was occurring in the vicinity of your capture. A prominent figurehead of the Kriv Clan was said to be present. If you can trade any further information, then we could discuss an amicable arrangement." The lines deepened on the shogun's forehead.

They moved Aaric carefully into a chair, and the white-garbed medical shinobi monitored his condition closely.

"I've never known anyone from the clan. I've never known much. Even if I had crossed paths with one, I would never have been told," Caenrya responded coldly. Her fists clenched under the metal biting into her skin. "The only thing I do know is that you managed to kill everyone who might have provided such details and captured the single one who is completely *useless*."

Rainer snapped, lunging forward several steps before the two others reined in his arms. Cursing at them, he snarled beside her, "You're lying!"

"Quiet, Rainer," the shogun shot at the man. "She was not responsible for the loss of Serillia. Your team confirmed that your wife passed at the hands of another. We won't get answers without first listening."

They were going to kill her.

An impossible hollowness brought her eyes to the ceiling. Try as she might, there was no reasoning with them when their verdict had already been made. All she could do was disassociate from her body to withstand any torture they tried.

She only hoped Verina would live. Caenrya's throat grew thick.

There was something to be said about devoting her entire life to achieve one tiny dream and for all of it to amount to *nothing*.

"Sit her up," the shogun ordered, motioning to the medical shinobi to adjust the frame.

The brunette medical shinobi avoided eye contact with Caenrya as she elevated the back of her cot, the latter steadying herself for whatever may be in store. Caenrya tensed as the shogun gestured once more, the indication sending a jolt of irrationality through her despite her best attempt not to react.

There was one thing she could never forgive in her years of servitude. The permanent reminder was etched into a story of shame on her back, something she never allowed anyone to see.

Jerking away from the woman, Caenrya bared her teeth in a violent promise. "If you touch my back, I swear I'll enjoy fragmenting your mind." A cornered frenzy lit her eyes.

Everyone quieted, the shogun's expression mellowing as he waved the woman away from Caenrya. "You're a slave then," he determined, knowing full well that each had a brand burned into their backs.

Caenrya only lifted her chin in response. Humiliation and resentment tightened her face.

"Why defend the lord you were escorting if freedom is this close? Why not expose his identity and divulge the information you've gleaned?"

Heartbeats thudded loudly in her ears. Caenrya met his heavy gaze, regaining her composure. "For every day I work in his service—do his bidding—I gain a day where my younger sister lives."

"What if I promised my aid in retrieving her?" That gold wing pin shone as his head inclined, catching the lighting.

Her body froze at the thought. Such a dangerous one.

Damn the shogun and her precarious situation. Damn her shrunken heart for skipping a beat at the thought, at the possibility, as faint and hopeless as it might be.

But the sliver of light must have shown in her distrusting eyes, for the shogun's fingers danced on the bed rail beside her. "In exchange for any details you can offer about your knowledge and experience thus far, however insignificant you might distinguish them to be, I can offer the Duša Clan's full efforts in this exertion."

Duša Clan. She'd never heard of the clan's name before. The shinobi who ambushed her were Duša then.

Caenrya's throat worked for a moment, Rainer's protests barely recognizable over the roaring in her ears. Shaking her head, she cautiously asked, "Why go to such lengths? You must stand to gain something."

"My clan has many enemies, both within our territory and in the surrounding lands. If I can mitigate the threat from any of them, the effort would pay dividends." His tone grew a hair darker, and his spine straightened. "We've lost many good shinobi in ongoing feuds, and if we continue on such a warpath, we'll be left defenseless against the other vultures awaiting our failure. With the Kriv Clan resting on a majority of my clan's border, their civil war is spreading through the edges of my land." Those imposing eyes weighed on hers. "I ask that you join our ranks."

The other shinobi protested along with Rainer. Caenrya's heart sank. She'd be trading one lord for another. But hadn't she already settled on the path she was inevitably fated to tread?

Holding a palm up, the shogun silenced his shinobi. Directing his next words at them, he said, "She already proved to overpower our strongest shinobi in the Kū nature, and she's capable of holding her own against a number of our jōnin-ranked shinobi. Such a bloodline gift would prove substantially advantageous." His thick brows lowered dangerously. "Would the other clans hesitate?"

Licking her lips, the auburn-haired female shinobi sighed. "No, Shogun Arundel."

The others ranged from reluctant to outright spiteful.

Caenrya debated her options, though common sense dictated she could only give one plausible answer.

Throughout her indentured years in the daimyo's care—if she could call it such a thing—whispers of the elusive clans reached the ears of every slave. Some stories were terrifying, detailing the ways many would hunt their own kind for deviating from a single rule or for forsaking their ancestors. Though Caenrya had a gut feeling there was some truth to those rumors, it was said their blood ran thick. Family above all else. A homeland that valued trivial things such as honor and loyalty.

She always resented them for never bothering to show that *honor* and *loyalty* to the victims in her discarded territory. But if there was the slightest chance Caenrya could enter their fold and bring her sister with her... wasn't it worth betting on those forbidden tales she gleaned from other slaves?

After all, she sold her soul once to spare Verina from a life fighting in the rings. Caenrya's life. Why not once more?

"I'll agree to your terms."

Caenrya started from the beginning, her eyes low to the floor. "My younger sister and I were kidnapped at such a young age I can barely remember anything. I don't know where from, but I do know we were sold upon arriving at a bidding event to the daimyo I've worked for." Caenrya fought the urge to touch her pointed ears. She circumvented many truths to prevent history from repeating itself. If these people knew everything...

Caenrya shivered.

"We were too young for fights, but our capacity was measured in various ways. I fought to be the best to leverage my worth. Eventually, I succeed at being the daimyo's prized possession." Her fists tightened. "His highest-earning fighter. In exchange for my efforts, he kept Verina, my sister, out of the fighting pits and separated her from the others." Everyone fended for themselves at Shikei, but she made sure Verina was given better treatment. "As for the daimyo, I learned about his routines. About some of those he made deals with. What he gained from it all."

Her eyes flicked up, catching how everyone was enraptured by her tale. Shogun Arundel nodded for her to proceed.

Caenrya recounted every memory to the tiniest detail, selecting to skip over a few minor things they need not know. But she kept her word, explicating many aspects of her daimyo—her *previous* daimyo—and the constant fighting she underwent at the arenas. She didn't know the daimyo's true identity. Only his face. One she described with a detail only the finest of artists could hope to capture. There were several other faces she'd memorized after frequent appearances at many of the fights she participated in. Some she carried out hits for. Their contracts took her deep into the warring lands, where men fought tooth and nail to climb higher than the rest up that mountain of prestige and power.

No one suspected death to be served by an unremarkable girl, and it was always her target's undoing. It made her daimyo very, very rich.

The shogun's face darkened when Caenrya recounted a number of her contracts. She was careful to leave out anything too damning, skipping over those she thought would raise far too many questions or may have been against one of their clan.

There wasn't much beyond speculation and the general location of her latest arena, as the daimyo had been excruciatingly careful to knock her out whenever they neared Shikei or any other remarkable location. However, from how these people drank up her words, she knew they gleaned something significant.

By the time she wrapped up her story, her shoulder healed by the brunette woman and cuffs unlocked, Caenrya had released her hold on Aaric's mind. They ushered his limp form to the infirmary for monitoring as he came to, leaving only her, the shogun, and Rainer in the room.

For a beat, Caenrya thought they'd double-cross her, laughing all the while at her gullible belief in them. She waited for it too, for a kunai to be sheathed in her heart and her existence to end.

But when the shogun extended a hand to help her ragged form rise from the cot, Caenrya speculated if she traded the devil she knew for the devil she didn't.

THE END OF CHAPTER 1

www.ingramcontent.com/pod-product-compliance
Lightning Source LLC
Chambersburg PA
CBHW031514010826
48973CB00013B/1267